Carl Horstmann, Henry Bradshaw

The Life of Saint Werburge of Chester

Carl Horstmann, Henry Bradshaw

The Life of Saint Werburge of Chester

ISBN/EAN: 9783337057978

Printed in Europe, USA, Canada, Australia, Japan

Cover: Foto ©Raphael Reischuk / pixelio.de

More available books at **www.hansebooks.com**

TEXTS PREPARING. GENERAL NOTICES.

The following Texts are preparing for the Original Series of the Early English Text Society :—

Anglo-Saxon and Latin Rule of St. Benet, ed. Dr. H. Logeman.
Anglo-Saxon Glosses to Latin Prayers and Hymns, edited by Dr. F. Holthausen.
An Anglo-Saxon Martyrology, edited from the 4 MSS. by Dr. G. Herzfeld.
Aelfric's Metrical Lives of Saints, MS. Cott. Jul. E 7, Part IV, ed. Prof. Skeat, Litt.D., LL.D.
All the Anglo-Saxon Homilies not accessible in English editions, including those of the Vercelli MS., edited by Prof. Napier, M.A., Ph.D.
The Exeter Book (A.-Sax. Poems), re-edited from the unique MS. by I. Gollancz, B.A. Cambr.
A Parallel-text of the 6 MSS. of the Ancren Riwle, ed. Prof. Dr. E. Kölbing.
The Sege of Jerusalem, edited from the MSS. by Dr. F. Kopka.
Two Fifteenth-Century Cookery-Books, edited from the MSS. by Mr. T. Austin. [At Press.
Early English Verse Lives of Saints, Standard Collection, from the Harl. MS., ed. Dr. C. Horstmann.
Supplementary Early English Lives of Saints, ed. Dr. C. Horstmann.
The Early and Later Festialls, ab. 1400 and 1440 A.D., ed. Dr. C. Horstmann.
Thomas Robinson's Life and Death of Mary Magdalene, ab. 1620 A.D. [At Press.
Q. Elizabeth's Translations, from Boethius, &c., edited from the unique MS. by Walford D. Selby. [At Press.
Early English Deeds and Documents, from unique MSS., ed. Dr. Lorenz Morsbach.
Merlin, Part IV., containing Preface, Index, and Glossary. Edited by H. B. Wheatley.
Beowulf, a critical Text, &c., ed. Prof. Zupitza, Ph.D.
Pilgrimage of the Lyf of Manhode, in the Northern Dialect, ed. S. J. Herrtage, B.A.
Early English Homilies, 13th century, ed. Rev. Dr. R. Morris.
The Rule of St. Benet: 5 Texts, Anglo-Saxon, Early English, Caxton, &c., ed. Rev. Dr. R. Morris.
A Chronicle of England to 1327 A.D., in Northern verse (42,000 lines), ab. 1350 A.D., edited from the unique Göttingen MS. by M. L. Perrin, B.A.

----

1 March, 1888. With this, go out four Texts : the two of the Original Series for 1887,— 1. Dr. Horstmann's re-edition of Henry Bradshaw's *Life of St. Werburghe*, A.D. 1521 ; 2. Dr. Horstmann's edition of the earliest MS. and form of the set of *Saints' Lives*, &c., containd in the Laud MS. ; 3. the third and last Text for the Extra Series, 1887, *The Torrent of Portyngale*, re-edited by Dr. E. Adam (with Prof. Kölbing's help) ; 4. the first Text of the Original Series for 1888 : Part I, the text and translation of Dr. Holthausen's edition of an early treatise on the *Vices and Virtues* from the Stowe MS. 240, ab. 1200 A.D. The other Original-Series Texts for 1888 will be Mr. Rhodes's re-edition of the Anglo-Saxon Glosses and Latin text of Bede's *Liber Scintillarum*, and Mr. Harsley's edition of Eadwine's early 12th century *Canterbury Psalter*, as to which see below. Both these texts are nearly all in type.

For the Extra Series, 1888, Bullein's *Dialogue on the Feuer Pestilence*, 1567, has been for a long while all in type and revised ; and it will go out as soon as its Editors, Messrs. A. H. and Mark Bullen, allow. The second book for this year will be a new edition of the first English *Anatomie of the Body of Man*, by Thomas Vicary, Serjeant of the Surgeons, and Chief Surgeon to Henry VIII, Edward VI, Q. Mary, and Q. Elizabeth, five times Master of the Barber-Surgeons' Company, and Chief Surgeon to St. Bartholomew's Hospital after its re-foundation in 1546-7 by Henry VIII. and the City of London. No copy of the first edition of this little book in 1548 is now known ; and therefore the unique copy of it, re-issued by the Surgeons of Bartholomew's in 1577, has been reprinted. Diligent efforts have been made to secure all accessible details of Vicary's life in its various aspects of—1. 'a meane practiser at Maidstone' ; 2. the head Court-Surgeon for over forty years ; 3. a member (1527-62) and Master of the Barber-Surgeons' Company ; 4. the re-organiser of the recreated Bartholomew's Hospital ; and 5. a private citizen. But though fair success has attended the searches under sections 2 and 5, little has been attained under 1 ; while for 3 and 4, delay is still needful.

Mr. D'Arcy Power has, by the kind leave of Mr. South's widow, lent the Society Mr. South's full extracts from the earliest Minute-Book of the Barber-Surgeons' Company; but the Governors of the Company have refused to allow the printing of any of the extracts, inasmuch as Mr. Sidney Young, a member of the Company, has long been compiling its history from its records, and he does not wish any of these printed before his book is publisht, which will be some years hence. With regard to Bartholomew's Hospital, Part I of its Records is now printing by two Officers of the Hospital; and till their First Part is out, the Society's book cannot be completed. This will therefore be issued in two Parts, of which the first (all now in type) will contain all Vicary's work, with its many illustrative Documents from the Public Record Office, the Guildhall Records, the Museum MSS., &c., while in Part II will be the Notes, Indexes, and Forewords, with a Life of Vicary. Nearly all the Forewords, save the Bartholomew's section—the old Surgeon's life at the Hospital in 1548-62—are in type. The New Shakspere Society has sold the Early English Text Society the right to print copies of its plates of Edward VI's Coronation Procession through the City of London in 1547, and Norden's Plan of London in 1593; and other illustrations will be given. The Editors are the Director, and his son Mr. Percy Furnivall, a student of St. Bartholomew's Hospital. It is hoped that Part I of the book will be ready in May.

Mr. Alexander J. Ellis has already in type over two hundred pages of Part IV of his great work on *Early English Pronunciation*, dealing with our modern dialects. This will be issued by the Philological and Chaucer Societies jointly with the Early English Text Society; but the date of publication must depend on the progress of the very intricate and laborious work, and the funds of the several Societies. The Part will undoubtedly be finisht this year.

Dr. Aldis Wright many years ago undertook the editing of the MS. Anglo-Saxon Psalters for the Society. As a preliminary, he copied the 12th century (? ab. 1150 A.D.) Trinity MS. of Eadwine's Canterbury Psalter, which has transitional forms like the change of Anglo-Saxon *c* to *ch* (*wyrchende* for A.Sax. *wyrcende*), the weakening of full vowels in the endings, *senfullen* for A.Sax. *synfullan*, &c. Dr. Aldis Wright also made notes of all the other Anglo-Saxon Psalters from the ninth to the twelfth century, and tentatively classified them by the Roman and Gallican versions which they respectively gloss. Meantime Dr. Hy. Sweet edited the oldest MS., the Vespasian, in his *Oldest English Texts* for the Society. The next step should have been to collate six or eight Psalms from all the MSS., and see whether one or (at most) two texts, with collations, would not have sufficed for the whole body. But as Mr. Harsley, to whom Dr. Aldis Wright kindly handed his whole material, wanted one text printed forthwith for his Doctor's Dissertation, leave was given for the late Canterbury Psalter to go to press; and now the text of it is all printed. Dr. Logeman then raised the question of how the other MSS. should be treated; and he was authorised to prepare a Parallel-Text edition of the first ten Psalms from all the MSS., to test whether the best way of printing them would be in one group, or in two—in each case giving parts of all the MSS. on one page—under their respective Roman and Gallican Latin originals. If collation proves that all the MSS. cannot go together on successive pages, there will be two Parallel-Texts, one of the A.Sax. MSS. following the Roman version, and the other, of those glossing the Gallican; but every effort will be made to get the whole into one Parallel-Text. This Text will be an extravagance; but as the Society has not yet committed one in Anglo-Saxon, it will indulge in one now. And every student will rejoice at having the whole Psalter material before him in the most convenient form. Dr. Logeman and Mr. Harsley will be joint editors of the Parallel-Text. The Early English Psalters are all independent versions, and will follow separately in due course.

Through the good offices of Prof. Arber, the books for the Early-English Examinations of the University of London will be chosen from the Society's publications, the Committee having undertaken to supply such books to students at a large reduction in price. The profits from these sales will be applied to the Society's Reprints. The *Ayenbite of Inwyt* is now reprinting under the supervision of its Editor, Dr. Richard Morris. Members are reminded that fresh Subscribers are always wanted, and that the Committee can at any time, on short notice, send to press an additional Thousand Pounds' worth of work.

Our *Jubilee Reprint Fund*, for which Mr. M. T. Culley of Coupland Castle has sent a Letter of Appeal to every Member, has as yet receivd but little support, tho' Mr. Mortimer Harris started it with a cheque for two guineas. Further Donations will be welcome. They should be paid to the Honorary Secretary, Mr. W. A. Dalziel, 67 Victoria Road, Finsbury Park, London, N.

The Subscribers to the Original Series must be prepared for the issue of the whole of the Early English *Lives of Saints*, under the editorship of Dr. Carl Horstmann. The Society cannot leave out any of them, even though some are dull. In many will be found interesting incidental details of our forefathers' social state, and all are worthful for the history of our language. The Lives may be lookt on as the religious romances or story-books of their period.

The Standard Collection of Saints' Lives in the Corpus and Ashmole MSS., the Harleian MS. 2277, &c. will repeat the Laud set, our No. 87, with additions, and in right order. The differences between the foundation MS. (the Laud) and its followers are so great, that, to prevent quite unwieldy collations, Dr. Horstmann decided that the Laud MS. must be printed alone, as the first of the Series of Saints' Lives. The Supplementary Lives from the Vernon and other MSS. will form one or two separate volumes. The Glossary to the whole set, the discussion of the sources, and of the relation of the MSS. to one another, &c., will be put in a final volume.

When the Saints' Lives are complete, Trevisa's englishing of *Bartholomæus de Proprietatibus Rerum*, the mediæval Cyclopædia of Science, &c., will be the Society's next big under-taking. Dr. Holthausen has kindly said that he will probably edit it. Before it goes to press, Prof. Napier of Oxford has been good enough to promise that he will edit for the Society all the unprinted and other Anglo-Saxon Homilies which are not included in Thorpe's edition of Aelfric's prose,[1] Dr. Morris's of the Blickling Homilies, and Prof. Skeat's of Aelfric's Metrical Homilies. Prof. Kölbing has also undertaken for the Society a Parallel-Text of all the six MSS. of the *Ancren Riwle*, one of the most important foundation-documents of Early English.

For 1889, Dr. Holthausen's Part II, the Introduction, Notes, and Glossary to the Stowe MS. *Vices and Virtues*, will probably be ready in January. What other books will follow, must depend on when any editor of one of the many works in preparation for the Society has a Part or the whole of it ready for issue. Lists of these Works are on the last page of the Cover and the first of this inside quarter-sheet.

In case more texts are ready at any time than can be paid for by the current year's income, they will be dated the next year, and issued in advance to such Members as will pay advance subscriptions. Last year's delay in getting out Texts must not occur again, if it can possibly be avoided.

---

[1] Of these, Mr. Harsley is preparing a new edition, with collations of all the MSS. Many copies of Thorpe's book, not issued by the Aelfric Society, are still in stock.
Of the Vercelli Homilies, the Society has bought the copy made by Prof. G. Lattanzi.

OTHER SOCIETIES.

Wyclif, founded by Dr. Furnivall in 1882, for the printing of all Wyclif's Latin MSS. *Hon. Sec.*, J. H. Standerwick, General Post Office, London, E.C. One Guinea a year.

Chaucer, founded by Dr. Furnivall in 1868, to print all the best Chaucer MSS., &c. *Editor in Chief*, F. J. Furnivall. *Hon. Sec.*, W. A. Dalziel, 67, Victoria Road, Finsbury Park, N. Subscription, Two Guineas a year.

New Shakspere, founded by Dr. Furnivall in 1873, to promote the intelligent study of SHAKSPERE, and to print his Works in their original Spelling, with illustrative Treatises. *President*, ROBERT BROWNING. *Director*, F. J. FURNIVALL. *Hon. Sec.*, K. Grahame, 65, Chelsea Gardens, Chelsea Bridge Road, London, S.W. Subscription, One Guinea a year.

Ballad, founded by Dr. Furnivall in 1868, to print all Early English MS. Ballads, and reprint the Roxburghe, Bagford, and other collections of printed Ballads. *Editor in Chief*, The Rev. J. W. Ebsworth, M.A., F.S.A. *Hon. Sec.*, W. A. Dalziel, 67, Victoria Road, London, N. One Guinea a year.

Shelley, founded by Dr. Furnivall in Dec. 1885, to promote the study of Shelley's Works, reprint his original editions, and procure the acting of his *Cenci*. *Chairman of Committee*, W. M. Rossetti. *Hon. Sec.*, T. J. Wise, 127, Devonshire Road, Holloway, London, N. Subscription, One Guinea a year.

Browning, founded by Dr. Furnivall and Miss Hickey in 1881, for the study and discussion of Robert Browning's Works, print Papers on them, illustrations of them, and to procure the performance of the poet's plays. *President*, Dr. Furnivall. *Hon. Sec.*, W. B. Slater, 249, Camden Road, London, N. Subscription, One Guinea a year.

Philological, founded in 1842, to investigate the Structure, Affinities, and the History of Languages. *Hon. Sec.*, F. J. Furnivall, 3, St. George's Sq., Primrose Hill, London, N.W. One Guinea entrance, and one a year. Parts I., II., and III. of the Society's English Dictionary, for which material has been collecting for 30 years, have lately been issued, edited by Dr. J. A. H. Murray, and publisht by the Clarendon Press, Oxford. Part IV (nearly ready) will complete vol. i. (A-B), and start vol. ii. (C-D). Mr. Henry Bradley is now joint Editor, and has begun vol. iii with E.

Wagner, to promote the study of his Musical and other works, and the performance of his Operas at Bayreuth. *Hon. Sec.* for England, B. L. Mosley, 55, Tavistock Square, London, W.C. Subscription, Ten Shillings a year.

———————

Shakspere Quarto Facsimiles, issued under the superintendence of Dr. Furnivall, 10*s.* 6*d.* each, or 6*s.* if the whole series of forty-three is taken, edited by F. J. Furnivall, Prof. Dowden, Mr. P. A. Daniel, Mr. H. A. Evans, Mr. Arthur Symons, Mr. T. Tyler, and other Shakspere scholars. B. Quaritch, 15, Piccadilly, London, W. (Thirty-five Facsimiles have been published, and eight more will be ready soon. The Series will be completed in 1888.)

The Life of
Saint Werburge of Chester.

BERLIN: ASHER & CO., 5, UNTER DEN LINDEN.

NEW YORK: C. SCRIBNER & CO.; LEYPOLDT & HOLT.

PHILADELPHIA: J. B. LIPPINCOTT & CO.

The Life of

Saint Werburge

of Chester,

By HENRY BRADSHAW.

———◇———

ENGLISHT A.D. 1513, PRINTED BY PYNSON A.D. 1521
AND NOW RE-EDITED

BY

CARL HORSTMANN.

———◇———

LONDON:
PUBLISHED FOR THE EARLY ENGLISH TEXT SOCIETY
BY N. TRÜBNER & CO., 57 & 59, LUDGATE HILL.
———
1887.

Original Series,
88.

R. CLAY AND SONS, CHAUCER PRESS, BUNGAY.

LYFE OF ST. WERBURGE BY HENRY BRADSHAW.

THE present legend is extant only in an edition by Pynson (London), 1521 (described in Dibdin's *Typogr. Antiq.* II. 491), of which five copies are known to exist[1]: one (the copy described by Dibdin as Heber's) in the British Museum, two in the Bodleian, one in the Minster library at York, and one in Mr. Christie Miller's collection (cf. Hawkins). It was carefully reprinted (in the type and shape of Pynson's ed., with all its faults, and without punctuation) for the Chetham Society, 1848, by E. Hawkins, with an introduction. Extracts had been given by Dibdin, and, not always correctly, by Warton (*Hist. of Engl. Poetry*, II. 371—380).

In Pynson's edition the poem is preceded by a prologue in the honour of St. Werburge by J. T. (whose name neither Herbert nor Hawkins were able to make out). This prologue in an acrostic of the two first stanzas, and in vv. 17, 23, 28, names Henry Bradsha, "sometyme monke in Chester," and servant of St. Werburge, as the author of the English legend. At the end of the book are appended three "balades" by different authors, the first of which, "A Balade to the auctour," written by an (official?) examiner to whom the book was sent for approbation (cf. p. 200, v. 8 ff), mentions that its author, "though vncertayne be

---

[1] It was mentioned by Maittaire (who in 1741 inserts it in a list of books not before noticed), and in Ames's *Typogr. Ant.* 1749, who must have had a copy before him. However, Heber, *Typog. Ant.*, I. 270, says, that a few years before he wrote, the very existence of the book was questioned; and Dr. Foote Gower, in his Sketch of materials for the history of Chester, 1771, also doubts its existence; cf. Hawkins.

his name,"[1] died in "the present yere of this translation MDxiii"—which implies that the legend was completed that same year (1513), shortly before the author's death; the second ballad, written, as it seems, by a friend of the author, perhaps an inmate of the same abbey, shortly after his death, calls him "Harry Braddeshaa, of Chestre abbay monke" (v. 24), and laments his premature death (v. 27). All these "balades" speak of the author and his work in terms of the highest praise, and testify to the admiration it must have inspired. So, then, Henry Bradsha(w) is the author of the English life of St. Werburge.

Of this poet nothing more is known than what is recorded by Anthony à Wood, who says (in his *Athenœ Oxonienses*, 1691, ed. Bliss, 1813, I. col. 18)—"he was born in the auncient town of Westchester, commonly called the city of Chester; and being much addicted to religion and learning, when a youth, was received among the Benedictine monks of St. Werburge's monastery in the said city. Thence at riper years he was sent to Gloucester college in the suburb of Oxon, where, after he had passed his course in theology among the novices of his order, he returned to his cell at St. Werburge, and in his elder years wrote *De antiquitate et magnificentia urbis Chestriæ chronicon*, &c., and translated from Latin into English a book which he thus entitled, *The lyfe of the glorious Virgin St. Werburge: Also many miracles that God had shewed for her*, London 1521, 4°. He died in 1513 (5 Henry VIII.), and was buried in his monastery, leaving then behind him other matters to posterity; but the subject of which they treat, I know not" (cf. Hawkins). The date of his death (1513) agrees with that stated in the

---

[1] There cannot be the least doubt that these words refer to the author of the English legend, not to that of its Latin source, as Hawkins maintains. It seems that the legend had been sent for approbation to the authorities without the author's name, or with his Christian name only, he being a monk. The mistake was caused by the word "author," v. 6, which Hawkins applies to the composer of the Latin source as Bradshaw modestly calls himself a translater only.

"Balade to the author."   He died just upon the completion
of his legend (cf. p. 200, v. 20), which does not betray any
traces of old age, nay, seems to have been written in his full
vigour.   This fact, and the expressions used in the second
"balade" (p. 201, v. 27), that death had "abbreged the lyfe
of this good clerke," seem to imply that he died not very
old.   His premature death would explain why a poet of his
talents left no more works from his pen.   Besides, he calls
"preignaunt Barkley, nowe beyng religious" (who died in
1552), and "inuentiue Skelton, poet laureate" (laureated
before 1490, died in 1529), his contemporaries (cf. p. 199, v.
2024).   Assuming him to have reached 45—50 years, the
date of his birth may be fixed about 1465.   Of his Latin
work quoted by Wood, *De antiquite et magnificentia urbis
Chestriæ Chronicon*, nothing is known; it was no doubt
preparatory to his *Life of St. Werburge*, and the substance of
it was embodied in the legend.[1]   "Of the 'other matters to
posterity' nothing more is positively known to us than to
Wood; but Mr. Herbert was in possession of a poem, *The
lyfe of St. Radegunde*, also printed by Pynson, of which he
says, 'although the name of the author or translator of this
book does not decidedly appear on the face of it, yet on comparing it with the life of St. Werburge, it may readily be
perceived that both were penned by the same person, Henry
Bradshaw, but hitherto omitted in every list of his works'"
—*Typogr. Antiq.* p. 294 (Hawkins).   Of this *Lyfe of St.
Radegunde*, ed. by Pynson, a unique copy is now in the

---

[1] Hawkins thinks it not improbable that some fragments dispersed
in various MSS. descriptive of Chester may have been extracted from
his chronicle.   He further remarks: "Mr. Cowper, in his Summary of
the Life of St. Werburge, quotes more than once the Latin life of this
lady by Bradshaw, and these extracts he derives from Leland's *Collec-
tanea*; but where this collector discovered his original authority does
not appear.   Mr. Cowper is probably mistaken in ascribing the work to
Bradshaw's own pen; it is much more probable that the extracts are
derived from the original chronicle or passionary which Bradshaw
translated; for he himself states distinctly that his poem was a translation from a Latin history preserved in his monastery."

possession of Mr. Miller, Britwell. I have in vain applied to
the possessor to be allowed to take a copy of it for the present edition, of which the *Lyfe of St. Radegunde* was to form
part, so making up the works of Bradshaw. As I have not
seen that book, I cannot say more about it than what I
have quoted from Hawkins.

The *Life of St. Werburge* is the work of Bradshaw's life,
finished only shortly before his death. This saint was called
the Patroness of Chester[1] (II. 1741); she was the patroness
of Bradshaw's abbey, where her bones rested. Local saints
at that time were the chief glory of their respective places,
their "legend" a subject of the deepest local interest; to
have their "legend" in Latin, or in the vernacular tongue,
was the chief object of local ambition.[2] Most of the Latin
Vitæ are due to this local interest. The original Life was
often subsequently enlarged by the history of the translation,
by additions and appendices containing more recent local
miracles. English literature abounds not only in legends,
but in local legends in prose and verse, written in the absence of a Latin life, or when that was deemed insufficient,
as being intelligible to the clergy alone, or deficient and
inadequate in style. Lydgate's *Edmund and Fremund*, and
Albon and Amphabell, were the standard works of this kind
in the preceding century. There were others which combined the legend of the saint with the history of the town
or monastery where he rested.[3] So Bradshaw undertook to
write the life of *his* local saint, a task for which he was
eminently qualified, both by inclination, parts, and studies.

[1] When the author calls her prioress and lady of Chester Abbey
(I. 99), which she never was, he can only mean it in the sense that
King Ethelred made her "lady ruler and president" over all the
nunneries in his kingdom; or perhaps he only calls her so because she
was enshrined there, and was considered its patroness.
[2] Bradshaw considers it as a sign of a good reign when "The lyues
of sayntes were soth in eche place, And written in legendes for our
comfort and grace," II. 1155.
[3] So *St. Editha, sive Chronicon Vilodunense* (ed. by me, Heilbronn,
1883).

As his book shows him, he was a man of a childlike, sweet temper, simple, pious, without affectation, warm-hearted, modest, sincere, a friend of the people, to whom he dedicated his work (II. 2016). He had a natural sense of beauty, an innate grace, a deep moral feeling. He was of a religious, poetic, and antiquarian cast. His life was spent in the narrow walls of his monastery, in the stillness of his cell, of his study, far from the tumult of the great world. He was not ambitious, but unregardful of the applause of the great. His interest centred in his native place, in his abbey, in its saint. He knew Latin, and was well versed in Latin literature ; he knew of course the Bible ; he was well acquainted with the English literature of his time—with Chaucer, Lydgate, Barclay, Skelton ;—but his chief delight was the chronicles and histories and legends of old. He had written in Latin a chronicle on the antiquities and magnifi-cence of Chester, and was Chester's best antiquary. So it was that, not feeling so bold as "to descrybe hye hystoryes," and scorning to write "bawdy balades, to excyte lyght hertes to pleasure and vanyte" (I. 91), he, to avoid idleness and make himself useful, undertook "to wryte a legende good and true, and translate a lyfe into Englysshe, I meane Blessed saynt Werburge, Protectrice of Chester and of the abbay" (I. 92 ff.).

The *Life of St. Werburge* is a legendary epic after the fashion introduced by Lydgate ; in two books, with the appar-atus of prologues and epilogues (Lenvoye), with episodic in-gredients—the lives of the immediate relations of his saint—with frequent descriptions, in the modern style full of "aureate terms," in the stanza used by Lydgate. But it is of a more comprehensive plan than the mere legendary epics of that poet, containing not only the life of his saint, and those of her relations, St. Audry, St. Sexburge, and St. Ermenilde, but connecting it with the history of the city of Chester and its abbey, and grounding the whole on the history of England and Mercia. It is the result of careful studies

of local history, and is of great antiquarian interest, the
more valuable as it rests on authorities partly unknown to us.
It is written for the people, not for the great, and in a more
popular and simple, though less refined style than Lydgate's,
in verses rich in alliteration, which remind us, in their rhythm,
of the old alliterative long-line still used in the North; thus
combining an artistic and popular element.   It is not a mere
translation, nor an imitation, but shows traces of an original
genius, of a truly epic tone, with a native simplicity of
feeling which sometimes reminds the reader of Homer.

I here give the contents of the poem.[1]

BOOK I.—In a prologue the author treats of the divers dis-
positions of men[2] and of his own motive in writing, and mentions his authorities.   He then begins with the Anglo-Saxon
invasion and the Heptarchy, and gives a description of the
kingdom of Mercia.   St. Werburge was daughter of Wulfere,
King of Mercia, and of St. Ermenilde, daughter of King Ercombert of Kent (whose mother was Emma of France), and of St.
Sexburge, who was daughter of King Anna of East Anglia by
St. Hereswith of Northumberland (and sister to St. Audry); so
that St. Werburge descended from the four chief Saxon kings
(besides that of France).   (The poet gives a complete and valuable genealogy of all these royal houses, so fertile in saints.)[3]
Wulfere was second son to Penda, King of Mercia (626—656),
and brother to Peada, St. Ethelred (afterwards king, father to
King Coelred), St. Merwald (father to Sts. Mildred, Milburge,
Milgide, and to Mereuin, by his wife Domneva of Kent), St.
Marcell, St. Keneburge, and St. Keneswyde.   He succeeded his
elder brother Peada, who was slain, after a three years' reign,
by his wife Elflede; and chiefly resided near Stone, in Stafford
shire.   He had, besides St. Werburge, three sons: Sts. Wulfade
and Ruffin, who died martyrs, and Kenred, who was king afterwards, and died at Rome in the odour of sanctity.   Wulfere was
a valiant and politic king, but of a fierce temper.   Peada had

---

[1] Cf. Alban Butler, *Lives of the Fathers*, &c., London, 1833, 3 Febr.,
who relies on Bradshaw, but differs in the circumstances of the death of
Wolfade and Ruffin.   Another summary of the life of St. Werburge,
with an historical account of the images carved on her shrine (now the
episcopal throne) in the choir of the Cathedral of Chester, was given
by W. Cooper, at Chester, 1749.

[2] The passage reminds of Horace, *Od.* 1. 1.

[3] There are some mistakes in the printed text: v. 289, read Dom-
neua instead of Ermenberge (cf. 448); v. 397, the name is Domneva in
the Vita.   The four holy daughters of King Ermenred: Ermenberge,
Ermenburge, Adeldryde (r. Domneva), Ermengyde, are wanting in the
Female Saints, but extant in the *Vita St. Werburgae*.

begun to plant the faith in Mercia; Wulfere had been baptized by the bishops Finanus and Jerumannus, and had on that occasion, and at his marriage, vowed to destroy all idolatry in his kingdom; he was a good Christian at first and assisted St. Cedda (Chad), whom he obtained from Archbishop Theodorus for the bishopric of Lichfield after Jerumannus, in building churches, but he afterwards became an apostate.   Young Werburge was an example of every virtue, full of humility, meekness, and piety, sober and grave, "still and womanly," and no wonder, she being of so good a stock.   For her beauty and singular qualities she was desired by many; the prince of the West Saxons wooed her, but she, "abasshed sore," answered that she had chosen the Lord Jesus for her spouse.   A mountain might sooner be moved "than she forto graunt to suche worldly pleasure."   The wicked Werebode, chief steward at her father's court, whom he had perverted, made use of his powerful influence with the king to obtain his assent to marry her, which he granted on condition he could gain that of his daughter.   But her mother Ermenilde, and her brothers, Wulfade and Ruffin, severely rebuke Werebode's temerity in making such a proposal, he being such a " carle."   Therefore he meditated revenge.   Wulfade, one day chasing a stag, happened to get to the oratory of St. Chad, who then lived in the wilderness.   By him, Wulfade was instructed in the faith, and baptized; so was his brother Ruffin. These princes frequently resorting to St. Chad, were espied by Werebode; who slandered them to the king, their father, as having forsaken their faith and as plotting his murder.   The king, to find out the truth, took Werebode to the oratory, but sent him there before him to warn the princes.   Werebode, however, finding them there, and neglecting his errand, hastily returned to the king, and incensed him so against them, that he, in a rage, slew his own sons.[1]   He had no sooner returned to his castle, than Werebode was seized by an evil spirit, and died miserably.   Whereupon the king repented, and, by the advice of his queen, went to St. Chad—whose vestments he saw hanging on a sunbeam—and did penance, and became a good Christian again; he destroyed all the idols, converted their temples into churches, and founded the Abbey of Peterborough, and the Priory of Stone, where his sons were buried.   Werburge, considering the wretchedness of this life, asked her father's consent to enter monastic life in the Abbey of Ely.   At first he refused, and advised her to marry, saying, "ryght ioyfull wolde I be To kysse a chylde of thyne, hauynge thy lykenesse, And so the also coronate as a myghty pryncesse;"[2] but she persisted, saying she had made a vow of chastity; and pleaded her cause so

---

[1] There is an old English "local" legend in verse on the martyrdom of Wolfade and Ruffin in MS. Cott. Nero CXII (ed. in *Altengl. Legenden*, Neue Folge, 1881, p. 308 –314), compiled about 1450 by one of the canons of Stone priory, who quotes as his authorities "the Cronakle" and a "Tablo" suspended in his church.   It differs in many particulars from the account given by Bradshaw.

[2] These words are, to me, of Homeric simplicity.

pathetically and with so many tears, that at last her father granted her request. He conducted her in great state, with the peers of his realm in attendance, to Ely, and was met at the gate of the monastery by the abbess Audry, with all her convent in procession, singing holy hymns. Werburge on her knees begged for admittance, and was received as a novice, and Te Deum was sung. The poet here inserts a splendid description of the festivities given by Wulfere in honour of the spiritual marriage of his daughter, in presence of her uncles and aunts, of King Egbryct of Kent, and Aldulphe of Eastanglia; of the decorations of the hall, hung with painted tapestry representing Old Testament stories, the orders of Angels, Mary, the apostles, martyrs, confessors, virgins, and the stories of Hector, Arthur, &c.; of the feast and the songs sung during the banquet by minstrels. Having been professed after her noviciate, St. Werburge lived a holy life at Ely, in prayer, penance, and contemplation; "her body upon erthe, her soule in heuen lent." O ye fair ladies, richly clad and "proud as a peacock," take example by this holy virgin, who, being a king's daughter, has exchanged her coronet, silk and velvet, for a coarse habit and a life in penance! —The poet then inserts the lives of (1) St. Audry, who, having been married twice, yet remaining chaste, entered Canwod abbey, was made abbess of Ely—her dowry—and built a new monastery there in 673, where she died in 679, 23 June; (2) of her sister, St. Sexburge, mother to Egbryct, Lothary, Ermenylde, and Erkengode; who, after her husband's death, entered Sheppey monastery (in Kent), built at her cost, and thence went to Ely, where she became second abbess after St. Audry, and died 16 years later, 6 July; and (3) of St. Ermenilde, Sexburge's daughter, who, after the death of Wulfere, also entered the house of Ely under her mother, and became third abbess of it, and died there (13 Feb.). The poet adds two miracles done by St. Ermenilde after her translation: how a prisoner's fetters were broken, and how a schoolmaster was lamed for punishing his pupils on the Saint's day, but restored at the Saint's shrine. Wulfere, who died after a 17 years' reign, and was buried at Lichfield, was succeeded by his brother Ethelred, his son Kenred then being a minor. This Ethelred made Werburge, his niece, principal or superintendent of all nunneries in his kingdom, and she left Ely. By his liberality she founded the houses of Trentham (in Staffordshire), of Hanbury (near Tutbury, in Staffordshire), and of Wedon, one of the royal manors in (North)hamptonshire. The same king also built the collegiate church of St. John in the suburbs of Chester, and gave to St. Egwyn the ground for the great Abbey of Evesham upon Avon. Having reigned 29 years, he, by the advice of St. Werburge, changed his life, and took the monastic habit in Bardney monastery in Lincolnshire, resigning his crown to his nephew Kenred, Werburge's brother. Kenred was a pious king, anxious to root out vice and strife. He gave to Egwyn 84 tenements and lands in Worcestershire for the maintenance of Evesham; and going to Rome on pilgrimage, with Offa and Egwyn, ceded that monastery to the pope, and on his return had his donation confirmed by a "seyn" (synod) at Alve. After a reign of five

years he resigned the crown to Coelred, his uncle's son; and
going to Rome in 708, entered the Benedictine Order. Werburge, consecrated abbess by Bishop Sexwulfus of Litchfield,
governed the monasteries in her care by word and example,
being "a mynyster rather than a maystres, a handmayd rather
than a pryores," a perfect model of humility, piety, and ab-
stinence; she would rise long before matins, and recite the
psalter on her knees, and after matins remain in contemplation
till daybreak; she never took more than one repast in the day.
For a pastime, she caused the Legendary or Vitas Patrum to be
read among her sisters, &c. She mostly resided at Wedon and
Trentham. Her holiness was confirmed by many miracles. Thus,
once, when wild geese (gauntes) wasted the lands of Wedon,
she had them penned by a servant, and loosing them the next
morning, restored to them a missing companion, which, as William of Malmesbury says, had already been roasted. When her
bailiff cruelly chastised her servant Alnotus, his head was turned
backward; but he was restored on asking forgiveness. Twice
she was miraculously saved from being oppressed, the last time
by an oak tree opening to conceal her. She cured many sick
people who visited her. When her end drew near, she foretold
her death, visited all places under her care, and gave her last
orders; she desired her body to be buried at Hanbury. In her
illness she thanked God for His visitation, and consoled her
sisters, teaching them how death was birth to another life and
freedom. On her last day she humbly received the sacrament
in presence of her sisters, exhorted them to keep their order in
charity and obedience, and recommended them to God. She died
at Trentham on the 3rd of February, angels conveying her soul
to heaven. Her body was brought to the church, and watched,
amid the lamentations of the sisters. The folk of Trentham, wishing to retain it, watched it with strong hand, but fell asleep
miraculously, and those of Hanbury came and brought it to
their place, as she had desired. The "third passionary" at
Chester Abbey speaks of many miracles done at Hanbury. Such
was the life of St. Werburge, "a princess, a virgin, a nun, and
a president." For her many miracles, her body was raised in
708, nine years after her death, in presence of Coelred, his
council, and many bishops, and being found entire and sweet
looking, was richly clothed and enshrined at Hanbury, 21 June,
where her body remained incorrupt 200 years, till the Danish
invasion.

Book II.—A prologue treats of the use of literature, and of
the contents of the second book. The poet then narrates the
Danish invasion, which, preceded by horrible tokens, was a
scourge for the sins of men. In 875, when the Danish fury
swept over Mercia, and these pirates had advanced as far as
Repton (in Derbyshire), within five miles of Hanbury, and expelled King Burdredus, the people of Hanbury, for fear of the
Danes, carried the shrine of St. Werburge to Chester. Here it
was solemnly received by the clergy, lords, and citizens in procession, singing Te Deum and welcoming the saint, and was de-
posited in the mother-church of Peter and Paul. The poet here
inserts a short history of his native place—called Caerleon by

the Britons, the City of Legions by the Romans, afterwards
Chester " quasi castria, being built like a comely castle "—of its
uncertain foundation, its early Christianity (since King Lucius),
which had been kept intact ever since, the meeting of St. Augustine and the monks of Bangor, the expulsion of the Britons by
King Offa. King Edward senior, Alfred's son and successor,
marrying his sister Elflede to Ethelrede, created him first Duke
of Mercia after the expulsion of its kings. This Elflede, holding
St. Werburge in special veneration, built and endowed with
secular canonries a stately minster—afterwards the Cathedral
—over the relics of St. Werburge, joining it to the old church,
which was now dedicated to the Trinity and St. Oswald,[1] and
translating the church of Peter and Paul to the centre of the
city, where a parish-church was built in their honour. Elflede,
in 908, rebuilt and enlarged the city of Chester, then nearly
decayed, walled it in, and fortified it with a strong castle.
After the death of her husband she rebuilt the churches and
towns of Stafford, Warwick, Tamworth, and Shrewsbury, and
founded the great Abbey of St. Peter's in Gloucester, whither she
translated the relics of St. Oswald, and where she herself was
buried in 919. The poet then relates part of the miracles done
since St. Werburge's translation to Chester. She saved that
place from the Welsh king Griffinus, and again from the
Danes and Scots under kings Harold and Maucolyn ; she thrice
cured a lame woman, Eadgida ; made a barren woman, Judith,
conceive ; helped another in labour ; restored a woman struck
blind for working on the Sabbath ; healed six blind and lame
persons ; delivered a man hanged unlawfully from the gibbet ;
saved corn, hoarded up in her park at Upton during a raid,
from being destroyed by the enemy's horses ; cured one of her
canons, Ulminus, who had broken his leg. Following the reigns
of the next kings, Athestan, Edmund, &c., the poet dwells on
the blessed reign of Edgar, " the floure of England," the reformer
of the Church ; who, at Chester, received the homage of eight
kings, and rowed with them up the Dee to the church of St.
John, and devoutly visited and enriched the church of St. Werburge. In the reign of Edward the Confessor, Leofric was Duke
of Mercia and Earl of Chester, who with his pious wife Godith
rebuilt many churches, founded the monastery of Leonence, near
Hereford, and that of Coventry, and repaired that of Evesham.
At Chester he rebuilt St. Werburge's minster, besides repairing

---

[1] The church of St. Oswald forms the south transept of the choir
of Chester Cathedral. It was set apart for the uses of the inhabitants
of the parish within which the monastery was placed. "The abbot
and convent afterwards, wishing to reattach it to the Cathedral, built
for the parishioners a small chapel, dedicated to St. Nicholas, on the
spot where the theatre now stands ; but they do not appear to have
been contented with their new place of worship, for in 1488 a composition was made between the abbot and the parishioners of St. Oswald
for their new church. They accordingly re-entered into the south
transept (which had been rebuilt by Abbot Ripley), and have ever since
used it as their parish church."—See *Chester Guide.*

the church of St. John. William the Conqueror gave to his kins-
man, Hugh Lupus, the earldom of Chester with the sovereign
dignity of a palatinate, on condition he should conquer it.
Having been three times beaten, he at last took the city, and
divided the conquered lands of the county among his followers.
In 1093, under William Rufus, Hugh dismissed the canons
regular of St. Werburge, and, in presence of St. Anselm, laid
the foundation of a magnificent abbey in honour of St. Werburge, which he handed over to Benedictine monks, brought
over from Bee in Normandy; he secured it by strong walls.
Miracles continued : St. Werburge appeared to a monk of her
abbey, Dan Simon, who was much abused by his fellows, ex-
horting him to bear wrong patiently. Earl Richard, son and
heir to Hugh Lupus, on a pilgrimage to St. Winifred's, at Holy-
well, was miraculously saved from being intercepted by Welsh-
men, the Dee giving passage to a force sent to his succour, near
Eilburghee; for which miracle Richard's constable, William,
the son of Nigell, gave to St. Werburge the village of Newton,
and founded the abbey of Norton on the Dee, near where his
army forded the river—which place is still called "The constable sondes." The same Richard was afterwards perverted by
his wife Matilda, niece to Henry I., so that he claimed abbey-
lands—the manor place of Salton—from the abbot, and intended
to have transferred that abbey to another order ; when, on his
return from Normandy, he, with his wife and company, was
shipwrecked and drowned near Barfleur ; St. Werburge herself
told her sacristan of their fate. In 1180 a great fire broke out
at Chester, which destroyed the minster of St. Michael, and
threatened to consume the whole city, but was suddenly extin-
guished when the shrine of St. Werburge was carried about in
procession.[1]

Conclusion (mostly in 8-lined stanzas).—(1) All these miracles, and many more, recorded in the third Passionary at Chester,
but which it would be tedious to relate, magnify this holy
virgin, who is justly called by the people Patroness of Chester,
and honoured there next our lady, "as is rehersed at masse in
her sequens." (2) O ye lords, citizens, and matrons of Chester,
remember the privileges granted by your forefathers, the protection given by St. Werburge, the punishments inflicted on the
violators of her abbey, and "to the monastery be never vn-

[1] What became of her shrine afterwards, is told by Butler : The
relics being scattered in the reign of Henry VIII., her shrine was converted into the episcopal throne in the same church, and remains in
that condition to this day. This monument is of stone, ten feet high,
embellished with thirty curious antique images of kings of Mercia and
other princes, ancestors or relations of this saint. See Couper's remarks
on each.—On the dissolution of the monasteries by Henry VIII.,
Chester was erected into an independent bishopric, and St. Werburge's
was converted into a cathedral church, which it has ever since remained
(dedicated to Christ and the Blessed Virgin Mary) ; a dean and six
prebendaries were installed ; the last abbot (Thomas Clarke) became
the first dean.

kynde." (3) O blessed Werburge, pray for thy servant, thy monastery, "I beseech thee, swete patrones!" (4, L'envoye) Go forth, little book, which art written not for clerks, but for the merchant men and rude people; Jesus be thy speed!

For this Life, the poet has most conscientiously collected all the materials then accessible. He himself mentions his authorities in general (I. 127—133), and quotes them in special at their respective places. They are partly legends, partly chronicles. His chief source he calls "the legend," "the true legend," "the true Passionary, A boke wherin her holy lyfe wryten is, Whiche boke remayneth in Chester monastery" (I. 694-6), "the thrid Passionary" (I. 3246; II. 1691)— which, therefore, seems to have formed an additional volume to an older Passionary containing the lives of the saints of the year. This book being now lost, it becomes difficult to form an estimate of it. The life contained in it is no doubt identical with the primitive *Vita S. Werburgæ*, ascribed to Goscelinus[1] by the Bollandists (Feb. 3), *but augmented by later additions, as the history of the translation to Chester, and the miracles done at Chester.* The life by Goscelinus is rather scanty in facts, containing only St. Werburge's descent from four kings (including that of France, but not the North-umbrian line), her holy life at home, and at Ely, where she is joined by her mother Ermenilde, both contending in

[1] This is the same Goscelinus who, after Will. of Malm., *Reg. Angl.* 4, 1, innumeras Sanctorum Vitas stilo extulit vel informiter editas comptius emendavit, post Bedam secundus in laudibus Sanctorum Angliæ enarrandis. The Bollandists remark: Floruit is c. a. MC, a S. Anselmo Archiep. Cantuar. aliisque ob doctrinam ac pietatem singularem in Angliam evocatus e Belgio, ubi ante monachus S. Bertini apud Audomaropolim varias Sanctorum vitas illustrarat easque inter etiam stylo cultiori emendarat Vitam S. Amelbergæ Virginis . . Eam autem Vitam dum hic Cap. 6 suo stylo recusam agnoscit, et huius se auctorem esse prodit. Utraque præterea vita eadem ratione suis est capitibus propriisque titulis distincta. . . Vixit Ramesiæ non procul a monasterio Eliensi. . . Perhaps he wrote the life of St. Werburge on the occasion of her translation to Chester, and instigated by St. Anselm. Hawkins, mistaking the "balade to the author" (p. 200) to have been written by Bradshaw to the author of the Latin life, doubts the authorship of Goscelinus, because it is said there that "uncertain was the author's name."

humility; her being appointed lady president of all nunneries;
two miracles related diffusedly (wild geese penned, a bailiff
punished for cruelty), her death, burial, and first translation.[1]
How much richer in details is Bradshaw's life! More particulars[2] he found in the *Vita SS. Wolfhadi et Ruffini
martyrum, auctore anonymo* (Act. SS. Bolland, 24 July,
p. 570), from which he took the character of false Werebode,
his marriage project, his intrigue, the death of the two princes
by their own father. Next he used Lives of St. Sexburge[3]
(6 July), of St. Etheldrede or Audry of Ely[4] (23 June), and
that of St. Ermenilde (probably by the same Goscelinus),
which is extant only in an abridged text in Capgrave's *Nova
Legenda Angliæ* (ed. 1516), where the same two miracles
recorded by our poet are found. Occasionally he quotes the
legend of St. Egwyn, I. 2408. Into the narrative of the
saint's life, so combined from different legends, he inserted
such additional matter—descriptions of Mercia and Chester,
notes on the Heptarchy, the Danish and Norman invasions,
a chronicle of English kings, anecdotes, &c.—as he was
pleased to extract from the various chronicles which he
mentions, from Bede, William of Malmesbury, Girardus
Cambrensis, Alfred of Beverley, Henry of Huntingdon (from
whom he quotes several passages in Latin verse), and Ranulph
Higden, his countryman and a monk of his own abbey (who
died in St. Werburge's abbey ab. 1363).[5] For the second book

---

[1] The contents of this life were, as usual, summarily repea'ed in
the sequence sung at Mass, which B. alludes to in II., 1689 ff., most
likely also in the hymns, &c. of the Officium.

[2] I cannot find from where he took the Prince of West Saxons, who
wooed St. Werburge ; or the miracles recorded in chap. 26 : perhaps
the latter were added in a marginal note to the Passionary. The
miracles done at Hanbury (cf. I., 3245 ff.) were, it seems, not specified,
but only generally mentioned in the Passionary.

[3] The Vita is lost ; the text in Capgrave Nov. Leg. Angl. contains
only a short encomium.

[4] Her Life in Act. SS. Boll. 23 June contains a detailed genealogy.

[5] He quotes Bede, I. 136 (Anglos. invasion), 432 (Penda's victories),
507 (Wulfer made king), 1072 (St. Chad), 1844 (St. Sexburge born
at Exning), 2472 (Kenred forsaking the world), II. 497 (St. Augustin

—Werburge's translation to Chester, and miracles done there, with a history of Chester and its abbey—his chief authority must be sought in the 3rd Passionary, or rather in the additions appended to the Life; which appendix seems also to have contained the changes affecting the Abbey of Chester, as the miracles are classified after the two periods of the abbey (miracles done in the time of canons regular, and in the time of Benedictine monks). The history of the translation may have been added soon after the fact; the miracles go as far as 1180 (when the great fire raged at Chester), and seem to have been added soon after that date (if not simultaneously with the facts) in chronological order. When the poet speaks of many more miracles recorded in the 3rd Passionary, which he thinks proper to omit, for they " wolde require a longe tyme and space, To the reders tedious, no meruayle sothly " (II. 1690), these miracles perhaps formed another set, added later or registered with the facts, and were merely ordinary cures, such as he had mentioned before. As to the history of Chester and its abbey, we must not forget that Bradshaw had written a Latin chronicle on the antiquities of Chester, which no doubt rested partly on local sources,[1] and also contained a history of Chester Abbey; so that he could rely on the results of former studies.[2] That he used local

and the monks of Bangor); William of Malmesbury: I. 2189 (first abbesses of Ely), 2379 (K. Ethelred made Abbot of Bardney), 2697 (the wanting goose roasted), II. 1209 (Leofric made Earl of Chester); Alfridus: II. 133 (beginning of the Danish invasion); Giraldus: I. 2318 (Ethelred builds the collegiate church of St. John at Chester); Ranulph Higden's Policronicon: I. 177 (the kingdom of Mercia), 3451 (date of the first translation of St. Werburge), II. 379 and 386 (foundation of Chester), 1213 (foundations by Leofric). The quotations from Henricus (Henry of Huntingdon), II. 364, 666, 1205, are not without some errors (cf. ed. Saville).

[1] There were several official books kept at Chester: 1. The Red Book, once in possession of the abbey of St. Werburge, containing the evidences of their endowments, copies of legal proceedings out of plea rolls: it is now carefully preserved in the archives of the Dean and Chapter; 2. A remarkable MS., *Annales Cestrienses*, Chester Annals, from Christ to 1255 (cf. *Chester Guide*).

[2] In II. 561 he gives the testimony of Archbishop Antoninus for the

sources is evident from II. 597, where he refers to a table preserved at St. John's in Chester, with the history of its foundation.   Several of the facts given by our poet are found elsewhere: Ranulph Higden (*Polic.* 5, 18) shortly mentions the translation of St. Werburge to Chester, and the institution of canons secular; the presence at Chester of King Edgar with eight kings is recorded by Florence of Worcester, and others; for Leofric, our poet quotes William of Malmesbury (II. 1201); for his foundations, R. Higden—the same foundations are also mentioned in *Vita S. Edwardi Conf.* (5 January), Cap. 7, including that of St. Werburge's abbey; Hugh Lupus is mentioned by William of Malmesbury, *Pont. Angl.* 4 (and *Reg. Angl.* 2, 13), and Higden.   But many of the particulars we can trace to Bradshaw only, who, in the absence of other sources, himself remains our chief authority.

I here give the text of the *Vita* by Goscelinus, to show how greatly its scanty materials are enriched in the English legend.

Vita Auctore Goscelino monacho ex Ms. Guilielmi Cambdeni.[1]
(Act SS. Bolland. Febr. 3, p. 391.)

Cap. I. Genealogia S. Wereburgae.
Cap. II. Conversatio in Elio monasterio.
Cap. III. Conversatio matris suae in eodem monasterio.
Cap. IV. Praeponitur monasteriis sanctimonialium Werburga a patruo suo Rege Æthelredo.   Idem Rex huius sanctitatis exemplo fit perbeatissimus monachus.
Cap. V. Werburga ut mater pia, ita fit omnium ministra pro magistra.
Cap. VI. Volatilium agmina praecepto captivat et relaxat.
Cap. VII. Humilitas ejus.   Carnificem retorta in tergum cervice increpat, et supplicem reformat.
Cap. VIII. Transitus ipsius iii Nonas Februarii.
Cap. IX. Corpus ejus Triccengehamenses custodientes obdormiunt, et Hamburgenses divinitus reseratis foribus auferunt.
Cap. X. Post novem annos elevata, inventa est toto corpore et vestibus ut vivens vernantissima.

Filia Regum, et sponsa Christi decentissima, Virgo Werburga in Cestria civitate requiescit, meritorum signis gloriosa.   Clara est in tota Anglia, et pura sanctitate, et regia dignitate, et virtutum attestatione, atque Anglicarum historiarum celebritate.   A primis

first gifts to St. Werburge's; he refers here, it seems, to a deed preserved in the abbey.

[1] A somewhat abridged text of this life is that in Capgrave, *Nova Leg. Angliae*, 1516.

Anglorum Regibus sublimiter splendescit ; a Rege vero Doroberniae, quod est Cantuaria^, potentissimo Ac helbrichto, qui primus
Anglorum Regum per Protodoctorem suum Augustinum Christo
sacrari meruit, imo a quatuor reguis altum et sanctum genus tra-
hit : quod hic sequenti ordine exponi dulce videtur, quo Dei gemma
carius appretietur, et quasi de praeviis sideribus haec matutina
stella clarius spectetur. Æthelbrichtus igitur ex Berta Regina
filia Regis Francorum, Eadbaldum cum Æthelburga filia pro-
creavit, quem suae pietatis et regni optimum haeredem reliquit.
Æthelburga vero Regina post proprii Regis Nordanhumbrorum
Ædvini interfectionem, reversa ad fratrem Eadbaldum in villa
Limminga monasterium aedificavit, in quo cum S. Æadburga
requiescit. Eadbaldus quoque ex alterius Regis Francorum filia
Emma Eormredum atque Ergombertum Principes sanctamque
Virginem Answytham, quae apud Folcanstam deposita vene-
ratur, propagavit. Eormredo autem ex inclyta conjuge Oslava
nati sunt Æthelredus, atque Æthelbrichtus, quos innocenter
jugulatos, splendida lucis columna de coelo prodidit Christi
martyres : quatuor quoque sibi filiae sanctae, Domneva, Ærmen-
berga, Ærmenburga, et Ærmengida, velut paradisiaci fontis
quadrifida emicuere flumina. Fratri vero eius, Ærgomberto
Regi, Annae Regis filia Sæxburga, soror perpetuae Virginis
Ætheldrethae, regaliter conjuncta peperit Ægbrichtum ac Lo-
tharium Reges, caeloque dignas Eormhildam atque Eorken-
godam Reginas. Eormhilda Wlfero Regi Marciorum, Pendae
Regis filio, tradita, splendidissimam Werburgam, cui haec par-
entalis purpura infloratur, generavit. Beatissima vero matertera
eius Virgo Eorkengoda amore sacrae religionis peregrinata trans
mare requiescit, ubi se a Domino susceptam tamquam advenam
suam multis virtutibus ostendit. At beata et regia Domneva regio
Wlferi germano Merwalae conjugata, ad summae Trinitatis gra-
tiam triplicem Virginitatis protulit lauream, sanctissimas scilicet
sorores Mildburgam, Mildrydam, et Mildgydam, quae distinctis
monasteriorum suorum lapidibus irradiant patriam. Natus est
ei et Merevin filius, qui ad sanctos innocentes a baptismate raptus
est parvulus. Almifluae quoque Werburgae generositatem ac
sanctimoniam proxime exornant sanctissimae amitae suae Pendae
Regis filiae, Kyneburga et Kynewida, quae cum propinqua sua
beatissima Tibba Burgensem superni janitoris Petri illustrant
ecclesiam. Suus vero genitor praenominatus ac patrui Reges,
id est, Peada, Ædelredus ac praedictus Merwala praedictarum
sororum fratres, Christianae institutionis non solum cultores,
verum etiam primi atque intensissimi fuere propagatores : et
sicut Ædelbrictus Doroberniae, ita Wlferus in Merciis Christi-
anitatem primus dilatavit. Sic itaque, ut praemisimus, ex quatuor regnis, et antiquis Regibus rosa Christi Werburga florescit :
a principe susceptae fidei Ædelbrichto Cantuariorum, a Berta
vel Emma Francorum, ab Anna Rege, et avia Sexburga Orien-
talium Anglorum, a patre vero luculentissima facta Merciorum.
Haec vero ad gloriam praedicandae Virginis praetitulantur, ut
de radice sancta ramum sanctitudo doceat sanctitudo, imo de con-
tempta regni excellentia maior adscribatur claritudo. Restat
nunc ut explicemus sanctam ipsius conversationem, et probabi-
lem in Domino fiuem.

A tenero ergo aevi flore, cum formae pulchritudo insigniter
responderet generositati suae, coepit speciosa facie cum
speciosissima mente ad illum, qui speciosus est forma prae filiis
hominum, contendere: cuius ut inaestimabilem dulcedinem
praegustare potuit, protinus in eius amorem anhelo pectore
exarsit, et, ut cervus ad fontes aquarum, virginalis anima eius
in ipso sitivit: adeo dulcis et suavis Spiritus Domini a Patre
dilectionis procedens illam attraxit, caelestes concupiscentias in
eius corde accendit, terrenas exstinxit. Illa amore perpetuae
virginitatis ad sponsum aeternae integritatis convolavit, procos
et amatores regificos angelica pudicitia repulit, imo Christus
electam sibi inhabitans omnibus appetitoribus eripuit. Sanctis-
sima parens non cessabat assiduis monitis irrigare hortum Domini,
et plantare in ea immarcescibilia germina paradisi, et accendere
lampadem eius oleo et flamma caritatis inextinguibili. Ad illam
enim vitam flagrantissimam prolem exercebat, quam ipsa adhuc
sub jugo maritali gemitibus inenarrabilibus suspirabat. Verum
altissima Dei providentia benigne dispensans omnia, matrem eam
in regno statuit omnium inopum, omnium necessitudinum refu-
gium, simul etiam ut piis visceribus pignus Deo gigneret accep-
tissimum et ampliorem coronam dilatorum tandem reciperet
desideriorum. Viluerant divitiae tam matri quam filiae; pala-
tium habebant pro monasterio: aurum, gemmae, vestes auro
textae, et quidquid fert pompatica mundi jactantia, onerosa sibi
magis erant quam gloriosa; et si forte his uti ad tempus regia
compelleret dignitas dolebant se potius vanitati subiectas tamquam captivas.

At vero virginalis B. Werburgae libertas, mox ut valuit, haec
vincula exuit, et ad Eligense monasterium cum officio sublimium
parentum hostia Dei commigravit: ubi primum beata et intemerata matertera sua Ætheldreda, ac deinde soror eiusdem Virginis,
sua ut praedictum est, avia, principabatur Sexburga. Illico ab-
jicitur cultus terreni nitoris, induitur habitus sacrae religionis,
vestis pulla pro ornamento gloriae, velum capitis humile pro
regni assumitur diademate. Ita praeclara Virgo certabat fastum
mundi calcare; mente et conversatione, velut hic peregrina, ad
supernam patriam tendere; tota animi summissione humillimam
Christi exhibere ancillam, quam ipse exaltare dignaretur in
sponsam. Omnes monasterii famulatus anticipabat: omnibus
se inferiorem exhibebat: erga omnium necessitates vulneratae
caritatis viscera impendebat.

Jam deo amabilis pater eius Wlferus, multarum ecclesiarum
aedificator, christianae fidei summus amator ac dilatator, quippe
qui etiam subiectos Reges, datis provinciis in mercedem, ad Christi
cultum attraxit, septimo decimo imperii sui anno de temporali
regno ad perenne transivit. Tunc beatissima Regina Eormenhilda
post pios fletus triumphans se solutam a mundiali catena, diu
desideratam conversationem arripuit, et cum beata filia in Eligensi
monasterio jugum Domini suave subiit. Hic deinceps tanta virtutum flagrantia in omni sanctitate et religione vixit infatiga-
bilis, ut et Virginibus exemplum esset castitatis ac totius virtutis.
Contendebant alterutra pietate mater et filia, quae humilior, quae
possit esse subiectior; mater sibi praeferebat eius quam genuerat,
virginitatem, Virgo matris auctoritatem: utrimque et vincere

et vinci gaudebant. Nunc autem in eodem coenobio ad saluti-
feram ipsius benignissimae parentis tumbam conspicue elucescit,
quibus clementiae visceribus se in cunctos diffuderit, dum cor-
poraliter vixit; adeo ut experti ipsius beneficia audeant fideliter
asserere, quod nullus credulus petitor frustretur eius ope.

Igitur patruus almae Werburgae Rex Æthelredus, qui fratri
Wlfero successerat, cum sancta mente totius sanctitatis esset
benignissimus, videns in beata nepte divinam prudentiam ac
sanctimoniam altius resplendere, qui nimirum virtutem poterat
ultra germanitatem diligere, tradidit ei monasteriorum Sanctimonialium, quae in suo regno pollebant, principatum. Pulchre
sane superna id actum est providentia, ut sacrae institutionis,
cuius perfecta erat discipula, in salutem multorum decentissima
foret magistra.

Rex vero magis ac magis coepit imperii taedere, dum se repu-
taret inter secularia negotia quasi animal accline terrae, illam
vero columbinis pennis meritorum ad caelum volitare, et quid
plura? Non quievit aestus spiritus sui, donec vigesimo nono
regni sui anno in Bardeniensi coenobio de Rege efficeretur
monachus, qui idem jam favore superno probatur meritis
venerandus.

Dilectissima autem Deo Werburga erga subjectos ita erat
magistra, ut potius videretur ministra : aequabat, vel magis
subjiciebat se infimis : malens, si liceret, locum extremitatis
quam praelationis. Portabat omnes quasi viscera sua, fovebat
acsi uterina pignora, erudiebat exemplo attentius quam im-
perio. Totam possederat dilectio et benignitas, pax et hilaritas.
Ad indigentes promptissima illi largitas : ad afflictos compatien-
tissima erat pietas : adversa ridebat patientia, vincebat fiducia,
calcabat caelesti laetitia : ad usum vero divinae sapientiae acci-
piebat prospera, abstinentiam pro deliciis, vigilias pro somno,
labores pro voluptate, lectiones et orationes sacras pro epulis
habebat : corpore in terris, animo conversabatur in caelis.

Sed jam forsitan lectorem lassamus, dum miracula suspendimus.
Majora miraculis sunt merita, quibus ipsa fiunt miracula :
quia possunt esse perfecta merita absque signis, signa vero nihil
sunt absque meritis. At vero multis mirabilibus effulsisse probatur dignissima Virgo, et in Eligensi coenobio, et quocunque
degebat loco. In Weduna autem regio patrimonio suo, quod est
in Hamtuna provincia, jocundum et celeberrimum a generatione
in generationem hoc eius miraculum asseritur ab ipsa plebe
tota.

Cum in ipsius Wedunae mansione moraretur regia Virgo,
agros eius solito infinita aucarum indomitarum, quas gantas
vocant, depopulabatur multitudo. Nuntiat domesticus ruricola
hoc damnum Dominae suae. Tunc illa magnanimi fide praecepit illi, ut omnes adduceret, et includeret, more scilicet ani-
malium qui depascunt alienas segetes. Vade, inquit, et omnes
hac volucres introduc huc. Itabat ille altius obstupescens, au
garriret, an deliraret haec jussio. Quomodo enim suspectus
advena tot volatilia ire gressibus in vincula cogeret, quibus per
caelum evadere liceret? Quomodo, inquit, ad primum accessum
meum in aethera fugientes huc convertam? Tunc virgo pro-
positum urgens: Vade, ait, quantocyus, et ex nostro jussu

omnes adduc in custodiam nostram. Ille timens vel super-
vacuum dictum divae praeceptricis negligere, post omnes vadit,
dicensque illis: Ite, ite ad Dominam nostram; omnes ante se,
acsi captiva pecora, agit. Nulla avis de tanto coetu pennam
levavit sed quasi implumes pulli vel alis excisae pedetentim se
permovebant, pedestri incessu summissis collis velut pro con-
fusione reatus sui adventabant: sic intra curiam judicis suae
trepidae et suppressae quasi damnatae se collegere, ibique retru-
duntur captivae, vel magis servantur indulgentiae.

Noctem illam filia lucis, uti consueverat, in hymnis caeles-
tibus ac precibus perpetuat. Mane omnes advenae elatis vocibus
concrepant ad Dominam, quasi veniam et emigrandi poscentes
licentiam. At illa, ut erat erga omnem Dei creaturam benign-
issima, absolutas jubet dimitti, interminans ne ultra auderent in
hunc locum regredi. Unam autem ex eis quidam ministrorum
exiens furto abstulerat, et occuluerat: cumque omnes elatis pennis in aera se sustulissent, seseque circumspiciendo requisissent,
damnum contubernii sui una absente percensent. Extemplo
universus exercitus supra domum Virginis glomeratur, ingenti
strepitu injuriam collegii sui conqueritur; caelum undique
diffusis copiis obtegitur, ut quasi hac voce humana judicium
miseratricis suae implorare viderentur: Quare, domina, cum
omnes nos relaxaverit tua clementia, una ex nobis tenetur
captiva? Et potest haec iniquitas latere in domo sancta tua, et
foeda rapacitatis valere sub tua innocentia? Egressa ergo
divina Virgo ad murmur tantae plebis et querimoniam, intel-
lexit caussam, acsi praefatis verbis auditam. Protinus per-
scrutatum furtum reus ipse publicat receptamque volucrem suae
genti pia conciliatrix associat, et abire simul praedicta conditione
mandat. Quibus nimirum sic gestiebat, dicebat benigno animo:
Benedicite volucres caeli domino. Nec mora; omnis illa concio
ita avolavit, ut nulla huius avicula in ipsa terra almae
Werburgae, ut famose memoratur, ultra reperta sit. Bene
ergo illi pecualis creatura parebat, quae omnium Creatori tota
devotione jugiter obtemperabat. Tale prorsus miraculum in
Vita beatissimae Virginis Amelbergae, quam nostro stylo recu-
dimus, legitur, quatenus in eodem opere eadem fides utriusque,
licet diverso tempore et loco exstiterint, comprobetur.

Quantae autem humilitatis fuerit, quantae etiam apud Deum
sublimitatis, in eodem loco Wedunensi aliis confirmatur indiciis.
Erat illi armentarius, vir piae conversationis, et quantum licuit
sub humana servitute sanctae vitae, qui et suis locis fama
meritorum perpetuatur ac recolitur festive, Alnotus nomine.
Hunc villicus Dominae cum forte laniaret cruentissimo verbere,
et ille omnia in Dei nomine toleraret mansuetissime, alma
Virginis compassio non ferens dolorem, proruit ad pedes in-
dignos lanistae, clamans cum prece et increpatione: Parce pro
Dei amore, quare excarnificas hominem innocentem, apud
altissimum Inspectorem omnibus nobis (ut credo) acceptiorem?
Cumque ille vel prae furore vel prae superbia tardius flecteretur,
continuo dura cervix et torva facies superna indignatione in
terga illi reflectitur. Sic demum quod magis debuerat, ipse ad
pedes Dominae provolvitur, et veniam, quam insonti negaverat,
suo reatu cum lacrymis deprecatur: statimque interveniente

Virginis clementia, in pristinum statum reparatur. Vir autem Domini memoratus jacet ad Stowam una legia a Buccabrive, quem in silva anachoreticam vitam ducentem latrunculi martyrizaverunt, et divina signa Deo acceptabilem, uti celebratur, prodiderunt.

Praeterea haud dubium est, amantissimam Deo Werburgam quam multis aliis signis emicuisse, et caelesti beneficio diversos aegros ac debiles curasse. Potuit etiam divina inspiratione plura praescire ac praedicere, diemque ultimum, quem semper prae oculis habebat totaque vigilantia cum flammanti lampade eminus observaverat, jam proximum ignorare nequibat. Cum ergo omni familiae et monasteriis sibi creditis prae nimia caritate jugiter optaret adesse; et econtra nulli tolerabile videretur sua dulci praesentia carere; elegit tamen divina praescientia et voluntate Heamburgae monasterio requiescere corpore, quae omnibus semper repraesentaretur mente. Quamobrem praecepit Heamburgensi familiae, ut ubicumque migraret ex hac luce, ipsi incunctanter venirent corpusque eius ad suum monasterium transportarent.

Venit ergo caelicolae Virgini diu desideratus finis terrenorum laborum ac dolorum, et ingressus caelestium aeternorumque gaudiorum: nox mortalitatis recessit, et dies aeternitatis illuxit: tenebrae transierunt, et lumen verum luxit, ac sol laetitiae perennis ortus est illi. Gaudebat beata anima quasi ad epulas invitata, videlicet de exilio ad patriam, de carcere ad regnum, de morte ad vitam, de captivitate ad triumphum, de tyrannide seculi ad illum quem desiderabat sponsum sempiternae gloriae transitura. Deposita itaque in coenobio quod Tricengeham appellatur, per languorem et mortem corporis ad immortalia solennia ab angelicis choris assumitur, et in caelestem curiam supernis concentibus triumphatur; cuius depositio tertio Nonas Februarii celebratur.

Corpus sacrum in ecclesiam defertur, et in medio populi Tricengehamensium obseratis diligentissime januis custoditur, certantibus nequidquam omnibus, ut Heamburgenses excluderentur, et per suum obsequium vel defensionem praeceptum vatidicae Virginis vinceretur, sacerque thesaurus in eodem loco perpetim retineretur. At non est sapientia, non est consilium contra Deum. Dum enim nocte ipsa attentius vigilarent, subito sopor gravissimus omnes occupat. Supervenit illico copiosa plebs Heamburgensium cum Dei ministris, extemplo omnia ostia monasterii, cadentibus in terram seris et vectibus, reserantur illis. Irruunt ergo, omni custodum turba somno sepulta, rapiunt nullo se adversae partis movente glebam Virginis et auferunt, secumque cum ingenti laetitia et gratiarun actione laudisona ad Heamburgense monasterium confusis rebellibus deducunt.

Quis itaque pensare sufficiat, quanta solemnitate ipsius anima suscepta sit Deo, cuius corpus ad requiem praeelectam transferri tanto dedit prodigio? In hoc ergo sacro loco Dei margarita cum debita reverentia et solemni jubilo tumulata, plurimis signorum indiciis se probat vivere in caelesti regia; sanitas aegrotis, lumen caecis, auditus surdis, sermo mutis restituitur: leprosi mundatione, et diversis languoribus oppressi una salute percepta gratulantur. Tot itaque post mortem suam vitae reformat quae tam sancte vivebat.

Post haec etiam inenarrabilis Domini gratia in ipsa carne virginali diutius incorrupta evidenter ostendere est dignata, qualiter sibi placuerit intemerata ipsius pudicitia cum mente qua Deum videbat mundissima. Post novem siquidem annos eius sepulturae, suggerentibus Heamburgensibus, placuit Regi Ceolredo, qui tunc regnabat Merciis, quatenus sacrosancta ipsius gleba de tumulo elevaretur, clamantibus cunctis indignum esse ut tanta lux multorum sub modio terrae absconderetur. Ablato ergo operculo speluncae, cum putaretur ab omnibus more humanae conditionis tota caro defluxisse et tantum nuda ossa superesse; inventa est potius Virgo integerrima quasi in dulci stratu obdormire; vestes nitidissimae et sanae, sicut primitus induta erat, omnino apparuere; facies candida, et genae roseae, tamquam in primaevo flore, amoto reverenter velamine, sunt visae. Attollitur clamor gratiarum in caelum, tantaeque gratiae admiratio in laudes Domini accendit frequentem populum. Assumitur ergo a Sacerdotibus solemniter adornatis, cum supplicibus votis et canoris chorizantis Ecclesiae modulis. Explorantibus adhuc diligenti studio, nulla penitus in ea laesio, nulla reperta est corruptio. Ita demum reconditur in theca sibi competenter parata, ubi conspicue fideles populos illustrat praeclara lampade sua.

Duravit diutius sub Angelica custodia hic honor illaesi corporis, usque ad tempora scilicet Paganorum et dira malorum, quando justissima Dei dispensatione haec patria Anglorum tradita est gladiis Gentilium. Tunc demum vitalis gleba voluit cedere mortali legi, atque resolvi, ne impiis manibus eam contingerent hostes, miraculorum Dei increduli et beneficiorum ingrati. Potuit plane Dei omnipotentia et in die malorum dilectam suam protegere, sicut servavit plerosque Sanctos huius patriae ab iniqua contagione, qui adhuc usque jam post quadringentos amplius annos vernant integro et incorrupto corpore, et poterunt indubitanter usque in finem pro Divino arbitrio perdurare. Verumenimvero mirabilis et gloriosus Deus in Sanctis suis, mira et inaestimabili providentia alios in majorem gloriam resurrectionis ad tempus resolvit, alios perpetua incorruptione in exemplum promissionis suae custodit. Tot nobilissimi Martyres et summi Sacerdotes Domini a bestiis, vel avibus, vel ignibus sunt consumpti. Posuerunt, inquit Psalmographus, mortalia servorum tuorum, Domine, escas volatilibus caeli, carnes Sanctorum tuorum bestiis terrae. Quo maior fuit ignominia, eo maior erit gloria. Summus Martyrum primicerius Stephanus, dum legitur multa signa in vita fecisse, non ibi tamen legitur mortuos suscitasse. Post mortis vero triumphum omniumque membrorum resolutionem, plerosque mortuos describitur vitae reddidisse, ut a mortis injuria major nasceretur vitae potentia. Magnae itaque gratiae Dei respectus erat in B. Werburgae corpore solido, sed major spes acternae renovationis restat in jam consumpto.—Celebremus ergo promptissima devotione sacratissimam ipsius festivitatem, quia omnis eius celebritas ad Christi Domini pertinet honorem, qui ita eam condignis meritis fecit celebrabilem quam nimirum nobis pro·

vidit ante se Interventricem, quatenus per dilectae suae venera-
tionem, suam mereamur propitiationem, qui non habemus
meritorum executionem. Tanto quippe benignius illam exaudiet
orantem pro nobis, quanto accensiores fuerimus in ipsius Deo
offerendis praeconiis. Annuat nobis semper memorandae Werburgae coronator, quatenus per eius sancta suffragia et hic
profutura desideria consequamur, et in aeternum beatae visionis
ac resurrectionis suae consortia mereamur. Annuat, inquam,
ipse Salvator, qui cum Patre et Spiritu sancto in omnia secula
regnat et dominatur. Amen.

Comparing Bradshaw's poem with the Latin *Vita*, and
the other sources used by him, we find how unjust it would
be to call him—as he modestly calls himself—a mere translator. Indeed, nothing would be falser. He had not only
to gather his materials from the most distant sources, and to
arrange all this mass of information, all these legendary, his-
toric, anecdotic ingredients, but he added largely of his
own, using freely his invention (save in facts) for poetic
purposes. His own are not only the prologues, "breue re-
hersalls," and epilogues (II. Capp. 21—24), but the many
descriptive parts, as the splendid description of the feast at
St. Werburge's spiritual marriage (I. Cap. 16), that of the
procession which brings her relics into Chester (II. 267—350),
that of the great fire at Chester (II. 1598 ff.), the descriptions of war, battle and siege, with ordnance and "artillarie";
his own, the fine lyric ingredients which mostly remind us
of popular songs, as the song at receiving holy communion
("Well-come my lorde, well-come my kynge," &c., I. 2963—
2990), the Lamentation of the Sisters at Werburge's death
(I. 3137 ff.), the "Welcome" to St. Werburge at the bring-
ing-in of her relics (II. 316 ff.); his own, nearly all the
numerous and long speeches (wooings, dialogues, exhortations, prayers, farewells, &c.), the apostrophe to the ladies
of his time (I. 1779—1806), the reflections; his own, all
the illustration, the *examples* taken from sacred and profane
history and from nature, the quotations from the Bible, the
proverbs, the metaphors, &c,[1]

[1] Examples taken from sacred and profane history are, for instance :
In beaute amyable, she was equall to Rachell, Comparable to Sara in fyrme

In his descriptions he conforms to the taste of his time, which, since Chaucer, through the influence of Italian poetry,

fidelyte, In sadness and wysedom lyke to Abygaell, Replete as Delbora with grace of prophecy, Equyualent to Ruth she was in humylyte, In pul-chrytude Rebecca, lyke Hester in lolynesse, Lyke Judyth in vertue and proued holynesse, I. 799—805; similar instances, I. 2171-5, 2178—2184; I. 1044 ff. : Lyke as Archythofell, chefe counselour to Absalon, Sundry tymes moeued hym vnto varyaunce, And with kynge Ass-uerus in fauour was Amon, Counseylynge hym euer vnto great mys-chaunce: In lyke cause Werbode, moeued to vengeaunce, was chefe counseler to Vulfer the kynge ; and II. 1500—1513 : It is red in scrip-ture howe quene Jesabell, Ambicious of honour agaynst all ryghtous-nes, Peruerted her lorde Achas, kyng of Israell, To sle Nabath for his vineyard doubtles ; Also Athalia, the bible sheweth expresse, Com-maunded to slee the kynges children all, That she myght regne sole princesse imperiall, &c. ; I. 1093—1099 : To Noe came comforte after the great deluge By a douue bryngynge a braunche of Olyue, To the prophet Hely a rauen dyd refuge, Brought hym his sustenaunce and saued hys lyue ; Vnto saynt Eustach full memoratyue Our lorde ap-pered in a hartes lykenes, To whome he obeyed gladly with mekenes—Of whiche *examples* prynce Vulfade gladde was ; I. 788 : The nobles . . . came for to seke her, lyke as to Solomon Quene Saba approched to here of his wysedome ; II. 1468 : Like as to Moises deuided the redde see And the water of Jordan obeyed to Josue, Ryght so the depe riuer of Dee made diuision ; I. 1345 ff.   From profane history : II. 1201, This Edgare was nominate in cronicles expresse The floure of Englande, regnyng as emperour, Lyke-wise as Romulus to Romains was of prowes, Cyrus to the Persis, to the Grekes their conquerour, Great Charles to Frenchemen, to Troians Hectour ; II. 1626 ff. : Alas, great heuynes it was to beholde The cite of Troye all flamyng as fire, More pite of Rome cite was manyfolde, Feruently flagrant, empoiryng the empire : As to the quantite the cite of Chestire myght be assembled this tyme in like case To the sayd citees. From nature : I. 724-8, Dothe not a royall rose from a brere procede, Passynge the stocke with pleasaunt dylecta-cyon ? The swete ryuer passeth by due probacyon His heed and foun-tayne : ryght so dothe she Transcende her parentes with great benygnyte ; cf. 610 ; 2003 : As the ryuer passeth oftetymes the heed-fountayne, The lytell graffe or ympe transcendeth the tree, Lykewyse theyr chyldren encresed certayne In mekenes, &c. ; 2949 ff. : The swete byrde closed in a cage a longe season Gladly entendeth to fly at lyberte, The prysoner fetered and cast in depe dongeon Euer supposes to be rydde frome cap-tyuyte : The soule of mankynde, moost dygne of dutye, Naturally desyreth . . . to be delyuered from bodyly pryson ; 1156 : He watched on them . . . Lyke as a hounde folowynge . . . or a dogge dothe a dere by sent of the chas ; 1233, he rored and yelled lyke a wylde bull ; 1805, prowd as a pecocke ; 1579, stones glyterynge as Phebus, and the beten golde lyke an erthly paradyse (the same simile 3125, 3377) ; 1790, shynynge lyke angels ; 3390, more white than the lile Mixt with rose

and the then growing arts of painting and music, had turned
to picturesqueness and melody. In his description of the
feast, the hall is hung with painted tapestry, paintings which
represent the whole celestial hierarchy in the order then used
in altar-pieces. The attitudes in which he produces his saint,
her way of address, her tone of feeling, sometimes remind us
of the Sancta-conversazione-pictures of the old masters, and
breathe the devotion which inspired a Fra Angelico 'da Fie-
sole.[1] His genuine and true English character appears more
in the lyric and dialoguic ingredients, in the sense of humour
which sometimes pervades his narrative, as in the miracle
of the geese (I. 2612 ff.), in the invective against the proud
ladies of his time (I. 1779 ff.); but more in the all-pervading
truth which makes him cling to facts rather than fictions, and
renders his performance more historical than legendary; in
the truth of his feeling, his warm heart, his earnestness, his
piety and devotion.

Bradshaw's powers have been very differently rated:
Warton speaks slightingly of him, Dibdin values him highly,

colour; 1814, Werburge professed to her rule full ryght, A redolent
floure . . As Lucyfer shynynge, a clere lampe of lyght. He compares
(like Lydgate) the virtues of his saint to the precious stones and flowers
(II. 313 ff., 1906 ff.), she is a myrrour of mekeness, a flower of chastyte, a well of clennes (I. 2521, 3140). He uses Venus for love (I. 44,
1884), goddes Cupyde (890); more frequently Phebus for sun (I. 1191;
bryghter than Phebus in his meridian spere II. 1389, shenyng more bryght
than radiant phebus in the triumphant trone I. 3330). Quotations
from the Bible: I. 855-60, 1149-52, 1352-6, 2851-7, 3009-11, 3196-9;
3485; II. 8 ff. Proverbs: Tho man prepose, god dysposeth all; Who
clymbeth to hye, often hath a fall, I. 930-1; Tho mankynde prepose
his mynde to fulfyll, Yet god dysposeth all thynge at his wyll, 3201-2;
A lad to wedde a lady is an inconuenyent, 1015; Good maners and
conynge maken a man, II. 7 (cf. Manners maken man, Quoth Wil'iam
of Wykeham); I. 76, 2750. On the whole his illustrations are not very
rich, but adapted to the purpose, and in the character of his time.

[1] It must also be remembered that the shrine of St. Werburge at
Chester was decorated with thirty images of kings of Mercia and other
princes, ancestors or relations of our saint (from which he took, perhaps, the Prince of West Saxons who wooed S. W.). Other instances
of the influence of painting are frequent in the poetry of that time, as
in Capgrave's *Life of St. Katharine*.

Hawkins takes a middle course.[1]   In my estimation he ranks among the best of old English poets.   Not only

[1] Warton, for instance, remarks : "Henry Bradshaw has rather larger pretensions to poetical fame than William of Nassington, although scarcely deserving the name of an original writer in any aspect. . . . B. is not so fond of relating visions and miracles as his argument seems to promise.   Although concerned with three saints, he deals more in plain facts than in the fictions of religious romance, and on the whole his performance is rather historical than legendary ; this is remarkable in an age when it was the fashion to turn history into legend. . . . But a greater degree of credulity would perhaps have afforded him a better claim to the character of a poet, and at least we should have conceived a more advantageous opinion of his imagination had he been less frugal of those traditionary fables in which ignorance and superstition had clothed every head of his argument.   The most splendid passage of the poem is the description of the feast made by Wulfer in the Hall of the Abbey of Ely. . . . If there be any merit of imagination or invention to which the poet has a claim in this description, it altogether consists in the application ; the circumstances themselves are faithfully copied by B. from what his own age actually presented.   In this respect, I mean as a picture of ancient life, the passage is interesting, and for no other reason.   The versification is infinitely inferior to Lydgate's worst manner. . . Bale, a violent reformer, observes that our poet was a person remarkably pious for the times in which he flourished.   This is an indirect satire on the monks and on the period which preceded the Reformation.   I believe it will readily be granted that our author has more piety than poetry.   His prologue contains humble professions of his inability to treat lofty subjects and to please light readers."   Dibdin says : "It is presumed that his name will stand among the foremost in the list of the poets of the period wherein he wrote.   His descriptions are oftentimes happy as well as minute, and there is a tone of moral purity and rational piety in his thoughts, enriched by the legendary lore of romance that renders many passages of his poem exceedingly interesting."   Hawkins: "If it is not allowed to rank B., according to Dibdin's estimate, among the foremost in the list of poets of his period, it is unjust to place him in so low a rank among his contemporaries as the severity of Warton seems to demand.   There is a tone of moral principle and devotional piety so unaffectedly pervading the whole volume, and so easily and naturally introduced, as to impress the reader with the conviction that they had an habitual influence upon his mind and heart, and exhibited themselves without an effort, and almost unconsciously in all his expressions.   There is much strength and apparent sincerity in his numerous exhortations to piety and devotion. . . His familiarity with the Latin language has been already noticed, and the reader can scarcely have failed to observe his intimate acquaintance with the sacred writings ; numerous Scripture personages are adduced as models and examples of the various virtues which adorn the Christian character ; and the language of Scripture is constantly

for his deep learning, his truth and sincerity, his warm
feeling, his piety, and the purity of his moral; not only
for the frequently happy and vigorous style of his narrative,
his lyric parts, his graphic descriptions, &c.; but for the
combination of all these powers; and because his poem is a
most successful attempt at a genuine and popular epic, rude
as its form may still be.   There is an attempt at epic style,
at epic copiousness, minuteness, and objectiveness, at epic
humour, which shows that the poet not only studied in the
school of Homer,[1] but had a natural talent for that kind of
poetry.   The poem is, to me, full of single charms, full of
happy traits of character and description (cf. f. i. I. 1301);
everything is to the point and interesting, nothing dry, tedious,
and diffuse (as in Capgrave), or showy and ostentatious (as
in Lydgate).   Even in his descriptions he observes the law

apparent in his exhortations and descriptions.   Moral maxims and proverbs, the concentrated wisdom of ages, seem to have been familiar to
him, and may be detected in many of his pages. . . The remark of
Warton is probably just, that had he had a greater degree of credulity,
he would have had a greater chance of being poetical; credulity indeed
does not seem to be his failing, for though he records many miracles,
. . . it is quite clear that he omits many marvellous tales which might
have been supplied by the original work, but which would be 'to the
readers tedious, no mervayle, sothly,' and to which he was not himself
quite prepared to give full credit. . . B. had evidently less faith in
the miracles of his monastery than had been enjoyed by his prede-
cessors; in truth, there appears to be occasionally a lurking humour in
his description which betrays as much disbelief in his own narrative as
the temper of the times and the still lingering credulity of his contemporaries would permit (?).   If his own good sense and the growing en-
franchisement of the period from the bondage of superstition and papal
imposition checked in him any tendency to imaginative flights and
poetic paroxysms, it will not be denied that he frequently exhibits con-
siderable strength of expression in his language, and great powers in his
vivid and graphic descriptions.   A goodly specimen of railing may be
found in the rebuke of Werbode for his presumption.   Many of the
miraculous cures are described with great force, and it will be difficult
to find in any contemporary author so lively, picturesque, and humor-
ous a narrative as that of the unhappy *Geese of Wedon*, 'who went
mekely as yf they had reason naturall, unto her presence,' &c."

[1] I may be mistaken in assuming that he read Homer; but Homer's
poems, certainly, were known at his time.

of epic progression, as when his persons move in procession one after another, according to their rank (as I. 1506 ff., II. 274 ff.). The simplicity of feeling and expression is (I think) sometimes truly Homeric (so I. 1415-23). His speeches breathe a sweetness and tenderness and delicacy characteristic of the genuine epic; even the formal way of address is truly epic. The poet is full of his subject, of his hero; all is steeped in that *admiration* and *devotion* which are the true sources of epic poetry. The details are executed with that *love* which springs from devotion. Sometimes, in his narrative, we even find the tone of *hilarity* peculiar to Homer (as in the miracle of the geese). These qualities cannot but excite our admiration, and impress the reader with agreeable feelings. There is even an attempt at epic composition; at least the inserted lives of St. Sexburge and St. Audry are, I think, intended as episodes. In giving at large the genealogy of his saint, he does exactly what Homer did before him. In other respects he is bound by the course of his narrative.

The poem is written in 7-lined stanzas (rhyme royal, introduced by Chaucer); sometimes a Latin verse is added as an 8th line: I. 2696, 3110, 3118, 3413; an English verse is added in II. 526. Once the two last verses of the 7-lined stanza are formed by Latin leonine verses: II. 1337-8. The concluding chapters (II. Cap. 21—23) are composed in 8-lined stanzas (the last verse forming the refrain), Cap. 21 with same rhymes throughout the chapter. The same change of. stanzas occurs in Lydgate, the 8-lined stanza being considered more fit for magniloquent passages, prayers, admonitions, &c. The Lenvoye (Cap. 24) is again written in rhyme royal (as in Lydgate).—The verses seem at first sight rather rugged and imperfectly built. Hawkins remarks: "He had clearly not a musical ear, his versification is not smooth and harmonious, and his naturally defective appreciation of rhythmical intonation has been much exaggerated by the awkward and difficult arrangement of the stanza which he has adopted; with an easier metre his lines might have flowed with more ease and grace." Indeed, the regular 10-syllable verses of Chaucer, with a regular change of toned and toneless syllables, are not frequently found. But he generally retains the old popular long-line (with four accents in two half-lines, and an arbitrary number of untoned syllables) used by the Anglo-Saxons, revived in the alliterative long-line of the 14th century, and still employed in the North at his time—verses which have a sort of anapæstic (or dactylic) rhythm.[1] This principle does not, however, seem to be strictly observed, and verses of the regular kind seem to be mixed up with the long-lines. In choosing the popular long-line he also retained the alliteration used with the long-line, and still popular in the North; not, as a rule, in each verse, but arbitrarily, and mostly attached to certain locutions and phrases (partly of old date, partly new formed).[2] Some-

[1] Hawkins remarks: "To produce anything of rhythmical composition, the accent must be laid strongly upon the very last syllable of the line, even in cases when, according to the modern mode of pronunciation, the last syllable is as little dwelt upon as possib'e; the following illustrations may be observed: gostly remedy, parte trinite, odour savour hour, body clergy verity," &c. This is true, and more so in French or Latin words, where the accent is mostly to be put on the last syllable, which is frequently the only rhyming one; but Hawkins does not understand the principle.

[2] Such phrases of old or recent date, are, for instance: brute beest, wylde wood, sharpe sword, bare bon, harde hert, wretched world, dere derlyng, doughter dere, louely lady, crowned kyng, chefe champyon, fa'se fend, poore peple, royall rose, royall reme, &c.; mayn and myght, churches and chapeles, wydowes and wyues, rentes and ryches, ryches and royalte, realme and royalte, vncles and auntes, prelatis and pr.nces, hawkyng and huntyng, fayr and fre, meke and mylde, wanton and wylde, sadde and sobre, secret and styll, well and wysely, to haue and holde, call and cry, sigh and sobbe, wayle and wepe, sing and say, mervayle and muse, gouerne and guye, conserue and saue, &c.; lyke a lady, feruent as fyre, flamyng as fyre, clerer than cristall, after cours of kynde, a lampe of lyght, lanterne of lyght, kyng of kynges, on payne of punyshment, in parte of payne, grace of god, for love of our lord, a well with water, deth with his darte, most of myght, kuelyng on kne, dredfully daryng, syngyng swetely, regnyng in regaly, reigne with reuerence, found fals, kept in clos, soth to say, to try out the truthe, to take in a trayne, semyng as on slepe, sorowe came vnsought, vertu to avaunce, moeued his mynde, &c. Many of these combinations are certainly new, as prynce prepotent, principall protectour, trusty

times, however, and mostly in descriptive passages, it is so
frequent that it occurs more than thrice in the same line, or
extends over two lines, or that two different alliterations are
found in one line. So the same popular element which
appears in the lyric parts, in the proverbs quoted, &c., also
figures in the metre of his verses, and in the alliterations.—
The rhymes are frequently defective: there are several
identical rhymes (tell tell, I. 1682; out out, II. 1161; playne
playne, I. 2608; cost (cost) cost (coast), II. 1157), or where the
rhyming syllable is identical (Englande lande, forsake sake,
past-tyme tyme, Oswolde wolde, Kenrede we rede, well-come
come, dyspleasure pleasure, olyue lyue, Eadfryde Osfryde,
Oxenforde Herforde, Werburge Milburge; also rhymes like
sadnesse gentylnesse, ydlenes busines mekenes, example
people, resonable impossyble, dygnyte beaute, suerte prosperite, mighty twenty, newly ghostly, reason pryson, &c.,
rhymes which are very frequent). There are many bad

treasure, charitable chanons, tortuous tormentour, taynted traytour,
redolent rose, power and policy, pleasant and profitable, floure of
femynyte, diamond of dignite, saphire of sincerite, sufficient to suffyse,
dygne of duty, submyttyng vnder subjeccyon, &c. Sometimes we find
two alliterative words in a line: Stande vp Werbode, kyng Vulfer than
sayd; It is well knowen thou arte comen of nought; Ledynge the
Israelites to the lande of promyssyon, &c.; sometimes more: The maker
of mankynde most in maieste; Called specyall prymate and pryncypall
presydent; With mynstrels melody and myrthes amonge; Our chyfe
champyon in all our chyualry; Thou cruell pagano presumynge at thy
pleasure; he lauded full lowly our lord; The people were prone and
punysshed therfore; Manyfest wyth myracles by meryte of her mekenesse; On a rocke they ranne no remedy myght fynde, &c. The same
alliteration in two lines: Her merytes were moche more commendable
Than were her myracles manyfest and playne (I. 2606), The messanger
merueyled and mused in his mynde Of this straunge message stode styll
in a study (2633), Also she refused her fathers realme and royalte All
ryches rentes pleasures possessions (1541). Heaped alliterations in two
lines: This wycked Werebode the bedyll of Belyall, The minister of
myschef & sergeaunt of sathanas (I. 1023-4). In French words the alliteration lies frequently in the first syllable before the tone, as in daily
desirynge, perceyuyng him penitent, she refused her realme, her preeminence caused no presumpcyon, our counsell therto consentynge; or
in the second-toned syllable, as in vertue to auaunce, conserue and saue,
aray and royalte (cf. fortune vnfrendly).

c

rhymes, as pylgrimage barge, express rehers I. 2206, doubtles
rehers (r. express?), princes rehers, porte harte, solemnysed
syde;[1] especially where *n* rhymes with *m*, as tyme ruyne,
exempt obedient, Rome alone.[2] Another licence (frequent in
the older popular Midland poetry) is, that he rhymes only the
last and toneless syllables, so even in endings, as, for instance,
gees feldes, I. 2619; churches richesse, II. 360; brethur tresur,
I. 2329; parte trinite, 3364; is bylcuys, 1113; resolued shryned,
II. 231; descended notyfyed, I. 589; possessed greued, 2844;
rehersed dede, or in heuyn Ruffyn, 1225; heuen (r. heuyn)
nyen, 2319; maydyn dyscyplyne, 764; lenton religyon,
martyr (r. marter) father, father syster, syster doughter,
bretherne (r. brether) aulter, 2226; maker daunger, foundere
clere; or in cases like doubtles folysshenes, doubtles quyetnes,
lady be, body satisfy, Ely heuy, cruelly dayly worldly, depely
monastery, evidently merveillously, consequently oratory,
euery robry, allmyghty glory, frosty sagittari, bull irefull,
knowlage rage, &c.; and so in French words in on, nce, er,
our, te, ure, ell, ous, y, all, &c. (as in power dyfferre, mariner
prisoner, discrecion consolacion, greuans pagans, protectour
benefactour, artylere vyctorye, dygnyte beaute she, solemnyte
dirige, batell befell, delycyous plentuous, beauteous, precious
in pontificalibus, continuall Paule, &c.); even in example
people;[3] also in Anna Delbora, I. 2813; Adda Duyna, Peade
thyrty, Sledde fre, 368; Whitbye lady, Ely desydery, Deiram
sam, Egnicius gracyous, &c.[4] Full rhymes, like mother
other, lolynesse holynesse, I. 805; Worcester Dorchester, are

---

[1] Complayne (subst.) certayne, I. 2626, is a sort of forced rhyme.

[2] There are many more instances of this kind: tyme doctrine, tyme
Collatyne, tyme Jurwyne, tyme diuine, baptyme ruyne, Salomon
wysedom, region Rome, alone whom, sone kyngdome, one fredom, disposicion martyrdom, religion custom, reason wysedom, barowne rowme,
rowme euerichone, renowne come, peticion come. Instances of the
same kind frequently occur in Midland poetry.

[3] The author probably wrote exampull pepull, or exampill pepill
(cf. fire Chestire, yere Alexandere).

[4] In all these cases the last rhyming syllable has of course the tone,
or a sort of undertone.

very rare. So in these rhymes again the poet uses the liberties of popular poetry. But in a great many cases the impurity of the rhyme is not due to the poet, but to the edition, as in realme (r. reme) Jerusalem, I. 560 ; paganes (r. pagans) penance, parentes (r. parens) conscyens, myscreauntes ordynaunce (cf. pagans Fraunce, Romans plesans), Ermenylde reconcyled begyled (r. reconcylde), heuen (r. heuyn) nyen, hande (r. honde) sounde, lande (r. londe) founde (r. fonde), strang (r. strong) among ; in many cases it is made good by restoring the dialectic peculiarities which the original presented (especially northern forms), as in eight right (r. reght), destroy (r. destry) edyfy, I. 868 ; bretherne (r. brether) aulter, matyns (r. matens) presens, 2545 ; martyre (r. martere) were, martyr father, eye (r. ye) kne (cf. ee : see Josue, II. 1466), herte (r. harte) parte, soule (r. saule) Paule (cf. Paule all specyall), slayne Finane, abbesse (r. abbas) place ; or by the pronunciation, as in Lyncolne mansyon I. 565, Johan extorcyon. It is clearly proved by the rhymes that *é* and *y* had a similar pronunciation[1] (in Mary fre chastite, Synaye see, Caunterbury countre, Gregorye natiuite, Elye she amyte, Dee partye, Mersee memorye, thyrty Peade, thyrte fre Sledde, lady be pite, party humilite kne, glorye virginite, victory charite, hystorye auctorite, myghtye royalte, mysery me, euaugely humilite, tyrannye tree, &c. ; cf. truly tui) ; wherefore we find frequently *e* written for *y* (as in womanle chastyte, gladle possibilite, truele me chyualre, trule he vanyte, solemle humilite, honorable chastyte, misere me cite, priore liberte, police chyualre, lile see, thyrte fre ; besides richely monastery, truly mysery, Ely heuy, I transitori, &c.). In this way we must also explain rhymes like vpone adowne (r. adone), I. 1302 ; crowne possessyon, 2360 ; towne alone, rowme euerichone, custome barowne rowme, renowne

---

[1] Compare also the spelling in eche and yche, quene and quiene, chefe and chyfe, succide ; Bede, however, is rhymed with Ethelred, clere with were. *í* had not yet the present pronunciation, as is proved by rhymes like nyen (r. nyne) heuen (r. heuyn), I. 2318, shrine virgine, tyme ruyne, syde Osfryde, &c. ; nyne rhymes with quene.

religion many-one; before foure honoure, sore sauyour, more rigoure (cf. hour auctour, floure coloure, hour restour succour), but also honour: pleasur tresour, I. 821 (cf. treasure endure, pleasure sure, Arthure endure sure); precious in pontificalibus. Besides, the dialect allowed the poet to use a variety of forms, as certayne playne, certan man Dunstan, certen men women; batell befell, batayle fayle, catall thrall; merciens consciens, mercians greuans; contre Canterbury, countray Journay; brether aulter, brethur tresur, I. 2329; hert and hart, almyghty and almyght, byfore and byforne, &c.

This leads us to consider whether Pynson printed the text exactly as written by the poet, or whether he altered it in some respects. His edition was made only a few years after the poem, and it is very readable, if we except some mistakes; so that we may trust that he did not materially alter the readings. There is, however, as little doubt that he modified the dialect of the original by introducing the forms used in the London press. There are still traces left which clearly prove that the dialect was marked more strongly in the original. Chester being situated on the confines of the Northern, Western, and Midland dialects, we may expect to find peculiarities of all these dialects. Indeed, there are traces of all these dialects, or at least may be gathered from the rhymes.[1] Bradshaw wrote lond hond sond (= sand) rhyming with fonde (= found) bonde sonde (= sound), as I. 23,518 (rhymes like hande sounde, I. 2275; lande founde, 246; Mercelande founde, londe founde, probably also Merslande hande, Englande vnderstande, must therefore be altered). He wrote Paule (rhyming with all, speciall), saule II. 588 (P soule), as in the North; abbas and abbesse; knowlage (I. 932); slayne and slane (: Finane, I. 866), certayne certan (northern) and certen (midland);

---

[1] It is chiefly owing to the influence of various dialects that the spelling is still very uncertain; we find Oswold and Oswald, trist and trust, perell and peril, batell and batayle, posturne and postrone, compassed and compassed, riall and royall, orison and orayson, &c.

he uses ee (or ye = eye), he I. 1004 (= high), distrye (as in the North); toyne (= tune). Forms like wete (: fete) I. 2212, smetyn, marter (: father were), matens (: presens), gebet, profet, perell, franches, viset were frequent in the North Midland; as also reght (P right : eight); myele, frequent in the latter half of the poem, is the northern form, as also correcke; whome (= home), II. 1464, is a spelling peculiar to some parts of the North Midland. In endings we find *u* in brethur Worcestur (: tresur), I. 2329, as in the West; *o* in lenton (: deuocion), comon songon lynon yron Oxonford (the same forms, used mostly in the West, are however frequent in Caxton and other printers); *y* in bylenys (: is) I. 1113, heuyn 1225, 2318, maydyn 764, Chestire (: fire) II. 1630, all of which are found in rhymes. The text has still frequent plurals in *is*, as tearis, hartis, prestis, princis, actis, Persis, &c., besides in *-es*, which is sometimes demanded by the rhyme (as in churches : richesse, feldes gees I. 2619), and *-s* in citizens, Romans, pagans, Merciens, &c. (all in rhymes). The rhyme mynisters : sterres seems to demand mynisteres; Ierarchyses, I. 1629, or Ierarcheses, has to be altered in Ierarchyse (northern spelling); childer, I. 3277, brether are northern forms. The second person of the present tense ends in *-s*, as in the West Midland (cf. thou knowes, does, hase); thou shall, was, dyd, suffered, gaue, toke, are without ending. The third person ends in *-eth* and *-es* (cf. dothe and serues in the same line, I. 952); the plural in *-en*, as in the Midland (cf. ben, lyen, shewen, obseruen). The infinitive still ends sometimes in *-en*, as waken; more frequently the participle, as letten, II. 1313, bounden, &c. Lent (from lenden to arrive, reside) I. 970, 1778, is a Northern form.[1] Bradshaw still uses some old and dialectic words, as layth (lightning), II. 12; drowed, II. 1856 (r. haue drowen, from dreoȝen, to suffer), anentes, bown, shalmes (I. 1689), seyn (= synod).

[1] Latin verbs in ate, st, have commonly no ending in the preterite and participle (as creat, cruciat, preparat, coronate, congregate, arrest, electe; but extincted).

If in these dialectic forms, as well as in his metre and in the use of alliterations, he shows himself to be a friend of the people and of the popular, he is more modern in other respects.   He imitates Lydgate's way of construction, his asyndeta, his omission of the auxiliary 'to be', even with the participle, his frequent use of the participle, his absolute participles (as well knowen and founde, I. 543, proued 2543, 3200, manyfest and playne 2606), &c.; though he is more natural, and not so abstruse and difficult as Lydgate.   He is still more modern in the use and formation of words. Since Chaucer and Lydgate it had been the fashion to introduce long and sonorous words from the French and Latin for the sake of melodiousness and picturesqueness; the ear delighted in the sound of words ending in aunce, oun, aunt, ous, all, able, ate, &c.; every poet tried to augment the stock of these 'aureate terms.'   Our poet stands not behind in this respect.   He uses words like alienat, ampliat, appropryat, confederate, congregate, consecrate, coronate, creat, cruciat, decorate, eleuate, endurate, illumynate, maculate, metigate, nomynat, conomynat, prenomynat, próbate, prostrate, roborate, regenerate, sacrat, tumylate, dylate, retrograt; vnyt, inhabyte, promyt, electe, extyncte; edyfy (= build), gloryfy, magnyfy, multyply, putryfy, specyfy, testyfy, veryfy; enterprise, psalmodise, solempnyse; dyscus, expulse; apperceyue, reuolue; sautynge, flourynge, pasturynge; corespondent, equypolent, equypotent, omnipotent, prepotent, redolent, resplendent, sufficient, remanent; constaunt, exuberaunt, rutilant, oppugnaunt, abundaunt, preignaunt, vernaunt, valeaunt; facundious, memorous, tymerous, dolorous, melodyous, tedyous, vyctoryous; celestiall, corporall, eternall (besides eterne), contynuall, historyall, imperiall, lynyall, marcyall, memorall, memoriall, monasticall, pudicall, sensuall, supernaturall, virginall, vitall, fragyll; commendable, comparable, incomparable, deceuable, fauourable, honorable, mercyable, odible; myssyue, memoratyue, primatyue; barbarike, polytike; alian, cotidian; dygne, condygne; caduce, transytory, interyor, interiously, senyor, remedyless ; sanctimoniall, moiniall, monyall (and moynes), coronall ; essentyals (sensuals) ; tuycyon, fruycyon, intrusyon, extorcyon, mynystracion, nomynyon, notycyon, collusion, suspection, recidiuacion ; dynydent, inconvenyent, encresement ; preheminence, magnificence ; audytour, enherytour, instructour ; valeaunce, puruoaunce ; spousage, parentage ; fortytude, pulchrytude ; femynyte, audacyte, lascyuyte, ambiguite, penalite, senyorite, sensualite, amyte, volupte ; desydery, lumynary, sagittari ; pensyuenesse ; musture, verdure, pasture, moynes, spouses ; homycyde, fysnamy, lygne, ayde, decour, vre, cubycle, subbarb, &c. Many of these words and formations have since disappeared or become obsolete, as recidiuacion, nomynyon, notycyon, suspection, volupte, encresement, desydery, spouses, moiniall, vre,[1] decour, cubycle, lygne, dygne, condygne, caduce, odible, vyctoryall, hystoryall, memorall, memorous, facundyous, remanent, interyously, promyt, psalmodise, apperceyue, sautynge ; as also formations like enuired, encronicled, depair (= impair), dyspent, reparel ; or have taken a different meaning, as tumylate, edyfy, recourse, transcende (a ryuer), dyuydent.   Some of them seem to have been introduced by Bradshaw, as perhaps caduce, volupte, nomynyon, more certainly cyrcumfulsed (I. 2038).   Many French words have still the French spelling, as enherytrice, protectrice, mediatrice, lygne, lygnage, promesse and promes, baptyme, sautyng, covent, &c.[2] French adjectives used adverbially, frequently omit -ly, as playne, sure, certayn, expresse, contynuall, specyall, consequent, &c.

The Glossarial Index to the text was added by Mr. W. M. Wood, for the convenience of readers, under instructions from the Director of the E. E. Text Society.

[1] vre seems first to occur in Lydgate.
[2] In French words also we frequently find double forms, as promyt (promyttnge) and promyse, descrybe and descryue, moynes and moiniall, memorall memoriall memorous, interyour interyously, suspicion and suspection, regalyte regaly (I. 407) realte, lynage and lygnage, discens and dyscent, &c.

CORRECTIONS.

p. 16, v. 221, *put* ; *after* delectab!e.
p. 19, v. 308, *put* [1] *after* Offryde.
p. 51, v. 1274, *put* . *after* syght.
p. 83, v. 2228, *read* matrone *inst. of* matronè.
p. 166, v. 1034, *read* Galway, Scot.
p. 184, headline, *read* Barfleur

¶ Here begynneth the holy lyfe and history of saynt werburge / very frutefull for all christen people to rede.

(Engraving of St. Werburg on title-page.)

¶ *The Prologe of .J. T. in the honour & laude of saint* ⊓. 2
Werburge / and to the prayse of þ *translatour of the
legende folowynge.*

1

H onour / ioye / and glorie / the toynes organicall,　　1
E ndeles myrthes wᵗ melodies ! / prayse ye all yᵉ princes,
N ourisshed in vertue / intact / as pure as cristall,
R elefe to all synners ! / o Werburge, lady maistres ;
I n grace thou passed / all other, and in goodnes,　　5
　Whan thou was present in this mundayne lyfe ;
　None was the lyke / wydowe / mayde / ne wyfe.　　7

2

B y diuyne grace / to vs a ryche present,　　8
R eioyce we may / in Werburge one and all,
A gemme of vertue / a virgin resplendent,
D ilect of our lorde (in ioye and blis eternall
S urely she is set) to intercede and call,　　12
H er mouth nat cessyng / for them to call and cryo
A nd in her trust / of synne to haue mercy.　　14

B

3

O good lady maistres / declyne thy syght a-fer   15
And graciously beholde / thy seruaunt chast and pure,
Henry Bradsha / sometyme monke in Chester,
Whiche only for thy loue / toke the payne and laboure
Thy legende to translate— / he dyd his busy cure,   19
Out of latine / in Englisshe rude and [1] vyle,   [1] P. ande and
Whiche he hath amended / with many an ornate style. 21

4

Alas, of Chestre / ye monkes haue lost a treasure,   22
Henry Bradsha / the styrpe of eloquence !
Chestre, thou may wayle / the deth of this floure;
So may the citezens / alas ! for his absence,
So may many other / for lacke of his sentence.   26
O swete lady Werburge / an holy Abbasse glorious,
Remembre Henry Bradsha / thy seruaunt most gracious. 28

5

In hym remayned no vice ne presumpcion,   29
Enuy and wrath / from hym were exyled,
Slouth ne Venus in hym had no dominion,
Auarice and glotony / he vtterly expelled;
No vice in hym regned / his felowes he excelled.   33
As clene as cristall / he bare these vertues thre :
Chastite / obidience / and wylfull pouerte.   35

6

O cruell deth / whiche art the perfite ende   36
Of this noble clerke / and euery mortall thyng,
Agaynst the / no man may hym defende ;
Thou causest wo / languor / and anguissyng.
And who on this / wolde haue remembryng   40
Howe from erth / to erth he must agayne,
Ho wolde dispise all thynges that be mundayne.   Vale. 42

3

The Table of this boke.

5

5

¶ A litel breue treatise of her hole lyfe / and how for
   her myracles shewed after her deth / the couent
   of Hamburi purposed to tranſlat her body by
   helpe of kyng Coelrede, reignyng in mercelande   Ca. xxxi.

¶ The solempne translacion of this glorious virgine
   saynt Werburge. and of the great myracles done
   at the same season by the might of god / and
   merite of this gracious lady . . . . Cap. xxxii.

¶ Howe the body of saynt Werburge continued hole /
   & substancial at Hambury after þͤ tranſlacion by
   the space of .CC. yeres / tyll the danes were
   comon to this lande / or it fell & resolued was
   vnto powder . . . . Cap. xxxiii.

¶ Here foloweth the lyfe of the gloryous virgyn
saynt werburge / also many miracles that
god hath shewed for her. / & fyrst the prologe of the auctour.

[Under this title the same engraving as on p. 1, and the same
engraving is also repeated at the back of the leaf.]

[BOOK I.]

1

WHan Phebus had ronne his cours in sagittari   1
    And Capricorne entred, a sygne retrograt,
Amyddes Decembre / þᵉ ayre colde & frosty,
And pale Lucyna / the erthe dyd illumynat,
I rose vp shortly / fro my cubycle preparat,   5
Aboute mydnyght / and cast in myne intent
How I myght spende / the tyme conuenyent.   7

2

I called vnto mynde / the great vnstedfastnes   8
Of this wretched worlde— / not by cours of nature—
How there be brought / some men to busynes,
Oppressed with pouerte / langour / and dyspleasure,
Some other exalted / to felycyte and pleasure.   12
The maker of mankynde / most in maieste,
Ruleth all at his wyll / it may non other be.   14

3

Beholde dyscretly / and se the fyrmament,   15
Consyder the sonne / and the mone also,
With all the planettes / and sterres resplendent,
How they kepe theyr cours / bothe to and fro,
Euer obedyent / theyr creature vnto ;   19
And byrdes besely / syngynge euery day,
Praysynge theyr prymate all that they may ;   21

4

The .iiii. elementes / in lyke condycyon,   22
The fyre / the water / the ayre / and the londe,
Obseruen theyr duty / after theyr creacyon
And buxum ben / and euer so be fonde.
Thus euery creature / as we vnderstonde,   26
Obeyeth to his creature / with humylyte—
Except dyssolute man / folowyng sensualyte;   28

5

If man wyll remembre / how he was create   29
To the lykenes and figure / of god almyghty,
And set in paradyse / a place moost delycate,
To haue the fruycyon / of eternall glory /
If not synne expulsed hym / to the vale of mysery,   33
But that he wolde enclyne / his naturall reason
To serue his maker / truely at due season.   35

6

Dyuers people / haue dyuers condicions :   36
Comynly proued / it is euery day :
Some set to vertu / and good disposycyons,
In penaunce / prayer / all that they may,
Some in contemplacyon / the sothe to say,   40
Some in abstynence / to chastyce the body
And make it subget / to the soule perfytely ;   42

7

Some other reioyce / in synne and ydelnes,   43
Some seruauntes to Venus / both day and nyght,
Other to couetyse / and worldly besynes,
Some to deceyue / by subtylte in syght,
Some vnto marchandyse / & wynnynge full ryght,   47
Some ferefull and tymerous / without audacyte,
Some sadde and sobre / and of great grauyte ;   49

8

Many haue pleasure to speke of rybaudry,   50
Some of fyghtynge / braulynge / and actes marcyall,
Other to flater / and paynt the company,

Some to syt bytwene the cuppe and the wall,
Some to blaspheme / and dyssemble withall,   54
To backbyte and sclaunder / by malyce and enuy,
Some to extorcyon / thefte and playne robry.   56

9

Thus after fraylte / and sundry compleccyons   57
Dyuers men dyuers in lyuynge there be,
Dysposed by a contrary dysposycyon,
Some vnto vertue / some vnto vanyte ;
Many maners of people / now we may se   61
Wauerynge in the worlde / without quyetnes,
As a shyp by tempest / is dryuen, doubtles.   63

10

Whan I reuolued / with due circumstaunce   64
The dyuers maners / and mutabylyte
Of worldly people / and the great varyaunce,
And how this lyfe / is of no suerte,
Now in great langour / now in prosperyte ;   68
yet after our meryte / we shalbe sure
To be rewarded / at our departure :   70

11

Than to vertuous labours / we shulde apply   71
And spende not our tyme / all in ydlenes ;
For, as a byrde is made / by nature to fly,
Ryght so we shulde vse / some good busynes
To our soule-helthe / with great mekenes ;   75
For tyme euyl spende / in labours vayne
Is harde to be well / recouered agayne.   77

12

But now, syth I am / a relygyous man,   78
For losynge of tyme / can not me excuse,
Therfore I purpose / to do as I can :
All suche ydlenes / whylom to refuse,
With the grace of god / the tyme for to vse   82
Some small treatyse / to wryte breuely
To the comyn vulgares / theyr mynde to satysfy.   84

13

To descrybe hỹe hystoryes / I dare not be so bolde,   85
Syth it is a mater / for clerkes conuenyent,
As of the .vii. aeges / and of our parentes olde,
Or of the .iiii. empyres / whylom moost excellent ;
Knowynge my lernynge / therto insuffycyent.   89
As for bawdy balades / ye shall haue none of me,
To excyte lyght hertes / to pleasure and vanyte.   91

14

But now in auoydynge / suche great folysshenes   92
I purpose to wryte / a legende good and true
And translate a lyfe / into Englysshe doubtles ;
I meane the spouse / of our lorde Ihesu,
Blessed saynt Werburge / replete with vertue,   96
A noble prynces borne / & vyrgyne pure and gloryous,
After an holy monyall / and an abbesse gracyous.   98

15

In the abbay of Chestre / she is shryned rychely,   99
Pryores and lady / of that holy place,
The chyef protectryce / of the sayd monastery
Longe before the conquest / by deuyne grace ;
Protectryce of the Cytee / she is and euer was,   103
Called specyall prymate / and pryncypall presydent,
There rulynge vnder / our lorde omnypotent.   105

16

And yf I vnworthy / begynne this lytell werke,   106
I praye all the reders / mekely of pardon,
To correcke and amende / syth I am no clerke,
Excuse my ignoraunce / and take the entencyon.
My mynde is to shewe / her lyfe and deuocyon,   110
That euery man and woman / ensample maye take
At this pure vyrgyn / synne to forsake.   112

17

And syth that she is / in blysse now gloryfyed,   113
It were no reason / her name be had in scylence,
But to the people / her name be magnyfyed,

To her laude and prayse / honour and reuerence.
Her parentes and bretherne / þᵉ floures of experyence, 117
Haue ben kepte in close / secrete many a day :
Wherfore I purpose / somwhat of them to say.   119

18

Fyrst I entende / to make playne descrypcyon   120
Of her fathers kyngedome / the realme of Mercyens,
How longe it endured / vnder his tuycyon,
Vnder how many kynges / it had prehemynens ;
Also of her petygre / the noble excellence—   124
For so many sayntes / of one kynred, certayne,
Is harde to be founde / in all the worlde agayne.   126

19

Vnto this rude werke / myne auctours these shalbe :   127
Fyrst the true legende / and the venerable Bede,
Mayster Alfrydus / and Wyllyam Maluysburye,
Gyrarde / Polycronycon / and other mo in deed.
Now gloryous god / graunt me to procede ;   131
Blessed vyrgyn Werburge / my holy patronesse,
Helpe me to endyte / I praye the, swete maystresse.   133

¶ *A descrypcyon of the realme of Mercyens / of bondes and
commodytes of the same.*

20

Ҭ He yere of our sauyoure / by full compu*tacyon*¹   134
Foure hundred / nyne & fourty frome his natiuite, ¹ P. compu-
As venerable Bede / maketh declaracyon,   lacyon
Duke Hengyst came to this lande in great royalte
With Saxons / Angles / Iutes / thre people myghtye ;   138
Desyred by Vortyger / than kynge of Brytons,
Came to defende [him] / fro greuous oppressyons.   140

21

Also the yeres of our blessed sauyoure   141
Syxe hundreth foure score and nyne expresse
The Brytons were expulsed / so sayth myne auctoure,

From Englande to walles / with great wretchydnes.
In Englande than ruled / seuen kynges, doubtles,   145
whose names we purpose / to shewe with lycens,
But pryncypally / of the kyngdome of Mercyens.   147

22

The fyrst realme of Saxons / began in Kent,   148
The yere of grace / foure hundreth fyue and fyfty ;
Where duke Engystus / in honour excellent,
With septre and crowne / fyrst reygned royally.
The seconde was Southsex / sayth the hystory,   152
Wher Adla and Ella / reygned full ryght ;
Whiche realme endured / but short tyme in myght.   154

23

The thyrde was Westsaxons / famous and myghty,   155
Where fyrst reygned / kynge Cerdicus,
The yere of our lorde / fyue hundreth one and twenty ;
Whiche realme by processe / and power vyctoryous
Subdued all other / to hym, full memorous.   159
The pryncypall Cytees / of his regalyte
Were in olde season / Wynchester and Salesburye.   161

24

The fourth was Estsex / Where duke Erchenwyn   162
Fyrst reygned kynge / hauynge domynacyon,
By the kynge of Merselande / brought ofte to ruyne ;
The chyef Cytee was Colchester / of his domynyon.
Also of eest-Englande / was the fyfth kyngdome,   166
Where Vffa crowned / had fyrst the sufferaynte
Of Northfolke and Southfolke / knowen in certaynte.   168

25

The syxthe was the kyngdome of Merslande,   169
Where Cryda was crowned / fyrst by auctoryte,
Hauynge nyne shyres / obedyent to his hande,
As after shall appere / more euydent to be.
The seuenth was Northumberlande / vnder Ida & Alle,   173
Whylom dyuyded / in sondry kyngdomes twayne ;   [175
The chyfe Cytee was yorke / wher þᵉ kynge dyd reygne.

26

The realme of Mercyens / by olde antyquyte,   176
As playnly declareth / Polycronycon,
Thre hundreth yeres / endured in auctoryte,
Vnder eyghtene kynges / worthy nomynyon,
Greatest of gouernaunce of all this regyon ;   180
Where Vulfer reygned / a kynge vyctoryous,
Father to saynt Werburge / vyrgyn moost gloryous.   182

27

The boundes and lorshyppes / of the sayd Mercyens,   183
As shewen dyuers bokes hystoryall,
Were large and myghty / and of great prehemynens,   -
Where the sayd kynge reygned by power imperyall.
This realme to dyscrybe / begyn we shall   187
At the Cytee of Chester / and the water of Dee,
Bytwene Englande and wales / of the west partye ;   189

28

And so transcendynge / vp towarde Shrewysbury   190
By the water of Sabryne / vnto Brystowe ;
The Eest-see mesureth / the Eest parte, truely ;
The water of Thamys / the south parte doth shewe,
Flowynge vnto London / who-so dothe it knowe ;   194
The water of Humbre / was on the north syde,
With the water of Mersee / theyr landes to dyuyde.   196

29

Of the foresayd ryuer / and water of Mersee   197
The kynge of Mercyens / taketh his name,
As moost sure dyuydent / to be had in memorye,
Mesurynge and metynge / the bondes with great fame
Of Mersee and Northumberlande / kynges of tho same, 201
Bitwene chesshyr & lancashyr theyr kingdomes, certayne,
As auncyent Cronycles descryben it full playne.   203

30

The sayd myghty kyngdome / of Mercyens dyd holde   204
Many noble Cytees / with townes and burghes royall,
Whiche Penda optayned / enlarged manyfolde ;

As Chester / Stafford / Lytchefelde / Couentre memorall,
Lyncolne and Huntyngdon / Northampton withall,   208
Leycester and Derby / Cambrydge and Oxonforde,
Worchester and Brystowe / with other mo, & Herforde. 210

31

Many royall ryuers / were conteyned in the same,   211
With sundry kyndes of fysshes / swete and delycyous—
It were tedyous to shewe / of them the dyuers name
In ryuers and in pooles / swymmynge full plentuous ;
Also forestes / parkes / chases large and beauteous,   215
And all beestes of venery / pleasaunt for a kynge
To cours at lyberte / be founde there pasturynge.   217

32

Also this royall realme / holdeth, as we fynde,   218
Habundaunce of fruytes / plesaunt and profytable,
Great plente of cornes / and graynes of euery kynde ;
With hylles / valeys / pastures / comly and delectable
The soyle and glebe / is set plentuous and commendable. 222
In all pleasaunt propurtes / no part of all this lande
May be compared / to this foresayd Merselande.   224

33

The people of Mercyens / the trouthe yf we dare saye, 225
Lordes / barons / knyghtes / with all the comunete,
In musture and in batayle / euer the pryce haue they
The kynges grace to serue / moost valyaunt in artylere,
In all actes Marcyall / euer hauynge the vyctorye,   229
With herte / mynde and harneys / redy day and nyght
Theyr enemyes to subdue / by power, mayne & myght. 231

34

If they be well ordred / vnder a sure capytayne   232
And set to suche busynesse / theyr honour to auaunce,
The tryumph they optayne— / knowen it is certayne
In Englande and Scotlande / & in the realme of Fraunce ;
Fewe of them haue countred / by manhode and valeaunce 236
Great nombre of enemyes / with knyghthode & polycy,
We meane them moost specyall / in the Weest-party. 238

35

Many other commodytes / pleasures and proprytes   230
This sayd realme / holdeth of olde antyquyte,
In royaltes and lordshyppes / landes and lybertes,
Honourably dylated / in worshyp and polyce,
Flourynge in wysedome / honours /and chyualre :   243
Veryfyed by kynge Offa / moost myghty and excellent,
Proued in his actes / by playne experyment.   245

36

This Offa subdued / in hystory as is founde,   246
The kynge[s] of Westsaxons / Northumberlande & Kent,
Droue Brytons to wales / out of this lande,
And made a depe dytche / for a sure dyuydent
Bytwene Englande and Wales / & to this day presente 250
Is called dytche Offa / so that no Bryton
On payne of punysshement / shulde entre this regyon. 252

37

Kynge Offa translated / as sayth Polycronycon,   253
By myghty power / the see of Canterbury
Vnto Lychefelde chyrche / with famous oblacyon,
For euer to contynu / confyrmed by auctoryte ;
Also he founded / saynt Albans monasterye ;   257
Fyrst of deuocyon / to Rome gaue Peter pens.
Thus royall somtyme / was the realme of Mercyens.   259

¶ *A descrypcyon of the Geanalogy of saynt Werburge, and
how she descended of foure kynges of this lande / & of
the royall blode of Fraunce.*

¶ *Regnum Merc'. ex parte patris.*

38

This noble prynces / the doughter of Syon,   260
    The floure of vertu / and vyrgyn gloryous,
Blessed saynt Werburge / full of deuocyon,
Descended by auncetry / and tytle famous

C

Of foure myghty kynges / noble and vyctoryous,   264
Reynynge in this lande / by true successyon,
As her lyfe hystoryall / maketh declaracyon.   266

39

The yere of our lorde / frome the natyuyte   267
Fyue hundreth .xiiii. and also .iiii. score,
Whan Austyn was sende / frome saynt Gregorye
To conuert this regyon / vnto our sauyoure,
The noble kynge Cryda / than reygned with honoure   271
Vpon the mercyens / whiche kynge was father
Vnto kynge Wybba / and Quadriburge, his syster.   273

40

This Wybba gate Penda / kynge of mercyens ;   274
Whiche Penda subdued / fyue kynges of this regyon,
Reygny[n]ge thyrty yere / in worshyp and reuerens,
Was grauntfather to Werburge / by lynyall successyon.
By his quene Kyneswith / had a noble generacyon,   278
Fyue valeant prynces / Peada,[1] and kynge Wulfer / 1 P. Penda
Kynge Ethelred / saint Marceyl / saint marwalde in-fere ;

41

And two holy doughters / blessed and vertuous :   281
Saynt Keneburge / and saynt Keneswyde the vyrgyn—
Whiche ladyes were buryed / full memorous
At peturborowe abbay / and now there lyen in shryne.
The sayd kynge Ethelrede / by sufferaunce deuyne   285
Had a prynce Cochede[1] / whiche after reygned kynge,
That translated Werburge / the .x. yere of her buryenge. 287

42   1 r. Coelrede

Saynt Merwalde specyfyed / vncle to saint Werburge,   288
By his quene saint Ermenberge, a prynces doughter of
    kent,
Gate .iii. holy vyrgyns / saint myldred, & saint mylburge,
Saynt Mylgyde the thyrde / of vertu equypolent ;
With a sone Mereum[1] / whiche frome the holy sacrament 292
Of baptym was taken /by myracle expresse   1 r. Mercuin
To the blys of heuen / to reygne there endelesse.   294

43

The seconde sone of Penda / we meane kynge Wulfere, 295
A noble valyant prynce / by lynyall dyscent
Reygnynge vpon the Mercyens with royalte & power,
Maryed saynt Ermenylde / þ⁰ kynges doughter of kent ;
Where[by] throughe the grace of god omnypotent   299
He ¹ had fayre yssue / saynt Werburge / saynt Kenrede,
Saynt wulfade / saynt Ruffyn / in story as we rede. ¹ ᴾ. They

¶ *Regnum Northumbrorum /*
ex parte matris.

44

The seconde realme of whom saynt Werburge dyd descende,
Was of saynt Edwyn / kynge of Northumberlande ;   [302
Whiche maryed Quadryburge / his ryghtes to defende,
Doughter of Cryda ¹ / kynge of Merslande.   ¹ P. Gryda
Bytwene them descended / as we vnderstande,   306
Two comly prynces / the fyrst we call Eadfryde,¹   ¹ ᵣ. Osfryde
The seconde sone, in batayle slayne, was named Offryde. 308

45

Kyng Eadfryde gate Hereryc, yᵗ was kynge of Deiram. 309
This Hereryc by Beorswyde, his quene fayre & fre,
Had saynt Hylde, the abbesse / saynt Bede sayth y⁰ same,
Lady, also foundresse / of the abbay of Whytbye.
This sayd kynge Hereryc / had another lady,   313
The quene of eest-Englande / saynt Heryswith she hyght,
Mother to saynt Sexburge / & thre other ladies bryght. 315

46

This holy Sexburge / full of grace and goodnes,   316
Was maryed to Ercombert / a noble kynge of Kent.
Bytwyx them descended / a precyous ryches :
The blessyd Ermenylde / humble and pacyent ;
Whiche for her vertue / was maryed full excellent   320
To Wulfer, kynge of Merciens / with great solempnyte,
And mother was to werburge / a swete floure of chastite. 322

c 2

¶ *Regnum Estanglorum /*
ex parte matris.

47

The thyrde noble kyngedome / of her parentage   323
Was the realme of eest-England / whylom in great degre.
Tytylus, kynge of the same / vyctoryous and sage,
Gate Redwald his fyrst sone / a chrysten prynce was he.
This Redwalde had .ii. sones / flourynge in chyualrye : 327
The fyrst was Kenuherus / a noble man of fame,
The seconde Eorpwaldus / called by his name.   329

48

This foresayd kynge Tytylus / had a seconde sone,   330
Called Egnicius / accepted as a martyre.
Whiche sayd Egnicius / by lynyall progressyon
Had .iii. noble prynces / that worthy euer were :
The fyrst was called Ethelwod / þᵉ seconde Adelhere,   334
The thyrde was saynt Anna / a kynge moost vertuous
In batayle slayne vnryghtfully / now a martyr gloryous. 336

49

This forsayd kynge Anna / maryed, as we rede,   337
The holy prynces Hereswith / for loue and amyte.
They had a noble yssue / to encrease theyr mede :
The blessed Sexburge / saynt Audry of Elye,   [341
Saynt Ethelburge the thyrd— / in Bryges now lyeth she—
Saynt Withburge the .iiii., yᵉ martyr saynt Iurwyne, [343
And Aldulph, after kynge / whiche regned a longe tyme.

50

The lady saynt Sexburge / eldest of them all,   344
A gracyous matrone / endurynge all her lyfe,
Was maryed to Ercombert / þᵉ kynge of Kent royall.
They brought fourth a progeny / noble to dyscryue :
The blessed Ermenylde / vertuous mayd and wyfe :   348
Whiche lady was mother / by grace of god almyght
Vnto blessed Werburge / our confort and our lyght.   350

¶ *Regnum Cancie et Francie / ex parte matris.*

51

The .iiii. myghti kyngdome / of whom this royal princes   351
Saynt Werburge descended / was the realme of kent ;
Where reygned fyrst Hengystus / by vyctory & prowes,
Whiche was the fourth man / by lygnage euydent
Procedynge fro Woden / a prynce full prepotent,   355
Of whom our *progenytours* / Angles / Iutes / & Saxons,
Lynyally succeded / kynges of dyuers nacyons.   357

52

This foresayd prynce Woden / as dyuers auctours sayne,
Was the .xv. fro Noe / by naturall progressyon,   [358
Of his eldest sone Sem / descendynge playne,
In saxons tongue Geaf / after ryte and custome,
Not of the lygne of Iaphet / by theyr opynyon.   362
Retourne we to Hengyst / and to his successoures
And speke of theyr royalte / to please the audytoures.   364

53

Ermenrycus, kynge of kent / reygned with great power   365
The yere of our sauyoure / fyue hundreth fyue & thyrte,
Vnto whome Engystus was great-graundfather.
This sayd kynge Ermenryc / had yssue fayre and fre :
A doughter called Ricula / which maried was to sledde,
Of Estsex and Mydylsex /gouernoure and kynge ;   [369
Of whom a myghty kynred / by proces was comynge.   371

54

This Ermenryc gate Ethelbryct full vertuous,   372
Whiche kynge reygned in kent / the yere of our sauyour
Fyue hundreth fyue & fyfty / & baptysed was gracyous
By blessyd bysshop Austyn / of Englande called doctour ;
He was fyrst crysten kynge / & pryncypall protectour   376
Of the fayth within this lande / and founder was also
Of dyuers holy places / and monasteryes both-tow.   378

55

This sayd kynge Ethelbryc / for the great habundaunce 379
Of ryches and honour / was maryed solemply

To the prynces Berta / the kynges doughter of Fraunce.
And of them proceded a vertuous progeny :   [383
Eadburg & Ethelburg saintes— / whiche Ethelburg, truly,
By Edwyne, kyng of North / had .iiii. prynces honorable,
And .iii. holy doughters / gracyous and commendable. 385

56

Also kynge Ethelbryct / had to his successoure   386
Kynge Eadbalde / in Kent reygnynge a longe space ;
He maryed lady Emma / of fraunce the chosen floure,
And by her had yssue / saynt Enswyde full of grace,
Also prynce Ermenred, his seconde sone / whiche wace 390
Maryed to quene Oslaua : / of them dyd procede
Two holy martyrs / Ethelbryct and Etheldrede.   392

57

This prynce Ermenred / had .iiii. ladyes bryght,   393
Lyke the .iiii. floodes of Paradyse / shynynge in vertu :
The eldest of the systers / saynt Ermenberge hyght,
The seconde saynt Ermenburge / the spouses of Ihesu,
The thyrde saynt Adeldryde / all vyces dyd subdu,   397
The .iiii. saynt Ermengyde / sayth theyr lyues hystoryall ;
Thre of them holy vyrgyns / the fourth matrone we call.

58   [399

This foresayd Eadbalde / a souerayne myghty kynge,   400
By Emma of Fraunce / had to his enherytoure
The noble kynge Ercumbert / full gracyous in lyuynge ;
Whiche maryed Sexburge / with worshyp & honoure,
The kynges doughter of eest-England specyfyed afore. 404
This prynce loued vertue / prayer and deuocyon,   [406
Commaundynge all his realme / to kepe þᵉ fast of Lenton.

59

Ercombert .xxx. yere / regnynge in his regaly   407
Had a noble progeny / in grace and all goodnes :
His prynce hyght Egbryct / his seconde sone Lothary ;
Whiche prynce reygned but ten yere / kynge expresse,
Lothary succeded hym / raynynge .xii. yeres doubtlesse. 411

Also he had two doughters / saynt Ermenylde þᵉ quene,
The other hyght saynt Erkengode / a moynes serene.   413

60

This lady Ermenylde / was maryed royally   414
To the aforesayd Vulfer / kynge of Mercyens ;
Bytwene them descended / full gracyously
A noble Margaryte / of hye magnyfycens,
A roose of Paradyse / full of prehemynens :   418
Moost blessed Werburge / the gemme of ·holynes,
Our synguler suffrage / and sterre of our clerenes.   420

¶ *A descrypcyon of the actes & chyualry of kynge Penda,*
   graundfather to saynt Werburge | & of his noble and
   vertuous yssue and progenye.   Ca. .iiii.

61

THe yere of grace .vi. C. syxe and twenty   421
     The foresayd prynce Penda / began for to reygne,
The tenth man fro Woden / a prynce in Saxony ;
Sone and heyre to Wybbe / sayth myne auctour playne.
Fyfty yeres of aege / that tyme he was, certayne,   425
Whan he was fyrst crowned / kynge of Mercyens ;
Thyrty yeres he reygned / with great reuerens.   427

62

Fyue kynges in batayle / this Penda dyd subdue :   428
Saintes Edwyn & Oswald / kinges of Northumberlande,
With Sygebert / Egnycius / and Anna full of vertu,
Thre noble kynges / regnynge in eest-Englande,
With helpe of Brytones / by Bede we vnderstande ;   432
Dylated his regyon / with worshyp and honoures,
Moche more than dyd / any of his predecessoures.   434

63

He maryed Keneswith / a lady fayre and bryght,   435
And by her had yssue / a goodly generacyon :
Peada his prynce / Vulfer a noble knyght,

Saynt Ethelred / and Merwalde full of deuocyon,
Also saynt Mersellyn / of holy conuersacyon,   439
Saynt Keneburge / also saynt Keneswyde,
Auntes to saynt Werburge / vpon the fathers syde.   441
                    64

Thre of his chyldren / as we vnderstande,   442
Prynce Peada / Kyneburge / and Ethelrede,
He maryed with Oswy / Kynge of Northumberlande,
To .iii. of his yssue / for loue and for mede.
Vulfer and Merwalde / the story sayth in dede,   446
Were maryed vnto / the royall blode of Kent : ¹ P. Domueue
To Ermenylde and Domneue ¹ / two ladyes excellent.   448
                    65

Soone after by grace / the myddyll parte of Mercyens 449
Vnder prynce Peada / were baptysed euery-chone ;
Whiche Peada maryed / Elflede with reuerens,
Doughter vnto Oswy / kynge of the North regyon.
Penda therto graunted / without contradyccyon,   453
Vnder a fre lycence / his people were at lyberte
Within all his regyon / baptysed for to be.   455
                    66

Also prynce Alfryde / sone to kynge Oswy,   456
Maryed saynt Keneburge / syster to prynce Peada.
Whiche sayd Peada / brought from the north party
Foure holy preestes / Ced / Beccy / and Adda,
To preche to his people / the fourth was Duyna ;   460
Whiche .iiii. selden seased / day / nyght nor tyme
To conuert the people / vnto chrystes doctryne.   462
                    67

Kynge Penda consented / as afore is sayd,   463
And permytted doctours / to preche in euery place
Thrughout his realme / and neuer it denayed,
To baptyse his subgectes / by fayth and ghostly grace ;
He ayded them with socour / and helpe in that case   467
That wolde be conuerted / for theyr synguler mede,
As sayth myne auctour / the venerable Bede.   469

68

But by the temptacyon / of our ghostly enemy   470
This sayd kynge Penda / this vyctoryous knyght,
Of valyaunt men in armure raysed a great company
And to the North partyes went / purposynge to fyght
And cruelly to slee / by power / mayne / and myght   474
The foresayd kynge Oswy / as he afore had slayne   [476
Say[n]t Oswalde, his brother / kynge and martyr playne.

69

Shortly was forgoten / the fauour of his affynyte   477
That fully was contracte / bytwene these kynges twayne
Ioyned at the maryages / of theyr chyldren thre,
Euer to haue endured / in loue by reason playne.
yet Oswy offered Penda / many ryche gyftes, certayne, 481
To auoyde his malyce / and for to kepe the peas ;
Whiche Penda refused / replete with wyckednes.   483

70

Bytwene these .ii. kynges / was a stronge myghty batell, 484
Not ferre frome yorke / ny the flood of Wynwed,
In the regyon of Leedes / where by fortune cruell
Kynge Penda perysshed / & carefully was leed,
And .xxx. dukes with hym / were slayne and lefte deed. 488
The kynge Oswy offered gladly / with good entent
His yonge doughter Edelfled / to god omnypotent.   490

71

He set her for doctryne / to the abbesse saynt Hylde, 491
Lady of Strenyshalt— / now called Whytby—
And gaue .xii. possessyons / a monastery to buylde—
Whiche place is from yorke / myles thyrty.
He gaue great landes / to his sone-in-lawe, Peade.   495
But the thyrde yere after / this sayd prynce was slayne
By treason of his wyfe Elflede / for certayne.   497

¶ *How after dethe of Penda & his sone, prynce Peada, his*
    seconde sone Vulfer | father to saynt Werburge, was
    electe to be kynge of all the Mercyens. Ca. v.

72

AFter that this Penda / of Mercyens kynge,   498
    In batayle by kynge Oswy / cruelly was slayne,
And his prynce Peada / after hym thre yeres reygnynge
Was put vnto deth / by his quene, in certayne,
These people of Mercyens / rebelled sore agayne   502
The foresayd Oswy / kynge of Northumberlande,
And hym refused / as ye shall vnderstande.   504

73

All the sayd Mercyens / by a generall counsell   505
Fortyfyed themselfe / with power, myght and reason,
And crowned prynce Vulfer / as Bede doth vs tell,
with honour / worshyp / and great renowne,
Whiche prynce to kynge Penda / was the seconde sone ; 509
This prynce was preserued / afore-tyme secretly
And saued by his subicctes / frome dethe and malady. 511

74

This valyaunt prynce / and redoubted knyght,   512
Kynge Vulfer thus crowned / with great prosperyte
Vpon the Mercyens regned / by tytle and myght—
Whiche realme was dyuyded / whylom in partes thre : [516
Fyrst in the West-marches / & in the South parte, truely,
The thyrde parte was nomynate / mydle-Englonde—
Ouer them all thre / he reygned, as is fonde.   518

75

This sayd kynge Vulfer / in honour famous,   519
Was deuoutely baptysed / with great solempnyte
By two holy bysshops / the blessed Finanus
And bysshop Ierumannus / saythe the hystoryc ;
The kynge made a vowe / of hye auctoryte   523
All temples of ydols / within his regyon
To destroy and chaunge / vnto chrysten relygyon.   525

76

This Vulfer was polytyke / replete with wysdom,　　526
Vyctoryous in batayle / proued by his chyualry,
His enemyes oppressed / by manhode and reason,
Subdued his aduersaryes / and had the vyctory ;
From his realme expelled / all cruell tyranny,　　530
Conquered in batayle / at Ashdum ryght famous
The kynge of West-Saxons / called Kenwalcus.　　532

77

Also he subdued / vnto his Empyre　　533
The Ilande Vecta / called the yle of wyght :
And after that he had / of it his desyre,
He gaue the sayd yle / by tytle full ryght
To the kynge of eest-Englande / to enlarge his myght, 537
Vnder that condycyon / that he baptysed wolde be ;
And was his godfather / of pure charyte.　　539

78

In lykewyse as this prouynce / of Mercyens　　540
Whylom was greatest realme / within Englande,
Many yeres contynuynge / in prehemynens,
Ryght so the spyrytualte— / well knowen and founde
How fyue bysshop-sees / within this sayd Merselande : 544
As at Chester / at Lychefelde / also at Worcester,
The fourth at Lyncolne / the fyfth at Dorchester.　　546

79

Forthermore after dethe / of Ierumannus,　　547
Bysshop of Lychfelde / Vulfer the sayd kynge
Desyred the archebysshop / and prymate Theodorus
To graunt them a bysshop / of holy lyuynge,
To gouerne the people / by spyrytuall techynge,　　551
To shewe to his subiectes / the ensample of vertu
And to preche and teche / the fayth of Chryst Ihesu.　553

80

This holy archebyssop / and prymate Theodorus　　554
Desyred saynt Cedda / of the kynge Oswy
For his perfeccyon / and lyuynge vertuous,

To be remoeued / to the prouy[n]ce of Mercy.
Kynge Vulfer was gladde / of his comynge, truly :   558
Ryght so were all / the people of his realme,
Thankynge therfore / the kynge of Ierusalem.   560

81

Kynge Vulfer graunted / to saynt Cedda the confessoure,
Than bysshop of Lychefelde / moche possessyon   [561
To edyfy chyrches / vnto chrystes honoure ;
But namely he gaue a certayne mansyon
In the prouynce of Lyndesy / ny vnto Lyncolne,   565
Suffycyent to suffyse / and well for to content
Fyfty seruauntes / of god,¹ relygyous, obedyent. ¹ P. good 567

82

This noble sayd prynce / and redoubted souerayne,   568
Flourynge in manheed / wysedome and polycy,
Excelled the peres / of this realme, certayne,
In person / fortytude / and proued chyualry ;
Lyberall to his seruauntes / gentyll in company,   572
Gracyous to the poore / and a sure protectour,
A founder of chyrches / and a good benefactour.   574

¶ *A lytell descrypcyon of the noble maryage bytwene Kynge
Vulfer & saynt Ermenylde, yᵉ kynges doughter of Kent
/ & of the solempnyte done at þᵉ same season.   Ca. vi.*

83

ℨN meane whyle the kynge / mynded maryage,   575
    By the sufferaunce of our lorde god omnypotent,
Issue to encrease / acordynge to his lygnage,
After hym to succede / kynge and presydent.
He mynded moost / the kynges doughter of Kent,   579
Prynces Ermenylde / nomynate she was ;
A beautefull creature / replete with great grace.   581

84

Certaynly her father / was called Ercomberte,   582
As afore is specyfyed / the kynge of Kent,
Her mother Sexburge / humble in her herte ;

Of whome Ermenylde / a lady excellent,
Lynyally descended / by tytle full auncyent ;   586
Her graundfather Edbalde / kynge Ethelbryctes sone,
The fyrst crysten prynce / of Saxons nacyon.   588

85

Of foure myghty kyngdomes / she is descended :   589
From the royall blode of Fraunce / also of Kent
Vpon her fathers party / as afore is notyfyed ;
And on her mothers syde / by lyne auncyent
Fromo the eest-Englande / famous and excellent,   593
Also of Northumberlande / flourynge in honour,
Conuerted and baptysed / vnto our sauyour.   595

86

This sayd Ermenylde / this floure of vertue,   596
Was euer dysposed / from her natyuyte
Vnto the dyscyplyne / of our lorde Ihesu ;
Enspyred with his grace / and benygnyte,
Refused this worlde / ryches and vanyte ;   600
He[1] vsed the maners / of sadde dysposycyon,   [1] r. She
Passynge fragyll youth / and naturall reason.   602

87

Suche synguler confort / of vertuous doctryne   603
In her so dyd water / a pure perfyte plante,
Whiche dayly encreased / by sufferaunce deuyne,
Merueylously growynge / in her fresshe and varnaunt,
With dyuers proprytes / of grace exuberaunt,   607
As sobrynes / dyscrecyon / and mekenesse vyrgynall,
Obedyence / grauyte / and wysedome naturall.   609

88

Euery tree or plante / is proued euydent   610
Whyther good or euyll / by experyence full sure,
By the budde and fruyte / and pleasaunt descent ;
A swete tree bryngeth forth / by cours of nature
Swete fruyte and delycyous / in tast and verdure :   614
Ryght so Ercombert / by his quene moost mylde
Brought gracyously forth / the swete Ermenylde.   616

89

She folowed her father / in worshyp and honoure,   617
At her mother Sexburge / she toke imytacyon
To lyue in clennes ; / presentynge in behauyour
Her father in power / her mother in relygyon.
Humble in herte / hauynge compassyon,   621
Pyteous and lyberall / where was necessyte,
Ioyfull to obserue / the dedes of charyte.   623

90

Forther of her lyfe / to make declaracyon,   624
As the true legende playnly dothe expresse,
Consyder the hystory / with good inspeccyon
Of blessed Sexburge / that noble pryncesse.
The sayd conuersacyon / and ghostly swetenesse   628
That is perceyued / in her holy mother,
The same perfeccyon / was in the other.   630

91

Neuerthelesse Ermenylde / escape ne myght   631
Worldely honours / and seculer dygnyte,
As requyred so noble a state of ryght,
Ryches / possessyon / namely her beaute.
But vnto maryage / compelled was she   635
Of her parentes / contrary to her entent ;
To whome she was founde / euer obedyent.   637

92

This noble lady / by deuyne prouydens   638
Elected to her / a spouse commendable,
A valyaunt prynce / the kynges sone of Mercyens,
Called kynge Vulfer / famous and honorable,
Reygnynge in Mercelande / with ioy incomparable,   642
Excellynge many other / prynces of this regyon
In ryches / retynu / fortune / honour / and wysdome.   644

93

At this maryage / was moche solempnyte.   645
Her father Ercomberte / and her frendes all,
Tho prynces her vncles / Egbryct and Lothary,

The kynge of eest-Englande / Aldulph in specyall,
Dukes / erles / barons / and knyghtes in generall : 649
Whiche sayd company / were redy that same day
To worshyp the matrymony / in theyr beest aray. 651

94

This royall maryage / was solempnysed 652
With synguler pleasures / ryches and royalte,
Theyr frendes, cosyns / redy on euery syde
To do theyr deuoyre / and shewe humanyte,
Nothynge wantynge / euery thynge was plente, 656
Of delycate metes / and myghty wynes stronge,
With mynstrels / melody / and myrthes amonge. 658

95

Whan this fayre prynces / resplendent in vertue, 659
Came vnto Mercelande / in the order of matrymony,
Than grace with good gouernaunce / dyd vyce subdue,
Vertue was maystres / chefe ruler and lady ;
The faythe of holy chyrche / dyd growe and multyply, 663
Relygyon encresed / honour and prosperyte,
In euery place pacyence / true loue and charyte. 665

96

At the solempne spousage / of this lady bryght 666
Kynge Vulfer promysed / on his fydelyte
Errours to correcke / by his wysdome and myght,
Clerely to expell / all sectes of ydolatrye
Frome his realme / and fulfyll by his auctoryte 670
The promyse truely made / at the fonte of baptyme :
The chyrche to conserue / and saue it from ruyne. 672

97

The myghty realme of Mercyens / also of Kent 673
That season were brought / bothe vnto vnyte,
And as one kyngedome / ruled full excellent,
Theyr subiectes and seruauntes / in tranquyllyte.
Kynge Vulfer by his quene / had a noble progenye : 677
Vulfade and Ruffyn / with prynce Kenrede,
And Werburge / of whome we purpose to procede. 679

¶ *A breue declaracyon of the holy lyfe and conuersacyon of*
saynt Werburge | vsed in her tender youthe | aboue the
comyn cours of nature. Ca. vii.

98

This blessed lady / and royall prynces,   680
    Descendynge of noble / and hye parentage,
Was doughter to Vulfer / the legende dothe rehers,[1]
Kynge of Mercelande / and of famous lynage,   [1] r. expres
Her mother Ermenylde / ioyned to hym in maryage ;   684
They dwelled somtyme / a lytell frome Stone
At a place in Stafforde-shyre / amyddes his regyon.   686

99

They had bytwene them / other chyldren thre :   687
Vulfade and Ruffyn / martyrs full gloryous,
Synt Kenrede his prynce / of greate auctoryte,
Tumylate at Rome / a confessour gracyous.
The lyues of these thre / we wyll not now dyscus,   691
But speke of the ghostly / and meke conuersacyon
Of blessed Werburge / now at this season.   693

100

For as declareth / the true Passyonary,   694
A boke wherin / her holy lyfe wryten is—
Whiche boke remayneth / in Chester monastery—
I purpose by helpe / of Ihesu, kynge of blys,
In any[1] wyse to reherse / any sentence amys,   [1] r. nane? 698
But folowe the legende / and true hystory,
After an humble style / and from it lytell vary.   700

101

This blessed Werburge / from her natyuyte   701
Folowynge the counseyll / of her noble parentes,
Dysposed her-selfe / euer to humylyte,
Obedyent to them / with all reuerens,
Loth to dysplease / or make any offens   705
Or dysquyet any reasonable creature—
Thus was her maner / in youthe, be ye sure.   707

102

Sadde and demure / of her countenaunce,   708
Stable in gesture / proued in euery place,
Sobre of her wordes / all vertu to auaunce,
Humble / meke / and mylde / replete with grace.
Many vertuous maners / in her founde there was,   712
And dyuers gyftes naturall / to her appropryate,
As was conuenyent / for so noble a state.   714

103

And as she encreased / moore and more in age,   715
A newe plant of goodnes / in her dayly dyd sprynge,
Great grace and vertue / were set in her ymage.
Wherof her father / had moche merueylynge ;
Her mother mused / of this ghostly thynge :   719
To beholde so yonge / and tender a may
From vertu to vertu / to procede euery day.   721

104

No merueyll it is / who-so taketh hede   722
In naturall thynges / the dyuers operacyon.
Dothe not a royall rose/ from a brere procede,
Passynge the stocke / with pleasaunt dylectacyon ?
The swete ryuer passeth / by due probacyon   726
His heed and fountayne : / ryght so dothe she
Transcende her parentes / with great benygnyte.   728

105

And tho her bretherne / delyted for to here   729
For theyr soule-helthe / ghostly exortacyon,
yet she them passed/ manyfolde more clere
In loue of our lorde / and meke conuersacyon.
And lyke as Phebus / in his heuenly regyon   733
Passed [1] other stretes / shynynge moost pure,   [1] r. passeth
So dothe this vyrgyn / aboue the cours of nature.   735

106

Lordes / dukes / barons / within the kynges hall   736
Merueyled on her maners / and constaunte sobrynes ;
The plente of wysedome / and dyscrecyon withall

D

In so tender age / they neuer knewe expresse ;
Her mynde so perfyte / auoydynge all ylnes ;   740
But they knewe well / it pretended by all reasone
Synguler grace and goodnes / to her comynge soone,   742

107

Affyrmynge on this wyse / yf she wolde contynu   743
With suche vertuous maner / in yeres of hye dyscrecyon,
That she sholde do honour / by the grace of Ihesu
Vnto all her kynrede / and synguler consolacyon,
An ensample of vertu / and humylyacyon,   747
Theyr conforte / theyr tresure / and sterre full bryght,
And chefe lumynary / shynynge day and nyght.   749

108

Fyrst in the mornynge / to chyrche she wolde go,   750
Folowynge her mother / the quene, euery day,
With her boke and bedes / and departe not them fro,
Here all deuyne seruyce / and her deuocyons say
And to our blessed sauyour / mekely on knees pray,   754
Dayly hym desyrynge / for his endeles grace and pyte
To kepe her frome synne / and preserue her in chastyte.   756

109

Where youthe is dysposed / of naturall mocyon   757
To dysportes and pleasures / full of vanyte,
This mayde was euer / of sadde dysposycyon,
Constaunt and dyscrete / styll and womanle,
Gladde in her soule / to here speke of chastyte,   761
Clennes and sobrenes / and ioyfull for to here
Ghostly exortacyons / to her herte moost dere.   763

¶ *How this yonge vyrgyn saynt Werburge was desyred of*
   dukes & erles in maryage / and of the answere she gaue
   to them / in auoydynge worldly pleasures.   Ca. viii.

110

.**A**S tender youthe passed / this blessed maydyn   764
     Dayly encreased / more and more in vertue,
In ghostly scyence / and vertuous dyscyplyne,

Obseruynge the doctryne / of our lorde Ihesu,
Had his commaundymentes / in her herte full tru ;　768
So that no creature / more perfyte myght be
In vertuous gyftes (by grace) than she.　770

111

She was replete / with gyftes naturall :　771
Her vysage moost pleasaunt / fayre and amyable,
Her goodly eyes / clerer than the crystall,
Her countenaunce comly / swete and commendable ;
Her herte lyberall / her gesture fauourable.　775
She, lytell consyderynge / these gyftes transytory,
Set her felycyte / in chryst perpetually.　777

112

She hadde moche worshyp / welthe / and ryches,　778
Vestures / honoures / reuerence and royalte ;
The ryches she dysposed / with great mekenesse
To the poore people / with great charyte.
But her sadnes / constaunce / and humylyte,　782
Vertue / gentylnes / so pacyent and colde,
Transcended all these other / a thousande folde.　784

113

The vertuous maners / and excellent fame　785
Of this holy vyrgyn / redoubted so ferre
In all this regyon / in praysynge her name,
That the nobles of this lande / wolde not dyfferre,
But with ryche apparell / and myghty power　789
Came for to seke her— / lyke as to Salomon
Quene Saba approched / to here of his wysedome.　791

114

So lyke-wyse some came / to her of her vertue,　792
Some of her sadnesse / and prudent dyscrecyon,
Some for her constaunce / so stable and true,
Some of her chastyte / and pregnaunt reason,
Some for her beaute / and famous wysedome ;　796
And some, that were borne / of kynges lygnage,
Desyred yf they myght / haue her in maryage.　798

115

In beaute amyable / she was equall to Rachell,   799
Comparable to Sara / in fyrme fidelyte,
In sadnes and wysedom / lyke to Abygaell:
Replete as Delbora / with grace of prophecy,
Equyualent to Ruth / she was in humylyte,   803
In pulchrytude Rebecca / lyke Hester in lolynesse,
Lyke Iudyth in vertue / and proued holynesse.   805

116

The prynce of Westsaxons / a pere of this lande,   806
Wyllynge to haue her by way of maryage,
With humble reuerence / as we vnderstande,
Sayd to her these wordes / wysely and sage :
' O souerayne lady / borne of hye lynage,   810
O beautefull creature / and imperyall prynces,
This is my full mynde / that I now rehers,   812

117

' From my fathers realme / hyder I am come   813
Vnto our [1] presence / yf ye be so content,   [1 r. your]
With worshyp and honour / and moche renowne,
In all honest maner / aperynge euydent ;
My mynde is on you set / with loue feruent,   817
To haue you in maryage / all other to forsake,
If it be your pleasure / thus me for to take.   819

118

' ye shalbe asured / a quene for to be,   820
ye shall haue ryches / worshyp / and honour,
Royall ryche appareyll / and eke the sufferaynte,
Precyous stones in golde / worthy a kynges tresour,
Landes / rentes / and lybertees / all at your pleasur,   824
Seruauntes euery houre / your byddynge for to do,
With ladyes in your chambre / to wayte on you also.'   826

119

With these kynde wordes / the vyrgyn abasshed sore   827
And with mylde countenaunce / answered hym agayne
The playnes of her mynde / to rest for euermore,

Sayenge : 'o noble prynce / I thanke you now, certayne,
For youre gentyll offer / shewed to me so playne,   831
ye be well worthy / for your regalyte
To haue a better maryage / an hundreth folde than me. 833
                  120
' But now I shewe you / playnly my true mynde: 834
My purpose was neuer / maryed for to be ;
A lorde I haue chosen / redemer of mankynde,
Ihesu, the seconde persone in trynyte,
To be my spouse / to Whome my vyrgynyte   838
I haue depely vowed / endurynge all my lyfe,
His seruaunt to be / true spouses and wyfe.   840
                  121
' Therfore, noble prynce / hertfully I you pray,   841
Tempte me no forther / after suche condycyon,
Whiche am so stedfast / and wyll be nyght and day
Neuer for to chaunge / nor make alteracyon.
Take ye this answere / for a sure conclusyon :   845
The promyse I haue made / and vowe of chastyte
Endurynge my lyfe / shall neuer broken be.'   847
                  122
Dyuers other astates / came her for to assayle,   848
Made instaunt requestes / vnto this vyrgyn fro :
For all theyr busynesse / they myght not preuayle,
So constaunt, fyrme & stable / in herte & mynde was she :
A mountayne or hyll / soner, leue ye me,   852
Myght be remoeued / agaynst the course of nature
Than she for to graunte / to suche worldly pleasure.   854
                  123
She well consydered / the texte of holy scrypture :   855
' Who byleueth her chast / for the loue of Ihesu,
The temple of god / they be clypped sure
And shalbe rewarded / for that noble vertu
An hundreth folde (by grace), vyces to subdu,   859
And heuen for to haue / at theyr departynge '—
Whiche she remembred wysely / aboue all thynge.   861

¶ *How þᵉ false Werbode desyred kynge Vulfer to haue*
   Werburge, his doughter, in maryage.   And how yᵉ kynge
   graunted therto.   Ca. ix.

124

AS afore is sayd / whan Penda the kynge   862
   By saynt Oswy kynge / at Leedes was slayne
And Vulfer his sone / the fourth yere folowynge
Was baptysed and crowned / By bysshop Fynane,
A solempne voue he made / faythfull and certayne,   866
All temples of ydolles / in his realme to destroy
And chaunge them to chyrches / and newe edyfy.   868

125

The same he promysed / as he was true knyght   869
Whan that he maryed / blessed Ermenylde,
Dredynge sore the iustyce / of god almyght
For his fathers demerytes / vnreconsyled
On hym to fall sodeynly / and so be begyled ;   873
Promysynge a-mendes / at his conuersyon
Vnto holy chyrche / with humble deuocyon.   875

126

Whiche kynge Vulfer / as was the more pyte,   876
By the wycked counseyll / of a fals knyght
Called Werbode / ranne soone in apostasy,
For a lytell whyle / wantynge perfyte lyght ;
The bryghtnes of the day / was tourned to nyght   880
Whan he gaue credence / that creature vnto,
Prolongynge the actes / he promysed to do.   882

127

Vnder kynge Vulfer / chefe stewarde of his hall   883
Was this false Werbode / ruler of euery porte.
Whome the lady Venus / brought vnto thrall,
Persed and wounded / so greuously his harte
Enflammed with loue / and with her fyry darte,   887
Plonget with sorowe / syghynge day and nyght :
The beaute of Werburge / moeued so his syght.   889

128

The blynde goddes Cupyde / vexed so sore his mynde 890
With interyor loue / and sensuall desyre
Of worldely affeccyon / that reste coude he none fynde ;
His spyryte was troubled / he brenned as dothe the fyre.
Vpon this holy vyrgyn / his loue was so entyre, 894
To haue her in maryage / was all his intent,
That euery houre was a moneth / after his iudgement. 896

129

Prouyded in his mynde / how that he well myght 897
Enforce hym wysely / with boldynesse and polycye
To shewe his full entent / in maner good and ryght,
No dyspleasure taken / vpon his lordes partye :
By this ymagynacyon / he fell vpon his knee 901
Afore his lorde and kynge / desyrynge a petycyon :
His mynde to declare / with fully grace of pardon. 903

130

'Excellent prynce,' he sayd / 'and moost worthy kynge, 904
That reygnes now within the realme of Englande,
Flourynge in chyualry / in honour encreasynge,
Transcendynge other prynces / of this forsayd lande !
My full intencyon / now ye shall vnderstande, 908
Requyrynge your grace / in this poore cyrcumstaunce
At my petycyon / to take no greuaunce. 910

131

'My synguler good lorde / hertfully I you pray 911
With instaunte request / and humble supplycacyon :
Graunte me your doughter Werburge / as ye maye,
To haue her in maryage / auoydynge all treason.
If your grace deny / this present petycyon, 915
Dethe me behoues / full soone and hastely :
My loue is so feruent / there is no remedy.' 917

132

'Stande vp, Werbode' / kynge Vulfer than sayd, 918
'Our chyfe champyon / in all our chyualry !
your humble desyre / shall not be denayd

Of Werburge, our doughter / now consent wyll we,
If ye may optayne / her wyll and mynde, truele,   922
Her mothers also / vnder that condycyon
We graunt her to you / at your meke suggestyon.'   924

133

Of this gracyous answere / a gladde man he was ;   925
Reioysynge in his herte / began to conspyre,
Castynge in his mynde / craftely by compas
How he myght optayne / to the hye empyre
And reygne after Vulfer / at his owne desyre.   929
But, ' tho man prepose / god dysposed all ';
' Who clymbeth to hye / often hath a fall.'   931

¶ *How the quene saynt Ermenylde wolde not consente therto /
& how her bretherne saynt Wulfade and Ruffyn were
agaynst the sayd maryage. Ca. x.*

134

OF this busynesse / whan the quene had knowlege,   932
    Namely of Werebode / the greuous presumpcyon,
How he had moeued / thrught his wycked rage
The kynge in suche causes [1] / by synguler petycyon,   [1] r. cause
And how the kynge consented / to his supplycacyon :   936
She was sore greued / at this prowde crafty knyght,
Called hym in presence / and sayd these wordes ryght : 938

135

'Thou wycked tyraunt / and vnkynde creature,   939
Folowynge thyne appetyte / and sensualyte,
Thou cruell pagane / presumynge at thy pleasure,
Blynded with ygnoraunce / and infydelyte,
Who gaue the lycence / and suche auctoryte   943
Our doughter Werburge / to desyre of the kynge,
Without our counseyll / therto consentynge ?   945

136

' Consyder ryght well / thy kynred and pedegre :   946
It is well knowen / thou arte comen of nought,
Nother of duke / erle / lorde / by auncetre,

But of vylayne people / yf it be well sought ;
Agaynst our honour / now that thou hase wrou₃ht,   950
Whiche consequently / shall be to thy payne—
For all thy labour / is spende in vayne.   952

137

'Thou knowes of a certayne / refused she hase   953
Many a ryche maryage / within this londe,
A thousande tymes better / than euer thou waso,
Is now orels shalbe / by any maner fonde.
Our doughter to the / shall neuer be bonde,   957
Nor suche a caytyfe / shall haue no powere
With kynges blode royall / to approche it nere.   959

138

'Vnder my souerayne lorde / and me also   960
An offycer thou arte / and of great royalte
To be a true seruaunte. / now thou arte our foo,
Tryed / proued / founde fals / in eche degre.
Thou hase well deserued / to be hanged on a tre   964
For thy mysdede / thou shall soone repent
Thy hye presumpcyon / proude and dysobedyent.   966

139

'As for our doughter / and dere derlynge,   967
By the grace of god / and our aduysement
Soone shalbe maryed / to the moost myghty kynge
That euer was borne / and in this erth lent,
We meane our sauyour / lorde omnypotent ;   971
Wherfore thy wretchydnes / wyll vpon the lyght.
Thou taynted traytour / out of our syght !'   973

140

With that saynt Werburge / came into presence,   974
Afore her mother / and all the company,
Doynge her duty / with all due reuerenc[e] ;
Folowynge her doctryne / full sapyently,
With lycence optayned / spake euydently,   978
After suche maner / that all the audyence
Reioysed to here / her lusty eloquence.   980

141

'O souerayne lady / and kynges doughter dere,   981
My dere mother / ouer all thynge transytory,
O gracyous prynces / and quene to kynge Vulfere,
To your ghostly counseyll / do me euer apply :
As I haue promysed / ryght euydently   985
To the kynge of kynges / and lorde celestyall,
I wyll obserue / endurynge this lyfe mortall.   987

142

'And thou false Werbode / folowynge sensualyte,   988
I meruayle greatly / thy hye presumpcyon
To moeue our father / with suche audacyte,
Knowynge my mynde / set on relygyon.
yet for thy soule-helthe / accepte this lesson :   992
Aske mercy and grace / of my spouse eternall,
Lest vengeaunce sodeynly / vpon the do fall.'   994

143

Wherwith her bretherne / Vulfade and Ruffyn,   995
Two noble prynces / manfull, sadde and wyse ;
Sore vexed with peyne / theyr hertes were within
At this false stewarde / whiche can so deuyse
Agayne theyr honour / to do suche preiudyse   999
As to attempte theyr father the kynge
In so great a mater / they not consentynge :   1001

144

They called Werebode / afore them all,   1002
Sayenge : 'thou caytyfe / who gaue the lycence
To moeue this cause / so he and specyall
Touchynge a lady / of suche prehemynence,
A kynges doughter / of moche magnyfysence,   1006
None comparable to hym / in all this regyon
In honour / royalte / power / and dyscrecyon ?'   1008

145

'And as our mother sayd / to the byforne,   1009
Loke well thy progeny / and all thy lynage ;
A vyllayne orels wers / sothly thou was borne,

Now our dere syster / wolde haue in maryage,
As semynge for a prynce / of hye parentage ;   1013
Than for suche a carle / by a prouerbe auncyent
'A lad to wedde a lady / is an inconuenyent.'   1015

146

'Therfore we charge the / vpon greuous peyne,   1016
Moue no suche mater / nor speke of it no more !
For yf suche mocyon / come to vs agayne
Of hye presumpcyon / as is done afore,
Thou shalt repent / the cause and dede full sore.   1020
Now we commaunde the / no forther to contryue,
But cease of suche busynesse / in peyne of thy lyue.' 1022

¶ *How the false Werbode complayned vpon Vulfade and
Ruffyn*[1] *to kynge Vulfare by malyce and enuy / and was
the cause of theyr dethe.* Ca. xi.   P. Fussyn

147

THis wycked Werebode / the bedyll of Belyall,   1023
     The minister of myschef / & sergeaunt of sathanas,
Consyderynge he was / despysed of them all
And sore rebuked / for his outragyous trespas,
He brenned in enuy / as a man without grace,   1027
Cast in his mynde / how he myght wroken be
Vpon her bretherne / by some subtylte.   1029

148

Euer from that tyme / he lay in wayte,   1030
Sekynge occasyons / on them to complayne ;
Dayly ymagyned / with subtyll deceyte
Them to subdue / and cause to be slayne,
Attendynge oportunyte / to take them in a trayne,   1034
By the false entysement / of his mayster Belyall
Prompte to all myschefe / as dyscyple naturall.   1036

149

In fauour of his prynce / by crafte he hym brought   1037
(As now is in custome)—with false flatery

Some please theyr mayster / and that is ryght nought ;
So dyd this Werebode / by subtyll polycy :
His vengeable mynde / was hymselfe to magnyfy   1041
And vtterly to lose / these prynces twayne
Or destroye hym-selfe / by mysfortune playne.   1043

150

Lyke as Archythofell / chefe counselour to absalon,   1044
Sundry tymes moeued hym / vnto varyaunce,
And with kynge Assuerus / in fauour was Amon
Counseylynge hym euer / vnto great myschaunce :
In lyke cause Werbode / moeued to vengeaunce   1048
Was chefe counseler / to Vulfer the kynge ;   [1050
Whiche brought hym-selfe to shame / and euyll endynge.

151

The elder prynce, Vulfade / in his dysporte   1051
Vsed haukynge, huntynge / for a past-tyme ;
But vnto huntynge namely / was his resorte
Euery day in the morowe / longe afore pryme.
And as it fortuned / vpon a tyme,   1055
A myghty harte reysed was / coursed a longe space ;
Whome Vulfade pursued / with pleasure and solace.   1057

152

This harte sore strayned / ranne for his socour,   1058
As all deer done / of theyr propryte,
To a well with water / after his great labour
Hym to reconforte / and the more fressher be,
Wherby saynt Cead / had his oratorye.   1062
The wylde harte there lay / full secrete and styll
And suffered this holy man / to do all his wyll.   1064

153

This blessed bysshop, moeued with pyte,   1065
Couered this sayd harte / with bowes and leues also,
Put a small corde / aboute his necke, trule,
And after commaunded hym spedly to go
To the wylde woodes / whens he came fro,   1069

His pasture to seke. / for saynt Cead knewe truly
It was a sygne folowynge / of some great mysery.   1071
154
(As Bede wytnesseth) this holy confessour   1072
Was bysshop of Lychefelde / and Couentre;
Whiche for the loue of. our sauyour
In wyldernesse dwelled / all solytarye,
Contented with fruytes / of the wylde tree,   1076
With rootes / herbes / water / for his sustentacyon,
Endurynge penaunce / with due contemplacyon.   1078
155
This venerable prynce / ensuynge this great harte   1079
Approched to his cell / with great dylygence,
Tenderly requyrynge / where and in what parte
This harte escaped / sò ferre out of presence.
This holy man answered / with all reuerence :   1083
'Beestes / byrdes / fowles / I kepe none at all,
But I knowe the instructour / of thy helthe eternall. 1085
156
'By this brute beest / thou shall perceyue well   1086
The sacramentes of holy chyrche euerychone,
To encrese thy byleue / by our ghostly counsell,
And so to be baptysed / and haue remyssyon :
By dyuers brute beestes / for mannes saluacyon   1090
Our lorde hath shewed / secretes mystycall
To his electe persones / by grace supernall.   1092
157
'To Noe came conforte / after the great deluge   1093
By a douue / bryngynge a braunche of Olyue;
To the prophet Hely / a rauen dyd refuge,
Brought hym his sustenaunce / and saued his lyue ;
Vnto saynt Eustach / full memoratyue   1097
Our lorde appered / in a hartes lykenes,
To whome he obeyed / gladly with mekenes.'   1099
158
Of whiche examples / prynce Vulfade gladde was,   1100

Thankynge god and saynt Cead / that he thyder come,
And sayd : 'holy father / fulfylled with grace,
If ye can supply / my instaunte petycyon
That the sayd harte / myght retourne hyder soone   1104
Whiche is now in wyldernesse / vnto our presence,
Than to your doctryne / I wyll gyue fully credence.' 1106

159

Saynt Cead vnto prayer / deuoutely went :   1107
And the wylde harte / frome the wood came hastely
With the corde in his necke / apperynge euydent,
And in theyr presence / stode full ryght soberly.
'My sone,' than he sayd / 'byleue than stedfastly.   1111
Vnderstande ye may / all thynge possyble is
To a faythfull persone / that perfytely byleuys.'   1113

160

Vulfade, conforted / and in the fayth probate,   1114
Fell downe to his fete / with humble deuocyon,
Desyrynge baptym / to be regenerate
Vnto our sauyour / for his soules saluacyon.
Saynt Cead blessed / the well that season   1118
And baptysed this prynce / in name of the trynyte,
Was preest and godfather / for want of companye.   1120

161

This chrysten prynce / taryed with hym all nyght   1121
In fastynge / prayer / and medytacyon,
And was refresshed / naturally in syght
With bodyly and ghostly sustentacyon ;
The next day receyued / the holy communyon,   1125
With lycence departed / to his father agayne ;
The harte to the forest / recoursed, certayne.   1127

162

The thyrde day after / his brother Ruffyn,   1128
Folowynge the same harte / by deuyne prouydence,
Was well instructed / in ghostly doctryne,
Baptysed by saynt Cead / & communed with reuerence,
And, as it fortuned / by playne experyence,   1132

Of all the proces done / to the elder brother
All thynge dyd happe / ryght so to the other. 1134
163
Afore this season / chrystes fayth moost gracyous 1135
Thrugh this lande / was preched in eue[r]y place
By bysshop Fynane / and Ierumannus—
Whiche Ieruman of eest-Englande / fyrst byssop was,
And with saynt Ermenylde / came hyder by grace ; 1139
yet fully conuerted / was not Mersee regyon
Clene frome ydolatry / vnto this season. 1141
164
These forsayd prynces / conuerted newly 1142
By blessed Cead / to chrysten relygyon,
Dayly to hym resorted / for counseyll ghostly,
To encreace in vertue / and holy perfeccyon ;
With lycence pretended / they wolde togyder come 1146
Vnto his oratory / from the kynges hall,·
Vnder colour of Huntynge / as they dyd it call. 1148
165
And as it is wryten / in holy scrypture 1149
' Who-so is a sure frende / loueth stedfastly,
And who is enemy / putteth dylygent cure
Myschefe to accomplysshe / moost studyously :'
The false Werebode, suspectynge / euydently 1153
The newe conuersyon / of these prynces twayne,
Prepared hym craftely / to take them in a trayne. 1155
166
He watched on them / secretely euery day, 1156
To knowe theyr resorte / and vnto what place,
Lyke[1] as a hounde folowynge / these prynces to bytray,
Or a dogge dothe a dere / by sent of the chas. [1] P. Kyke
Whan he had perceyued / how all thynge was, 1160
He compased in mynde / by false inuencyon
To complayne to the kynge / for theyr destruccyon. 1162
167
' My synguler goode lorde / and moost pryncypall,' 1163

Sayd this Werebode / the fals traytour,
'Pleaseth your goodnes / and grace specyall
To my supplycacyon / to be a protectour.
ye haue two prynces / myghty in honour,   1167
Whiche are my lordes / and euer shalbe,
If they wolde be true / to your soueraynte.   1169

168

'They haue refused— / the more pyte is,   1170
your auncyent lawes / and sectes euerychone,
And with your lycence / haue done yet more amys :
For now they be subiecte / to a newe relygyon,
Vtterly refusynge / your decrees and olde custome,   1174
Folowynge the counseyll / and mynde of a senyor,
Called bysshop Cead / theyr specyall auctor.   1176

169

'your strayte commaundymentes / they dayly despyce,   1177
And purpose, I tell you / in secretenes,
Vnto your persone / to do moche preiudyce,
To murther or poyson you / shortly, doubtles,
And so for to reygne / and gouerne your ryches,   1181
Bytwene them twayne / to dyuyde your lande,
By fals conspyracy / as ye shall vnderstande.'   1183

170

With these false tales / and many other mo   1184
The kynge was moeued / to malyce and yre,
By his compleccyon / as he was wont to do,
More cruell than a beest / as feruent as the fyre ;
Depely affyrmynge / that dethe shulde be theyr hyre,   1188
If he myght take them / in any place
They shulde be slayne / and suffer withouten grace.   1190

171

In the morowe after / whan Phebus began to clere,   1191
The kynge toke Werbode / with hym secretly,
To try out the truthe / and how it wolde appere,
Wheder his prynces / were gone to the oratory ;
If it were so / he sende hym pryuely   1195

To gyue them knowlege / of his entent,
For to remoeue / from his hasty Iudgment.   1197

172

The father had pyte / vpon his chyldren naturall,   1198
Wolde not haue slayne them / the sothe to say ;
Wherfore he sende / the seruaunt of Belyall
To conuay them fro thens / some other way.
The kynge knewe hym-selfe / not able that day   1202
To refrayne his yre / and cruell hastynesse,
Gyuen to hym of nature / in suche great dystresse.   1204

173

This wycked Werebode / came to the oratory   1205
And sawe these prynces / in great deuocyon ;
Counceyled his message / by malyce and enuy,
Retourned to the kynge / hastely and soone,
Newly complaynynge / by fals ymagynacyon   1209
A hundreth-folde worse / than at the fyrst tyme,
With new addycyons / to brynge them to ruyno.   1211

174

And whan the kynge / approched nygh the cell,   1212
Herynge the complayntes / of this fals knyght,
The chyldren perceyued / a voyce ryght well,
Cessed of theyr prayers / and came forth full ryght.
On whome whan Vulfere / had ones a syght,   1216
He was sore moeued / as hote as the fyre
Agaynst his [1] chyldren / that loued hym entyre. 1 p. her. 1218

175

But by the malyce / and wycked temptacyon   1219
Of the deuyll / mannes olde mortall enemy,
And what by the false crafty suggestyon
Of Wycked Werebode / fulfylled with enuy,
And by his owne hastynesse / and cruell fury,   1223
These prynces were slayne / Vulfade and Ruffyn—
Now gloryous martyrs / reygnynge in heuyn.   1225

176

After whan kynge Vulfer / approched his castell   1226

E

And vnneth was entred / into his hall,
Incontynently a spyryte / the false fende of hell,
Entred fals Werebode / afore [1] the people all,   1 P. after.
Inwardly hym vexed / with peynes contynuall,   1230
That his armes and handes / he dyd horrybly tere—
Whiche sodayne vengeaunce / all the courte dyd fere. 1232

177

He rored and yelled / lyke a wylde bull,   1233
Shewed all the myschefe / malyce and enuy
Done agaynst the martyrs / with a mynde yrefull—
So sore constrayned / with peynes greuously.
The deuyll ceased not / his dolours to multyply   1237
Tyll his fylthy soule / compelled sore was
For to expyre / for his hydeous trespas.   1239

¶ *How kynge Vulfer was conuerted & toke great repentaunce
for his offences. And by the counseyll of saynt Ceade
was a deuoute man / and a good benefactour to holy
chyrche / and a founder of dyuers holy places relygyous.
Ca. xii.*

178

THan Vulfer, consyderynge / with due dyscrecyon   1240
His cruell hastynes / and furyous mynde,
How ferre he had / abused his reason,
Agaynst his chyldren / by nature and kynde :
He sore repented / in hystory as we fynde,   1244
His greuous trespas / and homycyde vnnaturall,
In conscyence greued / for his synnes mortall ;   1246

179

Namely lamentynge / in soule his apostasy   1247
After his baptyme / and ghostly conuersyon,
And for the departure / of his prynces truly
Contrary to ryght / kynde and all reason,
The losse of his fame / thrugh this regyon,   1251
A dethe to his quene / and his louers all,
Greuous to his kynnesmen / and frendes naturall.   1253

180

All these consydered / with due cyrcumstaunce,   1254
He wayled and weped / sobbynge fullsore,
Plonged in sorowe / heuynes / and greuaunce,
Lamentynge his offence / a thousande tymes therfore ;
His intollerable peyne / encreased more and more,   1258
Wofully he went / to his bed by and by,
Supposynge some dethe / withouten any remedy.   1260

181

Some of his louers / beynge there present   1261
Gaue hym theyr counseyll / to hunte in the forest,
Some to dysportes / and pleasures euydent,
Some vnto melody / all thoughtes to degest.
But Ermenylde, his quene / whiche loued hym best,   1265
Counseyled hym truly / to take contrycyon
And mendes make / by due satysfaccyon.   1267

182

Of this ghostly counseyll / the kynge was very glad,   1268
And in the morowe after / prepared besyly
With mekenesse to seke / blessed saynt Cead.
So whan the kynge came / to his oratory,
The bysshop was at masse / and ryght consequently   1272
Fro heuen[1] descended / so gloryous a lyght   [1] P. henen.
That of the mystery / Vulfer had no syght,   1274

183

Whan masse was ended / saynt Cead his vestures caste   1275
Vpon the sonne-beame / by myracle there hangynge,
Supposynge on a forme / and made moche haste
To mete at the doore / mekely the sayd kynge,
Whiche laye there prostrate / penaunce desyrynge ;   1279
With reuerence hym eleuate / and gaue an exortacyon ;
The kynge was agreable / for to do satysfaccyon.   1281

184

The bysshop hym enioyned / in parte of penaunce   1282
To destroye all ydolles / and sectes of ydolatry
In all his realme / and the temples of paganes

E 2

To translate to the honour / of god almyghty,
With preestes and clerkes / to pray and synge deuoutly, 1286
Also peas and iustyce / to be kepte contynuall,
With the werkes of mercy / to be vsed in specyall.   1288

185

Forther he enioyned hym / of his charyte   1289
Monasteryes to make / of great perfeccyon,
Endowed with landes / possessed in lyberte,
Therin for to set / men of relygyon,
To pray to our lorde / for his saluacyon;   1293
Whiche Vulfer promysed / to fulfyll gladle,
As sooue as he myght / by possybylyte.   1295

186

Than the foresayd kynge / and the holy confessour   1296
Went to theyr prayers / in the oratory.
And as the kynge loked vp / to our sauyour,
The sayd sacrat vestures / he sawe euydently
Hangynge on the sonne-beame / full merueylously;   1300
His gloues / his gyrdell / the kynge had vpon,
Whiche shortly to grounde / falled adowne.   1302

187

Wherby he perccyued / the great holynesse   1303
Of blessed saynt Cead / and interyor deuocyon,
Desyred his prayer / dayly with mekenesse
To almyghty god / for his remyssyon;
Frome thens departed / with his benedyccyon,   1307
Ioyfull in his soule / to-warde his place,
Thankynge god mekely / of his great grace.   1309

188

As the kynge promysed / to our sauyour,   1310
Shortly he auoyded / all ydolatry,
Brenned theyr ydolles / correcked theyr errour,
Translated theyr temples / vnto god almyghty,
Founded monasteryes / of relygyon many,   1314
Of men and women / gaue them possessyons,
Landes / rentes / ryches / to encrese deuocyons.   1316

189

Namely he founded / a ryche monastery   1317
For dethe of the prynces / in satysfaccyon
To the honour of god / and saynt Peter, truly,
Called Peterborowe abbay / in all this regyon ;
Endowed it with rentes / lybertes / possessyon—   1321
A place where many / relygyous persones be,
Seruynge day and nyght / our lorde with charytc.   1323

190

Also there was founded / at Stone a pryore   1324
In the honour of god / and the martyrs twayne,
Possessed with landes / rentes and lyberte,
Where deuoute chanons / ben inhabyte, certayne.
Myracles and sygnes / haue ben shewed there playne   1328
To the laude and prayse / of god omnypotent
And of these holy martyrs / patrones there present.   1330

¶ *Of the feruent desyre & great deuocyon y* saynt Werburge*
    hadde to be relygyous | & of þᵉ dayly supplycacyons she
    made to the kynge, her father, for the same.   Ca. xiii.

191

A S this myghty prynces / encreased in age,   1331
    So dayly encresed / her good condycyons,
That greatly enioyed / her honorable lynage
Consyderynge in her / suche vertuous dysposycyons ;
In vygyls / prayers / and ghostly medytacyons   1335
Set all her mynde / power / myght / and mayne,
To serue our sauyour / day and nyght, certayne.   1337

192

She well consydered / with due dyscrecyon   1338
Of this present lyfe / the great wretchydnesse,
How dredefull it is / full of varyacyon,
Deceuable / peryllous / and of no sykernesse ;
The tyme vncertayne / to be knowen, doubtlesse ;   1342
For here is no cytee / nor sure dwellynge¹ place,   ¹ P. dwel-
                                                          lynge.
All thynge is transytory / in short proces and space. 1344

193

Wherfore this vyrgyn / gladde and benyuolent,   1345
Folowynge the counseyll / of blessed Mathewe,
Was on of fyue vyrgyns / euer redy present,
Had her lampe replete / with oyle full of vertue,
Redy for to mete / her spouse, swete Ihesu,   1349
With charytable werkes / in her soule contynuall—
Therfore she was taken / to his blys eternall.   1351

194

She well consydered / the wordes of the gospell   1352
' Who refuses pleasures / and naturall generacyon
For the loue of Ihesu / rewarded shalbe well
With a hundreth-folde grace / here for theyr guerdon,
And after this lyfe / haue eterne fruycyon ' :   1356
Whiche she remembred / and euer fro that day
On her father wolde call / and mekely to hym say :   1358

195

' Reuerent myghty prynce / and lorde honorable,   1359
Moost dere byloued father / my synguler helpe & socour,
My trust / tresure / and solace / to me moost amyable,
Instauntly I beseche you / for loue of our sauyoure
And of his mother mary / of vyrgyns the floure,   1363
With all the company / that in heuen be,
My humble petycyon / now graunt it vnto me.   1365

196

' Well-byloued father / this is my fully mynde,   1366
My instaunte desyre / and humble supplycacyon :
By the grace of god / maker of all mankynde,
And by your lysence / helpe / and tuycyon
I purpose to enter / into holy relygyon   1370
And vtterly refuse / all pleasures transytory,
To be professed / at the house of Ely.'   1372

197

' O my dere doughter ' / sayd this noble kynge,   1373
' My pleasure / solace / and hope of my gladnesse,
Moost dere byloued / and my synguler swete derlynge,

I well consyder / your vertue and sadnesse,
your instaunt request / and humble gentylnessc,   1377
And of your desyre / inwardly·I am gladde ;
But yet your mocyon / makes my herte full sadde.   1379

198

' All my ioye and conforte / now resteth in the,   1380
Syth thy dere bretherne / from vs ben agone ;
Thou arte the trusty treasure / to thy mother and mc,
Our synguler solace / and sure consolacyon.
Wherfore, swete derlynge / as for my heyre alone   1384
I wolde the mary / and a quene the make,
If thou wyll consent / and my counseyll takc.   1386

199

' Consyder and beholde / thrugh all this lande,   1387
Take the a maryage / at thyne owne pleasure,
A prynce moost valyaunt / moost noble to be founde :
And of helpe and ayde / I shall the assure,
With ryches / royalte / welthe / and tresure,   1391
Clothes of golde / and royall ryche apparell
And all thynges necessary / as man can of tell.   1393

200

' Remembre also / how after course of kynde   1394
Aege dothe sore greue / thy moder and me also.
Therfore naturall loue (swete chylde) dothe me bynde
To gyue the best counseyll / what thou shall do,
To honour and worshyp / how thou may come to :   1398
Whiche great renowne / and hye astate, certayne,
To se the a quene / wyll make vs yonge agayne.   1400

201

' God ordeyned matrymony / fyrst in Paradyse   1401
Bytwene man & woman / whan he the worlde dyd make,
That mankynde myght encrese / multyply, and ryse,
Eche persone at pleasure / a spouse for them to take ;
Now ioyned by holy chyrche / all other to forsake,   1405
The chylde of the father / to take his dyscyplyne,
And after that to teche / his yssue theyr doctryne.   1407

202

'Also man and beest / haue dysposycyon naturall   1408
To brynge forth theyr lykenesse / by generacyon ;
But man, hauynge reason / and fre wyll with-all,
As lawe requyreth / hath his procreacyon
Vnder true matrymony / by his owne eleccyon,   1412
Orels to obserue / and lyue in pure vyrgynyte,
For the greater meryte / and rewarde of glorye.   1414

203

'And yf all maydens / shulde kepe theyr chastyte   1415
As ye now do / how shulde the worlde encrese ?
Swete louely creature / ryght ioyfull wolde I be
To kysse a chylde of thyne / hauynge thy lykenesse,
And se the also coronate / as a myghty pryncesse l   1419
Enclyne, dere derlynge/thy mynde to myne entent,
And all these sayd honours / wyll folowe consequent.'   1421

¶ *Of the meke answere saynt Werburge gaue to her father whan*
she was moeued to maryage. Ca. xiiii.

204

THe holi mayd / whan she knewe her fathers mynde, 1422
   Her soule was replete / with woo & pensyuenesse,
And sore began to wepe / after cours of kynde—
The salte teeres dystylled / for payne and heuynesse [1426
By her ruddy chekes shynynge / full fayre, doubtelesse,
Pyteous to beholde. / but whan the foresayd mayde
Ceased of her sorowe / thus to hym she sayde :   1428

205

'Moost beest byloued father / nexte to god almyght, 1429
your kynde gentyll mocyon / wolde moeue inwardely
The mynde of any creature / to folowe you ryght,
Or any stony stomake / to relent and apply,
And resolue eche harde herte / to waylynge dolefully, 1433
Consyderynge on euery parte / with good dyscrecyon
To accepte or refuse / this harde eleccyon.   1435

206

'Father, I haue ben to you / meke and obedyent   1436
Euer syth I had / yeres of dyscrecyon,
Gladde to obserue / your hye commaundyment
With loue interyor / and humble intencyon—
And so wyll contynue / with lowly submyssyon,   1440
In this present lyfe / whyle I do endure ;
Of my loue and prayer / euer ye shalbe sure.   1442

207

'But, moost louely father / I pray you hertfully   1443
Take no dysplesure / pardon what I shall say.
My soule / my herte / and mynde / is set stydfastly
To serue my lorde god / nyght and also day,
Neuer to be maryed / by no maner of way :   1447
For sothly I haue vowed / my true vyrgynyte
Vnto Ihesu / the seconde persone in trynyte.   1449

208

'That is my spouse / and blessed sauyour,   1450
For whose loue refused/ in certaynte haue I
All worldely pleasures / welth / ryches and honour,
With all voyde busynesse / and cures transytory ;
My loue on hym is sette / so sure and feruently,   1454
That nothynge shall separate / my hert hym fro,
Sekenes nor helthe / pleasure / peyne / ne wo.   1456

209

'Also my full entent / was neuer otherwyse   1457
Than to be handmayde / to my lorde Ihesu
And of my soule and body / to make hym sacryfyce,
For my ghostly welthe / all vyces to subdue.
He is my dere spouse / solace / helthe moost true,   1461
On hym is all my herte / and hase ben set alway,
And euer shalbe / vnto my endynge day.   1463

210

'In this wretched worlde / we can not longe endure   1464
And of this present lyfe / we are in no suerte ;
As we haue deserued / so we shalbe sure

After this pylgrymage / rewarded for to be.
For mercy and grace / therfore mekely call we   1468
Whyle we haue tyme and space— / for than it is to late
Whan dethe with his darte / sayth to vs chekemate.   1470

211

'Wherfore, dere father / I shewe you now agayne   1471
All my hole herte / desyre and entent,
Whiche euer hath ben / and so shalbe, certayne,
For to be relygyous / chast / and obedyent,
Namely at Ely / for theyr vertue excellent.   1475
Father, I requyre you / for chrystes loue and charyte,
My meke supplycacyon / now graunte it vnto me.'   1477

212

The kynge well consydered / his doughters desyre,   1478
Her constaunte true mynde / and pure deuocyon :
Graunted her petycyon / with synguler loue entyre,
Trustynge by her prayer / and dayly supplycacyon
Vnto heuen-blysse / the rather for to come.   1482
Her mother Ermenylde / was gladde of this tydynge
And lauded full lowly / our lorde and heuen kynge.   1484

¶ *How saynt Werburge was made a moynes after her desyre*
at the monastery of Ely vnder saynt Audry / lady and
abbesse.   Ca. xv.

213

THan the kynge remembred / with due cyrcumstaunce
The excellent vertue / sadnes / and grauyte   [1485
Of his dere doughter / and the perfyte constaunce,
Her humble petycyon / and pure vyrgynyte ;
He thanked our lorde / with great humylyte   ·   1489
Of his infynyte grace / that so royall a floure
Frome hym descended / to his prayse and honoure.   1491

214

He sende messages / in all goodly hast   1492
With letters myssyue / thrugh his regyon,
Commaundynge his subiectes / they shulde full fast

By a day assygned / be redy euerychone
In theyr best maner / with hym for to gone   1496
To brynge his doughter / to the hous of Ely,
There to be relygyous / after her desydery.   1498

215

Whan the day was come / of theyr appoyntment,   1499
The nobles of the realme / and lordes were redy
To attende on theyr souerayne / at his commaundyment.
Kynge Vulfer prepared / all thynge pleasauntly
And of his court / had chosen a noble company   1503
In theyr best aray / royalte / and renowne,
To offer saynt werburge / to god and relygyon.   1505

216

The kynge on his Iourney / rode forthe royally,   1506
The quene hym folowed / as is the custome ;
Werburge succeded them consequently ;
The peeres and his counseyll / knewe well theyr rowme,
Dukes / erles / lordes / and many a worthy barowne, 1510
Knyghtes / squyers / gentyls / of her kynred also,   [1512
With ladyes and gentylwomen / & seruauntes both-two.

217

Whan the kynge approched / the sayd monastery,   1513
Saynt Audry, than abbesse / toke her holy couent
And mette the sayd kynge / and all his company
With solempne processyon / and gretynge benyuolent,
Praysynge our lorde god omnypotent   1517
Whiche of his goodnes / to that congregacyon [1] [1] P.congrecacyon
Sende them a syster / of suche perfeccyon.   1519

218

Wereburge requyred / by the order of charyte   1520
Mekely on her knees / to enter relygyon.
Saynt Audry receyued / of her benygnyte
And graunted fre lycence / after her petycyon.
Gladde were also / the hole congregacyon   1524
And sange (Te deum), with moche reuerence,
Magnyfyenge our lorde / of his prouydence.   1526

219

She was receyued / with moche solempnyte   1527
Into the holy order / after her entent,
To proue her sadnes / and humylyte
(As is the custome), and so be obedyent,
To lyue euer after / humble / chast / and contynent.   1531
Than dyd theyr Ioye / merueylously encreas,
Consyderynge her pacyens / and perfyte holynes.   1533

220

Her royall dyademe / and shynynge coronall   1534
Was fyrst refuted / for loue of our sauyoure,
The poore vayle accepted / and the symple pall,
The royall ryche purpull / reiected that same houre,
With other clothes of golde / sylkes of great honoure ; 1538
She toke lowe appareyll / vestures that were blake—
All her plesaunt garmentes / she clerely dyd forsake. 1540

221

Also she refused / her fathers realme and royalte,   1541
All ryches / rentes / pleasures / possessyon,
With all worldely honoures / full of vanyte ;
Lowly submyttynge her / vnder subieccyon,
Vertu to encrese / myndynge moost relygyon ;   1545
She refused yet more her owne proper wyll,
Put all to her abbcsse / her order to fulfyll.   1547

¶ *Of the great solempnyte kynge Vulfer made at the ghostly*
maryage of saynt Werburge his doughter / to al his
louers / cosyns / and frendes.   Ca. xvi.

222

Kynge Vulfer, her father / at this ghostly spousage   1548
    Prepared great tryumphes / and solempnyte,
Made a royall feest / as custome is of maryage,
Sende for his frendes / after good humanyte,
Kepte a noble housholde / shewed great lyberalyte   1552

Bothe to ryche and poore / that to this feest wolde come—
No man was denyed / euery man was well-come.   1554

223

Her vncles and auntes / were present there all :   1555
Ethelred and Merwalde / and Mercelly also—
Thre blessed kynges / whome sayntes we do call ;
Saint keneswyd / saint keneburg / theyr systers both-two,
And of her noble lygnage / many other mo   1559
Were redy that season / with reuerence and honour,
At this noble tryumphe / to do all theyr deuour.   1561

224

Tho kynges mette them / with theyr company :   1562
Egbryct, kynge of kent / brother to the quene,
The seconde was Aldulphe / kynge of the eest party,
Brother to saynt Audry / wyfe and mayde serene,
With dyuers of theyr progeny / and nobles, as I wene ; 1566
Dukes / erles / barons / and lordes ferre and nere
In theyr best aray / were present all in-fere.   1568

225

It were full tedyous / to make descrypcyon   1569
Of the great tryumphes / and solempne royalte
Belongynge to the feest / the honour and prouysyon
By playne declaracyon / vpon euery partye ;
But, the sothe to say / withouten ambyguyte,   1573
All herbes and floures / fragraunt, fayre and swete
Were strawed in halles / and layd vnder theyr fete.   1575

226

Clothes of golde and arras / were hanged in the hall, 1576
Depaynted with pyctures / and hystoryes manyfolde,
Well wrought and craftely / with precyous stones all
Glyterynge as Phebus / and the beten golde
Lyke an erthly paradyse / pleasaunt to beholde.   1580
As for the sayd moynes / was not them amonge
But prayenge in her cell / as done all nouyce yonge.   1582

227

The story of Adam / there was goodly wrought   1583

And of his wyfe Eue / bytwene them the serpent,
How they were deceyued / and to theyr peynes brought ;
There was Cayn and Abell / offerynge theyr present,
The sacryfyce of Abell / accepte full euydent ;   1587
Tuball and Tubalcain / were purtrayed in that place,
The inuentours of musyke / and craftes by great grace. 1589
228

Noe and his shyppe / was made there curyously,   1590
Sendynge forthe a rauen / whiche neuer came agayne,
And how the douue retourned / with a braunche hastely,
A token of conforte and peace / to man, certayne ;
Abraham there was / standynge vpon the mount playne
To offer in sacryfyce / Isaac, his dere sone,   [1594
And how the shepe for hym / was offered in oblacyon. 1596
229

The twelue sones of Iacob / there were in purtrayture,1597
And how into Egypt / yonge Ioseph was solde,
There was inprysoned / by a false coniectour,
After in all Egypte / was ruler (as is tolde) ;
There was in pycture / Moyses wyse and bolde,   1601
Our lorde apperynge / in busshe flammynge as fyre
And nothynge therof brent / lefe / tree / nor spyre. 1603
230

The ten plages of Egypte / were well embost,   1604
The chyldren of Israell / passynge the reed see,
Kynge Pharoo drowned / with all his proude hoost ;
And how the two tables / at the mounte of Synaye
Were gyuen to Moyses / and how soone to ydolatry   1608
The people were prone /and punysshed were therfore,
How Datan and Abyron / for pryde were lost full youre.1610
231

Duke Iosue was ioyned / after them in pycture,   1611
Ledynge the Isrehelytes / to the lande of promyssyon,
And how the sayd lande / was dyuyded by mesure
To the people of god / by equall sundry porcyon ;
The Iudges and bysshops / were there euerychone,   1615

Theyr noble actes / and tryumphes Marcyall
Fresshly were browdred / in these clothes royall.   1617

232

Nexte to hye borde-lorde / appered fayre and bryght 1618
Kynge Saull, and Dauyd / and prudent Salomon,
Roboas succedynge / whiche soone lost his myght,
The good kynge Esechyas / and his generacyon ;
And so to the Machabees / and dyuers other nacyon   1622
All these sayd storyes / so rychely done and wrought,
Belongyng to kyng Vulfer /agayn yᵗ tyme were brought.1624

233

But ouer the hye desse / in the pryncypall place,   1625
Where the sayd thre kynges / sate crowned all,
The best hallynge hanged / as reason was :
Wherin were wrought / the .ix. ordres angelycall
Dyuyded in thre Ierarchyses / not cessynge to call   1629
'Sanctus / sanctus / sanctus/ blessed be the trynyte,
Dominus deus sabaoth/ thre persones in one deyte.'   1631

234

Nexte in ordre suynge / sette in goodly purtrayture, 1632
Was our blessed lady / floure of femynyte,
With the twelue apostles / echeone in his fygure,
And the foure euangelystes / wrought moost curyously,
Also the dyscyples / of chryst in theyr degre,   1636
Prechynge and techynge / vnto euery nacyon
The faythtes of holy chyrche / for theyr saluacyon.   1638

235

Martyrs than folowed / ryght manyfestly :   1639
The holy innocentes / whome Herode had slayne,
Blessed saynt Stephan / the prothomartyr truly,
Saynt Laurence / saynt Vyncent / sufferynge great payne,
With many other mo / than here ben now, certayne ; 1643
Of whiche sayd martyrs / exsample we may take
Pacyence to obserue / in herte for chrystes sake.   1645

236

Confessours approched /ryght conuenyent,   1646

Fresshely enbrodred / in ryche tysshewe and fyne :
Saynt Nycholas, saynt Benedycte / and his couent,
Saynt Ierom / Basylyus / and saynt Augustyne,
Gregory the great doctour/Ambrose & saynt Martyne;   1650
All these were sette / in goodly purtrayture—
Them to beholde / was a heuenly pleasure.   1652

237

Vyrgyns them folowed / crowned with the lyly,   1653
Amonge whome our lady/ chefe presydent was ;
Some crowned with rooses / for theyr great vyctory :
Saynt Katheryne / saynt Margarete / saynt Agathas,
Saynt Cycyly / saynt Agnes / and saynt Charytas,   1657
Saynt Lucye / saynt Wenefryde / and saynt Apolyn ;
All these were brothered / the clothes of golde within.1659

238

Vpon the other syde / of the hall sette were   1660
Noble auncyent storyes / & how the stronge Sampson
Subdued his enemyes / by his myghty power ;
Of Hector of Troy / slayne by fals treason,
Of noble Arthur / kynge of this regyon ;   1664
With many other mo / whiche it is to longe
Playnly to expresse / this tyme you amonge.   1666

239

The tables were couered / with clothes of Dyaper,   1667
Rychely enlarged / with syluer and with golde ;
The cupborde with plate / shynynge fayre and clere.
Marshalles theyr offyces / fulfylled manyfolde.
Of myghty wyne plenty / bothe newe and olde,   1671
All-maner kynde / of meetes delycate
(Whan grace was sayd) to them was preparate.   1673

240

To this noble feest / there was suche ordynaunce,   1674
That nothynge wanted / that goten myght be
On see and on lande / but there was habundaunce
Of all-maner pleasures / to be had for monye ;
The bordes all charged / full of meet plente,   1678

And dyuers subtyltes / prepared sothly were
With cordyall spyces / theyr ghestes for to chere.   1680
241
The Ioyfull wordes / and swete communycacyon   1681
Spoken at the table / it were harde to tell,
Eche man at lyberte / without interrupcyon,
Bothe sadnes and myrthes / also pryue counsell,
Some adulacyon / some the truthe dyd tell;   1685
But the great astates / spake of theyr regyons,
Knyghtes of theyr chyualry / of craftes the comons. 1687
242
Certayne, at eche cours / of seruyce in the hall
Trumpettes blewe vp / shalmes and claryons,
Shewynge theyr melody with / toynes musycall.
Dyuers other mynstrelles / in crafty proporcyons
Made swete concordaunce / and lusty dyuysyons—   1692
An heuenly pleasure / suche armony to here,
Reioysynge the hertes / of the audyence full clerc.   1694
243
A synguler mynstrell / all other ferre passynge,   1695
Toyned his instrument / in pleasaunte armony
And sange moost swetely /the company gladynge,
Of myghty conquerours / the famous vyctory,
Wherwith was rauysshed/ theyr spyrytes and memory; 1699
Specyally he sange / of the great Alexandere,
Of his tryumphes and honours / endurynge .xii. yere. 1701
244
Solemply he songe / the state of the Romans,   1702
Ruled vnder kynges / by polycy and wysedome,
Of theyr hye iustyce / and ryghtfull ordynauns
Dayly encreasynge / in worshyp and renowne,
Tyll Tarquyne þᵉ proude kynge /with yᵗ great confusyon 1706
Oppressed dame Lucrece / the wyfe of Colatyne;
Kynges neuer reygned in Rome / syth that tyme.   1708
245
Also how the Romayns / vnder thre dyctatours   1709

F

Gouerned all regyons / of the worlde ryght wysely,
Tyll Iulyus Cesar / excellynge all conquerours,
Subdued Pompeius / and toke the hole monarchy
And the rule of Rome / to hym-selfe manfully;   1713
But Cassius Brutus / the fals conspyratour,
Caused to be slayne / the sayd noble emperour.   1715

246

After the sayd Iulyus / succeded his syster sone,   1716
Called Octauyanus / in the imperyall see;
And by his precepte / was made descrypcyon
To euery regyon / lande / shyre / and cytee,
A trybute to pay / vnto his dygnyte: 1720
That tyme was / vnyuersall peas and honour:
In whiche tyme was borne / our blessed sauyoure.   1722

247

All these hystoryes / noble and auncyent   1723
Reioysynge the audyence / he sange with pleasuer,
And many other mo / of the newe testament,
Pleasaunt and profytable / for theyr soules cure,
Whiche be omytted / now not put in vre.   1727
The mynysters were redy / theyr offyce to fulfyll
To take vp the tables / at theyr lordes wyll.   1729

248

Whan this noble feest / and great solempnyte,   1730
Dayly endurynge / a longe tyme and space,
Was royally ended / with honour and royalte,
Eche kynge at other / lysence taken hace,
And so departed from thens / to theyr place;   1734
Kynge Vulfer retourned / with worshyp and renowne
Frome the house of Ely / to his owne mansyon.   1736

¶ *Of the holy professyon & ghostly conuersacyon saynt*
 Werburge vsed at Ely in relygyon | vnder saynt Audry
 her abbesse and cosyn. Ca. xvii.

249

SO whan this vyrgyn / the spouse of Ihesu,   1737
    Had fully contynued / in holy relygyon
With mekenesse / pacyens / and all vertu
Fully the yere / of her probacyon,
Than she made instaunce / for her professyon   1741
Vnto saynt Audry / her lady and abbesse ;
Whiche soone was graunted / with great gladnesse.   1743

250

Ordynaunce they made / and great royalte,   1744
Her frendes were called / agaynst that season ;
She was professed / with great humylyte,
The obseruaunce done / with due deuocyon :
She made solempne vowe / of ghostly conuersacyon,   1748
Mekely to obserue / obedyence and chastyte
Endurynge her lyfe / and wylfull pouerte.   1750

251

By the exsample / of her perfeccyon   1751
Many dyuers persones / of her noble lynage
Refused this worlde / and entred relygyon,
Renounsynge vayne pleasures / ryches and maryage,
Enclyned to vertue / for theyr ghostly auauntage,   1755
As may be specyfyed / here after folowynge
Theyr names / theyr astate / and theyr good lyuynge. 1757

252

Now this gloryous vyrgyn / after her desyre   1758
Is ghostly maryed / to our lorde Ihesu,
Accordynge to her entent / and true loue entyre,
She dayly encresed / frome vertu to vertu,
With more strayter lyfe / vyces to subdu ;   1762
The longer she endured / in relygyon
The better she prepared / her herte to deuocyon.   1764

253

And tho this vyrgyn / clerely dyd forsake   1765
All ryches, honours / and pleasures worldly,
With all possessyons / for her lordes sake,
She thought than she reygned / moost lyke a lady,
Cause that she lyued / in chrystes seruyce dayly ;   1769
And certayne it is / holy scrypture recordynge,
'Who serues well god / dothe reygne lyke a kynge.'   1771

254

In prayer / penaunce / and / contemplacyon   1772
Was all her busynesse / and study alway,
Compasynge by what maner of medytacyon
She myght best please / our lorde to his pay,
Offerynge her persone / a true sacryfyce euery day ;   1776
No labour her greued / loue was so feruent ;
Her body vpon erthe / her soule in heuen lent.   1778

255

Swete / comly creatures / ladyes euerychone,   1779
Sekynge for pleasures / ryches and arayment,
Blynded by your beaute / and synguler affeccyon,
Consyder this vyrgyn / humble and pacyent :
A spectacle of vertue / euer obedyent ;   1783
Beholde how she hase / clerely layde away
Her royall ryche clothes / and is in meke aray.   1785

256

your garmentes now be gay and gloryous,   1786
Euery yere made / after a newe inuencyon,
Of sylke and veluet / costly and precyous,
Brothered full rychely / after the beest facyon,
Shynynge lyke angels / in your opynyon,   1790
Where lesse wolde suffyse / and content as well
As all that great cost / folowynge wyse counsell.   1792

257

A playne exsample / now ye may take   1793
Of this myghty kynges doughter dere,
Whiche for the loue of god / dyd forsake

All suche vayne pleasures / and garmentes clere ;
She gaue herselfe / to penaunce and prayere :   1797
Wherfore, fayre ladyes / do way suche vanyte,
Prepare your-selfe / to vertue and humylyte !   1799

258

Some of lowe byrthe / excellynge theyr degre   1800
Done couet to haue / as royall ryche vesture,
Worldly honours / also the sufferaynte,
As they were ladyes / by lyne of nature :
Of dredefull mysery / they bere the fygure,   1804
Prowde as a Pecocke / whelynge full bryght ;
All is but vanyte / contentynge the syght.   1806

259

Gloryous vyrgyn / replete with synguler grace,   1807
Endowed with souerayne gyftes celestyall,
Refusynge voyde pleasures / whan thou had space,
And honours transytory / whiche hath brought in thrall
A thousande persones / in ruyne to fall ;   1811
A myrrour thou arte / of vyrgynall clennes,
Of true obedyence / and perfyte mekenes.   1813

260

So Werburge professed / to her rule full ryght,   1814
A redolent floure / all vertue to augment,
As Lucyfer shynynge / a clere lampe of lyght ;
For whome her spouse / god sone omnypotent,
Shewed many myracles / to euery pacyent,   1818
A sygne her loue was / supernaturall,
Closed in our lorde / by grace supernall.   1820

261

The excellent goodnes / of this moynes,   1821
And fame of vertue / with humylyte,
Transcended all other / in perfyte holynes ;
So that sundry persones / approched that party
For ghostly conforte / counsell and remedy.   1825
Suche as to her came / pensyue / woo / and sadde,
Departed ioyfull / in soule mery and gladde.   1827

262

She dayly prouyded / for ghostly treasure   1828
To buylde her a place / a sure mansyon,
Euer to remayne / with ioye and endure
In pleasure perpetuall / without corrupcyon :
Whiche she optayned by her deuocyon   1832
After this departure / to reygne as a presydent
In eterne blys / with god omnypotent.   1834

*¶ A lytell treatyse of the lyfe of saynt Audry, abbesse of Ely /
    and of her holy couersacyon and great deuocyon / vnder
    whome saynt Werburge was made nonne / and professed.
    Ca. xviii.*

263

℘He yere of our lorde .vi. C. ix. and thyrty   1835
        Regned saynt Anna / kynge of eest-Englande ;
Whiche maryed saynt Hereswith / of the North party.
They had noble yssue / as we vnderstande :
Prynce Aldulph and Iurwyne / in story as is founde, 1839
Saynt Sexburge the quene / and blessed Audry,
Saynt Ethelberge / Withburge / —a holy progeny.   1841

264

This blessed Audry / called Etheldred,   1842
Of two great kyngedomes / lynyally descendynge,
Was borne in Suffolke / as sayth saynt Bede,
In a lytell vyllage / called Exmynge.[1]   ¹ r. Exmynge.
This noble prynces / and dere derlynge,   1846
With many great vertues / of grace illumynate,
Magnyfyed her parage / and royall astate.   1848

265

This blessed Audry / from her yonge aege   1849
Was dysposed euer / vnto sadnes,
Obedyent lowly / vnto her parentage,
Encreasynge in vertue / and constaunt sobrynes ;
Worldely pleasures / dysportes / and wantonnes,   1853

Lyghtnes of language / and all presumpcyon
In this sayd vyrgyn / had no domynacyon.   1855

266

Sad and demure / she was in countenaunce,   1856
Nothynge enclyned / vnto fragylyte ;
Benynge and pacyent / without perturbaunce,
Meke / curteys / gentyll / full of humylyte ;
Pryde / statelenes / and sensualyte   1860
Were not in her founde / by any condycyon,
Curteyse in byhauour / vnto euery persone.   1862

267

No man was greued / nor toke dyspleasure   1863
At this sayd mayden / in her fathers hall,
Euery honest persone / and reasonable creature
Were pleased with her / bothe one and all,
None dyscontent / pryuate nor generall ;   1867
She was so meke / and full of pacyence,
That people desyred / to come to her presence.   1869

268

She was beauteous / fayre and amyable,   1870
Pleasaunte to beholde / in gyftes of nature,
Her countenaunce comly / swete / louely / and stable ;
Nothynge dysposed / vnto worldely pleasure,
More lyke an angell / by all coniecture   1874
Than a fragyll mayde / of sensuall appetyte—
For in vayne pleasures / she had no delyte.   1876

269

Whan that she came / to yeres of dyscrecyon,   1877
Dyuers her moeued / in way of maryage ;
Some offered ryches / royalte / and renowne,
Some other possessyons / landes and herytage,
And some the sufferaynte / her mynde to asswage ;   1881
All these she refused / for the loue of Ihesu,
To whome she auowed / her chastyte full tru.   1883

270

After that Venus / had her longe assayled   1884

To peruerte her mynde / to worldly affeccyon,
And of all nettes and engynes / therof had fayled,
Than came to her presence / a prynce of renowne,
Called duke Tombert / of the eest regyon ;   1888
Whiche longe desyred / to haue her in spousage,
At the laste optayned / the wyll of her parentage.   1890
                        271
Vnto whiche thynge / he wolde neuer enclyne,   1891
For all the mocyon / of her hye parentes,
Tyll she was assured / by heuenly doctryne
To kepe her vyrgynyte / clere in conscyens ;
Than she consented / without concupyscens,   1895
And with the sayd duke / she lyued in chastyte,
Bothe mayden and wyfe / almost yeres thre.   1897
                        272
After whose dethe / she remayned in Ely,   1898
In fastynge / prayer / vygyls / and penaunce—
Whiche place was gyuen / to her Ioynt and dowry
By Tombert her husbande / with great pleasaunce.
This yle of Ely / by deuyne purueaunce   1902
With muddy waters / is compased aboute,
Theyr enemyes to greue / and strongely to holde out. 1904
                        273
Thyder came Egbyrct [1] / kynge of the north parte, 1905
To desyre saynt Audry / in matrymony.   [1] r. Egfrid.
To whome she wolde neuer / consent in herte,
For no maner counseyll / that myght be done, truly—
Tho her syster Sexburge / moeued her tenderly—   1909
Tyll the angell of god / assured her to be
Quene / wyfe / and mayde / kepynge vyrgynyte.   1911
                        274
Than Audry graunted / maryed for to be   1912
Vnto this foresayd / noble kynge Egfryde.
And at the maryage / was great solempnyte,
Tryumphes, honoures / on euery syde ;
Great cost and royalte / they dyd prouyde.   1916

Frome Ely departed / vnto his owne place,
In the North parte dwellynge / with great solace.   1918
275
By the grace of our lorde god / moost of myght,   1919
And helpe of his mother / blessed mayd mary,
By prayer of Audry / and by myracle ryght
Togyder they lyued / bothe in pure chastyto :
The naturall mocyon / of his lascyuyte   1923
Was shortly slaked / and feruent desyre,
By myracle / as water quencheth the fyre.   1925
276
Whan he apperceyued / her asured constaunce,   1926
Her perfyte holynes / and chast contynence,
His herte reiosed / of her contynuaunce.
Of whome she desyred / with humble reuerence
And synguler supplycacyon / to haue fre lysence   1930
At Canwod abbay / to enter relygyon ;
Whiche the kynge graunted / for her deuocyon.   1932
277
Saynt Ebba, syster / vnto saynt Oswolde,   1933
Was abbesse and ruler / of that congregacyon.
Where blessed Audry / ryght as she wolde,
Was reuerently receyued / into relygyon ;
And after the yere / of her probacyon   1937
Professed there was / by bysshop Wylfrydo ;
Where all worldly honours / she set on syde.   1939
278
Frome thens she departed / to the yle of Ely,   1940
More quyetly to lyue / out of busynesse,
For drede of the kynge / her husbande, truly,
Purposynge to take her / frome that holynesso.
She toke two maydens / with her, doubtlesse ;   1941
And in theyr Iournay / our lorde of his grace
Shewed dyuers myracles / at eche restynge-place.   1946
279
The archebysshop of yorke / Wylfryde, her confessour, 1947

Was depryued frome his benefyce / by the kynge cruelly ;
Obserued pacyence / laudynge our sauyour
And folowed saynt Audry / to the place of Ely—
Whiche (as afore is sayd) was her Ioynt and dowry·— 1951
And electe her abbesse / on that congregacyon,
Moost worthy to be / for her holy conuersacyon.   1953

280

Where Audry buylded / a chyrche of our lady,   1954
With helpe of kynge Aldulph / her brother naturall,
Dystaunt a myle / frome the olde monastery
Founded by saynt Austyn / for meryte spyrytuall ;
Whiche place all desolate / she edyfyed full specyall   1958
By her prouysyon / an other noble monastery,
The yere of grace / syxe hundreth seuenty and thre.   1960

281

Whan the werke was ended / as her wyll was,   1961
She endowed the abbay / with fraunches and lyberte
And gaue the hole yle of Ely / to that place,
With all commodytes / profettes / and yssues, fre
Frome all exaccyons / exempte clerely to be   1965
Of kynge and bysshop / confyrmed it at Rome,   [1967
With all prelates & prynces / consentynge of this regyon.

282

In short tyme and space / to Audry dyd resorte   1968
Relygyous men and women / a great company,
Professed in that place / for theyr ghostly conforte,
Renounsynge vayne pleasures / & honours transsytory ;
Amonge whome saynt Werburge / professed solemply, 1972
Promysed in audyence / to lyue a lyfe monestycall
After saynt Benettes rule / for the lyfe eternall.   1974

283   [1975

Also the yere of grace / syxe hundreth seuenty and nyne
In the moneth of Iulii / in the nynth kalendas
To heuen departed / saynt Audry the quene,
Than reygnynge in Kent / kynge Lothary by grace,

Aldulph in eest-Englande / her brother whiche was, 1979
Kynge Offryde ¹ her husbande / in Northumberlande,
Also kynge Ethelrede / than reygnynge in Mercelande. 1981

¹ r. Egfryde.

¶ *A breue rehersal of* þᵉ *lyfe of saynt Sexburge / graund-*
mother to saynt Werburge. And of her comynge to Ely
to her syster Audry from Shepay monastery. Ca. xix.

284

℧He holy matrone / and quene saynt Sexburge, 1982
    A kynges doughter / & moder to kynges twayne,
Syster to saynt Audry / & graundmother to Werburge,
Of noble parentage / is comen, certayne,
Of two realmes descendynge / lynyally and playne : 1986
By her father / from the realme of eest-Englande
And by her mother / frome Northumberlande. 1988
285
Her father saynt Anna / as sayth myne auctour, 1989
Was kynge of the eest parte / sone to Egnicius ;
Whiche Anna was maryed / with moche honour
To Hereswith / doughter to kynge Herericius
And syster to saynt Hylde / the vyrgyn gracyous ; 1993
To whome saynt Edwyn / the gloryous martyr,
Kynge of Northumberlande / was great-graundfather. 1995
286
This sayd kynge Anna / lyued a longe space 1996
In welthe / worshyp / honour / and prosperyte
With his quene Hereswith / by synguler grace,
Obseruynge Iustyce / pacyence / and equyte,
Kepte the preceptes / of god almyghte, 2000
Mercyfull and lyberall / to the poore in payne ;
Whiche kynge by Penda / was murdred and slayne. 2002
287
As the ryuer passeth / oftetymes the heed-fountayne, 2003
The lytell graffe or ympe / transcendeth the tree,
Lykewyse theyr chyldren / encresed, certayne,

In mekenes / pacyence / and perfyte charyte
Aboue theyr parentes / in vertue and benygnyte ;   2007
So that theyr name / lynage / and hye astate
By them was magnyfyed / praysed and decorate.   2009

288

Kynge Anna and Hereswith / had a noble yssue :   2010
Syxe goodly chyldren / pleasaunt to beholde—
None fayrer in this lande / myndynge all vertue
And to all good maners / dysposed manyfolde ;
yet was theyr fayrenes / not equall to be tolde   2014
To theyr deuocyon / and synguler goodnes ;
Whose names expressed / ben afore, doubtles.   2016

289

Sexburge, the eldest / of the systers all,   2017
Instructe by her parentes / in vertuous dyscyplyne,
Folowynge theyr counsell / in herte full specyall
Prepared her soule / after theyr doctryne
Fer[1] aboue the age / of so yonge a femynyne ; [1] P. For. 2021
So that euery day / by grace and wysdome
In her dyd growe / some plant of deuocyon.   2023

290

In all this realme / dylated was her fame ;   2024
That, whan she approched / vnto lawfull acge,
Prynces / dukes / erles / herynge of her name
Desyred to haue Sexburge / in maryage,
And busyly laboured / vnto her parentage.   2028
This mayd was maryed / with honour full excellent
Vnto Ercombert / the noble kynge of Kent.   2030

291

To whome kynge Ethelbryct / graundfather was,   2031
The fyrst chrysten kynge / of Saxons and chefe floure,
Baptysed by saynt Austyn / thrughe heuenly grace ;
He was to holy chyrche / a specyall benefactour :
Monasteryes and pryores / founded with great honoure. 2035
Kynge Eadbalde his sone / exemple of hym toke,
Whiche was father to Ercombert / as sayth my boke. 2037

292

This lady Sexburge / cyrcumfulsed with grace,　　　　2038
After her desyre / and vertuous entent
Had leuer the monastery / than the fayre palace,
The chyrche to vysyte / than with maryage be lent;
But to her parentes / she was euer obedyent,　　　　2042
Folowynge theyr counseyll / and of her frendes dere
In lawfull maryage / toke the sayd kynge her fere.　 2044

293

A noble generacyon / she hadde by the kyngo:　　　　2045
Egbryct and Lothary / two prynces prepotent,
And two holy doughters / in vertue shynynge,
Ermenylde and Erkengode / by lynyall descent.
This Ermenylde, maryed / with honour equyualent　　2049
Vnto kynge Vulfer / had a royall yssue :
The gloryous Werburge / replete with vertuo.　　　　2051

294

Her syster Erkengode / refused vtterly　　　　　　　2052
Honours / worshyp / and worldly possessyon,
Ryches / maryage / and pleasures transytory,
Went vnto Fraunce / with humble deuocyon,
At the Cytee of Burges / entred relygyon,　　　　　2056
Where Ethelberge her aunt / was ruler and abbesso ;
Togyder they lyued / in perfyte holynesse.　　　　　2058

295

This honorable Sexburge / and blessed matrone,　　　2059
Refusynge worldly honours / and solempnyte
Preferred mekenesse / and perfyte deuocyon
Aboue all ryches / power and dygnyte,
Auoyded ambycyon / obserued humylyte,　　　　　　　2063
Vpon poore people / euer had compassyon
And them releued / with due mynystracyon.　　　　　2065

296

She made her palace / manytymes an hospytall,　　　2066
Her pryuate cubycle / a deuoute oratory ;
As a kynde mother amyable / in courte and in hall

Mekely fulfylled / the seuen werkes of mercy ;
Oftetymes in the chyrche / selde amonge company ;   2070
yet euer whan she myght / haue tyme and space,
Magnyfyed and praysed / our lorde in secrete place.   2072

297

She instructe her husbande / in ghostly vertu,   2073
To great lolynesse / and synguler perfeccyon.
So by her counseyll / with the grace of Ihesu
Frome infydelyte / purged was that regyon ;
Destroyed theyr ydolles / theyr sectes euerychone,   2077
Restaured temples / vnto chrystes honour,
Founded monasteryes / by her cost and labour.   2079

298

The kynge by her mocyon / commaunded straytly   2080
All his people and subiectes / vpon sharpe correccyon
To obserue prayer / and penaunce deuoutely
And truly for to fast / the holy tyme of Lenton.
The archbysshop Theodorus / and fathers of relygyon,   2084
Consyderynge her pacyence / and benygnyte
Reioysed in her dedes / and praysed the trynyte.   2086

299

Whan the famous Ercombert / the sayd kynge of Kent,   2087
Foure & twenty yere had reygned / in honour full royall
With blessed Sexburge / his quene excellent,
Than he departed / frome this lyfe mortall.
The quene prepared / the obsequyes funerall,   2091
With great lamentacyon / and great royalte,
As was conuenyent / for his state and degre.   2093

300

After that Sexburge / refused worldely pleasure,   2094
Entred relygyon / professed chastyte,
At Shepay monastery / in Kent full sure,
Buylded at her cost / full honorable.
After electe Abbesse / and ruler of that companye ;   2098
To whome she was / a myrrour of mekenes
And exemple of vertue / and proued holynes.   2100

301

As she was occupyed / in medytacyon,   2101
An heuenly messanger / to her was sent,
Shewynge how for synne / and transgressyon
Englande shulde suffer / great punysment
And be subdued / with greuous torment.   2105
Wherfore she lefte / in good rule that place
And dyd electe to them / an other abbace.   2107

302

Sexburge toke lycence / of her systers all,   2108
Commendynge them / vnto the trynyte,
And so departed / fro her chyldren spyrytuall ;
With labour attayned / to the hous of Elye,
There to be subiecte / to Her syster Audrye   2112
And to her doctryne / apply her entent,
Vnto relygyon / euer founde obedyent.   2114

303

Saynt Audry was gladde / of her systers comynge ;   2115
In lyke maner / were all the hole congregacyon,
With myrthes and solace / in soule reioysynge
To haue the presence / of so worthy a persone.
There lyued togyder / in perfyte deuocyon,   2119
Tyll blessed Audry / frome this lyfe mortall
Departed was / to the lyfe eternall.   2121

304

After whose buryall / Sexburge was electe   2122
To be abbesse and ruler / ouer that couent.
Whiche to all vertue / her mynde dyd erecte ;
And the .xvi. yere after / with labours dylygent
She translate saynt Audry / that noble presydent,   2126
Beynge hole incorrupte / also substancyall
In body and in vesture / by grace supernall.   2128

¶ *How saynt Ermenylde after the dethe of kynge Vulfer, her*
husbande, was made a nonne at Ely | vnder her mother
saynt Sexburge abbesse | and Werburge her deuoute
doughter. Ca. **xx.**

305

OF Mercyens the kynge / whan the foresayd Vulfere
    Had regned in honour / worshyp and royalte   [2129
With saynt Ermenylde his quene / fully .xvii. yere,
Vnto euerlastynge blysse / departed than he
And buryed was / with moche solempnyte   2133
In Lychefelde chyrche. / after hym there dyd succede
In-to the kyngdome / his brother Ethelrede.   2135

306

The quene for her husbande / made great lamentacyon, 2136
Dolefully lamentynge / nyght and day his departure,
As nature enquyred / endurynge a longe season,
Remayned in wydohode / and mournynge vesture;
yet after all heuynesse / penaunce / and dysconfyture 2140
She reioysed in soule / to be at lyberte,
Entendynge relygyon / by grace of the trynyte.   2142

307

Soone she departed / to the hous of Ely,   2143
Refusynge this worlde / pleasures, possessyon,
Instauntly requyred / with perfyte humylyte
To be a moynes / accèpte in relygyon.
Gladde was the abbesse / of her conuersyon   2147
And thanked our lorde / of his specyall grace;
So dyd all the systers / within the sayd place.   2149

308

Her naturall mother / blessed Sexburge,   2150
That tyme was lady / and chefe presydent;
There was professed / her doughter Werburge,
An exemple of mekenes / to all the couent.
Ermenylde thanked god / and was obedyent   2154

To her mother Sexburge / a myrrour of vertu,
Also to her doughter / the spouses of Ihesu.   2156

309

It passeth mannes reason / playnly to expresse   2157
Her vertuous lyfe / and ghostly conuersacyon,
In prayer / penaunce / and proued mekenesse,
In perfyte obedyence / and synguler deuocyon,
In vygyls / abstynence / and in hye perfeccyon,   2161
The cotydyane labours / her body to chastyce,
That her soule may be / to god true sacryfyce.   2163

310

Bycause that Werburge / in order was senyoure,   2164
Her mother Ermenylde / gaue her the sufferaynte,
Preferrynge her doughter / with mekenes and honoure ;
But yet her doughter / of a naturall amyte
Preferred her mother / with humble senyoryte ;   2168
And so bytwene them / was a swete contencyon
Wheder shulde more subiecte be / to other in relygyon.   2170

311

Afore, whan Ermenylde / was vnder maryage,   2171
Vnto holy matrones / she was comparable :
Sara / Rebecca / Rachell / and Sybell sage,
And saynt Elysabeth / with other mo honorable ;
Now in relygyon / she is moost notable,   2175
Knowen by her vertues / and sadde dysposycyon
What vnder matrymony / was her intencyon.   2177

312

Ermenylde subdued / by synguler deuyne grace   2178
All fragyll mocyons / and sensualyte,
Lyke maner as Iudyth / Olofernes slayne hace ;
She mortyfyed all pleasures / lustes and volupte,
Lykewyse as Iaell / dyd the prynce Sysare ;   2182
A duches of vertue / as whylom was Delbora ;
Vsed the oratory / in prayer as dyd Anna.   2184

313

After the departure / and wofull buryall   2185

G

Of Sexburge, her mother / abbesse and lady,
Her doughter Ermenylde / the blessed monyall,
Was chosen abbesse / and ruler of Ely—
As sheweth dan Wyllyam / of Maluysbury   2189
How fyrst was Audry / than Sexburge, her syster,
Afterwarde was abbesse / Ermenylde, her doughter.   2191

314

The lyfe of Ermenylde / was euer vertuous,   2192
Pleasaunt to god / and her systers euerychone ;
In the syght of god / her dethe was precyous,
Playnly notyfyed / by her conuersacyon.
She vertuously gouerned / her congregacyon,   2196
Frome this lyfe departed / to eternall glory,
As sayth her legende / the Idus of February ;   2198

315

And buryed was / with moche lamentacyon   2199
In the holy monastery / and house of Ely
Amonge her parentage / and congregacyon ;
Where she is shryned / with her aunt saynt Audry
And with her mother / saynt Sexburge rychely ;   2203
For whome our sauyour / of his specyall grace
Sheweth dayly myracles / in that sayd place.   2205

316

One of the myracles / we shall now rehers   2206
Our lorde for her shewed / at Ely abbay
After her translacyon / the story dothe expres.
It fortuned in Whytson weke / vpon a thursday,
An Englysshman was bounden / in wofull aray,   2210
Fetered with yrons / bothe on handes and fete,
Wrongfully accused / as ye may all wete.   2212

317

By instaunt request / he gate hym lycence   2213
To vysyte the tombe / of saynt Ermenylde.
Whome he requyred / with humble reuerence
And meke petycyon / frome the herte full mylde,
To be delyuered / and fully reconsylde.   2217

Whose humble desyre / and synguler supplycacyon
Was fully graunted / to his consolacyon.   2219

318

At this tyme / whan this holy man was prayenge,   2220
Whan the Deken redde the holy gospell,
By meane of Ermenylde / to our lorde and kynge
Frome his handes and fete / the yrons done fell,
By grace aboue nature / merueylously to tell,   2224
That the sayd yrons / in syght of all the bretherne
Sprange vp sodenly / and lyght vpon the aulter.   2226

¶ *Aliud miraculum.*

319

A N other myracle / declare now may we,   2227
    Done at the sayd Ely / by this holy matronè,
In presence of the pryor / and all the fraternyte,
Whiche pryor of this mater / had best notycyon.
A scole-mayster of Innocentes / after the custome   2231
Gaue lysence / vpon saynt Ermenyldes day
To all his chyldren / to sport them in play.   2233

320

Whan the feest / and solempnyte was done,   2234
The yonge tender chyldren / wanton and neclygent,
Dredynge theyr mayster / for fere of correccyon
To the holy shryne / they assembled full dylygent,
Trustynge therby of pardon / after theyr entent,   2238
Desyred theyr mayster / for saynt Ermenyldes sake
To pardon theyr trespas / and no dyspleasure take.   2240 .

321

The mayster, fulfylled / with hastynes and enuy,[1] [1 P. euny.] 2241
Toke them frome the tombe / with great indygnacyon,
Without dyscrecyon / punysshed them greuously,
Gyuynge no honour / to the saynt ne deuocyon
Rebuked them sore / sayenge with insultacyon :
'Trowe ye to be spared / from punyshment this day
For saynt Ermenyldes sake ? / nay, nay, do way !'   2247

322

After all this done / the nexte nyght folowynge,   2248
Whan the sayd mayster / to his bedde was gone,
His great vnkyndenes / saynt Ermenylde remembrynge
Rewarded[1] hym Iustly / after his guerdon :   [1] P. Rewarned.
His handes and his fete / prompte to persecucyon,   2252
Were sodenly smytten / made lame / contracte also ;
No power had to ryse / to moeue nor to go.   2254

323

This sodayne punysshement / langour / confusyon   2255
Vexed hym greuously in all his body,
Moost terryble of all / of helthe desperacyon
Inwardly hym troubled / with peynes horryble.
But yet by grace / he thought best remedy   2259
Sende for his chyldren / vpon the other day,
Humble asked them pardon / in a wofull aray ;   2261

324

Desyrynge his scolers / for loue and charyte   2262
To cary hym moost carefull / to her sepulture,
To requyre for hym grace / helthe and prosperyte
Of god and saynt Ermenylde / with all theyr cure.
They toke hym tenderly / ye may me leue full sure,   2266
Amonge them all / with mynde dylygent
And brought to the shryne / this wretched impotent.   2268

325

They prayed for hym / to our blessed sauyour   2269
And to saynt Ermenylde / a longe tyme and space,
Knelynge on theyr knees / wepynge full sore,
In prayer and psalmody / for his helthe and solace :
And so contynuynge / by our lordes great grace
He that afore was lame / bothe on fote and hande,
Restored to helthe / departed hole and sounde.   2275

¶ *How kynge Ethelrede, seynge the holy conuersacyon of Werburge, his nece | made her lady and abbesse at Wedon | Trentam | and Hambury.[1] And by her counseyll and exsample was made monke at Bardeney abbay.* Ca. xxi.   [1] P. Humbury.

326

THe famous prynce / and foresayd Ethelrede,   2276
   Brother to kyng Vulfer / as lawfull enherytour
To the sayd kyngedome / dyd nexte hym succede,
Electe of his peeres / with worshyp and honour,
Permytted by his chyrche / to be theyr gouernour,   2280
Bycause prynce Kenrede / his brother sone,
Was yonge and not able / to rule his kyngdome.   2282

327

This sayd kynge Ethelrede / clerely consyderynge   2283
With due cyrcumstaunce / the hye perfeccyon
Of Werburge, his nece / and vertuous lyuynge,
Her great holynesse / and ghostly conuersacyon,
Dayly encresynge / with feruent deuocyon,   2287
The excellent fame / and myracles full ryght
Shewed by our sauyour / bothe day and nyght :   2289

328

These good exsamples / grounded in vertu,   2290
Moeued kynge Ethelrede / in soule and in mynde :
And clerely conuerted / throwe the grace of Ihesu
To despyse this worlde / wretched and blynde,
Pryncypally by grace / wryten as we fynde,   2294
For her great goodnes / and vertues excellent
He made her lady / ruler / and presydent   2296

329

Ouer all the nonnes / of euery monastery   2297
Within his realme / to gouerne and to guyde,
To instructe and informe / and to exemplyfy,
To encrese deuocyon / vpon euery syde,
Vertue to exalte / to subdue vyce and pryde ;   2301

That holy relygyon / pleasaunt to chryst Ihesu,
Myght dayly encrese / frome vertu to vertu.   2303
330
Also he gaue Werburge / great possessyon,   2304
Landes / and rentes / ryches withall,
To edyfy and repayre / places of relygyon
After her desyre / with fauour specyall.
Wherwith she buylded / famous memoryall   2308
Two fayre monasteryes / Trentam and Hambury,[1]   [1] P. Hambury.
Possessed with rentes / landes / and lyberte.   2310
331
Also by sufferaunce / of the sayd kynge, truly,   2311
She translate the kynges maner of Wedon,
Whiche was in Hamptonshyre / vnto a monastery
Of holy women / obseruynge relygyon,
Suffycyently endowed / with lybertes / possessyon.   2315
Of whiche sayd places / she had the gouernaunce,
As worthy maystres / all vertue to auaunce.   2317
332
The yere of grace / syxe hundreth foure score and nyen,
As sheweth myne auctour / a Bryton Giraldus,   [2318
Kynge Ethelred / myndynge moost the blysse of heuen,
Edyfyed a collage-chyrche / notable and famous
In the subbarbes of Chester / pleasaunt and beauteous, 2322
In the honour of god / and the Baptyst saynt Iohan,
With helpe of bysshop Vulfryce / and good exortacyon. 2324
333
Also at the humble / and synguler supplycacyon   2325
Of blessed Egwyn / bysshop of worcestur,
This kynge gaue a place / for a fundacyon
To buylde a monastery / to relygyous brethur
At Eusam vpon Auen / for heuenly tresur,   2329
With a large precynct / to compas all the abbay,
More quyetly to serue / our sauyour nyght and day.   2331
334
After this tyme / Ethelrede the kynge   2332

By his counseyll maryed / a beautefull lady,
Called quene Ostryde / a woman of good lyuyngo,
Borne in the North parte / doughter to kynge Oswy—
To whome saynt Oswalde / was vncle, truly.   2336
The yssue bytwene them / after to succede
Was a noble prynce / nomynate Colrede.   2338
                335
Agaynst his enemyes / the kynge gate vyctory,   2339
Fortunate in batayle / sore oppressed Kent.
In all this regyon / famous was his chyualry;
Namely he subdued / at the water of Trent
Egfryde of Northumberlande / a kynge auncyent,   2343
His brother-in-lawe / whan Egfryde agaynst reason
Entred his landes / by subtyll intrusyon.   2345
                336
Dut after that Ostryde / his quene, was slayne   2346
By people of the North parte / moost cruelly,
The kynge frome that tyme / by grace, certayne,
Chaunged his maners / and lyuynge dayly
Frome temporall cures / and busynesse worldly   2350
To ghostly werkes / and contemplacyon,
Sekynge for heuen / with pure deuocyon.   2352
                337
Specyally he folowed / saynt Werburge counsell,   2353
Vsynge hym after / her swete ghostly doctryne;
The clere exsamples / as we afore dyd tell,
Moeued his conscyence / to ghostly dyscyplyne
With suche contrycyon / by specyall grace deuyne,   2357
That all vayne pleasures / and honours transytory
Were clere expulsed / and put out of memory.   2359
                338
This kynge refused / his septre and crowne,   2360
Clothes of Tyshew / and purpull full royall,
With ryches / lybertes / pleasures / possessyon,
For the loue of Ihesu / in herte pryncypall [1] /   [1] P. pryncaypall.
And for the meryte / of his soule-helthe withall.   2364

So whan he had reygned / nyne and twenty yere,
He chaunged his habyte / sayth the story clere;   2366

339

At a relygyous place / nomynate Bardenay,   2367
In Lyncolne-shyre / vnder his domynyon,
Synguler byloued / of hym alway,
Desyred the habyte / with meke supplycacyon
And was receyued / professynge relygyon,   2371
Euer after to obserue / the essencyals thre :
Obedyence / chastyte / and wylfull pouerte.   2373

340

He assygned his crowne / and temporall dygnyte   2374
Vnto prynce Kenrede / his brother sone,
As true enherytour / to haue regalyte.
For in pure obedyence / prayer and medytacyon
Ethelrede encresed / with feruent deuocyon;   2378
And as declareth / wyllyam of Maluysbury,
After was made abbot / of the sayd monastery.   2380

*¶ The holy conuersacyon of kynge Kenred, brother to saynt
Werburge / & how he refused his crowne / and was made
monke at Rome / & ther departed a holy confessour.
Ca. xxii.*

341

SO whan kynge Etheldrede / by heuenly grace   2381
        At Bardenay abbay / professed relygyon,
Than prynce Kenrede / his successour was
And toke the Empyre / the septre and the crowne
With moche worshyp / royalte / and renowne,   2385
As nexte of inherytaunce / by law naturall
To be kynge of Mercyens / by dyscent lynyall.   2387

342

This noble kynge Kenrede / replete with vertu,   2388
Brother to Werburge / obserued truly
The commaundymentes of god / & his lawes moost tru,

Obedyent to our sauyour / and lorde almyghty,
Loued holy chyrche / moost tenderly, 2392
Mynystred Iustyce / to his subiectes all,
Mercyfull to the poore / pyteous and lyberall. 2394

343

In all his realme / was no dyuersyte, 2395
Malyce was subdued / rancour and debate,
Vertue encreased / true loue and charyte,
Enuy was exyled / and all pryuy hate ;
Thefte / murthur / robry / were founde at no gate, 2399
True men myght lyue / without vexacyon ;
Pollers / promoters had no domynacyon. 2401

344

He gaue to our sauyour / and bysshop Egwyn 2402
For ghostly meryte / with moche honoure
Of tenementes and landes / playnely to determyne,
Within worcetur-shyre .iiii. score and foure,
To maynteyne the monastery / spoken of before, 2406
Euesham vpon Auen / byfore lawfull wytnes,
As the legende of Egwyn / truly dothe expres. 2408

345

To the courte of Rome / kynge Kenred went; 2409
So dyd Offa kynge / of the eest-Saxons,
Also bysshop Egwyn / by one assent,
Deuoutly to vysyte / all the hole stacyons
Of the cytee of Rome / with humble supplycacyons, 2413
Thankynge our lorde / of his mercy
Hath them preserued / and all theyr company. 2415

346

This holy bysshop / and kynge Kenrede 2416
Offered to our holy father / pope boneface
With mekenes, deuocyon / for ghostly mede
Afore his collage / wytnes in that case,
The foresayd monastery / and relygyous place, 2420
Frome that day euer after / to be clerely exempte,
To the popes holynes / immedyatly obedyent. 2422

347

Whan they had optayned / perfyte expedycyon   2423
Of all theyr bulles / after theyr entent,
They toke lycence / and had the popes beneson,
And towarde Englande / retourned and went,
Praysynge our lorde / with herte and loue feruent   2427
For theyr good spede / and prosperous Iournay,
Preserued in good helthe / all to theyr countray.   2429

348

After all this done / Kenrede the sayd kynge   2430
Commaunded to be had / a counseyll generall,
By letters myssyue / his peeres and lordes cytynge
Shortly to be present / with hym, one and all,
As well the spyrytualte / as the temporall.   2434
The Seyn was kepte / at a place called Alue,
And thyder assembled / his prelates of degre.   2436

349

Berthtunaldus / the archebysshop of Canturbury,   2437
The archbysshop of yorke / called Wylfryde,
With bysshops / suffreganes / archdekens many,
Dukes / erles / barons / vpon euery syde,
Knyghtes / esquyers / and comunes that tyde   2441
Were redy to knowe / the kynges mynde and pleasure,
Well ordred in place / and scylence kepte sure.   2443

350

This gloryous Kenrede / crowned with golde,   2444
Clothed in purpull / rose vp fro his place,
After due salutacyon / the cause mekely he tolde
Why he for them sende / and wherfore it was:
That they shulde testyfy / with hym in this case   2448
What landes he gaue / towarde the fundacyon
Of the sayd monastery / with grete deuocyon,   2450

351

And how for that abbay / he went to Rome   2451
And made the place subiecte / immedyatly
To our father boniface / and gate an exempcyon

For euer to remayne / to the sayd monastery,
With pardons and pryuyleges / there redde openly,　2455
And many other benefytes /of great commodyte,
Wryten in theyr grauntes / who lyst them to se ;　2457

352

Requyrynge the lordes / spyrytuall and temporall　2458
To graunte to the same / with good entent
And it to confyrme / and roborate specyall
With charters and dedes / and seales patent.
To whose petycyon / they dyd all consent,　2462
Made confyrmacyons and grauntes them amonge,
With a terryble sentence / who dothe the place wronge. 2464

353

Kynge Kenrede, consyderynge / the great holynes　2465
Of his noble parentes / his vncles euerychone,
Theyr royall progeny / the sufferaunt[1] goodnes,　[1] r. sufferane.
From this lyfe transytory / to heuen agone ;
Namely the vertue / and feruent deuocyon　2469
Of his syster Werburge / and his auntes all
Moeued his mynde / to seke for lyfe eternall :　2471

354

And, as saynt Bede sayth / whan this noble kynge　2472
Had regned fyue yere / in great prosperyte,
He forsoke this worlde / and chaunged his lyuynge,
Refusynge his crowne / septre / and dygnyte,
All vayne honours / ryches and regalyte,　2476
And made his vncles sone / prynce Coelrede,
To take his empyre / after hym to succede.　2478

355

So with all gentylnes / and humylyte　2479
The kynge of his subiectes / toke leue specyall,
Commendynge his people / to the trynyte
Them to conserue / spyrytuall and temporall.
Of his departure / dolorous were they all.　2483
Thus for the loue / of our sauyoure
He refused this worlde / pleasures and honoure.　2485

356

And went to Rome agayne / the yere of grace   2486
Seuen hundreth and eyght / by full computacyon,
Vysytynge the stacyons / frome place to place ;
There was professed / to saynt Benettes relygyon,
Vsed vygyls / fastynges / prayer / medytacyon ;   2490
Where this holy monke / frome this lyfe transytory
With vertu departed / to eternall glory.   2492

¶ *Of* þᵉ *feruent & ghostly deuocyon of saynt Werburge / &*
   vertuous gouernaunce of her places / & of þᵉ *great humi-*
   lite she vsed to her sisters / & al other creatures.
   Ca. xxiii.

357

This venerable Werburge / & moynes gracyous,   2493
   For her great vertue / and perfyte holynesse
Electe to be gouernour / ouer the nonnes relygeous
By her vncle kynge Ethelrede / of his goodnesse
Ouer dyuers monasteryes (as is sayd) expresse,   2497
Was consecrate abbesse / and lady gracyous
By the bysshop of Lychefelde / nomynat Sexwulfus.   2499

358

And thus she departed / fro the hous of Ely,   2500
Wherin she vsed / heuenly medytacyon,
With lycence optayned / in mynde sad and heuy ;
So were the systers / and all the congregacyon
Of her departure / knowynge her conuersacyon ;   2504
But, as wolde charyte / they had great gladnes,
Knowynge by her vertue / relygyon to encres.   2506

359

The spouses of Ihesu / and floure of benygnyte   2507
Consyderynge her-selfe / a lady and presydent,
Ordered her monasteryes : ryght well and wysele,
Receyued in systers / chast / humble / obedyent,
Ouer them made rulers / vertuous / and pacyent,   2511

Her subiectes to instructe / and counseyll day and nyght,
Vertue to exalte / and vyce depryue aryght.　　　　2513
360
This noble abbesse / remembrynge her duty,　　　　2514
What charge it is / to rule a congregacyon,
Humble requyred / the grace of god almyghty
And dylygently prepared / to supple her rowme ;
Pryncypally she gaue / to them euerychone　　　　2518
Perfyte exsample / of vertue in her dede,
With vertuous doctryne / the same to procede.　　　2520
361
A myrrour of mekenesse / she was to them all,　　　2521
A floure of chastyte / and well of clennes,
The fruyte of obedyence / in her was specyall ;
Refusynge vayne pleasures / honours and ryches
Content with lytell / an exsample of lowlynes　　　2525
As dothe belonge / vnto wylfull pouerte ;
Pryde had no resydence / but all humylyte.　　　　2527
362
She was a mynyster / rather than a maystres,　　　2528
Her great preemynence / caused no presumpcyon ;
She was a handmayd / rather than a pryores,
Seruynge her systers / with humble subieccyon ;
Subduynge her body / to penaunce and afflyccyon,　　2532
Subiecte to the soule / as reason wolde shulde be,
A true sacryfyce / offered to the trynyte.　　　　2534
363
It was no merueyll / tho all her couent　　　　　2535
Vnder suche a ruler / encreased in vertu,
Seynge her exsample / afore them dayly present,
Euer augmentynge / throwe the helpe of Ihesu ;
Worldy desyres / she clerely dyd subdue ;　　　　2539
She neuer ware lynon / by day or by nyght,
All ryche vayne vestures / she set by them but lyght. 2541
364
In prayer, medytacyon / the tyme she dyspent,　　　2542

Proued :. for euery nyght / longe afore matyns
She [1] wolde vpryse / at an houre conuenyent   [1] P. The.
And deuoutely say / afore our lordes presens
Dauyd spalter holly knelynge / with great reuerence,   2546
Or that her systers / came to the oratory
To say dyuyne seruyce / fyndynge her all redy.   2548

365

At after matyns / she vsed contemplacyon,   2549
Contynually abydynge / vnto the day-lyght
Prostrate on the grounde / or knelynge in deuocyon,
Wepynge full tenderly / with teeres downe ryght ;
Many holy oraysons / she sayd day and nyght ;   2553
Pyteous / mercyable / and full [1] of charyte   [1] P. fulll.
To the poore people / in theyr necessyte.   2555

366

This lady obserued / suche sharpe abstynence   2556
That one dayly repast / wolde her well suffyse ;
Delycate dysshe meetes / were put out of her presence ;
So nature were content / in moost humble wyse,
The Worde of god / was moost delycate seruyse ;   2560
Myndynge moche more / the soule to satysfy
Than please and content / her enemy, the body.   2562

367

These sayd exemples / with many other mo   2563
Pleasaunte vnto Ihesu / she taught her couent,
Them to preserue / frome theyr mortall fo,
By synguler vertue / grace to augment.
Her precepte and lyuynge / were euer corespondent,   2567
She neuer commaunded syster / do any thynge
But it was fulfylled / in her owne doynge.   2569

368

She exorted her chyldren / euer to deuocyon,   2570
With manyfolde doctrynes / ydlenes to exchewe ;
Lyke a tender mother / had pyte and compassyon,
She dayly fedde them / and nourysshed in all vertue,   .
And dylygently prayed / our sauyour Ihesu   2574

Them to preserue / of his infynyte grace
Frome peryll of peryshynge / in blysse to se his face. 2576

369

Also the .xii. degrees / of humylyte,   2577
Pacyence / quyetnes / and great perfeccyon
Were well obserued / with true loue and charyte,
Amonge her systers / the hole congregacyon ;
And the thre essencyals / of relygyon :   2581
Wylfull pouerte / chastyte / and obedyence,
were truly fulfylled / proued by the consequence.   2583

370

As for a pastyme / amonge her systers all   2584
She caused to be redde / auoydynge ydlenesse,
The swete legendary / for a memoryall,
And Vitas patrum / shewynge great swetenesse,
With other narracyons / of grace and goodnesse.   ˙2588
Ofttymes to her couent / she had a comyn sayenge :
'Please god and loue hym / and doubte ye nothynge.' 2590

371

All reders excuse me / tho I can not expresse   2591
For lacke of lernynge / the vertues morall,
The hye perfeccyon / and proued holynesse
Of this pure vyrgyn / and sanctymonyall,
Wherwith was decorate / her lyfe monestycall,   2595
Manyfest with myracles / by meryte of her mekenesse,
As the true hystory / playnly dothe expresse.   2597

372

The worthy myracles / of this vyrgyn pure   2598
Dylated were / thrugh all this regyon,
By deuyne sufferaunce / aboue nature,
Profytable / to euery chrysten synguler persone ;
In sekenesse / trouble / peyne or vexacyon   2602
Of her they haue refuge / helpe / and socoure
By her merytes / and prayer / that euery honoure (!). 2604

373

Her merytes were / moche more commendable   2605

Than were her myracles— / manyfest and playne :
For why by her merytes / famous and notable
Sygnes and myracles / were shewed full playne,
In the house of Ely / by grace of our sufferayne   2609
And in euery place / where she kepte resydence.
Of whome parte folowen / in this rude sentence.   2611

¶ *How at Wedon wylde gees were pynned by her commaundy-*
ment / & also releshed & put at lyberte. Ca. xxiiii.

374

THis holy vyrgyn / whan she dwelled at Wedon,   2612
   In Northamptonshyrn / with a deuoute couent—
Whiche place somtyme / was the kynges mansyon,
Translated to an abbay / by her commaundyment—
A myracle was done / by this noble presydent,   2616
As the true legende / playnly dothe vs say
And all the inhabytauntes / vnto this present day.   2618

375

A great multytude / somtyme of wylde gees—   2619
Comunely called Gauntes— / made great destruccyon [1]
Vpon her landes / pastures / waters / and feldes,   [1] P. descrypeyon.
Deuourynge the cornes / and fruytes of Wedon,
Greuous to her subiectes / within that possessyon ;   2623
The people coude fynde / no suffycyent remedy,
But shewed theyr complaynte / to Werburge theyr lady.2625

376

Whan Werburge had herde / this greuous complayne 2626
How the cornes were wasted / þᵉ tenauntes hurte therby,
Her herte was moeued / with charyte than, certayne,
To saue her fruytes / and helpe her company ;
Wherfore she commaunded a seruaunt go hastely   2630
To dryue those wylde gees / & brynge home to her place,
There to be pynned / and punysshed for theyr trespace.2632

377

The messanger merueyled / and mused in his mynde   2633

Of this straunge message / stode styll in a study,
Knowynge it well / it passed course of kynde
Wylde gees for to pynne / by any mannes polycy,
Syth nature hath ordeyned / suche byrdes to fly ;   2637
Supposynge his lady / had ben vnreasonable
Commaundynge to do / a thynge vnpossyble.   2639

378

With wordes of conforte / she sayd to hym agayne : 2640
' Go in my name / do my commaundyment.'
The seruaunt went forth / thynkynge all but vayne,
Vnto the foldes / where the byrdes were lent,
And sayd his message / with mynde and good entent : 2644
' My lady commaundes you / byrdes euerychone,
Afore me to go / vnto her proper mansyone.'   2646

379

A merueylous thynge / transcendynge nature :   2647
Vnto his wordes / the gees were obedyent,
Not one departed / fro thens, ye may be sure,
Of all the nombre / that there were present ;
Towarde her place / afore hym they went,   2651
Mekely / as yf they had reason naturall ;
Vnto her presence / he brought the gauntes all.   2653

380

Dredefully darynge / comen now they be,   2654
Theyr wynges traylynge / entred into the hall,
For great confusyon / after theyr kynde and propryte,
Mournynge in theyr maner / abydynge one and all
Her wyll and Iudgment / with mercy specyall ;   2658
Lamentynge all nyght / there in captuyte
Tyll the morowe after / withouten lyberte.   2660

381

All that same nyght / Werburge dyd contynue   2661
In deuoute prayers / and ympnes celestyall,
After her olde custome / vsed in all vertue.
In the mornynge after / the byrdes that were thrall
With hye voyces (as yf it were) on her dyd call   2665

H

For grace and pardon / of theyr offence,
And of departure / to haue fre lycence.   2667

382

Than she, full pyteous / to euery creature,   2668
Vpon these byrdes hauynge compassyon
Delyuered them / frome all daunger and cure,
Frely to departe / vnder this condycyon
That none of them / vpon the lordshyp of Wedon   2672
Shulde make destruccyon / nor lyght by any way
On cornes or fruytes / neuer after that day.   2674

383

Neuertheles a seruaunt / one of the gees dyd take   2675
And pryuely hydde it / agaynst iustyce and ryght,
Vnknowynge to Werburge / suche brybry to make.
The byrdes departed / moost glad to take theyr flyght,
From theyr tender Iudge. / but whan they sawe in syght
One of theyr felawes / taken frome theyr company,   [2679
The sayd great nombre / of gees retourned hastely.   2681

384

They flewe ouer / this blessed vyrgyns hall   2682
Mournynge and waylynge / after theyr entent,
And wolde not departe / but fast on her dyd call—
yet they durst not lyght / for drede of her commaundyment—
But in theyr maner & kynde they sayd / ‘ o swete presydent,
Why suffer ye suche wyckednes / done for to be   [2686
Anendes our felawe / agaynst all ryght and charyte?’ 2688

385

Werburge went fyrst / to knowe wherfore and why   2689
These byrdes retourned / so hastely, certayne.
By grace she perceyued / the cause of it, truly,
And tryed out the truthe / of all the mater playne.
She restaured the byrde / to his felyshyp agayne,   2693
And gaue them a lesson / or they went her fro,
How they shulde prayse / theyr maker and sufferayne, 2695
Sayenge (benedicite volucres celi domino).

386

But, as Wyllyam Maluysbury / sheweth expresse,   2697
The goos that was taken / and stollen afore away,
Was rosted and eten / the same nyght, doubtlesse ;
So whan it was asked / for vpon the other day,   1 P. after
The bare bones were brough[t] / afor[1] this lady, veray : 2701
And there by the vertue / of her benedyccyon
The byrde was restaured / and flewe away full soone. 2703

387

Certaynly, frome that tyme / vnto this present day, 2704
As all the people knowe / dwellynge aboute Wedon,
The foresayd wylde gees / attempten by no way
To hurte theyr fruytes / ne lyght in that possessyon.
No merueyll it is / remembrynge the deuocyon   2708
And true loue she had / to god omnypotent :
For vnto vertue / all thynge is obedyent.   2710

¶ *How a tyraunt without pyte punyshynge an Innocent was
punyshed / & after made hole.   Ca. xxv.*

388

FOrther to declare / the pacyence and humylyte   2711
  And the synguler grace / grounded in this abbas,
As in the true legende / playnly ye may se
We shall parte rehers / to augment your solas.
Werburge had a seruaunte / whiche named was   2715
Alnotus, a man / of meke conuersacyon,
Knowen by his merytes / after due probacyon.   2717

389

Also a baylyfe she had / a cruell tyraunt ;   2718
Whiche pyteously punysshed / without reason
And wounded greuously / Alnot, her seruaunt,
Without any greuaunce / at the place of Wedon.
Werburge for pyte / and great compassyon   2722
Afore this caytyfe / kneled on her knee,
Prayenge hym to cease / for loue of the trynyte ;   2724

390

Sayenge : ' why does thou punysshe / this innocent, 2725
Causeles, without mercy / whiche I byleue playne
Is more acceptable / to our lorde omnypotent
Than many other be / for his mekenesse, certayne ? '
The baylyfe at her prayer / wolde not refrayne, 2729
But punysshed hym styll / in his fury and pryde ;
Tyll the vengeaunce of god / fell on hym that tyde. 2731

391

Incontynente his heed / his necke / and his face 2732
Were tourned backwarde / lyke a persone monstruous,
Contrary to nature / for his great trespace,
Crucyate with sorowe / and peynes hyduous,
Contynually encreasynge / to beholde pyteous. 2736
At the last remembred / of the best remedy :
Fell prostrate to the fete / of Werburge, his lady, 2738

392

And cryed vpon her / with wofull chere, 2739
Wepynge / lamentynge / his great inyquyte :
' My louely lady / and maystres moost dere,
Helpe me, swete abbesse / in this necessyte !
I haue offended god / now pray for me, 2743
And I wyll neuer / endurynge all my lyfe
Dysplease no more / man / mayde / ne wyfe.' 2745

393

Whan Werburge consydered / his great contrycyon, 2746
His woofull herte / and lamentable crye,
Vpon hym she had / tender compassyon ;
Beholdynge his greuaunce / and tender[1] agony,   [1] r. terrible ?
' Good brother,' she sayd / ' who-so wyll haue mercy 2750
Must be mercyable / as in prouerbe wryten is ;
Who is without mercy / of mercy shall mys. 2752

394

' Call vnto mynde / thy owne wycked dede 2753
In punyshynge this poore man / without offence ;
To se his punyshment / my herte sore dyd blede,

I kneled afore thy fete / desyrynge indulgence ;
Thou toke no regarde / to my prayer ne presence,　2757
Wherfore the Iustyce / of god almyghty
Vpon the is fallen / for thy synne soday[n]ly.'　2759

395

Whan she had ended / her ghostly exortacyon,　2760
Perceyuynge hym penytent / with great humylyte,
Gladde to amende / vyce and transgressyon,
Anone vnto prayer / she went with charyte,
Opteyned forgyuenesse / of the blessed trynyte :　2764
His fysnamy / restaured to his kynde agayne,
Bothe bodyly and ghostly / cured was, certayne.　2766

396

This forsayd Alnotus / by synguler grace　2767
Refused this worlde / pleasures and vanyte,
Went vnto wyldernesse / and anchoryte [1] was. 1 P. inachoryte.
Whome theues martyred / to heuen blysse went he,
At Stow besyde Bukbrydge / buryed was, trule ;　2771
For whome our lorde / of his infynyte goodnes
Shewed many myracles / affyrmynge his holynes.　2773

¶ *How dyuers prynces folowynge sensualyte, intendynge to
violate this vyrgyn bi power / bi myracle were put to
confusyon.* Ca. xxvi.

397

HNother sygne was shewed / by the kynge of blys 2774
　　Of a wanton prynce / folowynge sensualyte
And his fragyll appetyte / in doynge amys ;
Entendynge by vyolence / power / and auctoryte
To depryue Werburge / of her vyrgynyte,　2778
Espyed a season / to fulfyll his entent,
Whan she was solytary / and no man there present.　2780

398

By force than he began / this mayd to assayle.　2781
But she trustynge in god / to be her protectour,
Escapynge his presence / cast her sacrat vayle

For lyghtnesse and ease / to fle from the traytour :
The sonne-beame receyued it/whiche hanged that houre.2785
Whiche myracle sene / the prynce fledde away ;
That vyrgyn was preserued / by grace that day.   2787

399

¶ An other myracle / was done in Kent   2788
In the vyllage of Hoo / yet full memorous.
A sensuall prynce / of wycked consent
Purposed to maculate / this vyrgyn gloryous,
Consyderynge her persone / so fayre and beauteous ;   2792
Taryed the season / to fynde her solytary,
By power to oppresse / this gracyous lady.   2794

400

Whan the tyme was comen / he thought conuenyent, 2795
After her furyously / he ranne a fast pace.
She, knowynge his mynde / and[1] vnchast entent,   [1 P. add]
Seynge no remedy / by man in that place
Called to our sauyoure / for his helpe and grace,   2799
Sayenge : 'blessed lorde / for thy endeles pyte
Defende me this daye / and saue my chastyte !'   2801

401

And as she fledde / frome this cruell persone,   2802
She ranne for socour / to a great oke-tree.
By grace the sayd tree / opened that same season,
Sufferynge this mayd / to haue sure and fre entree ;
Wherby she escaped his / wycked tyrannye.   2806
Whiche tree to this day / endurynge all the yere
By myracle is vernaunte / fresshe / grene / and clere. 2808

402

Of the sayd oke-tree / is a famous opynyon :   2809
That no man may entre / the sayd concauyte
In deedly synne bounden / without contrycyon ;
But in clene perfyte lyfe / who-soeuer he be,
May entre the sayd oke / with fre lyberte.   2813
And nygh to that place / a chyrche is now dedycate
In the honour of god / and werburge immaculate.   2815

403

¶ Many other myracles / our blessed sauyour   2816
Shewed for this vyrgyn / of his goodnes,
Conforte to the people / in sekenes and langour
That to her wyll seke / in theyr dystresse.
Her excellent vertue / and great holynesse   2820
By sygnes and myracles / were dayly manyfest
To many a creature / with peynes opprest.   2822

404

The fame wherof sprange / so fast aboute,   2823
Notyfyed playne / in all this regyon :
The people approched / withouten doubte
To knowe her blessed / and holy conuersacyon
And of these myracles / to haue probacyon,   2827
By the syght wherof / they myght all gloryfy
With ioy and gladnesse / our lorde god almyghty.   2829

405

There was no sekenesse / nor infyrmyte   2830
That mankynde had / nor vexacyon,
But by her prayer / and humylyte
Makynge for them / to our lorde intercessyon
They were restaured / to helthe and saluacyon   2834
All, by the meryte / of this vyrgyn pure,
A synguler refuge / vnto euery creature.   2836

406

To the dombe was gyuen / speche and language,   2837
To blynde theyr syght / to defe theyr herynge,
To halte and lame people / helthe, in euery aege,
By deuyne grace / and her ghostly lyuynge.
The people approchynge / nygh to her in dwellynge,   2841
By cally[n]ge to her / in the name of Ihesu
Had theyr petycyon / by her synguler vertu.   2843

407

Some other that were / fully possessed   2844
With wycked spyrytes / vexynge the mynde,
Or with sekenes incurable / myserably greued,

By her dayly prayer / aboue course of kynde
Of theyr dyseases / they shulde remedy fynde,   2848
And from her departe / in soule with gladnesse
Whiche to her came / sory in peyne and wretchednes. 2850

¶ *How saynt Werburge gaue knowlege to her systers of her*
   departure, & how she ordered in vertue her sayd monas-
   teryes afore her dethe. Ca. xxvii.

408

THis blessed abbesse / and vertuous floure,   2851
    The well of clennes / and humylyte,
Called to mynde / the wordes of our sauyour
Rehersed by Mathewe / in his euangely :
'The vyctoryall crowne / of eterne glory   2855
Is gyuen to them / that be redy eche houre,
Wysely attendynge / whan they be sende fore.'   2857

409

This texte was euer / in her memoryall,   2858
Prompte alway redy / as a true spouses
To wayte on her spouse / whan he wyll call,
Her lampe replete / with oyle of mekenes.
Synguler gyftes / she had of chrystes goodnes :   2862
Inspyred with the spyryte / of prophecy,
Secrete thynges to come/ knowynge therby.   2864

410

She knewe the season / was hastely comynge   2865
Of her departure / fro this lyfe mortall.
Wherfore she ordred / sadly euery thynge
Within her monasteryes / and charges spyrytuall,
Vysytynge her couent / with her presence personall   2869
Gaue knowlege to them / that soone and hastely
She shulde departe / frome this lyfe transytory.   2871

411

Afore her were called / the systers of yche place,   2872
And were apoynted / who shulde succede

After to be gouernour / ruler / and abbesse
To the pleasure of god / and theyr ghostly mede ;
Specyally commendynge / vertue, as we rede,   2876
What meryte they shall haue / of god almyghty
In spyrytuall cures / that done well theyr duty.   2878

412

All other offycers / within eche monastery   2879
Were assygned by Werburge / theyr presydent,
And vnder obedyence / charged full depely
Theyr offyce to execute / vertue to augment,
For the synguler profyte / of all the couent.   2883
She gaue to yche place / landes and possessyon
Suffycyently to serue / all the congregacyon.   2885

413

Whan she had ordeyned / eche place in charyte,   2886
Dyschargynge her conscyence / chargynge them all
To obserue relygyon / with perfyte humylyte
After her exemple / and doctryne pryncypall,
She had perfyte knowlege / by grace supernaturall   2890
Her body shulde rest / in the place of Hamburgens
After her departure / by deuyne prouydens.   2892

414

Wherfore she commaunded / the couent of Hambury   2893
Wysely to attende / with all theyr dylygence
Vpon the ende / of her lyfe transytory,
Wheresoeuer it be / to come with benyuolence
And incontynent take / her body with reuerence   2897
And brynge it shortly / vnto theyr monastery,
There to be tumylate / after her desydery.   2899

415

As it pleaseth our lorde / and celestyall sufferayne 2900
To sende to his seruaunte / his vysytacyon—
The day was apoynted / the houre incertayne
Of her departure / frome worldly vexacyon :
The messanger of dethe / the ende of trybulacyon,   2904

Oppressed this lady / moost worthy fame
Ryght at her monastery / nomynat Trentame.   2906

416

She thanked her maker / sayenge day and nyght   2907
'Well-come be the vysytacyon / of god almyghty.'
She called her systers / present afore her syght,
Her entente rehersynge / to them tenderly,
Desyrynge all them / to folowe dylygently   2911
The lawes of god / with honour and reuerence
And to her counseyll / to gyue fully credence ;   2913

417

Sayenge : 'dere byloued systers / in our sauyour,   2914
O spyrytuall chyldren / my derlyngos moost dere,
Whiche haue refused / all worldly honour
To serue our lorde / with herte and mynde clere,
Suffer no synne / in your soule to apere,   2918
But wasshe it away / by bytter contrycyon,
With prayer, penaunce / and true confessyon.   2920

418

'And trust ye well, your true obedyence,   2921
your chast lyuynge / and wylfull pouerte,
your dayly prayers / vygyls / and abstynence
That ye haue obserued / her vnder me,
Shalbe recompensed / a thousande-folde, trule,   2925
Whan ye shalbe taken / fro this lyfe transytory ;
your rewarde shalbe / with immortall glory.   2927

419

'As for my dethe / whiche approches nere,   2928
I drede nothynge / tho nature ferefull be :
I knowe for certayne / who departeth well here
Is newe-borne agayne / to Ioye and felycyte.
Iche chrysten man hath / a threfolde natyuyte :   2932
Fyrst of his parentes / by cours of nature
Borne to many troubles / and sorowes, sure ;   2934

420

'By the seconde byrthe / whiche is more excellent,   2935

At fonte of baptym / we haue regeneracyon,
By fayth professed / to god omnypotent
And made the chyldren / of ghostly saluacyon,
To auoyde by grace / all wycked temptacyon,　2939
To be inherytours / of Ioy perpetuall,
Folowynge the counseyll / of holy chyrche withall;　2941

421

'The thyrde byrthe / moost ferefull and to be dredde, 2942
Is whan the soule / departeth fro the body
To payne or blysse / and leues the corps dedde
To tourne agayne to erthe / to wast and putryfy.
In this thyrde byrthe / by callynge aferre [1] for mercy 2946
Our soule shall lyue in blysse / euerlastynge,　　　[1] r. afore?
Crowned with vyctory / for our chast lyuynge.　2948

422

'The swete byrde, closed / in a cage a longe season,　2949
Gladly entendeth / to fly at lyberte;
The prysoner fetered / and cast in depe dongeon
Euer supposes / to be rydde frome captyuyte:
The soule of mankynde / moost dygne of dutye,　2953
Naturally desyreth / proued by reason,
To be delyuered / frome bodyly pryson.'　2955

¶ *Of þᵉ ghostli exortacyon saynt Werburge made to her
systers in her sekenesse / and how deuoutely she receyued
þᵉ sacramentes of holy chyrche byfore her deth.
Ca. xxviii.*

423

THe day knowen / to her by reuelacyon　2956
Of her departure / by sygnes euydent,
She sende for all / the hole congregacyon,
And in presence / of all her holy couent
She called for the blessed sacrament;　2960
To whome she sayd / with wordes expresse
With wepynge teeres / and great mekenesse:　2962

424

'Well-come my lorde / well-come my kynge,   2963
Well-come my sufferayne / and sauyour,
Well-come my conforte / and ioy euerlastynge,
My trust / my treasure / my helpe and socour,
Well-come my maker / and my redemptour,   2967
The sone of god / moost in maieste,
Withouten begynnynge / and endeles shalbe.   2969

425

'I byleue that thou / for all mankynde   2970
Frome heuen descended / of thy charyte
And was incarnate / scrypture dothe mynde,
In the vyrgynall wombe / of blessed marye,
And suffered dethe / to make vs all fre,   2974
Descended to hell / roose the thyrde day,
Ascended to heuen / and our raunson dyd pay;   2976

426

'And I knowlege to the / with pure entent :   2977
On Shorpthursday / after thy passyon
Thy moost blessed body / in sacrament
Thou gaue to vs / for our communyon,
To be our defence / and ghostly tuycyon,   2981
Now present here / in forme of breed,
To Iudge mankynde / bothe quycke and deed.   2983

427

'O sufferayne sauyour / replete with grace,   2984
I the beseche / haue pyte vpon me
And in my soule / make a dwellynge-place,
Expulce all vyce / synne and mysery ;
Defende my soule / frome our aduersary,   2988
Saue and protecte me / from peynes infernall
And brynge thrugh thy mercy / to ioye perpetuall.'   2990

428

Thus with reuerence / and great humylyte   2991
She receyued / the blessed sacrament,
The seconde persone / in trynyte,

In perfyte fayth / hope / and loue feruent,
With great contrycyon / as it was apparent,   2995
Her herte lyfte vp / to-warde heuen on hye
Abydynge the wyll / of god almyghty.   2997
429

She exorted / her systers euerychone   2998
That were there present / in companye,
Desyrynge them all / with supplycacyon
To remembre her / sayenge with humylyte :
' My systers in god / now knowe may ye   3002
My dayes ben ferre past / comynge is the houre.
Wherfore I betake you / fyrst to our sauyour ;   3004
430

' Prayenge you tenderly / for the loue of me   3005
In deuyne seruyce / loke ye contynu ;
Obseruynge pacyence / mekenes / and chastyte,
Encresynge in relygyon / by the grace of Ihesu—
" Who-so perceuers / in herte and mynde true   3009
Vnder obedyence / to the extreme day,
Is sure to be saued " / scrypture so doth say.   3011
431

' Also remembre / that all worldly royalte,   3012
Honour / ryches / pleasure / possessyon,
If ye consyder / are but a vanyte,
Nothynge assured / to trust therupon ;
Wherfore dyspose you / to vertue alon   3016
Whyle ye endure / in this lyfe mortall,
Tyll that ye come / to Ioy perpetuall.   3018
432

' Secondly ' she sayd / ' systers, I you pray   3019
Kepe [1] well the order / of perfyte charyte,   [1] P. kept
Neuer declynynge / fro it by no way,
As ye haue taken / exemple of me ;
Iche loue other / and worshyp in theyr degre,   3023
So that no murmure / nor dyssymulacyon
Be founde amonge / this holy congregacyon.   3025

433

Be euer lowly / humble / and obedyent	3026
With due reuerence / worshyp and honoure,	
Folowe the mynde / of your presydent,	
Vnto your [1] heed / and ghostly gouernoure.	[1] r. you
Kepe well chastyte / that precyous floure,	3030
So that no thought / of sensualyte	
Corrupte your mynde / to breke vyrgynyte.	3032

434

Se that ye vse / dyscrete temperaunce,	3033
Abstenynge frome vayne superfluyte ;	
Se that amonge you / be founde no varyaunce,	
Kepe well the degrees / of humylyte.'	
These and many other / exemples of charyte	3037
She taught her couent / of synguler deuocyon,	
How they shulde optayne / to hye perfeccyon.	3039

435

Thyrdly she prayed / sayenge with mynde dylygent :	3040
' O blessed sauyour / I desyre the	
Saue and defende / my hole couent	
And theyr monasteryes / of thy great pyte	
Frome peryll of peryshynge / and frome enmyte,	3044
That all the subiectes / of our congregacyon	
May well obserue / theyr holy professyon.	3046

436

' And graunt me, swete lorde / throwe thy goodnes :	3047
Who-so in thy name / vpon me dothe call	
In langour / mysery / in peyne / or sekenes,	
Also women with chylde / in peynes thrall,	
May haue remedy / and helpe specyall ;	3051
And people in pryson / halte / blynde / and lame	
By me may magnyfy / thy gloryous name.'	3053

437

Than she requyred / with humylyte	3054
The spyrytuall sufferage / of holy vnccyon,	
Her soule to conforte / frome all aduersyte ;	

She toke her leue / and kyssed them ycheon.
Alas, what herte / myght shewe the lamentacyon,   3058
The wepynge / waylynge / and wofull heuynes
At the departure / of theyr swete maystres?   3060

¶ *Of the departure of saynt Werburge vnto heuen at the abbay
of Trentam / fro this myserable lyfe / & what lamentacyon her systers made for her dethe.   Ca. xxix.*

438

ƷN all her infyrmyte / peyne and busynesse   3061
     She vsed prayer / and medytacyon,
Callynge for mercy / by interyor mekenesse
With wepynge eyes / and great lamentacyon ;
Remembrynge in herte / our lordes passyon ;   3065
Commendynge her couent / vnto our sauyour
To be theyr defence / ayde / and protectour.   3067

439

The peynes encreased / of her infyrmyte,   3068
The panges doubled / her peyne to augment,
Nature decayed / vnto suche debylyte
That the sygnes of dethe / appered euydent.
The houre approched / after all Iudgment :   3072
Wherfore all thynges / were redy preparate,
As was conuenyent / for so noble a state.   3074

440

Her spouse Ihesus / hauynge pyte and cure   3075
Vpon his spouses / in extreme dystresse,
Wolde not suffer her peyne / longer endure,
But sende his angels / with great lyghtnesse
To conforte his seruaunt / in peyne and sekenesse,   3079
To dyssolue her wo / and great penalte
And brynge vp her soule / to eterne felycyte.   3081

441

There derknes was tourned / all vnto lyght,   3082
Langour and trouble / vnto prosperyte,

The day was gouernour / ouer the nyght
Whan that she passed / this lyfe transytory,
Bondage and thraldome / were brought to lyberte.   3086
The tyme of [1] Ioye / and euerlastynge pleasure   [1] P. ef
Was approchynge to Werburge / euer to enduro.   3088

442

A multytude of angelles / shynynge moost clere   3089
Were redy to gyde / with humble reuerence
The soule of werburge / as truly dyd apere,
And brought it to blys / vnto the hye presence
Of almyghty god / moost of magnyfycence,   3093
Clerely releashed / frome peynes of purgatory
To be rewarded / with euerlastynge glory.   3095

443

This blessed vyrgyn / gloryous and pure,   3096
In stedfast fayth / hope / loue / and charyte
The thyrde day of February / ye may be sure,
Expyred frome this lyfe / caduce and transytory
To eterne blysse / coronate with vyctory,   3100
Chaungynge her lyfe / myserable and thrall
For infynyte ioye / and glory eternall.   3102

444

With moche honour / these spyrytuall mynysters   3103
Conueyed the soule / aboue the fyrmament,
Passynge the seuen planettes / and all the sterres,
Vnto the presence / of god omnypotent,
Syngynge full swetely / theyr songes equyualent   3107
Of pleasaunt armony / of conforte and blys,
Salutynge her mekely / with wordes reuerent   3109
Veni dilecta : veni coronabiris.

445

The thre Ierarcheses / were redy present   3111
With heuenly melody / to receyue this monyall,
The quere of vyrgyns / mette her incontynent
With great solempnyte / and processyon royall,
Presentynge her soule / with myrthes angelycall   3115

To Ihesu, her spouse / to whome he sayd, truly,
'Well-come, dere doughter / to blysse celestyall,   3117
Intra in gaudium : domui tui.'

446

In meane tyme and space / this venerable body   3119
(The soule departed) lay whyte / streyght / and colde,.
Semynge as on slepe / she had ben, verely,
With swete odours fragrant / passynge manyfolde
All spyces and herbes / in erth may be tolde;   3123
The place was so pleasaunt / full of delyce
Lyke as it had ben / an erthly paradyce.   3125

447

This forsayd venerable congregacyon   3126
With wepynge teeres / and syghes lamentable
Wasshed the swete body / after the olde custome,
And dressed the corps / with clothes honorable,
Prepared all necessaryes / pleasaunt and commendable ; 3130
To churche she was brought / solemply in syght,
With feruent deuocyon / to be watched all nyght.   3132

448

And as they watched / with due mynystracyon   3133
Ouer the sayd corps / deuoutly prayenge,
They made great mournynge / and lamentacyon
Euerychone to other / for her departynge ;
'Alas,' they all sayd / with wofull waylynge,   3137
'Our solace / our helthe / is clere gone away I
Alas for sorowe / what shall we now say ?   3139

449

'The sterre of our conforte / is extyncte clere,   3140
The lanturne of our lyght / is taken vs fro,
The floure of chastyte / is layd vpon a bere,
The myrrour of mekenes / now lyeth full loo,
The treasure of relygyon / from vs now is ago.   3144
Our sorowe encresed / wretchednes / and mysery,
Syth thou arte departed. / alas, what remedy ?   3146

I

450

'Our hertes ben plonged / in great wo and peyne,   3147
Our myndes are medled / with heuy langour;
How shulde we now rest / frome mornynge, certayne,
Beholdynge now deed / whylom our protectour?
Swete lady, thou art gone / frome vs for euermore;   3151
Our deedly sorowe / replete with bytternes,
For waylynge and wepynge / can neuer ceas.   3153

451

'With herte, mynde and voyce / to the we do call: 3154
O blessed Werburge / our moost dere maystres,
O sufferayne lady / and ruler of vs all,
Why hase thou vs lefte / in suche heuynesse?
If thy wyll had ben / it is knowen expresse,   3158
Thou myght haue taryed / with vs by petycyon.
Alas, remedylesse / is our lamentacyon!   3160

452

'Frome vs thou arte taken / and gone is our solace,   3161
The myrrour of vertue / is deed now with the,
The tryed stock of truth / and the grounde of grace
Is pyteously decayed / our hope and sufferaynte.
O blessed sauyour / vpon vs haue pyte,   3165
Sende vs our conforte / by thy great myght agayne
As thou hase reysed many / from dethe to lyfe, certayne.3167

453

'O dredefull dethe / cruell enemy to nature,   3168
With dolefull heuynes / on the we may complayne,
Takynge our heed frome vs / to our great dysconfyture,
Hath brought vs to thraldome / wofulnes and peyne;
Nother kynge ne emperour / thy fauour may optayne,   3172
But he must departe / arested with thy launce.
Thanke we god of all / for it is his pleasaunce.'   3174

¶ *How the hamburgenses toke the blessed body of Werburye
frome Trentam by myracle & brought it to Hambury | &
of þᵉ buryall of werburge | & of manyfolde myracles
shewed for her merytes .ix. yere after her translacyon.
Ca. xxx.*

454

☊His gloryous vyrgyn / and moost blessed abbace   3175
    Departed from this lyfe / caduce and transytory
(As afore is sayd) the yere and tyme of grace
Almoost seuen hundreth / the thyrde day of February,
To celestyall blysse / and infynyte glory ;   3179
Her subiectes oppressed / with wylfull pensyuenesse,
With great trybulacyon / care and heuynesse.   3181

455

But where werburge gaue / in commaundyment   3182
To bury her corps / at place of Hambury,
As was the wyll / of our lorde omnypotent ;
Her subiectes of Trentam / whiche had her body,
Purposed her wyll / and entent to deny,   3186
Prepared to kepe / the corps by stronge hande,
With them to remayne / as ye shall vnderstande.   3188

456

The sayd people of Trentam / watched full dylygent   3189
Her corps, fulfyllynge / the obsequyes funerall,
Entendynge to auoyde / and frustrate her testament
Gate a great company / by power Marcyall,
Closed fast theyr doores / and gates one and all,   3193
Made sure yche place / by theyr prouydens
For to kepe the corps / excludynge Thamburgens.   3195

457

But, as Salomon sayth / sentencyously,   3196
'There may be no counseyll / power ne prudence,
Wysedome of man / nor naturall polycy,
To derogate or chaunge / deuyne sentence ;'
Proued euer[y] day / by true experyence :   3200

'Tho mankynde prepose / his mynde to fulfyll,
yet god dysposeth / all thynge at his wyll.'   3202

458

And as they watched / the same sayd nyght   3203
Moost busyly / to execute they[r] wyll and entent,
By deuyne prouydence / passynge mannes myght
Sodeynly on slepe / was all that couent,
Theyr company and mynysters / that were there lent, 3207
Hauynge no power / for to waken, doubtles ;
God so prouyded / for theyr great maystres.   3209

459

Than shortly resembled / vnto that sayd place   3210
The people of Hamburgens / a great company,
With the mynysters of god / people full of grace :
And anone by the wyll / of our lorde almyghty
The lockes and the barres / of that sayd monastery   3214
Fell downe to the grounde / by power supernall,
Without mannes hande / that enter they myght all.   3216

460

Whiche myracle proued / the people of Hambury   3217
Entred Trentam abbay / with mynde reuerent,
And founde there on slepe / all the other company,
Man / woman / and chylde / all that were present.
They kneled all downe / and worshypped the sacrament,3221
Praysynge our maker / of theyr good spede,
Theyr specyall socour / euer at theyr nede.   3223

461

Her blessed body / from Trentam they dyd take,   3224
Gladly departynge / out of the monastery—
Nother man nor woman / had power to wake,
Tyll they were passed / all greuous Ieopardy ;
Magnyfyenge our lorde / of his grace deuoutly,   3228
Solemply syngyng their songes celestiall
With infinite gladnes / and comfort spirituall.   3230

462

After all this done / this holy congregacion   3231

With reuerence / honour / and solempnite,
With wepynge tearis / for pure affection,
With lamentable songes / masse and dirige
Buried the corps / of this blessed ladie   3235
Right in the chauncell / of the sayd abbay,
There bodily to rest / as her wyll was alway.   3237
                        463
All obsequies ended / therto belongynge   3238
As was agreable for suche a president,
The systers departed / with clamour and mournynge,
Plonged in heuynes / and to their celles went,
To wepe and wayle secretly / their hartis to content, 3242
Criynge : 'alas, alas / nowe buried haue we
The exemple of vertu / mekenes / and chastite l'   3244
                        464
And as the history of her lyfe / doth expresse   3245
In a boke nominat / the thrid Passionary,
After the buriall of this patronesse
The place was decorat / with myracles many,
Manifest to the people / of euery progeny   3249
Howe god almyghty of his speciall grace
Hath done for his seruant / in short tyme and space. 3251
                        465
For many people greued with infirmite,   3252
Dolorous of hert / and interiour tribulacion,
Heuynes of mynde / or other penalite,
To her graue resortyng / with feruent deuocion,
Sekynge for remedy / with great contricion,   3256
Anon by her prayer / vnto our sauyour
They were released from peyne and langour.   3258
                        466
Also by her merite, suffrage and peticion   3259
Euery humble creature had helpe and succour ;
To distract persons / was yelded reason,
wikked spirites expulsed were that same hour,
Impotent and feble to helth she dyd restour,   3263

Halt and lame had passage / the blynde had perfect syght,
The dombe had speche / the deffe herynge ryght.   3265

467

Women with childe / beynge in great ieopardy,   3266
Namely in trauelyng / greued with wo and payne,
Whan they myght nat come / sendyng to her oratorye,
Makynge true oblacion / restaured were, certayne,
To helth and prosperite / from wo delyuered playne; 3270
And if they obteyned a relique from the place,
The mother and childe / by it founde speciall grace. 3272

468

The deuout pilgrym / the perfit maryner,   3273
The true laborer / the marchant with richesse,
The carefull pore man / the peynfull prisoner
Were sondry tymes delyuered from wo and distresse;
Men / women / childer / sekynge with mekenes   3277
This glorious virgyn / with humble supplicacion,
Founde soone remedie / helpe and consolacion.   3279

¶ *A litle breue rehersall of her lyfe / and howe for her myracles shewed þ^e couent of Hambury purposed to translate her body / by the helpe of Mercyens.*   Ca. xxxi.

469

THis gloryous lady / and gemme of holynesse   3280
     Of fyue myghty kynges / descended lynyally,
A prynces / an enherytryce / replete with mekenes
Refused all pleasures / pompe / and vayne glory,
Entred relygyon / professed at Ely,   3284
A spectacle of vertue / dwellynge in that place
And a floure of chastyte / electe by synguler grace. 3286

470

Her honorable vncle / kynge Ethelrede,   3287
Consyderynge her vertue / and hye deuocyon
Made her gouernour / for ghostly helthe and mede
Ouer all the monasteryes / within his regyon,

For the sure encresement / of perfyte relygyon ; 3291
Foure of these monasteryes / we haue in memory :
As Wedon / Trentam / Repton / and Hambury. 3293

471

Whan she was ruler / and chefe presydent 3294
Of these sayd places / vnder god almyghty,
Than vertue and goodnes / dayly dyd augment
By heuenly grace / to the soule-helthe of many,
And by her exemple / and doctryne ghostly 3298
Kynges / lordes / barons / refusynge theyr royalte
Entred relygyon / with great humylyte. 3300

472

Her lyfe and doctryne / agreed bothe in one, 3301
Proued in effecte / by specyall gyftes of grace :
Many she conuerted / vnto contemplacyon,
To prayer and penaunce / whyle they had here space.
Her couent and subiectes / within euery place 3305
By her excellent vertue / and hye dyscrecyon
Were gratiously gouerned / for theyr saluacion. 3307

473

Her dwellynge was most at the place of Wedon, 3308
Where many myracles were shewed openly ;
And at Trentam abbay / of her foundacion,
From peyne she departed to eternall glory ;
After her entent was buried at Hambury ; 3312
Of whom it may be sayd / ' here lyeth nowe present
A princesse / a virgin / a nonne / and a president.' 3314

474

The deuout couent of her congregacion, 3315
Whiche hath long wayled / with sorowfull payne,
Nowe haue great cause to make consolacion
And gyue due honour to our lorde and sufferayne,
Knowynge that Werburge / in blysse is nowe, certayne,
For them all dayly a true mediatrice [3320
In the heuynly trone / afore the hie Iustice. 3321

475

Our sauiour Iesus / graunter of all goodnes,   3322
Consyderyng the mekenes / and pure virginite
Of Werburge his spouse / and proued holynes,
By speciall grace / preserued her body
To his laude and honour / his name to magnifye,   3326
Both hole and sounde / from naturall resolucion,
As her soule was clere from vice and corruption.   3328

476

This immaculat mayde / shenyng more bryght   3329
Than radiant phebus in the triumphant trone,
With the quere of virgins / prayseth day and nyght
The blessed trinite with due adoracion,
Of perpetuall pleasure hauyng the fruycion,   3333
A singular intercessour for her seruauntes all
That here in erth mekely to her wyll call.   3335

477

And though her body do rest nowe in graue,   3336
yet notable signes contynually be done :
Some warned in their slepe comfort to haue
By visityng her place / callynge her vpon,
With contrite hert makyng true oblacion.   3340
Whiche thynge contynued by space of .ix. yere
With meruailous myracles euydent and clere.   3342

478

The couent, consyderyng suche great company   3343
From diuers partes / resortynge to theyr place
In pylgrimage to Werburge / for helpe and remedy,
Entended to translate this glorious abbasse,
To exalte her body replet with great grace   3347
To her great honour / comfort to eche creature—
Pite that suche a relique shulde lye in sepulture.   3349

479

To the prayes and honour of god omnipotent   3350
And of saint Werburge laude and reuerence
The couent and the people by one assent

Desired Coelrede, than kynge of merciens,
For aide in this case / helpe and diligence.   3354
(Whiche thynge graunted) the day appointed was ;
The clergy and the comons reioised with solace.   3356

¶ *Of the solempne translacion of this glorious virgyn saynt*
   Werburge / and of the great myracles done at the sayd
   season by the myght of god and merite of this gracious
   lady. Cap. xxxii.
                                        480
At the day appoynted of her translacion   3357
Kyng Coelred and his counsell were redy-present,
With bysshops, and the clergy, men of deuocion,
Her systers and subiettes, a religious couent ;
The comon people from eche place thider went   3361
With great gladnes / the hole for pleasure gostly,
The seke and impotent for helth and remedy.   3363
                                        481
The bysshops and clergy stode vpon one parte   3364 ˙
Of her holy graue / and her systers echone,
Syngynge and praysynge the blessed trinite ;
The kyng and his counsell with great deuocion
Stode on the other parte in contemplacion.   3368
The graue was opened, eleuat was the chest
Wherin her holy corps .ix. yere fully dyd rest.   3370
                                        482
Whan this sayd monument discouered was,   3371
Suche a suauite and fragrant odoure
Ascended from the corps by singular grace,
Passyng all wordly swetnes and sauour,
That all there present that day and hour   3375
Supposed they had ben / in the felicite
Of erthely paradise / without ambiguite.   3377
                                        483
And as eche man thought[1] by naturall reason ¹ P. thaught 3378
Nothyng shulde remayn of that blessed body

But the bare boones / all els to resolucion :
The couerture remoued by the sayd clergy,
The corps hole and sounde was funde, verely,　　3382
Apperyng to them / on slepe as she had ben,
Nothyng depaired / that ther coude be seen.　　3384

484

Her vesture appered hole, clere and white,　　3385
No parte consumed / for all the longe space,
Fragrant in odoure / repleit with delite,
As at the fyrst season whan she buried was ;
But whan discouered was her swete face,　　3389
Beautye appered more white than the lile,
Mixt with rose colour / moost faire for to se.　　3391

485

Her louely countenaunce / so comly to beholde,　　3392
And her swete fisnomy / with fairenes decorat
As fresshely apparant / moost pleasant to be tolde,
As at the fyrst day / whan she was tumulat.
No doubt therof / for she, with synne nat maculat,　　3396
Vsyng all her lyfe in clennes and virginite,
From bodily corruption / by grace must saued be.　　3398

486

The clergy, yet serchyng more diligently　　3399
Her precious body / and interiour vesture,
Eleuat the corps full reuerently
With moche worchip, honour and cure,
Founde nothynge perisshed in shap nor figure　　3403
For all the long space, tyme and contynuaunce
She lay in sepulture by diuine ordynaunce.　　3405

487

Whiche famous myracle / notified so clere,　　3406
The clergy with her systers in ioy and honour,
The kyng and his counsell all therat present were,
With voice melodious made a great clamour,
Praysyng and magnifiyng our blessed sauiour　　3410
With celestiall songes / and hymnes full of blys,

Deuoutly rehersyng / with all thoir deuour   3412
Mirabilis deus in sanctis suis.   3413
488
With that the comon rude people euerychone   3414
In the sayd churche-yarde standyng without,
Heryng the clergy syng with suche deuocion,
Towarde heuen they cried / and busely dyd shout,
The space of .iii. houres / or nere there-about,   3418
Worshippyng our lorde / with voice shrill and loude
In hert, wyll and mynde / as well as they coude.   3420
489
After all this done / her blessed body   3421
Was wasshed and reclothed with vesture precious
By the sayd couent of the place of Hambury.
The bysshops were reuesshed in pontificalibus,
And all the clergy syngyng with voice melodious   3425
Kneled all downe and gaue due reuerence,
Honour and worship to her corporall presence.   3427
490
Thus they resceyued with perfit humilite   3428
This sacrat relique, hole and substanciall,
And layd it in a shryne with great solempnite,
Enowrned with riches sumptuous and roiall,
Prepared by the kyng / and ordeyned inspeciall,   3432
Entendyng that this relique and gostly treasure
Perpetually with them shulde remayne and endure.   3434
491
People oppressed with greuous infirmite,   3435
Distract persons / halt, blynde and lame,
Resortynge to her shryne with humilite
Shortly were cured by callynge of her name ;
Impotent creatures (the legende sayth the same)   3439
Touchyng her tumbe / were cured from payne ;
Whiche tumbe remayneth at Hambury, certayne.   3441
492
After she was translate / knowen it is well,   3442

The clergy to[1] procession / went after to mas,   1 r. in
Honoryng and praysyng / the kyng of Israell
And blessed Werburge / with moche solace.
Whan diuine seruice duely ended was,   3446
The bisshops gaue theyr holy benedictions ;
The people departed glad to their mansions.   3448

493

This holy sayd fest of her translacion   3449
Was ordeyned and celebrate with solemnite,
As sayeth Ranulphus in his policronicon,
About the yere of grace .vii. hundreth and .viii., sothle,
The .xi. Kalendas of the moneth Iulii ;   3453
Regnyng in mercelande the said Kyng Coelrede,
Than bysshop of Lichefelde was Hedda / as we rede. 3455

¶ *Howe the body of saynt Werburge contynued hole | and
    substanciall at Hambury after the translacion by the
    space of two hundreth yeres | tyll the danes were comon
    to this lande | or it felle and was resolued vnto powder.*
    The .xxxiii. Chapitre.

494

This rutilant gemme and specious floure   3456
Hole and substanciall remayned at Hambury
Two hundreth yeres in beaute and colour,
By singular grace / and angelicall custodye,
Tyll the danes were comon of malice and misery,   3460
Of ire and myschief / as we vnderstande ;
We meane the comyng of pagans to this lande.   3462

495

Whiche danes by sufferaunce and dispensacion   3463
Of almyghty god / for synne and iniquite
Punysshed vnpiteously all this region
with a wofull plage of great crudelite,
The sharpe swerde of deth / hauynge no pite,   3467
Spared no creature / prest nor religious,
Long tyme duryng in their malice odious.   3469

496

Than this vitall glebe by diuine ordinaunce   3470
Voluntary permytted naturall resolution,
Lest the cruell gentils / and wiked myscreauntes
With pollute handes full of corrupcion
Shulde touche her body / by indignation ;   3474
Whiche pagans were enemyes to our lorde Iesu,
Robels to holy churche, vnfeithfull and vntrue.   3476

497

Howe-be-it the power of our swete sauyour   3477
Myght haue continued the body of his syruant
All that longe season in worshyp and honour,
As he preserued of his grace abundaunt
Many sayntes of this realme hole, fresshe and vernant 3481
viii. hundreth yeres agon / to this present day,
And like so to endure / hole and clere alway.   3483

498

Sothely to considre / our lorde omnipotent,   3484
Glorious in his sayntes / scripture doth specifie,
Of his diuine prouidence / pleasure and intent
Some haue resolued / for the greatter glorie
Of their resurrection for the tyme, truly,   3488
Some other to continue without corruption,
To the true example of his promission.   3490

499

Many holy martyrs / for Christ haue byn slayne,   3491
The hie prestis of god murdred cruelly,
Some with wylde bestes deuoured, in certayne,
Some cast in fiers, on cooles to broyle and fry,
Vpon many other byrdes fedyng openly—   3495
Of whom the prophet clerely doth reherce :
'The more peyne here and wo / the more glory, doubtles.' 3497

500

The glorious martyr Stephan (as is red)   3498
In this present lyfe dyd myracles many,
Neuertherles / he raised no people that were deed ;

But after the resoluynge of his blessed body
He raised deed men to lyfe agayne, truely,   3502
That the great power of lyfe myght sprynge
From iniurie of deth / by our heuen kynga.   3504

501

Great was the respect of diuyne grace   3505
In the body of Werburge / without resolucion,
Shewed by her myracles / for mannes helth and solace ;
But greatter was the hope of the eterne renouacion[1] [3509
In her body resolued to naturall consumption,   [1] P. rououeclon
Whiche for her merites to this present day
Helpeth all her seruantes that to her wyll praye.   3511

502

Therfore worshyp we with singular deuocion   3512
The holy lyuynge of this virgin gratious ;
For why / all the halowynge of her conuersacion
Belongeth to the honour of our lorde Iesus,
Whiche of his grace hath made her so glorious   3516
And graunteth his mercy / and of synne remyssion
To all them / for whom / she maketh intercession.   3518

503

Blessed pure virgin / moines and abbasse,   3519
O venerable werburge / mekely we the pray,
Make thou supplycacyon / to the graunter of grace,
After this lyfe present / that all we may
Come to heuen-blysse / whiche lasteth for ay,   3523
There to beholde / the gloryous trynyte,   [3525
To whom be laude / worshyp / honour / & endeles glorye.

[BOOK II.]

¶ The table of the seconde boke of þᵉ gloryons vyrgyn saynt Werburge.

[BOOK II.]

1

ⁿOw whan we consyder / with mynde dylygent   1
    The merueylous maners / & synguler condycion
Of the comyn people / symple and neclygent,
Whiche without lytterature / and good informacyon
Ben lyke to Brute beestes / as in comparyson,   5
Rude / wylde / and boystous / by a prouerbe, certan,
‘ Good maners and conynge / maken a man.’   7

2

Saynt Paule sayth / shewynge to the Romans   8
How all thynge wryten / in holy scrypture
Is wryten for our doctryne / and ghostly ordynans,
For our great conforte / and endeles pleasure.
All thynge is knowen playnly / by lytterature,   12
Morall vertues / be noted by it full playne
Frome vyce and neclygence / to abstayne, certayne.   14

3

What were mankynde / without lytterature ?   15
Full lytell worthy / blynded by ignoraunce.
The way to heuen / it declareth ryght sure
Thrugh perfyte lyuynge / and good perseueraunce ;

By it we may be taught / for to do penaunce   19
Whan we transgresse / our lordes commaundyment ;
It is a swete cordyall / for mannes entent.   21

4

How shulde the seuen / scyences lyberall   22
Haue ben preserued / vnto this day,
The wysdome / of the phylosophers all,
But alone by lernynge / it is no nay.
The notable actes / of our fathers, I say,   26
(yf litterature were nat) myght nat nowe be tolde,
Nor auncient histories and cronycles olde.   28

5

The lawe of ciuile / and of holy canon   29
By study be preferred with moche honour
To execute iustice / and for due reformacion ;
The most blessed doctrine of our sauiour,
The actis of the apostoles / with the doctours four,   33
Be preserued by wrytyng / and put in memorie,
With the lyues of saintes many a noble storie.   35

6

Of whiche histories we purpose speciall   36
To speke of saint Werburge / vnder your protection,
Declaryng the ende of her lyfe historiall
As we haue begon / and made playne mencion
In the fyrst volume by breue compilacion,   40
There playnly descriuyng her liniall discens
Of .iiii. myghty kyngdomes by true experience ;   42

7

Also we haue shewed in the sayd littell boke   43
Her goodly maners / and vertuous disposicion
Of her yonge age / who-so lyst theron to loke ;
And howe her bretherne suffred martyrdome ;
Of her fathers realme a litell discripcion ;   47
Howe she was professed in the place of Ely ;
Of her conuersacion within the sayd monastery ;   49

8

After for her vertue / howe she was made abbasse   50
Of diuers monasteries, flouryng in vertue ;
And of the great miracles whiche there done was
For her great charite / by the grace of Iesu ;
Howe diuers of her kynrede dyd clerely exchewe   54
All wordly pleasures and honours transetory,
Professynge obedience at the place of Ely ;   56

9

Also we haue shewed vnder your licence   57
Of her departure from this lyfe mortall,
And of her sepulture at the place of Hamburgence ;
The manyfolde myracles shewed by grace supernall,
The wofull lamentacion of her systers all ;   61
And howe after .ix. yere of her translacion
By diuine ordinaunce miracles were done.   63

10

We humble require you of your charite   64
To this seconde abstract to graunt pardon,
Consyderynge we omytte whilom the historie
And speke of cronicles / makyng a digression ;
It is of no ignoraunce / nor presumption,   68
But to enlarge the mater and sentence,
To gladde the auditours / and moue their diligence.   70

11

In oure seconde boke expresse nowe wyll we,   71
Vnder your licence and speciall tuicion,
Of this blessed virgin / flourynge in chastite,
Why and wherfore she came to Chestre towne,
Principally by miracle / and diuine prouision,   75
And howe for synne / vice / and wykednes
Danes oppressed this lande with wretchednes,   77

12

And howe she was receyued at Chestre citie ;   78
Of the fyrst foundacion of towne and the place ;
Of the great myracles there shewed openlie

To chanons and monkes / by singular grace,
Vnto euery creature in extreme case,   82
Howe Werburge delyuered the towne from enmite,
From dredfull fire / and plages of miserye.   84

13

Also encronicled foloweth here expresse   85
A brefe compilacion of kynge Edwarde seniour,
Of kyng Ethelstam / the great worthynes,
Of humble kyng Edgare [1] regnyng as emperour,   [1 P. Ergare]
Of his comyng to Chestre / of his great honour ;   89
And howe Erle Leofrice repared of his charite
The mynstre of Werburge, gyuyng therto liberte ;   91

14

   Of the seconde foundacion of the sayd monastery   92
From secular chanons to monkes religious
Soone after the conquest, sayth the historye,
By the erle of Chestre nominat Hug. Lupus,
With counsell and helpe of blessed Anselmus ;   96
And of the great compas of the sayd abbay,
Enuired with walles myghty to assay ;   98

15

Howe Richard [1] erle of Chestre by myracle ryght [1 P. Ric'] 99
Was preserued from daunger of Walshemen,
And howe he was drowned about mydnyght
Purposyng to distroye the monastery, certen.
Celestiall signes were shewed to men and women,   103
To children and innocentes by singular grace
Of blessed Werburge, patronesse of the place :   105

16

These miracles specified / and many other mo   106
This virgin shewed within Chestre cite,
Whiche at this tyme we let ouer go,
Lest to the reders tedious it shulde be.
Almyghty god, both one two and thre,   110
Sende vs of theyr grace to make a good ende :
Helpe, lady Werburge, this warke to amende.   112

¶ *Of the comynge of cruell pagans to this lande / and howe*
saint Werburge longe lyenge hole and incorrupt at
Hambury, than was resolued to pouder.   And howe the
kynge of merciens was chased from his lande.   Ca. i.

17

Fore the comyng of danes to this lande   113
  Merueilous signes were shewed in syght,
To conuert the people (as we vnde[r]stande) :
Sterres in the heuen shynyng full bryght,
Dyuersly mouynge apperyng day and nyght,   117
Rennynge in the ayre dredfull to beholde,
By longe continuaunce, sayth the story olde ;   119
18
Flamyng fire / dragons in the ayre fleynge,   120
Thondryng / and layth / erth-quake moost terrible,
With many other signes / as cometis blasynge,
Were seen in the ayre / to nature horrible ;
Vpon clothynge of people bloddy dropes odible   124
Euydently appered : the yere of grace
vii. hundreth .lxxxvi. in many a place.   126
19
By whiche sayd signes wonderfull to se   127
Two plages of pestilence folowed incontinent :
The first was great derthes, hungre and pouerte,
The seconde was the greuous and sore punysshement
Of the cruell danes, cursed and fraudulent ;   131
Whiche trouble began the .iiii. yere of Bricticus,
Kyng of westsaxon[s] / saith maister Alfridus.   133
20
The thyrde yere folowyng these signes, in certen,
Danes and Norwaies enterprised this lande,
In the north partie, an hoost of armed men,
Whiche cruelly spoiled and distroied holy Ilande,
With Tynmouth abbay / and all that myght be fonde,   138

Drowned and slewe the people euerychone,
Brenned churches / townes / spared no religion. 140

21

In short tyme after the prenominate pagans 141
At tamysmouth reentred this realme agayne,
Destroyed many cites by their myghty ordynaunce,
Oppressed London / Canturbury by power, certayne ;
The kynge of Merciens to escape was fayne ; 145
Kyng Adoulfus made the danes a batell,
To whiche kyng by grace the victorye befell. 147

22

   yf ye wyll consydre the cause wherfore and why 148
Our lorde suffred pagans to punysshe this region,
The treuth was this : for synne specially.
For in the primatiue churche / with great perfection
Kynges / quienes / dukes entred religion, 152
Professed obedient, chaste, without propurte,
Vertue to encrease / true loue and charite : 154

23

That tyme was iustice ministred with mercy, 155
True loue and amite founde in euery place ;
Dissimulacion / pride and fals enuye
Durst nat appere in halle nor in palace,
Extorcion, pollynge opteyned no grace ; 159
The commaundementes of god were obserued a-ryght,
Charite was feruent / encreasynge day and nyght. 161

24

By proces of tyme / as sayth myn auctour, 162
Through great possession / power / and liberte
Vertue decreased in holy churche day and houre,
Holy religion decayed pitiousle,
Charite was colde / iustice and equite, 166
Extorcion, disceyte were vsed euery day,
Couetise / pride / lechery were ryued[1] alway :   1 r. ryue 168

25

Therfore our lorde of his great ryghtwisnes 169

Suffred cruell people to entre this region,
A scourge, to correct synne and wykednes ;
Like a swarme of bees from dyuers nacion,
Whiche had no pite, mercy nor compassion :   173
Danes, Gotes, Norwayes, and scottes also,
Pictes and the wandeles, with mony other mo.   175
26
These foresayd fearfull and cruell nacions,   176
Moost cruell pagans, dyd great persecucion,
From the begynnyng of Adelwlfe, kyng of westsaxons,
Tyll the comynge of normans vnto this region,
The space enduryng by full computacion   180
Two hundreth yeres complet .xxx. also,
With the swerde of vengeaunce, fire and moche wo.   182
27
The yere of our lorde .D.CCC. fyfty and one   183
At Tamysmouth arriued a great hoost of pagans
With .iii. hundreth ships, and .l. men of armes echone ;
Whiche destroied Douer / and put the lande to greuans ;
Agayne Bernulphus, the kyng of Mercians,   187
The paynyms preuayled / and caused his hoost to flo ;
Whiche fortune enforced them more bolder to be.   189
28
But the yere of grace .D.CCC. sixe and sixtie   190
The greattest noumbre of the pagans all,
viii. kynges, entred this realme by victorie,
Norwaies / gootes / Wandels / danes in especiall,
With many other nacions within in generall ;   194
Kyng Hingware and Hubba than came to this lande,
Whiche slewe saint Edmunde, kyng of Estenglande.   196
29
The cruell paynyms and tyrauntes moost furious,   197
Repleit with malice / pride / and enuye,
Seruauntes to satan and ministres malicious,
Purposed to desolate holy churche wyckedly :
Brenned monasteries and spoiled vtterly   201

Many churches, chapels, of a mortall hate,
Slewe religious men, and nonnes dyd violate.   203

30

The people were punysshed in euery place ;   204
To olde, sicke and impotent they shewed no mercy,
yonge soukyng children coude fynde no grace,
Wyddowes and wyues were put to vilany,
Maydens were corrupt / and slayne chamfully.   208
So all this realme endured confusion,
Put to greuous peyne / deth / and affliction.   210

31

After these infidels had ben at London   211
And there accomplisshed theyr cruell entent,
They soone proceded towarde Lincolñ region,
From thens directly with hasty iugement
To the realme of Merciens, noble and auncient,   215
Right vnto Repton, where the kynge lay ;
Robbyng and spoilynge all in theyr way.   217

32

This kynge of Mercelande, called Burdredus,   218
Regnyng .xxii. yere vpon the merciens,
Was clerely expulsed by the pagans furious,
And went vnto rome with pure conscience ;
Where he is buried by diuine prouidence —   222
Whiche kyng was cosyn by discent liniall
To blessed Werburge so glorious and pudicall.   224

33

This gracious virgin and preelect abbasse,   225
Buried at Hambury (as is sayd before)
Continued incorrupt and hole in that place
In vesture and body .ii. hundreth yere and more ;
But whan the danes came with suche rigour   229
To Repton abbay / than she was resolued,
And of deuocion full richely shryned.   231

¶ *Howe the people of Hambury brought the shryne to Chestre | and of the solemne receyuyng of it by all the inhabitauntes of Chesshyre.* Cap. ii.

34

ℨN meane tyme the danes pitously destroyed   232
   The monasteries of Werburge / Trentam & Wedon,
As they many other places had euyll oppressed
In the north and eest part of this region ;
The kyngdome of Kent suffred lyke punicion,   236
The Ile of Wyght endured moche turment :
So dyd the Westmarches / for punysshement.   238

35

The people of Hambury, wysely consyderyng   239
The comynge of danes vnto Repton,
And of the departure of Burdred, theyr kyng,
Howe all Englande was in great affliction,
And howe they were next to endure punicion—   243
Whiche forsayd Repton was distaunt from Hambury
The space of .v. mile, sayth the history—   245

36

The Hamburgenses with all the comons and clergy,   246
Dredynge full sore the pagans flagellacions,
Of their lyues desperate / but for the shryne specially,
To our blessed sauiour made dayly inuocacions
With vigils, prayers and feruent meditacions,   250
To preserue the countrey / the relique / the shryne
From daunger of enmite and miserable ruyne.   252

37

As they continued in cotidian prayer,   253
The best remedie sekyng for to fynde
To auoide vexacion and all greuous daunger
Of theyr great ennemies cursed and vnkynde,
The holy goost inspired theyr mynde   257
To take the shryne with great humilite
And brynge it to Chestre from perill and enmyte.   259

38

They toke this riall relique of reuerence   260
With great mekenes, deuocion and feruour,
Through the grace of god, theyr helpe and defence,
Came to-warde Chester with diligence and honour—
A place preordinat by our sauiour   264
Where her body shulde rest and worshipped be,
Magnified with miracles next our ladie.   266

39

¶ Whan the clergie of Chestre and the citezens   267
Herde tell of the comynge of this noble abbasse,
They made preparacion and great diligence,
In theyr best-maner worship and solace
To mete this relique of singular grace ;   271
The great estates / and rulers of the countray
Were redy to honour saint Werburge that day.   273

40

First was ordeyned a solemne procession,   274
With crosses / and baners / and surges clere lyght,
The belles were tolled for ioye and deuocion ;
The ministres of god in coopes redy dight,
With censours of siluer / to encense her body right ;   278
All prestis and clerkes redy to say and synge
Proceded in ordre / this holy virgin praysyng.   280

41

Next to the clergie approched in degree   281
The lordes of the shyre, knyghtes, barons, all ;
With feruent deuocion / praysyng the trinite
Whiche sent to them suche comfort spirituall.
The citezens ensued with gladnes cordiall,   285
With bokes and beades / magnifieng our maker
For this great treasure to kepe them from daunger.   287

42

Venerable virgins next sette in ordre clere,   288
With lilies in theyr handes / coronate with chastite,
Good widowes and wyues appoynted well were,

Gyuynge true thankes vnto this virgin fre.
Nex[t] them assemble all the commonte   292
In all goodly maner, dyuised by discrecion,
Praysynge saynt Werburge with humiliacion.   294

43

Whan they approched to her hie presence   295
And comon were afore this relique most riall,
They kneled all downe with mycle reuerence,
Salutynge the shryne with honour victoriall,
Magnifiyng with melodye and tunys musicall   299
This glorious virgin / nothyng done amis,
Syngynge Te deum to the kyng of blysse.   301

44

The lordes / the cite3ins / and all the commons   302
Mokely submytted them-selfe to the shryne,
With manyfolde prayses and humble supplicacions,
With interiour loue / and morall discipline,
Trustyng all in her to saue them from ruyne,   306
From greuous daunger / and cruell enmite
By her entercession vnto the trinite.   308

45

They gaue due thankes vnto this abbasse,   309
Deuoutly sayenge knelyng vpon kne :
' Welcome, swete lady, replet with grace,
The floure of mekenes / and of chastite,
The cristall of clennes and virginite ;   313
Welcome thou art to vs euerychone,
A speciall comfort for vs to trust vpon !   315

46

' Welcome, swete princesse / kynges doughter dere,   316
Welcome, faire creature / and rose of merciens,
The diamonde of dignite / and gemme shenyng clere,
Virgin and moiniall of mycle excellence ;
Welcome, holy abbasse of hie preeminence,   320
The rutilant saphire of syncerite,
Welcome, swete patronesse, to Chestre cite !   322

47

'Thou art our refuge / and singular succour,   323
Oure sure tuicion, next to the trinite,
Oure speciall defence at euery houre
To releue thy seruauntes in all necessite ;
Thou art our solace and helpe in eche degre,   327
Oure ioye / trust / and comfort / and goostly treasure :
Welcome to this towne, for euer to endure ! '   329

48

¶ Agaynst her comynge into Chestre cite   330
The stretes were strawed with flours fragrant,
The mancions and halles edified rialle
Were hanged with arras precious and pleasaunt,
Torches were caried on eche syde flagrant ;   334
Also ouer the shryne was prepared a canaby
Of cloth of golde and tissewe riche and costly.   336

49

Thus with great worship, decoure and dignite   337
Of all the clergie, lordis and citezens
She was receyued with great humilite
Into the cite with humble reuerence,
The clergie syngyng with mycle diligence,   341
The comons prayeng with loue feruent,
Folowynge this relique after their entent.   343

50

In procession they passed all in to the towne,   344
With ioye and great gladnes, ye may be sure,
In ordre togyther, in charite and deuocion,
Praysyng our sauiour and this virgin pure ;
They brought full solemple with gostly p[l]easure   348
This riall relique to the moost noble place
Within all the cite, as our lordes wyll was.   350

51

This seconde translacion of this virgin bright   351
From Hambury abbay vnto Chestre cite
Was celebrate, with ioye and gladnes full right,

The yere of our saueour in his humanite
viii. hundreth complet .v. and seuentie ;   355
Alured regned than kyng of this region,
Victorious and liberall / coronate at London.   357

52

This kyng deuyded in .iiii. partes his richesse :   358
One parte to the poore, the seconde to religion,
The thyrde part to scholers / the fourth to bild churches ;
And of a day naturall / he made trium diuision :
viii. houres to rede and praye with feruent deuocion,   362
viii. houres occupied with businesse naturall,
And other .viii. houres to rule his realme riall.   364

henric'. li°. v.

Nobilitas innata tibi probita[ti]s honorem,
Armipotens Alurede, dedit / probitasq3 laborem,
Perpetuumq3 labor nomen : cui mixta dolori
Gaudia semper erant : spes semper mixta timori.
Si modo victus erat / ad crastina bella parabat,
Si modo victor erat / ad crastina bella pauebat ;
Iam post transactos regni viteq3 labores /
Christe [1] ei sit vera quies / sceptrumq3 perenne.   1 r. Christus

¶ A litel descripcion of the foundacion of Chestre / and of
    the abbay-churche within the sayd cite / where y° holy
    shryne by grace remayneth. Cap. iii.

53

Two cites of legions in cronicles we fynde :   365
One in south-Wales / in the tyme of Claudius
Called Caeruska / by britons had in mynde,
Orels Caerleon / buylded by kyng Belinus ;
Where somtyme was a legion of knyghtes chiualrous. 369
This cite of legions was whilom the bysshops se
Vnto all south-wales / nominat Wenedocie.   371

54

Another cite of legions we may fynde also   372

In the west part of Englande / by the water of Dee,
Called Caerlleon of britons longe ago,
After named Chestre, by great auctorite;
Iulius the emperour sende to this sayd cite   376
A legion of knyghtes / for to subdue Irelande;
Like-wyse dyd Claudius (as we vnderstande).   378

55

The founder of Chestre / as sayth Policronicon,   379
Was Lleon Gauer / a myghty stronge gyaunt,
Whiche buylded caues and dongions many one,
No goodly buyldyng / propre ne pleasaunt;
But the Kynge Leil, a briton sure and valiaunt,   383
Was founder of Chestre by pleasaunt buyldyng,
And of Caerleil also / named by the kynge.   385

56

Ranulphus in his cronicle yet doth expresse   386
The cite of Chestre edified for to be
By the noble romans prudence and richesse
Whan a legion of knyghtes was sende to the cite,
Rather than by the wysdome of Britons or policie;   390
Obiectyng clere agaynst the britons fundacion,
Whiche auctour resteth in his owne opinion.   392

A° gratie. lxv.

57

Kyng Marius, a bryton, regnyng in prosperite   393
In the West partie of this noble region,
Ampliat and walled strongly Chestre cite
And myghtyly fortified the sayd foundacion.
Thus eche auctour holdeth a singular opinion.   397
This Marius slewe Reodric, kyng of pictis lande,
Callyng the place of his name Westmarilande.   399

58

This 'cite of legions,' so called by the Romans,   400
Nowe is nominat in latine of his proprete
Cestria quasi castria / of honour and pleasance:
Proued by the buyldynge of olde antiquite

In cellers and lowe voultes / and halles of realte   404
Lyke a comly castell / myghty, stronge and sure,
Eche house like a toure, somtyme of great pleasure.   406

59

Vnto the sayd Chestre all northwales subiect were   407
For reformacion, Iustice and iugement ;
Theyr bysshops see also it was many a yere
Enduryng the gouernaunce of brutes auncient ;
To saxons and britons a place indifferent ;   411
The inhabitauntes of it manfull and liberall,
Constant, sad and vertuous / and gentyll continuall.   413

60

Of frutes and cornes there is great habundaunce,   414
Woddes / parkes / forestes / and beestis of venare,
Pastures / feeldes / comons / the cite to auaunce,
Waters /pooles/ pondes / of fysshe great plente ;
Most swete holsome ayre by the water of dee ;   418
There is great marchandise / shyps / and wynes strang,
With all thyng of pleasure the citezens amonge.   420

61

The yere of our lorde a hundreth sixe and fyfty   421
Reigned vpon this lande a briton kyng Lucius,
Whiche with great desire required instantly
His realme to be baptized of pope Eleutherius.[1]   1 P. Eleutherius
Whose charitable mocion was harde full gratius :   425
The pope enioyed / graunted his peticion
And sende .ii. doctours to conuerte this region.   427

62

The doctours by prechyng and singular grace   428
In short tyme conuerted the greatter Britayne ;
The people confessed their synne and trespase,
Baptized all were / forgyuenes dyd attayne ;
Idolatrie cessed through-out this lande, certayne ;   432
With grace circumfulced and lyghtned was Englande,
By faith to god professed was all Wales and scotlande. 434

L

63

Kynge Lucius ordeyned / by the doctours mocion   435
xxviii. bisshops in this realme for to be,
And .iii. archebisshops, for gostly exhortacion,
To reduce the people to vertue and humilite.
At London was set the chiefe archebisshops se,   439
The seconde in south-Wales at cite of legions,
The thyrde was at yorke, all subiect to the britons.   441

64

Churches were edified in many a place   442
Here in the more Britayne with diligent labour,
Christis faith encreased by speciall grace,
Faithfull religion delated euery hour;
Diuine seruice was songon & sayd with great honour,   446
True faith and deuocion were dayly encreasynge,
Namely in Chestre by grace continuall abidynge.   448

65

Certaynly, sith baptym came to Chestre cite,   449
Soone after Lucius / and afore kynge Arthure,
By the grace of god and their humilite,
The faith of holy churche dyd euer there endure
Without recidiuacion and infection / sure;   453
Wherfore it is worthy a singular commendacion,
Aboue all the citees and townes of this region.   455

66

The perfect begynnyng and fyrst foundacion   456
Of the monasterie within the suyd cite
Was at the same tyme by famus opinion
That baptym began within this countre;
The great lordes of Chestre of landes and auncetre   460
First edified the churche for comfort spirituall
In honour of the apostels Peter and Paule.   462

67

Whiche churche was principall to all the citie,   463
And the mouther-churche called withouten doubt;
It was their buriall by great auctorite,

To all this sayd cite / and .vii. myle without ;
The cemiterie was large to compase it about.   467
But what by sufferaunce and processe of tyme
Many olde customes ben brought now to ruyne.   469
68
In whiche mother-churche of Peter and Paule   470
All holy sacramentes ministred dayly were,
With great encreasement of vertues all,
Continuall endurynge more than .CCC. yere,
In the britons tyme / of blodde noble and clerc,   474
Afore the comyng of saxons to this lande,
Whiche with apostasie enfected all Englande.   476
69
So after that the Angles / Iutes / and saxons   477
By fortune of batell / power and policie
Had clerely subdued all the olde britons
And them expulsed to wales and wylde countre,
The faith of holy churche remayned at chestre cite   481
In the sayd churche, truely, by singular grace alone,
Like as the faith of Peter neuer fayled at Rome.   483
70
  What tyme saint Austin, the doctour of Englande,   484
Had baptiȝed Ethelbrut,[1] kynge of Kent,   [1] r. Ethelbrict
And by relacion dyd fully vnderstande
That the faith of Christ most digno and excellent
In the citie of legions was truely remanent,   488
In the churche of the apostoles Peter and Paule,
He magnified our lorde with thanke speciall.   490
71
That season there was a noble monasterie   491
xii. myles from Chestre, nominate Bangour,
Where religious monkes lyued vertuouslye,
Almost .iii. thousande / obedient euery houre,
Without possessions / lyuyng by theyr labour :   495
Vnto whiche place he sende for helpe at nede,
To conuert the saxons (sayth venerable Bede).   497

72

Saynt Austin approched the cite of legions,	498
Where the sayd couent afore hym were present :	
Whom he required to preche to the saxons	
The faith of holy churche and baptym diligent.	
To whose humble prayer / they were disobedient,	502
Obseruyng no charite. / yet for theyr great pride	
Many of them were slayne by kyng Ethelfride.	504

73

That season the britons remayned vnder licence	505
Of Angles and saxons within the sayd cite,	
Tyll the dayes of Offa, kynge of merciens,	
Regnyng in the west marche with great victorie ;	
Whiche kynge expulsed by power and chiualrie	509
All brutes and walshemen clere out of his londe,	
In peyne of punysshement none there to be fonde.	511

74

Whan the said churche, hauynge great liberte,	512
Dayly augmented in vertue and holynes,	
Prestis and clerkes praysed the holy trinite	
And the sayd apostoles with great mekenes,	
The cite encreased in worshyp and ryches ;	516
Churches were edified with feruent deuocion	
In sondrie places within the sayd towne.	518

75

This noble kyng Offa agaynst the pagans	519
Of .xvii. batels had euer the victorye ;	
Confederate was with great Charles, kyng of Fraunce,	
And edified saint Albans monasterye ;	
Of Englande first toke the hole monarchie ;	
Gaue Peter pens vnto the court of Rome ;	524
Translate to Lichefelde the se of Canturbury ;	
xxxix. yere regned fully in this region.	526

¶ *A brefe rehersall of the first foundacion of the mynstre of Chestre / and of the institucion of secular chanons in the tyme of kyng Edwarde senior.* Cap. iiiL

76

͡He yere of grace .D.CCC. seuynte and fyue,   527
    Kyng Alured regned ¹ vpon ² this region,   ¹ r. regning.
                                    ² P. vupon.
The relique, the shryne full memoratyue
Was brought to Chestre for our consolacion,
Reuerently receyued, set with deuocion   531
In the mouther-churche of saint Peter and Paule,
(As afore is sayd), a place moost principalL   533

77

In whiche holy place vnto this present day   534
She bodilye resteth by diuine prouidence,
And so by his grace shall continue alway,
In honour, worshyp / and mycle reuerence ;
A deuout oratorie of vertue and excellence,   538
Prepared by our lorde / where speciall remedy
Is agayne all greuans in soule and in body.   540

78

The primatyue gyftes gyuen to the place   541
Immediatly were after her comynge
Of deuout people replet with grace
In the dayes of the forsayd Alured kyng:
Of landes and libertes they made moche offerynge   545
To god and saint Werburge / after theyr possession,
Tristyng to her prayer and sure protection.   547

79

The people with deuocion and mynde feruent   548
Gaue diuers enormentes vnto this place :
Some gaue a coope / and some a vestement,
Some other a chalice / and some a corporace,
Many albes and other clothes offred ther was,   552
Some crosses of golde / some bokes / some belles ;
The pore folke gaue surges / torches / and towelles.   554

80

The cite3ens offered to the sayd virgine	555
For the great miracles amonge them wrought	
Many riall gyftes of Iewels to the shrine,	
Thankynge our lorde, that hath vs all bought,	
And blessed Werburge in worde, dede, and thought—	559
Women and children she mynded full gracious,	
As testifieth the archebisshop Antoninus.	561

81

Diuine seruice was obserued deuoutly	562
Euery day, encreasyng with feruent adoracion	
As the feest required / and the solemnite,	
To the honour of our lorde and hie glorificacion ;	
Preistis and clerkes with pure meditacion	566
Obseruynge their dutie gaue vertuous example	
Of great perfection to the comon people.	568

82

After kyng Alured / regned his son	569
Edwards senior, by liniall discence,	
Crowned the yere of grace .ix. hundreth and one,	
with wordly glorie and great preeminence ;	
Buylded castels, townes of myghty defence,	573
Subdued the danes .vii. tymes in batell ;	
Encreased his realme manfully and well.	575

83

That tyme the realme of merciens was translate	576
By the kynge / and gyuen to duke Ethelrede,	
A noble man of auncetre / politicke and fortunate,	
Whiche maried his syster, lady Elflede,	
Doughter to the forsaid valiant kynge Alurede ;	580
The sayd gentilman was wyse and vertuous,	
Sad and discrete, pacient and famous.	582

84

This lady Elflede, duchesse of merciens,	583
Had speciall loue and singular affection	
To blessed Werburge, and true confidence :	

Wherfore she mynded with great dilectacion
To edifie a mynstre, a place of deuocion,   587
To this holy virgin, for profite of her soule,
Enlargynge the churche of Peter and of Paule.   589

85

She moued her husbande with great mekenes   590
To supplie the same dede of his charite,
And diuers other nobles of theyr goodnes
For aide in that cause after their degree.
Ioyfull was the duke of the mocion gostle,   594
Glad were the nobles within all the shire
To founde a mynstre after her desire.   596

86

Afore the holy roode in a table writen is   597
At saint Iohans churche without the sayd cite,
Howe that prince Edmunde, the thyrde son e-wis
Of Edwarde senior, true foundour shulde be—
To whom lady Elflede was aunt by auncetre.   601
So betwix twayne was founded in short space
An holy mynstre, of vertue full and grace.   603

87

They sende for masons vpon euery syde,   604
Counnynge in geometrie / the foundacion to take
For a large mynstre, longe, hie, and wyde,
Substancially wrought / the best that they can make,
To the honour of god / for saynt Werburge sake;   608
At the est ende taken theyr sure foundacion
Of the apostoles churche / ioynynge both as one.   610

88

Whan it was edified / and curiously wrought   611
And all thyng ended / in goodly proporcion,
Than riche enormentes were offred and brought
Of the said nobles with great deuocion;
Temporall landes / rentes / possession   615
Were gyuen, for euer to mayntayne the place
Of blessed Werburge by singular grace.   617

89

Spirituall ministres were elect also :   618
Secular chanons, of great humilite,
To synge and psalmodise oure sauiour vnto,
Within the sayd mynstre hauynge a perpetuite ;
Prebendes were assigned to that fraternite,   622
With townes / borowes / and fredomes manifest,
Continually encreasyng vnto the conquest.   624

90

And the olde churche of Peter and of Paule   625
By a generall counsell of the spiritualte
With helpe of the duke moost principall
Was translate to the myddes of the sayd cite ;
Where a paresshe-churche was edified, truele,   629
In honour of the aforesayd apostoles twayne,
Whiche shall for euer by grace diuine remayne.   631

91

Also we may note, holdyng none opinion,   632
This lady Elflede of her charite
Of the sayd mother-churche translate the patron,
Caused the sayd oratorie reconciled to be
In the honour of the most blessed trinite   636
And of saynt Oswalde, martyr and kyng,
For the loue she had to hym continuynge.   638

92

   The yere of our lorde .ix. hundreth and .viii.   639
This noble duchesse with mycle royalte
Reedified Chestre / and fortified it full ryght,
Churche / house / and wall, decayed piteousle.
Thus brought vnto ruyne was Chestre cite   643
First, by Ethelfride, kyng of Northumberlande,
And by danes / norwaies, vexyng all Englande.   645

93

Also she enlarged this sayd olde cite   646
With newe myghty walles stronge all-about,
Almost by proporcion double in quantito

To the further byldynge brought without dout ;
She compassed in the castell enemies to hold out   650
Within the sayd Walles, to defende the towne
Agaynst danes and walshemen, to dryue them all downe. 652

94

After the deth of her husband Ethclrede   653
She ruled the realme of mercelande manfully,
Buylded churches / and townes repared in dede,
As Staforde / Warwike / Thomwort / and Shirisbury ;
Of newe she edified Runcorñ and Edisbury.   657
The body of saynt Oswalde also she translate
From Bardeney to Gloucetur, there to be tumulate :   659

95

Where she edified a noble monastery,   660
With licence of her brother afore nominate,
In honour of saint Peter / ouer the blessed body
Of the sayd saint Oswalde / kyng and martyr coronate.
In wiche monastery this lady was tumulate,   664
The yere of our lorde .ix. hundreth and nyntene ;
Whom myn auctour prayseth in this wordes serene :   666

            henric'. li.ᴺ v.

O Elfleda potens / o terror virgo virorum :
    Victrix nature, nomine digna viri.
Te quoqȝ splendidior fecit[1] natura puellam, [1] r. Tu quo sp. fleres
    Te probitas fecit nomen habere viri.
Te mutare docet[1] sed solum[2] nomina sexus, [1] r. decet, [2] solam
    Tu regina potens / rexqȝ trophea parans.
Iam nec cesarei tantum meruere triumphi,
    Caesare splendidior virgo virago.   Vale.

¶ *Of the notable myracles of saynt Werburge shewed in the*
    tyme of chanons / and fyrst howe she saued Chester from
    distruction of walshemen.   Cap. v.

96

This glorious Werburge and virgin pure   667
    By singular grace of god omnipotent
Shewed many myracles to euery creature,

To blynde / dombe / halt / lame / and impotent,
In the cite of Chestre / whan her shryne was present, 671
Like-wyse as in her lyfe at Wedon / at Hambury—
Witneseth the same her true legende and history.   673

97

Wher[for]e¹ to the honour / prayse / and laudacion   674
Of Iesu / the seconde persone in trinite,   ¹ P. Where
And of this virgin a¹ speciall commendacion,   ¹ r. to?
We purpose to reherse nowe with charite,
Vnder the protection of you that shall the reders be, 678
Parte of the myracles / with mynde diligent
In this humble stile / and sentence consequent.   680

98

The first myracle / that our blessed sauiour   681
Shewed for his spouses / after her translacion
To Chestre : was nye the tyme of Edwarde seniour,
Son to kyng Alured, famous of renowne.
The Name of britons was chaunged that season,   685
Were named walshemen, in the montaynes segregate,
Euer to the saxons hauynge inwarde hate.   687

99

The Walshemen that tyme had ouer them a kyng   688
Called Griffinus / to be theyr gouernour,
Electe by the comons their appetite folowyng,
Endurate with malice / couetise and rancour,
Ennemies to englisshemen / as is said before.   692
This kyng entended by mortall enuy
The cite of Chestre to spoyle and distrye.   694

100

A myghty host discended from the mountans,   695
Well armed and strongely approchyng the cite,
Prepared for batell, with them great ordinaunce.
The sayd Griffinus and all his company
With his power passed ouer the water of Dee—   699
Whiche ryuer adioynneth to the sayd towne,
Betwene Englande and Wales a sure diuision.   701

101

This kynge layd siege vnto Chestre cite   702

With all his great host / there honour to wyn—

By policie of warre / encreasynge myghtyle.

For whiche the cite3ens remaynyng within

were sore disconsolate, like for to twyn :   706

With wofull heuy hartes they dyd call and crye

Vpon blessed Werburge for helpe and remedye.   708

102

The charitable chanons with great deuocion   709

Toke the holy shryne of theyr patrones,

Set it on the towne-walles for helpe and tuicion,

Trustynge on her to be saued from distres.

But one of the ennemyes with great wyckednes   713

Smot the sayd shryne in castyng of a stone,

And it empaired / piteous to loke vpon.   715

103

Anone great punysshement vpon them all lyght :   716

The kyng and his host were smytten with blyndnes,

That of the cite / they had no maner of syght ;

And he that smote the holy shryne, doubtles,

Was greuously vexed with a sprite of darkenes,   720

And with hidous payne expired miserably—

The kynge was sore a-dred / and all his company.   722

104

Shortly the kynge remoued his great host,   723

Departed from the cite without any praye,

And gaue in commaundement in euery coost

Saynt Werburge landes to meynteyne alway,

Assigned her possessions euer after that day   727

With the signe of the crosse, a token euident,

In pleasyng this virgin / for drede of punysshement.   729

¶ *Howe saynt Werburge cured and healed a woman thre
tymes (whiche was halte and lame) to helth and
prosperite agayne.*   Cap. vi.

105

ꝛN the cite of Chestre (the legende doth expresse)   730
    An honest matrone dwelled / Eagida nominat,
Whiche by continuaunce / and payno of sickenes
Was made halt and lame / of helth all desperate ;
yet to saynt Werburge her hart was eleuate,   734
Instantly required with humble supplicacion
This holy virgin for helth / and preseruacion.   736

106

Anone by the merite of this lady clere   737
The pacient restored to helth and prosperite,
Gaue honour and thankes to Werburge and prayer,
Entendyng euer after her true seruaunt to be
And truely continue lyuyng in pure chastite.   741
But shortly she brake her promesse made in syght,
Folowyng her appetite and carnall lustes full ryght.   743

107

She had great riches, welth and prosperite   744
And maried with pleasure after her entencion ;
Wher[for]e thries she endured her olde infirmite,
And thries was cured, by meke intercession,
To helth of body from peynfull contraction.   748
Thus by the merite of this virgin pure
She was deliuered from peyne thries to pleasure.   750

108

This forsayd Eadgide, prudently ponderyng   751
These notable miracles with her gostly eye,
Gaue great commendacion and speciall thankyng
To almyghty god / with feruent humilite
And to saynt Werburge, knelynge on kne,   755
Came to her oratorie and gaue an oblacion
To the holy shryne with singular deuocion.   757

¶ *Howe saynt Werburge saued Chestre from innumerable*
barbarike nacions / purposynge to distroye and spoyle the
sayd cite vtterly.   Cap. vii.

109

AN other tyme innumerable barbarike nacions   758
   Came to spoyle Chestre, to robbe it and distry,
(Sayth the historye) from diuers regions :
Harolde kyng of danes / the kynge of gotes & galwedy,
Maucolyn of Scotlande, and all theyr company,   762
With baners displayed, well armed to fyght ;
Theyr tentes rially in hoole heth were pyght.   764

110

They set theyr ordinaunce agaynst the towne   765
Vpon euery side / timorous for to se,
Namely at the northgate they were redy-bowne
By myght, police to haue entred the cite.
The citezens dredyng to be in captiuite,   769
Made intercession vnto this holy abbasse
For theyr deliueraunce in suche extreme case.   771

111

The deuout chanons sette the holy shryne   772
Agaynst theyr enemies at the sayd northgate,
Trustynge to Werburge to saue them from ruyne
And shewe some myracle to them disconsolate.
For the citezens were of their lyues desperate,   776
Passynge mannes mynde to escape theyr daunger
But all-only by merite of this virgin clere.   778

112

As the kynges were sautynge this forsayd cite,   779
Trustyng for a praye to haue it euery hour,
One of the sayd ennemies, replet with iniquite,
Nat worshyppyng y* virgin / nor dredyng our sauiour,
Smote this riall relique with a stone in his rancour,   783
Brake therof a corner, curiously wrought,
Cast all to the grounde : than sorowe came vnsought.   785

113

The sayd malefactour nat passynge the place   786
Vexed with the deuill for his greuous offence,
Roryng and yellyng his outragious trespase,
Tore his tonge a-sonder in wodely violence,
Miserable exspired afore them in presence;   790
Satan ceased nat to shewe great punysshement
Vpon his soule and body / by signes euident.   792

114

These kynges consideringe this soden vengeaunce   793
Amonge them all lyght so soone and hastely,
Shortly remoued theyr great ordinaunce,
Departed from the cite with theyr company;
Callyng on this virgin fast for grace and mercy,   797
Promyttynge neuer after to retourne agayne
To disquiete her seruauntes and cite, in certayne.   799

¶ *Howe saynt Werburge by her merite sent frute to a*
   barrayne woman by syngular prayer made vnto her.
   The .viii. chapitre.

115

A Noble gentilman / a consul in office,   800
    Descendyng of the hie and riall blodde of costy,
Elected a spouses at his owne deuice,
A swete faire gentilwoman, curtes and comly,
Nominat Iudith / ioynned to hym in matrimony;   804
With whom this lady lyued a longe season
Barrayn and fruteles of generacion.   806

116

She daily lamented her great wretchednes,   807
As woman infortunate full of miserye,
Prayed to saynt Werburge with interiour mekenes
For remedy and helpe agaynst that wofull infamye,
Desired to haue issue and frute of her bodye,   811
If it pleased god / and this virgin also,
Most greattest comfort to brynge her hert from wo.   813

117

Saynt Werburge appered to her in vision,	814
In white bright vesture / clere as the cristall,	
Expressynge wordes of great consolacion,	
Most ioyfull to Iudith to make rehersall :	
Commaundyng her by the effect speciall	818
To go to her churche with singular deuocion	
And praye our sauiour with humble supplicacion,	820

118

Also for to compasse her holy aulter	821
With a linen cloth / knelyng on her kne,	
And after for to take the same cloth in-fere	
And compas her wombe about reuerentle.	
This Iudith was ioyfull / and rose vp yerle	825
And truely fulfylled this gostly vision ;	
From thens departed to her propre mancion.	827

119

Soone after this wyfe afore-rehersed	828
Conceyued a childe and had succession,	
Praysyng this virgin in hart, worde and dede ;	
And after the tyme of her purificacion	
Of the same faire cloth she made oblacion,	832
Richely set in syluer / well wrought in compas	
With many riche enormentes she sende to this place.	834

120

After came her-selfe vnto the monastery	835
With many of her neyghbours / there nye dwellyng,	
Praysyng and laudyng this glorious lady,	
With cordiall thankynges makyng theyr offeryng,	
Of this great myracles [1] true witnes bearyng ; [1 r. myracle]	839
Departed from the place with ioy and deuocion	
All the sayd company / eche to theyr mancion.	841

¶ *Of a woman great with childe with peyne brought out of*
her wytte / by saynt Werburge was restoured to reason
agayne.   Cap. ix.

121

3N the prouince of Chestre / knowen it is of olde,   842
   A certayne man dwelled / of great honeste,
Whiche had a doughter disposed manyfolde
To sondrye vertues / clennes / and humilite.
This humble mayde ioyned was in matrimonye   846
To an honest yong man / of whom she conceyued
And was great with childe / openly perceyued.   848

122

Whan the tyme approched of her deliueraunce,   849
Vexed she was with mycle wo and payne,
Continually enduryng / with suche hidous greuaunce
That out of her mynde she went, incertayne ;
All phisike and medicyns were founde to her in vayne : 853
No comfort in erth, helpe nor remedye
For her myght be founde in suche extremite.   855

123

Her father and mother / and her frendes all   856
Brought theyr dere doughter with great deuocion
To saynt Werburge churche / requiryng speciall
This blessed virgin / with humble intercession
To helpe the pacient from all vexacion,   860
Promyttynge an oblacion to this lady bryght
Whan she vnto reason were comen a-ryght.   862

124

And as she slepped at the aulter ende,   863
Wofully cruciat with peynes hiduous,
Passyng mannes cure it for to amende :
Anone by the merite of this virgin glorious
She was released from all payne greuous   867
And fully restored to her reason agayne,
Had good deliueraunce / and spedde well, in certayne. 869

125

Whiche myracle knowen / her frendes euerychone   870
And all the good matrons of the sayd cite
Came holly togyther with theyr oblacion
To the holy shryne, thankyng with hart fre
This blessed virgin of her benignite,   874
Whiche is so redy a mediatrice alway
To helpe her true seruauntes both nyght and day.   876

¶ *Howe an other woman vnlaufully wurkynge was made*
blynde / and by saynt Werburge restored was to her
syght agayne. Cap. x.

126

Within the same cite afore the abbay-gate   877
Dwelled a woman / which brake the commaundement
Of god and holy churche / hye sabbot-day dyd violate
Vnlaufully wurkynge : wherfore great punysshement
Fell vpon this woman with peynes equiualent,   881
Sodaynly smytten / wurkynge full busely
With greuous blyndnes / and mycle miserye.   883

127

This woman, consyderynge her syght was gone,   884
The pleasure of this worlde, her helpe and succour,
Hauynge to lyue by / small riches or none,
Cried maynly 'out out, alas' euery hour,
'Wo is me wretche, fulfylled with dolour !   888
Alas, I was borne to abyde this wofull day
My maker to displease ! / alas, what shall I say ?'   · 890

128

She called to memorie with hye discrecion   891
The myracles that Werburge shewed to mankynde :
By grace she repented / with suche contricion
That water distilled from her eyes blynde,
Dolefully lamentynge / that she was so vnkynde ;   895
Ruthfully was brought to Werburge oratory,
Trustyng in this virgin to haue remedy.   897

M

129

As she continued in her supplicacion,   898
Wofully wepynge / abidyng the great grace .
Of blessed Werburge / with singular inuocacion,
Anone she was cured to helth and solace,
Restored to her eye-sight / she passed the place,   902
Praysed our lorde and this virgin pure,
Was a holy woman after, ye may be sure.   904

¶ *How saint Werburge restored to helth and prosperite vi.*
   lame and halt persons by singular grace.   Cap. xi.

130

The excellent fame of this glorious lady   905
     Dilated was through all this region,
Manifest by myracles full honorably :
Therfore from diuers partes came many a person
For helth of body and gostly conuersacion,   909
Some to be cured from payne intollerable
And some of olde sores that were incurable.   911

131

Amonge whom there came vnto her place   912
Sixe wofull persones / cured for to be,
Halt, blynde and lame, besekyng her of grace
With humble supplicacion vpon them haue pite,   1 P. treares.
With wepynge teares[1] sayenge / 'o souerayn ladie,   916
O imperiall princesse / and kynges doughter dere,
Heele our disease by thy instant prayer !   918

132

'O blessed virgin and holy moiniall,   919
O glorious abbasse / and worthy gouernour,
O pereles parens and ministre spirituall,
O celestiall gemme resplendent with honour,
Praye for vs wretches vnto our sauiour,   923
That we may opteyne here mercy and grace,
Cured of our sekenes / after to se thy face.   925

133

'Thy name transcendeth this realme, swete lady,   926
Thy myracles magnifien thy great goodnes,
Thy worshyp encreaseth with honour and glorie
Daily euermore through thy great holynes :
Shewe nowe thy power / cure vs from sekenes,   930
That by the we may prayse the kyng of blis,
As thou hast cured many one or this.'   932

134

By these meke prayers / in hert full penitent,   933
And many other orisons sayd priuatly
Callyng on this virgin with deuocion feruent,
For certayne / or they passed the monastery
They were all cured from peyne and malady.   937
In wytnes wherof / and triall as it was
Theyr staues remayned longe after in the place.   939

¶ *Howe a yonge man thries hanged vnlaufully, was thries
   delyuered by saynt Werburge from dethe to lyfe and
   lyberte.*   Cap. xii.

135

HLmyghty god gaue in commaundement   940
   By moises lawe / to his people echone,
No innocent to slee by wrongfull iudgement
Nor causeles to punysshe by greuous oppression,
Also to beware of lyght suspection.   944
Wherof a myracle we shall nowe expresse,
Done in Chestre cite by Werburge theyr patronesse.   946

136

A certayne yonge man dwelled in the cite,   947
Honest in maners / and of good conuersacion,
Disposed to vertue and humilite :
Was arrest and taken of a lyght suspicion
By the officers and rule[r]s of the sayd towne,   951
Gyltles accused most innocently,
Condemned and iudged to deth shamfully.   953

M 2

137

After sentence gyuen / ministres were all redy   954
Vpon the iudgement to do execucion :
He was fettred and brought to the gebbet by and by
And as a stronge thefe hanged ther-vpon.
His frendes and cosyns for hym made great mone—   958
Alas, what tonge myght expresse the wo
They made that tyme departynge hym fro ?   960

138

And as this innocent hang in his payne,   961
He called to mynd the manyfolde goodnes,
The myracles of Werburge, shewed her, certayne,
Howe she had saued many in great distres :
So, whan he myght no wordes expresse,   965
In mynde he required her / and humblie dyd pray
From shamfull deth to saue hym that day.   967

139

Whan all the officers departed were thens   968
Supposynge the soule seperate from the body,
A white doue[1] descended afore them in presence   [1 P. done.]
And lyght vpon the gebbet immediatly ;
The byrde with his byll brake the rope, truely,   972
The prisoner escaped that tyme from deth,
Shortly reuiuynge toke naturall breth.   974

140

Whiche thynge notified, so meruailous in syght,   975
The ministers returned / theyr labour in vayne :
Toke this innocent by power and myght,
Vpon the sayd gebbet hanged hym agayne.[1]   [1 One stanza missing here ?]
Thus[1] he was delyuered by myracle from payne : [1 r. Thries ?]
The tortuous turmentours cessed their tyrranny,
Permytted the prisoner to go at liberte.   981

141

Whiche myracle knowen / his frendes and cosyns all   982
Returned agayne with glad mynde and chere.
The prisoner mette them, louyng god in spec'all

And blessed Werburge in his best manere.
The deuout citezens approched them nere, 986
Went all to the shryne the virgin thankyng;
The belles were tolled for ioy of this thyng. 988

¶ *Howe at the maner-place of Vpton saint Werburge restrayned*
wylde horses from distruction of cornes put in by theyr
ennemyes. Cap. xiii.

142

A̶Lso the thyrde season approched to Chestre cite 989
  Many cruell ennemyes in the part of Wirall,
Purposyng to spoyle / and distroy all the countre,
The people and theyr frutes / theyr corne and catall.
The citezens, dredyng to be captyue and thrall, 993
Fortified the cite with men of armes bright,
Hauynge sure artillarie for to defende and fight. 995

143

The husbandes of the countrey about there dwellyng, 996
Agaynst the sayd ennemyes makyng sore prouysion
Brought their corne & cattell / their husolde remaynynge,
In assurance to be / to the parke of Vpton,
Saynt Werburge landes, from all distruction— 1000
Whiche parke from Vpton was distaunt a myle space,
A prebende to a chanon of her mynstre and place. 1002

144

These wycked ennemies fulfylled with malice, 1003
Agaynst all conscience and ordre of charite,
In no-maner wise dredynge the hie iustice
Entred the sayd parke with mycle cruelte,
Pulled downe the paale at pleasure and liberte, 1007
Put in theyr horses, made great distruction
Of cornes and catell, of a hie presumpcion. 1009

145

Werburge, remembrynge theyr great wyckednes, 1010
Theyr malice and myschief agaynst her possession,
By myracle shewed her power and goodnes,

Preseruynge her seruauntes from all vexacion
And punysshyng her ennemies with great affliction, 1014
As she hath done many seasons or this
By mean to her spouse, our lorde kyng of blis. 1016

146

Whan the corne-sheuys laye broken afore them playne, 1017
The horses had no power any part to take :
For why ? by myracle / theyr heedes all, in certayne,
Were vp holden in the ayre / theyr bodyes sore dyd quake,
They touched no frutes / wast they dyd none make. 1021
Of the principall doers / some raged out of mynde,
Some smetyn with palsy / some lepre, halt and blynde. 1023

147

Whiche punysshement knowen vnto all the host, 1024
The rulers and captens without any delaye
Knyt agayne the sheuys / that none shulde be lost,
With tremblynge hartes humbly began to praye
This holy virgin to saue them that daye ; 1028
Vpon a condicion / escapynge from payne :
Endurynge theyr lyfe neuer to turne agayne. 1030

148

From that tyme furth ther dare no nacion, 1031
Consyderyng the power of this virgin pure,
Approchyng Chestre cite to make derogacion ;
Denmarke, Goet, nor Galway-scot, ye may be sure,
Cruell danes nor walshemen dare nat procure. 1035
Wherfore the citezens haue cause to loue the place
And thanke this virgin for her helpe and grace. 1037

¶ *Howe a chanon of Chestre hauyng his leg and thie broken,*
was restaured to helth by saynt Werburge, hys
patronesse. Cap. xiiii.

149

Within Chestre-mynstre, that holy place, 1038
Dwelled a chanon nominate Vlminus,
Sad of disposicion by syngular grace,

Humble and pacient / discrete and vertuous,
Liberall and honest / gentyll and piteous; 1042
And for a pastyme this was his pleasure,
To hunt and to hauke to confort nature. 1044

150

And as this chanon rode for his solace 1045
On huntyng with other honest company,
By fortune vnfrendly— / the more pite was,
Both horse and man fell to grounde sodendly,
In perill of theyr lyues standynge in ieoperdye : 1049
The horse downe lyenge oppressed the chanon,
Brake his leg a-sondre / with blod great effusion. 1051

151

Whan by his company the chanon was vp take, 1052
He fell in a swowne for anguisshe, wo and payne,
All wordly riches redy to forsake
For one hour of quietnes to be had agayne ;
Vnto his mancion they brought hym, certayne, 1056
Where he continued in mycle wo and langour,
Abydyng allonly the mercy of our sauiour. 1058

152

Counnyng surgeans were sought vpon euery syde, 1059
To cure this gentylman from penalite ;
But none of them / by wysdome coude prouyde
Clerely to heele hym / and do hym remedye.
Thus he remediles / in extreme ieopardye 1063
Prayed to saynt Werburge, his patronesse,
For helth and remedye / of her great goodnesse. 1065

153

Whose humble prayer with inward loue feruent 1066
Was graciously harde of her charite :
For right soone after appered euident
A byrde like a doue, most clere for to see,
Into the chanons chambre the byrde flow, trule, 1070
Among the company / and anone, doubtles,
The place was repleit with odour and swetnes. 1072

154

Soone after the company euerichone	1073
Were sadly on slepe, a thynge meruaylous,	
And afore the pacient by playne vision	
Saynt Werburge appered in his syght full glorious,	
Sayeng : 'my chaplayne and seruaunt vertuous,	1077
Why be ye absent from diuine seruice,	
Nat doynge your dutie accordyng to iustice ?'	1079

155

'Ma dame,' he sayd / 'and swete president,	1080
It is well knowen to all the cite	
Of my mysfortune and harmes euydent,	
Howe my horse almost had oppressed me.	
Wherfore an impotent I endure mysere ;	1084
It is no feyned cause / that I do expresse.	
I beseke you of helpe nowe, swete maistres.'	1086

156

Saynt Werburge, euer piteous and merciable	1087
Vpon her seruantes in great distresse,	
Conforted her chaplayne with wordes delectable,	
Proued in effect by her excellent goodnes	
To his syght and felynge, as he dyd expresse :	1091
She touched the foote / that sore and broken was,	
Cured it holly from payne by singular grace.	1093

157

Whan she had cured thus this impotent,	1094
Anone she departed out of his syght.	
The chanon gaue honour to god omnipotent	
And to this virgin and lady bryght	
Of this gostly vision, comfort and lyght ;	1098
All peyne was past, sekenes, vexacion,	
Helth was come, by playne probacion.	1100

158

The chanon rose vp the same mydnyght	1101
And went to mattens, as custome was.	
His bretherne were glad with all theyr myght,	

Praysed our lorde of his singular grace
And Werburge, patrones of the sayd place ;　　　　1105
Also with honour, reuerence and humilite
The bretherne sange te deum solemle.　　　　　　1107

¶ *A brefe rehersall of certayne kynges / and how kyng
Edgare came to Chestre. Also howe Leofrice, Erle of
Chestre, repared diuers churches.* Cap xv.

159

After the decesse of kynge Edwarde seniour　　　　1108
Ethelstan his sonne was coronate at London
Kyng of this lande / regnyng in honour
With power, regalite by true succession ;
Valeant in chiualry and actes euerychone,　　　　1112
Subdued danes / scottes / norwayes / britons all,
Opteyned triumphe / and dignite imperiall.　　　　1114

160

The fourth yere of his reigne / and the yere of grace　1115
viii. hundreth .ii. and seuenty by full computacion
Guy erle of Warwike by fortune slayne hase
Colbrond the gyaunt / floure of danes nacion.
The sayd kyng Ethelstan by power and renowne　　1119
Thries subdued danes / and slewe the kyng of Irelande,
Nominat prince Anlaff / as we vnderstande.　　　　1121

161

This noble Ethelstan was good and gracious　　　　1122
To all-holy churche / namely to religion,
Ryghtfull in iudgement / liberall and piteous
To his true subiectes through his dominion ;
To mynstres and holy places had great affection,　　1126
Confirmed theyr foundacions with libertes clere,
Whose noble actes bo touched a lytell here :　　　　1128

> Regia progenies produxit nobile stemma,
> Cum tenebris nostris illuxit splendida gemma,
> Magnus Ethelstanus, patrie decus / orbita recti,
> Illustris probitas a vero nescia flecti.

162

After Ethelstan regned Edmunde, his brothur,   1129
Fyue yeres in honour / hauyng great victory.
Princis Elred and Edwyn succided eytherothur,
In great busines with scottes and danes, truly.
Next whom meke Edgare / sayth the history,   1133
xvi. yere of age / coronate at Kyngston,
With peace and quietnes first ruled this region.   1135

163

In whose natiuite the blessed Dunstan   1136
Herde angels singe with mycle melody :
'Peace is nowe come to Englande, certan,
Quietnes / and rest / honour / and victory.'
Of cornes and frutes that tyme was plentie ;   1140
Danes / norwaies / scottes / britons in euery place
Submytted them-selfe to the kynges grace.   1142

164

Science encreased, true loue and amite,   1143
Vertue was exalted in all this region ;
Monasteries were edified of his benignite,
Endowed with riches / and riall possession :
xl. religious places by famous opinion   1147
Were newly buylded by the sayd noble kyng,
In sondry places of this realme standyng.   1149

165

Secular prestes expulsed sothely were   1150
From diuers monasteries with great discrecion,
Religious persones, repleit with vertue clere,
Entred their places cause of deuocion ;
Charite was feruent and holy religion ;   1154
The lyues of sayntes were soth in eche place,
And written in legendes for our comfort and grace.   1156

166

Many shyps were made vpon the kynges cost   1157
To serche by the se all his lande about,
That no alian entre in no-maner cost,

By policie and manhod to holde all his ennemies out.
Danes / norwaies / scottes durst nat ones loke out— 1161
Suche drede all nacions had ensuynge the tyme
That kyng Edgare regned by prouidence diuine.   1163

167

In progresse he passed ones in the yere   1164
Eche quarter of the realme with his company,
To se that his subiectes well ordred were
And the lawe obserued / iustice with mercy.
Than was none oppression, wronges nor iniury,   1168
Debate, malice, rancour myght nat be founde ;
True loue and charite was in all the londe.   1170

168

Kynge Edgare approched the cite of legions,   1171
Nowe called Chestre / specified afore ;
Where .viii. kynges mette of diuers nacions,
Redy to gyue Edgare reuerence and honour,
Legiance and fidelite depely sworne full sore   1175
At the same cite : after to be obedient,
Promyt at his callyng to come to his parliament.   1177

169

From the Castell he went to the water of Dee   1178
By a priue posturne through walles of the towne ;
The kyng toke his barge with mycle rialte,
Rowyng vpwarde to the churche of saynt Iohñ ;
The forsayd .viii. kynges with hym went alone :   1182
Kynge Edgare kept the storne / as most principall,
Eche prince had an ore to labour with-all.   1184

170

Whan the kynge had done his pylgrimage   1185
And to the holy roode made oblacion,
They entred agayne into the sayd barge,
Passynge to his place with great renowne.
Than Edgare spake in praysyng of the crowne :   1189
' All my successours may glad and ioyfull be
To haue suche homage, honour and diguite.'   1191

171

Also it is to be had in memory   1192
That this sayd Edgare and his princis all
Came with great reuerence vnto the monastery,
To worshyp saynt Werburge with mynde liberall;
Where he gaue fredoms and priuileges speciall,   1196
With singular possessions of his charite,
Confirmynge the olde grauntes by hye auctorite.   1198

172

This Edgare was nominate in cronicles expresse   1199
'The floure of Englande' / regnyng as emperour,
Lyke-wise as Romulus to romains was of prowes,
Cyrus to the persis / to the grekes their conquerour,
Great Charles to frenchemen / to troians Hectour ;   1203
Famous in victorye, preignant in wysdome,
Vertuous and pacient / feruent in deuocion.   1205

henric'. li°. v.

Auctor opum, vindix scelerum / largitor honorum,
   Sceptriger Edgarus regna superna petit.
Hic alter Solomon / legum pater / orbita pacis,
   Quod claruit bellis / claruit inde magis.
Templa deo / templis monachos / monachis dedit agros :
   Nequitie lapsum / iusticieᵹ locum.

173

Also from the byrthe of our blessed sauiour   1206
A thousande fyfty yere / and seuyn expresse,
In the tyme of saynt Edwarde kyng and confessour,
As William Maluesbury beareth wytnes,
Than Leofricus, a man of great mekenes,   1210
Was erle of Chestre and duke of merciens,
Son to duke Leoffwin by liniall discence.   1212

174

This noble Leofric, sayth policronicon,   1213
Of his deuocion and beningne grace,
Namely by the counsell and vertues mocion

Of his lady Godith, countes whiche was,
Reedified churches decayed in many a place,   1217
Also he founded the monastery of Leonence,
By the towne of Herforde / and the place of Wenlecence.1219
175

This erle repareled a noble olde monastery,   1220
Euesham vpon Auen / gaue them great riches ;
Also founder was of the abbay in couentre,
Made the cite free, for loue of his countesse :
At the cite of Chestre of his great goodnes   1224
He repared the College-churche of saynt Iohn̄,
Endowed it with riches and enormentes many on.   ·1226
176

This erle of Chestre, the sayd Leofricus,   1227
Of his charite / and feruent deuocion
To the honour of god / reedified full gracious
The mynstre of Werburge within the sayd towne,
Gaue vnto it riches and singular possession,   1231
Endowed the sayd place with fredoms and liberte
And speciall priuileges, confirmed by auctorite.   1233
177

So the sayd place encreased in honour,   1234
In great possessions / fredoms / and richesse ;
With singular deuocion vnto our sauiour
And prayse to saynt Werburge, theyr patronesse,
The chanons obserued vertue and clennes,   1238
Daily augmentyng by diuine sufferaunce
Vnto the comyng to this lande of normans.   1240

¶ Of the comyng of Willyam conquerour to this lande, and
   howe Hug. Lupe, his syster sonne, was founder of Chestre
   monasterye. Cap. xvi.
178

THe yere of grace .M. sixe and thre-scour,   1241
   The .xiii. day of the moneth of october
The duke of Normandy / William conquerour,

Pight a stronge batell / displayed his baner,
Of normans and frenchemen hauynge great power,   1245
Subdued kyng Harolde / opteyned all the londe,
Was coronate at London / made saxons all bonde.   1247

179

For diuerse great causes he came to this countre :   1248
First for deth of Alured, his nere kynsman ;
The proscripcion of Robert archebisshop of Canterbury ;
The periury of Harolde agaynst conscience playne ;
The promys of saynt Edwarde made to hym, certayne,1252
That the sayd Wylliam shulde enioye the crowne,
If the kyng departed without succession.   1254

180

A generall counsell was celebrate at London,   1255
That all bysshops sees by helpe of the conquerour
From borowes shulde be translate to a famous towne
Within their diocese / to the greatter honour.
Ryght so they all were / sayth myn auctour ;   1259
Also the see of Lichefelde was translate to Chester,
By helpe and sufferaunce of the bysshop Peter.   1261

181

  With Wylliam conquerour came to this region   1262
A noble worthy prynce nominate Hug. Lupus,
The dukes son of Britayne / and his syster son ;
Flourynge in chiualry, bolde and victorious,
Manfull in batell / liberall and vertuous :   1266
To whom the kyng gaue for his enheritaunce
The counte of Chesshire, with the appurtinaunce,   1268

182

By victorie to wynne the forsayd Erledom,   1269
Frely to gouerne it as by conquest right ;
Made a sure chartre to hym and his succession,
By the swerde of dignite to holde it with myght,
And to calle a parlement to his wyll and syght,   1273
To ordre his subiectes after true iustice
As a prepotent prince / and statutes to deuise.   1275

183

This valeant knyght with a myghty host   1276
Descended from London to wynne the sayd counte.
But the lordes of Chesshire rose from euery cost,
Agaynst hym made batell and had the victorie;
Thries they preuayled agaynst the erle, trulie.   1280
After he optayned to his fame and honour
The erledome of Chestre, entred as a conquerour.   1282

184

He gaue to his knyghtes after theyr desire   1283
Lordshyps and franches / and great possession,
With riche mariages, within all Chesshire,
Exalted his seruauntes to hye promocion;
Vnto holy churche had special deuocion,   1287
Maynte[in]ynge iustice / commendyng vertue,
Deposyng vice by the helpe of Iesu.   1289

185

After the departure of his vncle, the conquerour,   1290
Whan William Ruff. toke the regalite,
Than blessed Anselme, the famous doctour,
Dyd viset this lande oft-tymes of his charite,
Glad to refourme / and brynge vnto vnite   1294
Where was debate / and mycle diuision,
By diligent labour / and good exhortacion.   1296

186

This forsayd erle of his benignite,   1297
Interiously louynge holy religion,
Repleit with vertue and feruent charite,
Sende for saynt Anselme vnto London,
To come to Chestre at his peticion   1301
And there for to founde a religious place
In honour of Werburge by diuine grace.   1303

187

Blessed Anselme at the erles supplicacion   1304
Came vnto Chestre with gladde chere shortly:
Where he founded an abbaye of holy religion,

A pleasaunt place and a noble monasterye,
In worshyp of god / and saynt Werburge, sothely,   1308
The yere of grace by full computacion
A thousande .iiii. score .xiii. yere alon.   1310

188

All secular prestes / and chanons also,   1311
Within the sayd place afore-tyme dwellyng
Were clerely dismyssed / and letten go ;
Religious monkes, perfect in lyuynge,
Receyued were gladly their rule professynge.   1315
Saynt Anselme ordeyned Richard of Beccense
To be their abbot with great preeminence.   1317

189

Landes / rentes / libertes / and great possession,   1318
Franches / fredoms / and priuileges riall
Were gyuen mekely to that foundacion,
Maners / borowes / townes / with the people thrall,
And many faire churches / chapels withall,   1322
Wardes and mariages were gyuen that season
To god and saynt Werburge, cause of deuocion ;   1324

190

Kyng Wyllyam Ruff, son to the conquerour,   1325
Confirmed the foundacion / with great auctorite,
Endowed the monastery with mycle honour
Of fredoms / franches / also liberte.
The place that tyme was made as fre   1329
As the sayd erle was in his castell,
Or as hert myght thynke / or tonge myght tell.   1331

191

Saynt Anselme departed thence vnto London   1332
And was made archebisshop of Canturbury.
To the place he gaue a sure confirmacion,
With singular priuileges to be had in memory ;
Of whom it is written here folowyng, truly :   1336
Hic vir dum vixit, extirpantes maledixit
Werburge iura presentia siue ¹ futura.   ¹ P. sine.   1338

192

This noble prince gaue of his charite   1339
Riall riche enormentes vnto the sayd place,
Coopes / crosses / Iewels of great rialte,
Chales / censures / vestures / and landes dyd purchace ;
A librarie of bokes to rede and synge there was—   1343
Of whiche riall iewels and bokes some remayne
Within the sayd monastery to this day, certayne.   1345

193

The founder also buylded within the monasterie   1346
Many myghty places / conuenient for religion,
Compased with stronge walles on the west partie
And on the other syde with Walles of the towne,
Closed at euery ende with a sure postron,   1350
In south part the cimiterie inuironed rounde about,
For a sure defence ennemies to holde out.   1352

194

The .ix. yere aftre this riall foundacion,   1353
This noble founder the .xxvii. day of Iuly
Departed to-warde the heuenly mancion.
Next whom his son Richarde succeded, truly,
Than regnyng in honour the first kyng Henry.   1357
Also the place had their fraunches and fredom
Afore the sayd cite a hundreth yere and one.   1359

¶ *Howe saynt Werburge taught her monke and chaplayne to
kepe paciens for his greatter merite and glorye to come.*
Cap. xvii.

195

AFter the translacion of Chestre monasterye   1360
     From secular chanons to monkes religious
By helpe of Anselme archebisshop of Canturburye,
Supportyng therto the foundei Hug. Lupus,
As afore is specified full memorous,   1364
A monke there dwelled of vertuous disposicion
Vnder obedience / nominate dan Symon.   1366

196

This brother Simon, his tyme well vsyng,   1367
Nowe in vertuous study / nowe in contemplacion,
Nowe in deuout prayer / nowe busely wryttynge,
Somtyme in solace / and honest recreacion,
Obserued deuoutly his holy religion,   1371
Obedience / pacience / and wylfull pouerte,
Mekenes / meditacion / with pure chastite.   1373

197

For whiche examples and signes of vertue   1374
Diuers of his bretherne repleit with enuy
Were fully confederate, entendyng to subdue
This honest prest by malice and policy :
They layd to his charge open wronges and iniury,   1378
They punysshed & oppressed hym with great affliction,
Dayly augmentyng by subtyll collusion.   1380

198

Dan Symon, offendyng no brother at all,   1381
Obserued pacience / euer callynge for grace,
Wepyng, lamentyng with syghes cordiall
His fortune vnfrendly, remediles / in that case ;
Entended to depart to some other place,   1385
Of a scrupulous conscience / seyng no redresse,
Was redy to procede plonged in heuynes.   1387

199

Werburge appered to this monke in vision,   1388
Rryghter than Phebus in his meridian spere :
' My seruaunt,' she sayd, callyng hym vpon,
' Why be ye so sad / and heuy of chere ?
Wheder entende ye? shewe the mater clere ! '   1392
' Alas,' he sayd, ' ma dame and patronesse,
For sorowe I can nat my peynes expresse.   1394

200

' Diuers of my bretherne ben greued at me,   1395
Vexyng me dayly with great tribulacion,
Causeles on my part deserued, trule,

In worde or en dede gyuyng none occasion.
I can nat be quiet amonge that congregacion ;   1399
Wherfore, swete lady, vnder your licence
I purpose to departe in sauynge my conscience.'   1401

201

Saynt Werburge pacified his mynde and entent   1402
With wordes of comfort and holy scripture,
Made hym be humble in hert and pacient,
'Thy sufferaunce shalbe great ioye and pleasure,
And for thy pacience thou maist be sure   1406
To haue rewarde in blis perpetuall
At thy departure from this lyfe mortall.'   1408

202

Wherwith saynt Werburge departed sodeinl[y]   1409
To the blys of heuyn euer-endurynge.
The monke was meke in hert and mery,
Obserued her doctrine this lyfe continuyng,
Gaue good example of perfect lyuynge   1413
Vnto his bretherne / and at his departure
For his pacience passed to eternall pleasure.   1415

¶ *Howe sondes rose vp within the salt see agaynst Hilburghee
by saynt Werburge at the peticion of the constable of
Chestre.* Ca. xviii.

203

THe seconde erle of Chestre after the conquest   1416
   Was erle Richard / son to Hug. Lupus :
Whiche Richarde entended all thyng to the best ;
To visite saynt Winifride in hert desirous,
Vpon his iourney went / myn auctour sayth thus,   1420
Deuoutly to holy-well in pylgrimage,
For his great merite and gostly aduantage.   1422

204

Whan the wicked walshemen herd of his comyng   1423
After a meke maner vnto that party,
They made insurrection, inwardly gladdyng,

Descended from the mountaynés most furiously,
Agaynst the erle raised a cruell company ;   1427
Bytwxt hym and Chestre lettynge the kyngis way,
Purposynge to slee or take hym for a praye.   1429

205

The erle son perceyued theyr malicious entent :   1430
In all hast possible sende to Chestre secretly,
To warne his constable by loue and commaundem[en]t,
Wyllyam the son of Nigell / to rayse a great army,
To mete hym at Basyngwerke right sone and spedely 1434
For his deliueraunce from deth and captiuite
Of the wyld walshemen / without humanite.   1436

206

The constable congregate in all goodly hast   1437
A myghty stronge host / in theyr best arraye,
To-warde Hilburghee on iourney ridyng fast,
Trustyng vpon shippes all them to conuaye—
Whiche was a riall rode that tyme, nyght and daye. 1441
And whan they theder came, shyppyng none there was
To carie all them ouer in conuenient space.   1443

207

Alas, what hert may thynke / or tonge well expresse 1444
The dolorous greuaunce / and great lamentacion
That the host made / for loue and tendernes,
Knowynge their great maister in suche persecucion ?
Some wept and wayled without consolacion,   1448
Some sighed and sobbed / some were in extasy,
Without perfect reason. / alas, what remedy ?   1450

208

Wyllyam the constable, most carefull man on lyue   1451
Of his mysfortune, in suche extreme necessite
Called to hym a monke there dwellyng contemplatyue,
Required hym for counsayle and prayer for his charite.
The monke exhorted hym to knele vpon his kne,   1455
Humblie to beseke Werburge, his patronesse,
For helpe and remedy in suche great distresse.   1457

209

The constable content anone began to praye : 1458
'O blessed Werburge and virgin pure,
I beseke the mekely, helpe me this day,
That we may transcende this ryuer safe and sure,
To saue and defende my lorde from discomfiture ; 1462
And here I promytte to god and the alone
To offre to the a gyfte at my comyng-whome.' 1464

210

Whiche prayer ended, with wepyng and langour, 1465
Beholde and consydre well with your gostly ee
The infinite goodnes of our sauiour :
For like as to Moises deuided the redde see,
And the water of Iordan obeyed to Iosue, 1469
Ryght so the depe riuer of Dee made diuision,
The sondes drye appered in syght of them echone. 1471

211

The constable consyderynge / and all the company 1472
This great myracle transcendyng nature,
Praysed and magnified our lorde god almyghty
And blessed Werburge, the virgin pure.
They went into wales vpon the sondes sure, 1476
Deliuered their lorde from drede and enmite,
Brought hym in safe-garde agayne to Chestre cite. 1478

212

The said Wyllyam constable came to the monasterye, 1479
Thanked saynt Werburge with meke supplicacion,
Fulfylled his promes made in extremite :
Offred to the place the village of Neuton ;
Afterwarde he founded the abbay of Norton. 1483
And where the host passed / ouer betwix bondes,
To this day ben called 'the constable sondes.' 1485

¶ *Howe Matilde countesse of Chestre, counsellyng her husbande
agaynst the monastery of Chestre, was drowned at
Barflewe, with many other mo.* Cap. **xix.**

213

AFter the decesse of Hug. Lupe prenominate   1486
    Richarde, his son, .vii. yeres of age,
Was elect Erle by the kyng, and creat ;
With counsaile gouerned his landes and heritage.
At yeres of discrecion he toke in mariage   1490
The lady Matild / nece to the first kynge Henry,
Doughter to erle Stephan, (sayth the history).   1492

214

At his begynnyng he was a benefactour,   1493
A founder to the place by landes and possession,
By franches and libertes / ayde / helpe / and succour,
Gyuen to the abbay / augmentyng the foundacion :
Proued by his actes of singular deuocion   1497
Enduryng long tyme / tyll that his lady
By wycked counsaile moued hym the contrarye.   1499

215

It is red in scripture howe quene Iesabell,   1500
Ambicious of honour agaynst all ryghtousnes,
Peruerted her lorde Achas / kyng of Israell,
To sle Nabath for his vineyard, doubtles ;
Also Athalia / the bible sheweth expresse,   1504
Commaunded to slee the kynges children all,
That she myght regne sole princesse imperiall :   1506

216

Ryght so this Matilde, clerely refusyng   1507
The steppes of Sara / Rebecca / and Rachell
And other good matrons : but imitacion [1] takyng   [1] P. mutacion
Of these wycked women Athali and Iesabell,
Peruerted her husbande by her subtyll counsell   1511
To aske of the abbot the maner-place of Salton
With the appurtinaunce / by famous opinion.   1513

217

Thabbot, by counsell of his bretherne all,	1514
Denyed to graunt their propre possession,	
The patrimony of Christ, and their landes seuerall	
To the sayd erle Richarde and his succession,	
Gyuen by his father at the first foundacion.	1518
For whiche thyng the erle and Matilde, his lady,	
Hated thabbot / the bretherne / and the monastery.	1520

218

The erle and his countesse went to Normandy,	1521
To viset their frendes and cosyns naturall ;	
So dyd the princis / their father kyng Henry,	
With many estates of the blodde riall.	
These princis fauored no saxon at all ;	1525
The erle conominat in malice and hate	
Agaynst the monasterie / as a man endurate.	1527

219

Satan sende forth his seruauntes in hast	1528
To enfect the erles hert with venomous poison.	
The bedyls of Belial attempted full fast	
The erle and his countesse / to kepe theyr opinion ;	
Detractours, flaterers, cause of promocion,	1532
Trustyng therby to opteyne fauour and grace	
Excited their myndes agaynst the sayd place.	1534

220

The erle sore attempted by his gostly ennemy,	1535
By wycked people callyng hym vpon,	
Namely by the counsell of Matilde, his lady,	
Entended to alter and chaunge the foundacion	
Of the sayd abbay to a nother religion,	1539
Confirmed the same, sweryng most depely,	
At his whom-comyng to Englande / from Normandy.	1541

221

Thabbot and couent, knowyng this great perell	1542
By speciall louers and frendes secretly,	
Were pensyue and sorowfull (it was no meruell),	

Their hertes plonged in wo and misery,
By naturall reason hauyng no remedy,   1546
Consyderyng his malice encreased more and more
Agaynst the monastery / with wordes of rigour.   1548

222

They had their hope, trust and confidence   1549
In blessed Werburge, their patronesse :
With wepyng eies, clere in conscience
They called her vpon in all their distresse :
'O glorious virgin, lady and swete maistres,   1553
Metigate the malice by thy benignite
Of Richarde our lorde / mekely we praye the.   1555

223

'Suffre hym neuer to distroye thy place   1556
By wycked consell, malice and enuy,
Founded and dedicate by heuenly grace
In honour of god / and the specially ;
Protect / defende / and saue thy monastery,   1560
Thy landes / thy libertes / and thy seruauntes all,
As thou afore·tyme hast done continuall.'   1562

224

   In meane tyme the erle entended spedely   1563
From thens to depart / and retourne agayne,
To fulfyll his entent agaynst the monasterye,
By the subtyll mocion of his countesse, playne.
A ship was prepared / all thyng redy, certayne ;   1567
The prince of England / the erle and his lady
Toke shippyng at Barflewe, and all their comp[any].   1569

225

Certaynly, they sayled but a lytell space   1570
Whan agaynst them roose a contrarie wynde.
The mariners to gyde the ship had no grace,
The stormes so great, hiduous agaynst kynde ;
On a rocke they ranne / no remedy myght fynde ;   1574
Incontinently the ship barst all in-sondre ;
The erle and his feliship were turned all vndre.   1576

226

No man ne childe scaped from deth that tyme,	1577
But one pore seruaunt, whiche swamme to the londe.	
Suche was theyr fortune by sufferaunce diuyne.	
Many of theyr bodis [1] were neuer fonde.	[1] P. bedis.
Thus was their power made thrall and bonde,	1581
Theyr lyues were lost within a s[h]ort space	
Whiche were cruell ennemyes vnto her place.	1583

227

On saynt Katharins day at after mydnyght,	1584
Whan matens were ended / and bretherne gon,	
Some mournyng, waylyng for drede full ryght,	
Some busie in prayer and contemplacion :	
Werburge appered to the secristan alone,	1588
Sayenge : ' ye may be ioyfull in god and mery :	
Erle Richarde is drowned, your mortall ennemy.'	1590

228

The same glad tidyng shewed an honest woman	1591
Tollyng at the churche-dore the sayd day and hour,	
As she was commaunded by Werburge, in certan,	
To thabbot and couent plonged in great langour.	
(Whiche myracle herde) they pray[s]ed our sauiour	1595
And blessed Werburge / with hert deuoutly,	
Syngyng Te deum full solemply.	1597

¶ *Howe a great fire, like to distroye all Chestre, by myracle ceased / whan the holy shryne was borne about the towne by the monkes.*   Cap. xx.

229

FRom the incarnacion of our sauiour	1598
A thousand / a hundreth yere, .lxxx. also,	
On sonday in mydlenton / the .viii. houre,	
Whan euery paresshen theyr churche went to	
As all christen people of dutie shulde do,	1602
A fyre by infortune rose vp sodeinly,	
All flamyng feruent or the people dyd espy.	1604

230

This fearefull fire encreased more and more,	1603
Piteously wastyng hous / chambre / and hall ;	
The citezens were redy their cite to succour,	
Shewed all their diligence / and labour continuall,	
Some cried for water / and some for hookes dyd call,	1600
Some vsed other engins by crafte and policy,	
Some pulled downe howses afore the fire, truly.	1611

231

Other, that were impotent / mekely gan praye	1612
Our blessed lorde / on them to haue pite ;	
Women and children cried ' out and waile-a-way,'	
Beholdyng the daunger and perill of the cite ;	
Prestes made hast diuine seruice to supple,	1616
Redy for to succour their neyghbours in distres	
(As charite required) and helpe their heuynes.	1618

232

The fire contynued without any cessynge,	1619
Feruently flamyng euer contynuall,	
From place to place meruaylously rennyng,	
As it were tynder consumyng toure and wall.	
The citezens sadly laboured in vayne all ;	1623
By the policie of man was founde no remedy	
To cesse the fire so feruent and myghty.	1625

233

Alas, great heuynes it was to beholde	1626
The cite of Troye all flamyng as fire ;	
More pite of Rome cite was manyfolde,	
Feruently flagrant / empeiryng the empire :	
As to the quantite, the cite of Chestire	1630
Myght be assembled this tyme in like case	
To the sayd citees, remedeles, alas !	1632

234

Many riall places fell adowne that day,	1633
Riche marchauntes houses brought to distruction,	
Churches and chapels went to great decay ;	

That tyme was brent the more part of the towne ;
And to this present day is a famous opinion   1637
Howe a myghty churche, a mynstre of saynt Michaell,
That season was brent and to ruyne fell.   1639

235

Whan the people sawe their power insufficient,   1640
By diligent labour / wysdome and policye
To subdue the fire / but styll dyd augment :
To almyghty god they dyd call and crye
And to saynt Werburge, the gracious lady,   1644
For helpe and succour in suche wretchednes,
Wepyng and waylyng for woo and heuynes.   1646

236

Thabbot and couent of the sayd monasterie,   1647
Religiously lyuyng in holy conuersacion,
Repleit with mekenes and feruent charite,
Toke the holy shryne in prayer and deuocion,
Syngyng the letanie bare it in procession,   1651
Compasyng the fyre in euery strete and place,
Trustyng in Werburge for helpe, aide and grace.   1653

237

Whan they had ended the holy letanye   1654
From place to place procedyng in stacion,
Anone a stremyng sterre appered sodaynlye,
A white doue descended afore the congregacion
Approchyng as to helpe them / a signe of consolacion. 1658
The people reioysed of that gostly syght
And praysed saynt Werburge with power and myght. 1660

238

So by the merite of this blessed virgin   1661
The fire began to cesse— / a myracle clere—
Nat passyng the place / where the holy shryne
Was borne by the bretherne / as playnly dyd appere.
The citeȝens dyd helpe in their best manere ;   1665
The feruent great fire extincted was in-dede
By grace aboue nature / in story we may rede.   1667

239

The clergie, the burges / and the comons all,	1668
Consyderyng the goodnes of this virgin bright,	
With tendernes of hert and loue in speciall	
Magnified and praysed our lorde god almyght	
And blessed Werburge by day, also nyght,	1672
Whiche hath preserued of her great charite	
Chestre from distruction in extreme necessite.	1674

240

Vnto her shryne the people all went,	1675
The clergie before, in maner of procession,	
Thankyng this virgin with loue feruent	
For her mercy and grace shewed them vpon ;	
Deuoutly knelynge there made oblacion,	1679
Sayeng full sadly / 'we shall neuer able be	
The place to recompence for this dede of charite.'	1681

¶ *A breue rehersall of the myracles of saynt Werburge after
her translacion to Chestre.*   Cap. xxi.

241

T Hese fore-sayd myracles and signes celestiall,	1682
By diuine sufferaunce shewed manifestly,	
Magnifien this virgin and blessed moiniall	
With mycle worshyp, honour and victory,	
Playnly declaryng vnto your memory	
What singular grace / worshyp / and excellence	1687
Our sauiour shewed for his spouse openly,	
As is rehersed at masse in her sequens.	1689

242

To expresse all myracles written in the place	1690
In a boke nominate the thrid passionarye,	
It wolde require a longe tyme and space,	
To the reders tedious (no meruayle sothly).	
Wher[for]e we omytte to writte of them specially,	
But touched in generall vnto your audience,	1695

To reioyse and comfort your hertes inwardly,
As ye may considre in her sequens. 1697

243

Certaynly, it is knowen by bokes expresse : 1698
Sith that saynt Werburge came to Chestre cite,
By the power of god and myracle, doutles,
She hath defended the towne from ennemite,
From barbarike nacions full of crudelite,
Of whom we haue shewed with diligence, 1703
Preseruyng her seruauntes / and the monastery,
As is declared in her true sequence. 1705

244

Also of her goodnes preserued she hase 1706
The sayd towne from fire in extreme necessite ;
Many diuers tymes to their ioye and solace
Releuyng the cite3ens in wo and penalite.
For it is well knowen, by olde antiquite
Sith the holy shryne came to their presence, 1711
It hath ben their comfort and gladnes, truly,
As playnly appereth in her sequens. 1713

245

Also to blynde men she hath gyuen syght, 1714
To dombe men speche right perfectly,
To deffe men their heryng pleasaunt and right,
And helth to sicke men repleit with debilite,
Delyuered prisoners from captiuite,
Passage to lame men / to mad men intelligence ; 1719
Suche myracles shewed this blessed lady,
As ye may vnderstande in her sequens. 1721

246

Women with childe by her had good delyueraunce, 1722
Virgins defended from shame and vilany ;
Her seruauntes were cured from wofull greuaunce,
Marchantes and mariners delyuered from ieopardye ;
Other were saued from hangyng shamfully ;
A speciall comfort, succour and defence 1727

To all carefull creatures sekyng for remedy,
By singular grace / as sayth the sequens.   1729

247

No wofull person in payne and wretchednes,   1730
Man, woman, childe / who-so-euer they be,
Comynge to the abbay with perfit mekenes,
Makyng supplicacion to this lady free,
But they departed ioyfull and merie
To theyr dwellyng-place by her beniuolence,   1735
And for their lyuyng had all thyng necessarie,
As written is playnly in her sequens.   1737

248

For whiche great myracles and signes continuall   1738
This blessed Werburge, floure of humilite,
Of the people is called for grace supernall
' Patrones of Chestre ' / protectrice of the countre.
Where next our sauiour and his mother Marie
She hath great honour, prayse and preeminence,   1743
As most condigne to beare the principalite,
In witnes wherof recordeth her sequens.   1745

249

This holy abbasse and lady imperiall   1746
Hath ben president in Chestre monasterie,
Theyr trust / theyr treasure / and defence speciall
In mycle reuerence .vii. hundreth yere, trulie ;
And so shall continue, by grace of god almyghty,
To the worldes ende in hie magnificence.   1751
To whom be honour, worship and glorie
Euer to endure / as sayth her sequens.   1753

¶ *A charitable mocion and a desyre to all the inhabytauntes
within the countie palatine of Chestre for the monasterie.
Cap. xxii.*

250

Ⓞ ye worthye nobles of the west partye,   1754
   Considre in your mynde with hye discrecion
The perfite goodnes of this swete ladye,

We mean saynt Werburge, nowe at this season,
Whiche hath ben your helpe and singular tuicion,
And so euer wylbe— / haue this in your mynde   1759
Whan ye to her call with humble supplicacion :
Wherfore to the monasterye be neuer vnkynde.   1761

251

Remembre / at the foundacion of the sayd place   1762
your predecessours and fore-fathers redy were
To gyue for their soule-helth by singular grace
Parcell of their landes and possessions mere
To our sauiour and to saynt Werburge clere,
Redy to offre them with humble hert and mynde   1767
In perfit oblacion, with Hug. Lupe their foundere :
Wherfore to the monasterie be neuer vnkynde.   1769

252

Many helde their landes of the sayd monasterie   1770
By tenure grand-seriante / and some by homage,
By tenure franke-almoigne / other by fealtie
With seruice de chiualere / and some by escuage,
Some by petit-seriant / and by tenure burgage,
As in their euidentes and grauntes they may fynde :   1775
Tres maners de rentes / with tenure villenage :
Wherfore to the monasterie be neuer vnkynde.   1777

253

The place hath speciall franches and liberte,   1778
Hauynge certayne wardes of landes and mariage
Of diuers gentilmen within the sayd counte ;
All theyr tenauntes and seruauntes haue fre passage
Within all chesshire without tolle and pillage—
Suche auncient fredoms in their dedes they fynde,   1783
Gyuen by theyr founders for gostly auauntage :
Wherfore to the monasterie be neuer vnkynde.   1785

254

The erle gaue the place many great fredoms   1786
Within Chestre cite / whiche ben knowen of olde,
With singular priuileges and auncient customs,

Saynt Werburge faire / with profites manyfolde,
That no marchandise shulde be bought ne solde
Enduryng the faire-dayes (in writyng as we fynde)   1791
But afore thabbay-gate / to haue and to holde :
Wherfore to the monasterie be neuer vnkynde.   1793

255

Therfore, lordes, barons / ye rulers of the countre,   1794
We you nowe exhorte in our sauiour,
Discretly considre with your gostlie eie
The myght of this mayden and chaste floure,
Shewed by myracles euery day and hour—
Whan she was required with true hert and mynde,   1799
In all busines she hath ben their protectour :
Wherfore to the monasterie be neuer vnkynde.   1801

256

Whan your forefathers haue ben in great perell,   1802
In ieoperdie of lyfe on see and on londe,
Or like to be slayne by ennemies in batell,
Or taken by warre in prison fast bonde :
Vnto this virgin / as we vnderstonde,
Whan they called and cryed with contrite mynde,   1807
They escaped all daunger / cam whom safe and sonde :
Wherfore to the monasterie be neuer vnkynde.   1809

257

Marchauntes passynge with marchaundise,   1810
From lande to lande truly entendyng,
If they were taken with cruell ennemyse
Orels were put in perill of perisshyng :
If they to this virgin deuoutly praying
Made supplicacion with humble hert and mynde,   1815
Anone they opteyned theyr humble askyng :
Wherfore to the monasterie be neuer vnkynde.   1817

258

If any of you [was]¹ vexed with infirmite,   ¹ om.   1818
With sekenes incurable / or other vexacion,
As ¹ wronges, iniuries, and other maladie.   ¹ P. Ar.

Vnto saynt Werburge makyng intercession
And to her place promysyng an oblacion
With contrite hert and penitent mynde,   1823
They were soone cured from all affliction :
Wherfore to the monasterie be neuer vnkynde.   1825
259
And you, honest matrons, remembre you all   1826
The goodnes of this virgin full of grace :
Whan ye in trauelyng vpon her do call
Or haue any relique sende from the place,
ye fortune and spede well in short tyme and space ;
And diuers maydens louyng a chaste mynde   1831
From vilany ben saued by her purchase :
Wherfore to the monasterie be neuer vnkynde.   1833
260
But eche contray / shire / and congregacion,   1834
Some be disposed to vertues generall,
And some to the contrarie, proued by reason :
Folowyng their mynde and appetite sensuall
Haue shewed[1] vnkyndnes to the place spirituall,   [1] P. sheweb
And haue ben sore punysshed / take this in mynde,   1839
To all other folowynge and[1] example speciall :   [1] r. an
Wherfore to the monastery be neuer vnkynde.   1841
261
There was neuer man of high nor lowe degree,   1842
Lorde / baron / knyght / marchaunt / and burges,
Attemptyng to infringe their rightes and liberte,
Remaynyng in the same malice and wyckednes,
But if they repent shortly theyr busynes
Askyng absolucion to theyr conscience blynde,   1847
Vengeance on them doth lyght, doutles :
Wherfore to the monastery be neuer vnkynd.   1849
262
Diuers malefactours agayne good conscience   1850
Attemptyng[1] to take there seuerall possession   [1] r. attemptyd
By subtell policy and wrong-feyned euidens,

o

By proued periury and fals collusion,
Whiche in theyr iniury and wronge mesprision
Without repentauns in theyr consciens blynde .   1855
Sodenly haue ben drowed a sharpe punycion :
Wherfore to the monastery be neuer vnkynde.   1857
263
Other haue be glad to alienat the patronage   1858
Of certayne churches by malice and enuy,
By a fals enquest for theyr owne auauntage,
Defraudyng the right of the holy monastery :
Suche euill doers remaynynge in theyr tyranny,
Without satisfaccion, in their consciens blynde,   1863
Lyke wretches expired moste myserably :
Wherfore to the monastery be neuer vnkynde.   1865
264
Other haue ben besy serching day and nyght   1866
To infringe theyr fraunchis and fridome auncient
By fals recordes, oppugnant to ryght,
As hath ben proued by persones indifferent ;
yet they haue procured and sought wronge iugement
Agaynst their libertes, in conscience blynde :   1871
Sodayne and euyll deth folowed them consequent :
Wherfore to the monasterye be neuer vnkynde.   1873
265
Some other haue be, parauenture on late,   1874
Studious to disquiet the place, the company,
And diuers libertes haue alienate,
Also tolled their franchis fraudulently,
From the sayd place well knowen in memory ;
Suche mysdoers we moue in conscience blynde   1879
To mende [1] their wronges, lest payne come sodeynly : [1] P. maende
Wherfore to the monasterie be neuer vnkynde.   1881
266
Suche malefactours considre nat discretly   1882
Howe all suche landes, libertes and fredoms
Were gyuen to Christ and ben his patrimonye,

And nat allonly to religious persons ;
For all suche fraunches, priuileges, possessions
Of charite were gyuen, of pure conscience and mynde 1887
To god and saynt Werburge with great deuocions :
Wherfore to the monasterie be neuer vnkynde. 1889

267

Nowe for to make a finall ¹ conclusion,   ¹ P. small   1890
We well perceyue in auncient bokes olde,
All suche transgressours / holdyng their opinion,
Obstinate in malice, indurate and bolde,
Some haue ben slayne / some drowned in water colde,
Some shamfully hanged rebukyng their kynde, 1895
Some wretchedly departed / some cruciat manyfolde :
Wherfore to the monasterie be neuer vnkynde. 1897

¶ *A litell orison or prayer to the blessed virgine saynte*
Werburge by the translatour of this werke. Ca. **xxiii.**

268

Ⓝ Blessed Werburge and virgin glorious,   1898
   Descended by auncetrie of blod victoriall,
Doughter to kynge Vulfere / and Ormenilde vertuous,
O sufferayne lady and famous moiniall :
With hert and true mynde on the I call,
Thou art my succour / my helpe in all distres : 1903
Defende and saue me from peynes infernall
By thy meke prayer, swete patrones. 1905

269

O rutilant gemme clerer than the cristall, 1906
O redolent rose repleit with suauite,
Whiche for the loue of thy spouse eternall
Refused hast all vayne pleasures transetore,
Honours / riches / and secular dignite ;
Nowe regnyng in heuyn as a quene, doutles, 1911
Praye for thy seruaunt to the lorde of mercy,
Mekely I beseke the, swete patronesse. 1913

270

O sufferayne lady full of singular vertue,   1914
Myndyng most religion from thy infancy
Elect to the a spouse our sauiour Iesu,
Professed obedience at the house of Ely,
Where thou obserued the sensuals [1] thre   [1] r. essencials
By grace aboue nature, playn to expresse :   1919
Opteyne me power to haue victory
Ageynst myn ennemyes, swete patrones.   1921

271

O floure of virgins and comly creature,   1922
Syngyng with angels in the heuenly toure,
Transcendyng the saphir and diamounde pure
In worship, praisyng, beaute and decur ;
What tong can reherse thy ioy and honour,
Whiche is ineffable for man to expresse ?   1927
Beseke thy spouse, our blessyd sauiour,
To graunte me mercy, swete patrones.   1929

272

For thy great vertu and hie discrecion   1930
Chosen thou was a pyler here to be
Of diuers monasteryes, to encrease religion
By thy gostly doctryne and humilite ;
Exsample thou gaue of perfit charite
Vnto thi subgettis as a kynde maistres :   1935
Helpe me thy seruaunt of thy benignite
To please my maker, swete patrones.   1937

273

No maruell it was thought thy subgettis all   1938
Were vertuous and perfect in contemplacion,
Vnder suche a ruler, a hed and principall,
Whose gostly example and exortation
Were corespondent, accordyng in one—
Thy precept and deed were vnit with mekenes :   1943
In this vale [of] misery be my protection,
I humble the require, swete patrones.   1945

274

Glorious abbasse and floure of chastite, 1946
Carboncle shenyng bothe day and nyght,
All this region by thy noble progenie
And by the is decorat vnder god almyght ;
The presens of thy blessyd body right
Reioisith thy seruauntis in all distres, 1951
Thou art our refuge and lanterne of light :
Succour thy seruauntes, swete patrones. 1953

275

O pereles princes, lady imperiall, 1954
O gemme of holynes and noble president,
Comfort to all creatures in paynes thrall,
Releuyng all secke, feble and impotent ;
A myrrour of mekenes to euery pacient,
Whose myracles magnifien thy great goodnes : 1959
Defende thy seruaunt[es] from greuous turment
By thy supplicacion, swete patronesse. 1961

276

O noble sufferayne and singular protectrice 1962
Of thy true subiectes by speciall grace,
In all necessite a sure mediatrice,
From greuous oppression preseruyng thy place,
A lanterne of lyght in eche wofull case
To illumine thy people plonged in heuynes 1967
With great consolacion and gostly solace :
Nowe lyghten our conscience, swete patronesse. 1969

277

Swete louely lady, mekely I the praye, 1970
For thy great mekenes and perfect charite,
Make thou intercession both nyght and day
For thy true seruauntes vnto the trinite,
That we may opteyne here grace and mercy
And of our synne to haue forgyuenes, 1975
Afterwarde to come to eternall glorie ;
Helpe nowe and euer, swete patronesse. 1977

¶ *A breue conclusion of this litell werke vnto the reders, by the translatour. Cap. xxiiii.*

278

With tremblynge penne / and hand full of drede   1978
In termes rude translate nowe haue we
The noble historye of saynt Werburge in-dede,
Besekyng all them for their good humanite   '
Whiche this litell proces shall beholde and se,   1982
For to adde and minisshe and cause reformacion
Where nede requireth after your discrecion.   1984

279

At her lyfe historiall example may take   1985
Euery great estate / quene / duches / and lady,
To encreace in vertue / and synne to forsake,
To obserue mekenes and prayer deuoutly,
With pacience of hert / and almesdede, truly.   1989
If thou be widowe / her lyfe well folowyng
Thou mayst be sure in blis to haue a wonnyng.   1991

280

If thou be religious / wearyng blacke vesture,   1992
Take good example at this holy abbasse ;
Her lyfe wyll teche the how thou shult[1] endure   [1] r. shalt
In holy religion / opteynyng mycle grace
With mekenes / meditacion / mesure in eche place,   1996
And howe thou shalt kepe thy sensuals thre
Consideryng in heuen thy rewarde to be.   1998

281

If thou be a virgin, of hie or low degre,   1999
Takyng imitacion of this virgin bright
Thou mayst well obserue the floure of chastite
And thy spouse shalbe the lorde most of myght ; |
On whom if thou attende redy day and nyght,   2003
Thou shalt haue merite, as recordeth scripture,
With .v. wise virgins after thy departure.   2005

282

The cause mouyng vs this werke to begyn,   2006
It was to auoyde slouth and idelnes,
And most for the loue of this holy virgin,
Whiche is our sufferayn lady and patrones.
As for baudy balades full of wretchednes,   2010
And wanton wylde gestis / we purpose none to make,
For drede of losyng tyme / clothed in vesture blake. 2012

283

Go forth, litell boke / Iesu be thy spede   2013
And saue the alway from mysreportyng,
Whiche art compiled, for no clerke in-dede,
But for marchaunt men / hauyng litell lernyng,
And that rude people therby may haue knowyng   2017
Of this holy virgin / and redolent rose,
Whiche hath ben kept full longe tyme in close.   2019

284

To all auncient poetes, litell boke, submytte the,   2020
Whilom flouryng in eloquence facundious,
And to all other / whiche present nowe be,
Fyrst to maister Chaucer / and Ludgate sentencious,
Also to preignaunt Barkley / nowe beyng religious,   2024
To inuentiue Skelton and poet laureate ;
Praye them all of pardon both erly and late.   2026

285

If there be any thynge within this litell boke   2027
Pleasaunt to the audience / contentyng the mynde,
We praye all reders / whan they theron do loke,
To gyue thankes to god maker of mankynde,
Nat to the translatour ignoraunt and blynde ;   2031
For euery good dede / done in any cost
It cometh allonly of the holy gost.   2033

286

Almyghty god, both one two and thre,   2034
We desire the with humble supplicacion,
Saue holy churche of thy benignite,

And all ministres in holy religion ;
Preserue the kyngis grace, the Peeris, the region,   2038
Defende our monasterie and thy seruau[n]tes all,
And graunt vs by grace to come to blis eternall !   2040

FINIS.

A balade to the auctour.

287

O thou disciple of Tully most famous
Nowe flourisshyng in the floures of glorious eloque*n*ce,
Like as appereth by your stile facundius,
Full worthe laude, prayse and preeminence,   4
Put forth your werkes full sure of sentence—
Whose auctour / what though vncertayne be his name
Of all the reders exalted shalbe in fame.

288

Alas, why shulde this delicious werke,   8
Thus surely sette by pured science,
To be examined by my rudenes all derke,
Whiche knowe full well myn insufficience,
Sith I haue lerned by longe experience   12
That dulled age in werkes of poetry
Must nedes gyue to poetes place and victory.

289

Glorious god and kynge eternall,
We magnifie thy name as is but ryght,   16
Sith thou gaue to vs a floure most riall,
Redolent in cronicles with historicall syght ;
Whiche nowe is departed from this temporall lyght
The present yere of this translacion   20
M.D. xiii. of Christis incarnacion.
Cuius anime propicietur deus.

An other balade.

290

O frutefull histore / o digne memoriall,
Enbawmed with doctrine of virtues infinite,

With termes exquised / and sence retoriall,
To spirituall hertes a singular delite,   4
Fragrant and facunde / of englisshe exquisite,
Holsome in doctrine / for those that it desire :
Auaunce you to rede it / for it is exquisite,
Folowynge theffect to kepe you from hell-fire.   8

291

Reioyse Chestre / reioyse ye religious
And thanke your maker of his beniuolence
That hath you gyuen suche treasure preciouse,
Aduocatrice / in your most indigence !   12
O virgin werburge / of double excellence,
Conserue thy seruauntes dayly familier,
Preseruyng them from inconuenience,
The for tensue / that art theyr lode-sterre.   16

292

Amonges the whiche to thyn honour
One of thy clientes / with morall retorique
Hath chaunged newly / o mayde most swete flour,
Thy legende latine / to our language publique :   20
Preserue his soule / and make hym domestique
Within the heuyns / in whiche that thou art sonke—
With deth preuent / he myght nothyng replique :
Harry Braddeshaa, of Chestre abbay monke.   24

293

O cruell deth / o theffe vindicatyfe,
To persons vertuous ennemy mortall,
Of this good clerke thou hast abbreged the lyfe,
Preuentyng hym with thy dede stronge fatall.   28
yet in dispite of thy most venomus gall
He hath translate this legende profitable
And left it for holsome memoriall
To all his sequaces— / a gyft most couenable,   32

294

With polysshed termes / and good sence litterall,
No place there voyde / but vertue abundeth.

Theffect is manifest : for science ouer all
Rethorically thy sentence groundeth,   36
All vices surely it confoundeth.
Shewynge the legende of this mayde pure,
Her shenyng lyfe eche-where redoundeth.
Suche steppes folowyng / we hope in them tendure.   40

An other balade to saynt werburge.

295

 With hert contrite accepte my supplicacion,
Aydynge my fraylete and lyfe vacillaunt,
Renegate and contumace in all obstinacion,
Bewrapt with all synne /. detestable and recreaunt ;   4
Vouchsafe to supplie Iesu and geat graunt
Remyssion to haue of my synnes generall,
Greuous and thrall / that I may the auaunt :
A, gentill Werburge / to thy doctrine me call.   8

296

Wherfore thy father / thy mother Ermenilde
Enclined both to dedes catholique,
Ruffine and Kenrede / thy bretherne were fulfilde
Both with great grace / through martyrdome both like, 12
With diuers of thy kynne magnifique
Redact in the catholique papall :
Geat me suche grace to voyde all synnes inique
And gentill Werburge, to thy doctrine me call.   16

297

With faithfull clennes / thy soule was sure preserued,
Euer contynuynge in doctrine celicall,
Refusyng vanite / from vertue neuer swarued
But in all grace remaynyng principall ;   20
Vnto thy deth exhortyng great and small
Ruled to be / to the preceptes diuine—
Gouerned by grace / were thy disciples all :
A, gentill Werburge, call me to suche doctrine.   24

298

Wordly felicite abiect from my courage ;
Enuy and pride / with lustes voluptuous,
Rancorous cupidite myn hert sore do aswage,
Bryng oyntmentes sanatiue for my sores dolorous ;   28
Vnclose thy succours / and be beniuolous,
Redy to be preseruyng me from pyne :
Gouerne my lyfe from all actes daungerous,
And gentill Werburge, call me to thy doctrine.   32

299

Be nowe beniuolent / whan I shall on the call,
Vnto thy slaue / as my trust hath ben sure ;
Leue vnto me for a memoriall
Knowlege effectuall of thy lyfe pure,   36
Lyuynge ther-after / and so tendure,
Euer in purite my lyfe to contynue,
yeldyng thankes for thy most holsome lure—
Christ ouer vs holde his hande / al vices teschue.   Amen.   40

¶ *And thus endeth the lyfe and historye of saynt Werburge.*
Imprinted by Richarde Pynson | printer to the kynges
noble grace / With priuilege to hym graunted by our
souerayne lorde the kynge.   A° M.D. xxi.

(Engraving on the last page, with the printer's monogram.)

GLOSSARIAL AND GENERAL INDEX.

By W. M. WOOD.

asured, 36/820, assured, satis-
fied.
at, 30/618, from.
attempten, *pl.*, 99/2706, attempt.
attempted, 183/1535, tempted,
goaded.
auctoryte, 14/170, authority.
auctours, 21/358, authors.
Audry, St. (= St. Etheldred),
abbess of Ely, daughter of
St. Anna, 20/340; receives
St. Werburge as a nun, 59;
life of, 70 *et seq.*
audytoures, 21/364, hearers or
readers.
aulter, 83/2226, altar.
auncetry, 17/263, ancestry.
auncyent, 15/203, 48/1171,
ancient.
Austyn, 18/269, St. Augustine;
at Chester, 148/498.
auaunt, 202/7, advance, magnify.
auauntage, 191/1784, advant-
age.
auoyde, *v.*, 115/3191, make void.
auaunce, *v.*, 16/233, advance.
aydynge, 202/2, aiding.
ayre, 10/23, air.

Bangour = Bangor monastery,
147/492.
baptym, 18/293, 146/449, bap-
tism.
barbarike, 157/758, barbaric.
Bardenay Abbey, 88/2367.
barowne, 59/1510, baron.
barrayn, 158/806, barren.
barst, 184/1575, burst.
batell, 147/478, 174/1266;
batayle, 16/227, battle.
bawdy balades, 12/90, ribald
tales.
baylyfe, 99/2718, bailiff.
Beccy, a holy priest, 24/459.
Bede, the venerable, 13/128.
bedes, 34/752, beads.
bedyll, 43/1023, 183/1530,
beadle, sergeant, servant.
beestes of venery, 16/216, beasts
of the chase.
beestis, 145/415, beasts.

begon, 132/39, begun.
ben, *pl.*, 10/25, 109/3003, be.
benedyccyon, 52/1307, benedic-
tion.
beneson, 90/2425, benison.
Benettes (St.) rule, 74/1974.
beniuolence, 190/1735, benevo-
lence.
beniuolons, 203/29, benevolent.
benynge, 71/1858, benign.
benyuolent, 54/1345, benevolent.
Beorswyde, the queen of
king Hereryc, 19/310.
bere, 113/3142, bier.
Berta, the wife of king Ethelbryct, 22/381.
besyly, 51/1269, busily.
besynes, 10/45, business.
beseke, 181/1460, beseech.
besekyng, 198/1981, beseech-
ing.
besely, 9/20, busily.
beten, 61/1579, beaten.
bewrapt, 202/4, clothed.
Bishoprics established in England, 27/544.
bitwene, 15/202, between.
blake, 60/1539, black.
blasynge, 135/122, blazing.
blod, 195/1899, blood.
bloddy, 135/124, bloody.
blynde, 103/2838, blind.
bokes hystoryall, 15/184, books
of history, historical books.
bonde, *v.*, 41/957, bound.
bondes, boundes, 15/183, bound-
aries.
borde-lorde, 63/1618, lords of
the feast, seated at the high
table.
bordes, 64/1678, tables.
borowes, 152/623, boroughs.
both-tow, 21/378, both too =
also.
bowes, 44/1066, boughs.
boystous, 131/6, boisterous,
ignorant.
Bradsha, Henri, compiler of
this book, acrostic on his
name, 1.
braulynge, 10/51, brawling.
brenned, 39/893, burned.

brent, 187/1636, burnt.
brere, 33/724, briar.
brethur, 86/2328, brethren.
breue, 132/40, brief.
breuely, 11/83, shortly.
brothered, 64/1659, embroidered.
browdred, 63/1617, embroidered.
brutes, 148/510, Britons.
Brystowe, 15/191, Bristol.
Brytons, 13/139, Britons.
brybry, 98/2677, bribery.
bulles, 90/2424, bulls, Papal ordinances.
Burdredus, king of Mercia, cousin of St. Wurburghe, expelled from Britain, 138/218.
burges, 188/1668, burgesses.
burghes royall, 15/205, royal boroughs.
buryenge, 18/287, burial.
buxum, 10/25, buxom.
byforne, 42/1009, before.
byleue, 45/1088, belief.
byleuys, v., 46/1113, believes.
byloued, 54/1360, beloved.
byn, 125/3491, been.
bysshop-sees, 27/544, bishoprics.
byssop, 47/1138, bishop.
bytter, 106/2919, bitter.
bytwyx, 19/318, betwixt, between.

caduce, 112/3099, 115/3176, caducous, falling early or by chance.
Caerleil, 144/385, Carlisle, the city of, founded by king Leil.
Caerlleon, the ancient name of Chester, 144/374.
canaby, 142/335, canopy.
captens, 166/1025, captains, officers.
carbonele, 197/1947, carbuncle.
catall, 165/992, cattle.
cause, 170/1153, because.
caytyfe, 41/958, caitiff.
Cead (Ced, 24/459, Cedda, 27/555), St. = St. Chad, instructs Vulfade and Ruffyn

in the Christian faith, 44 et seq.; miracle worked by, 61 et seq.
celicall, 202/18, heavenly, celestial.
cemiterie, 147/467, cemetery.
censours, 140/278, censures, 177/1342, censers.
Cerdicus, first king of the West Saxons, 14/156.
cesse, 186/1625, cease.
cessed, 49/1215, ceased, stopped.
chales, 177/1342, chalices.
chamfully, 138/208, shamefully.
chanons, 53/1327, canons.
Charles = Charlemagne of France, 148/521.
chartre, 174/1271, charter, agreement.
chastyce, v., 10/41, chastise.
chekemate, 58/1470, checkmate.
chere, 178/1391, countenance.
Chesshyr, 15/202, Cheshire.
chest, 121/3369, coffin.
Chester, the reception of the shrine of St. Werburghe at, 141 et seq.; the foundation of, 143 et seq.; called a "city of legions," 143/372; the city of, saved from king Griffinus, 154; also from innumerable barbaric nations, 157; the burning of, 186.
Chester cathedral, the foundation and building of, 149 et seq.
chyfe, 14/175, 39/916, chief.
chyrches, 28/563, churches.
cimiterie, 177/1351, cemetery.
citeȝens, 2/25, citizens.
"City of legions," two places so named, 143/365.
ciuile, 132/29, civil (law).
clene, 47/1141, clean.
clennes, 69/1812, 104/2852, cleanness.
clerke, 12/108, scholar.
clercly, 93/2539, clearly.
clothes. 63/1617, tapestry.
clypped, 37/857, called, elected.
Cochede [? Coelrede], a son of king Ethelrede, 18/286.

Dee, the river, 15/188 ; miracle of its drying up, 181.

defe, 103/2838 ; deffe, 189/1716, deaf.

degest, 51/1264, disperse.

Deiram, Hereryc, the king of, 19/309.

deken, 83/2221, deacon.

delated, 146/445, increased.

Delbora, 36/802, Deborah.

delyce, 113/3124, delight.

delyted, 33/729, delighted.

demerytes, 38/872, faults, sins.

denayed, 24/465, denied.

depaired, 122/3384, impaired.

depaynted, 61/1577, pictured.

depely, 105/2881, deeply, carefully.

derke, 200/10, dark.

derlynge, 41/967, darling, loved one.

derogate, v., 115/3119, make void, overturn.

derogacion, 166/1033, disparagement.

descriuyng, 132/41, describing.

descryben, v.pl.,15/203,describe.

despyce, 48/1177, despise.

desse, 63/1625, dais.

destruccyon, 96/2620, destruction.

desydery,59/1498,desideration; 105/2899, desire, request.

dethe, 39/916, death.

deuyne, 72/1902, divine.

dight, 140/277, dressed.

digne, 200, last line but one, worthy.

dilated, 162/906, spread abroad.

dilect, 1/11, loved.

dirige, 117/3234, mournful dirge.

discens, 132/41, discence, 150/570, descent.

disceyte, 136/167, deceit.

distract, 117/3261, distracted.

distrye, 154/694, destroy.

doctours, 132/33, doctors, but here the four Evangelists are meant.

does, 100/2725, dost.

dolours,50/1237,troubles,pains, misery.

dombe, 103/2837, dumb.

Domneue [?Domueue], wife of Merwald, 24/448.

done, pl., 44/1059, 69/1801, do.

dongions, 144/381, dungeons.

doutles, 193/1848, doubtless.

doune, 45/1094, dove, pigeon.

dredde, 107/2942, dreaded.

dropes, 135/124, drops.

drowed,194/1856,read drowned.

due, 50/1240, diligent, circumspect.

Dunstan, St., 170/1136.

Duyna, a holy priest, 24/460.

dyaper, 64/1667, diaper.

dyfferre, 35/788, defer.

dygne, 107/2953, worthy.

dylated, 17/242, 23/433, spread out.

dyscrecyon, 83/2243, discretion.

dyscryue, 20/347, describe.

dyscus, 32/691, discuss.

dyspent, 93/2542, spent.

dysshe, 94/2558, dish.

dystylled, 56/1425, ran down.

dytche Offa, 17/251, Offa's ditch between England and Wales.

dyuised, 141/293, devised.

dyuydent, 15/199, a divider (said of the Mersey as separating the kingdoms of Mercia and Northumberland); see also 17/249.

Eadbalde, king of Kent, 22/387.

Eadburg, St., 22/383.

Eadfryde, a son of king Edwyn, 19/307.

Eadgide, Eagida, miraculously cured by St. Werburge, 156.

echeone, 63/1634, echone, 181/1471, each one.

eche-where, 202/39, everywhere.

Edelfled, daughter of king Oswy, 25/490.

Edgar, king of England, 170/1133 ; receives the homage of eight kings at Chester, 171.

Edmunde, prince, one of the

P

210   GLOSSARIAL AND GENERAL INDEX.

founders of Chester minster, 151/599.
Edwyn, king of Northumberland, 19/303.
edyfy, v., 28/563, build.
ee, 181/1466, eye.
Eest-Englande, the fifth Saxon realm, 14/166.
Eflede, the duchess, one of the founders of Chester minster, 150/583.
Egnicius, a son of king Titylus, 20/331.
Egbyrct (= Egfrid), king, second husband of St. Audry, 72/1905.
Egbryct, son of king Ercombert, 22/409.
Egwyn, bishop, 89/2402.
cies, 184/1551, eyes.
electe, 154/690, elected.
elected to, 30/639, chose for.
Eleutherius, the Pope, 145/424.
eleuat, 121/3369, cleuate, 51/1280, elevated, raised up.
Elflede, wife of Peada, 25/497.
Ella, a South Saxon king, 14/153.
embost, 62/1604, embossed, depictured.
Emma, wife of king Eadbalde, 22/388.
empaired, 155/715, damaged.
empeiryng, 186/1629, impairing.
enbawmed, 200, last line, embalmed.
enbrodred, 64/1647, embroidered.
encense, 140/278, incense.
encresed, 88/2378, increased.
endurate, 154/691, endowed, filled with; 183/1527, enraged.
Engystus, Duke, rules in Kent, 14/150.
enherytour, 88/2376, inheritor.
enherytryce, 118/3282, inheritrix.
enioyed, 53/1333, found favour with; 145/426, filled with joy.

enormentes, 149/549, 151/613, ornaments.
enowrned, 123/3431, ? put in an urn, or environed, surrounded, or adorned.
enquest, 194/1860, inquiry.
enquyred, 80/2138, required.
ensample, 12/111, example.
enspyred, 29/599, inspired.
ensued, 140/285, followed.
Enswyde, St., son of king Eadbalde.
enterprised, 135/135, entered, overran, endeavoured to make prize of.
entree, 102/2805, entry, entrance.
entysement, 43/1035, enticement.
enuired, 134/98, environed, surrounded.
Eorpwaldus, a son of Redwalde, 20/329.
equypolent, 18/291, having power.
equyualent, 36/803, equivalent.
Erchenwyn, first king of the Eastsaxons, 14/162.
Ercombert, king of Kent, 19/317 (Ercumbert, 22/402).
Erkengode, daughter of king Ercombert, 23/413.
erle, 40/948, earl.
Ermenberge, St., wife of St. Merwalde, 18/289.
Ernenberge, St., daughter of prince Ermenred, 22/395.
Ermenburge, St., daughter of prince Ermenred, 22/396.
Ermengyde, St., daughter of prince Ermenred, 22/398.
Ermenred, a son of king Eadbalde, 22/390.
Ermenrycus, king of Kent, 21/365.
Ermenylde, St., wife of king Wulfere, 19/298.
Ermenylde, daughter of king Ercombert, 23/412.
Ermenylde's reply to the audacious request of Werebode, 40 et seq.

knowen, 16/234, known.
knowes, 41/953, knowest.
knowlege, 108/2977, acknow-
ledge.
Kyneswith, the queen of king
Penda, 18/278.
kynred, 13/125, kindred.

lad, 43/1015, lout, ungainly
fellow.
Lancashyr, 15/202, Lancashire.
lanturne, 113/3141, lantern.
lande of promyssyon, 62/1612,
Land of Promise.
lascyuyte, 73/1923, lascivious-
ness.
layth, 135/121, lightning.
leed, 25/487, laid (i.e. buried).
lefe, 62/1603, leaf.
legiance, 171/1175, allegiance.
Leil, a British king, the founder
of Chester and Carlisle,
144/383.
lent, 41/970. It means that
"the most mighty king that
ever was born" (i.e. the
Saviour) was only lent to the
world.
Lenton, 78/2083, Lent.
Leofric, Earl of Chester,
172/1213, re-edifies the minster of Chester, 173/1230.
lepre, 166/1023, leprous.
lernyng, 199/2016, learning.
letanie, 187/1651, litany.
letten, pl., 176/1313, let.
lettynge, 180/1428, stopping,
hindering.
leue, v., 37/852, 84/2266, believe.
leues, v., 107/2944, leaves.
leues, n., 44/1066, leaves (of
trees).
lile, 122/3390, lily.
liniall, 132/41, lineal.
Lleon, 144/380, Llewellyn.
lolynesse, 36/804, 78/2074, low-
liness, humility.
lorshyppes, 15/183, lordships.
Lothary, son of king Ercombert, 22/409.
louers, 50/1252, friends, kins-
men.

Lucius, a British king, causes
the realm to be baptized,
145/422.
Lupus, Earl of Chester,
174-175.
lycence, 79/2108, leave.
lycens, 14/146, licence.
lyen, v. pl., 18/284, lie.
lygnage, 21/354, lineage.
lygne, 21/362, line, lineage.
lyght, 93/2541, little.
lyght, v., 83/2226, lighted.
lyghtned, 145/433, enlightened.
lynon, 93/2540, linen.
lynyall, 18/277, lineal.
lysence, 54/1369, licence, leave.
lytell, 12/106, 70/1845, little,
small.
lytterature, 131/4, literature,
letters.
lyue, 43/1022, life.

ma dame, 168/1080, madam,
my lady.
maculate, v., 102/2791, stain,
defile; 122/3396, stained,
defiled.
maende, v., 194/1880, mend.
magnifien, 188/1684, magnify.
magnifique, 202/13, magnificent.
maners, 176/1321, manors.
manfull, 42/996, 145/412,
manly.
manheed, 28/569, manhood.
mansyone, 97/2646, mansion.
Marceyl, St., a son of king
Penda, 18/280.
margaryte, 23/417, pearl.
Marius, a British king, ampli-
fies the city of Chester,
144/393.
marriage feast of St. Werburge,
description of the solemnities
at the, 60-66.
Marwalde, St., a son of king
Penda, 18/280.
maryed, 67/1759, married.
Matilda, Countess of Chester,
182-185.
Maucolyn = Malcolm of Scot-
land, attempts to capture
Chester, 157.

may, 33/720, maid.

maydyn, 34/764, maiden.

maynteynge, 175/1288, maintaining.

maystres, 86/2317, maystresse, 13/133, mistress.

mede, 20/339, happiness; 89/2418, merit.

mediatrice, 119/3320, mediatress.

medicyns, 160/853, medicines.

medled, 114/3148, oppressed.

meetes, 64/1672, meats.

melody, 51/1264, music, mirth.

memoratyue, 45/1097, memorable.

memorous, 14/159, memorable

memoryall, 104/2858, memory, mind.

mendes, 51/1267, amends.

Mercia takes its name from the river Mersey, 15/197.

mercyable, 94/2554, merciful.

Mercyens = Mercians, description of the realm of the, 13-17.

Mereum [? Merenin], a son of St. Merwalde, 18/292.

Mersee, 15/196, the river Mersey.

Merslande = Mercia, the sixth Saxon realm, 14/169.

meruailous, 164/975, marvellous.

meruayle, 42/989, merueyll, 33/722, marvel.

mesprision, 194/1854, misprison.

metigate, 184/1554, mitigate.

minisshe, 198/1983, take from.

Miracles of St. Werburge, 153-169.

mocyon, 55/1379, intention; 56/1430, proposition.

moder, 75/1983, mother.

moeued, 38/889, moved.

moines, 126/3519; moynes, 23/413, 61/1581; moiniall, 141/319; monyall, 12/98, 82/2187, nun.

mone, 9/16, moon.

monestycall, 74/1973, monastic.

montaynes, 154/686, mountains.

monye, 64/1677, money.

moost, 108/2968, most.

more Britayne, 146/443, greater Britain.

most, 9/13, greatest.

mouther-churche, 146/464, mother-church.

mundayne, 1/6, worldly.

musture, 16/227, mustering together for warlike purposes.

musyke, 62/1589, music.

mutabylyte, 11/65, changeableness.

mutacion, 182/1509, imitation.

mycle, 141/297, much.

myddyll, 24/449, middle.

mydlenton,185/1600,the middle of Lent.

myghty, 64/1671, strong.

Mylburge, St., a daughter of St. Merwalde, 18/290.

Myldred, St., a daughter of St. Merwalde, 18/290.

Mylgyde, St., a daughter of St. Merwalde, 18/291.

mynded, 28/575, made up his mind to.

mynstre, 134/91, minster (church).

mynystred, 89/2393, administered.

myrthes angelycall, 112/3115. angelical mirth.

myschefe, 50/1234, treachery, wickedness.

mysere, 168/1084, misery.

myssyue, 58/1493, missive, fit for sending.

nat, 1/13, not.

natyuyte, 106/2932, nativity.

ne, 1/7, nor.

nece, 182/1491, niece.

neclygent, 83/2235, 131/3, negligent.

Noe, 21/359, 45/1093, Noah.

nomynate, 26/517, named.

nomynyon, 15/179, remembrance.

nonnes, 138/203, nuns.

porte, 38/884, part.
postron, 177/1350, posturne, 171/1179, gate.
power imperyall, 15/186, imperial power.
praye, 155/724, prey.
prayes, 120/3350, praise.
prehemynens, 13/123, preeminence.
preiudyse, 42/999, prejudice.
prenominate, 136/141, beforenamed.
preordinat, 140/264, preordained.
preparat, 9/5, preparate, 64/1673, 111/3073, prepared.
prepotent, 21/355, 76/2046, very potent, most potent.
presens, 197/1950, presence.
prestis, 125/3492, priests.
preuayled, 137/188, prevailed, got the better of.
primatyue, 149/541, earliest.
princes put to flight by St. Werburge's miracles, 101, 102.
priue, 171/1179, privy, secret.
probate, 46/1114, on probation.
professed, 54/1372, make public profession.
profettes, 74/1964, profits.
prolongynge, 38/882, delaying, putting off.
promoters, 89/2401, informers.
promyssyon, n., 62/1612, promise.
promyt, 171/1177, promised.
promyttynge, 158/798, promising.
prone, 62/1609, inclined.
propre, 159/827, proper, own.
propurtes, 16/223, proprytes, 17/239, properties.
protectryce, 12/101, protectress.
prymate, 9/21, head, maker, God.
pryme, 44/1054, early morning time.
prynces, pl., 53/1318, princes (i.e. the martyrs Wulfade and Rulfyn).
prynces, 12/97, princess.

pryores, 76/2035, priories.
pryue, 65/1684, private, privy.
psalmodise, 152/620, sing psalms.
pudicall, 138/224, bashful, modest.
punicion, 139/236, punishment.
punysment, 79/2104, punishment.
pured, 200/9, made pure.
purpull, 90/2445, purple.
purtrayed, 62/1588, portrayed.
purtrayture, 62/1597, portraiture.
putryfy, 107/2945, putrefy.
purueaunce, 72/1902, providence.
pyctures, 61/1577, pictures.
pyght, 157/764, pitched.
pyler, 196/1931, pillar.
pyne, 203/30, pain, trouble.
pynned, 96/2632, impounded.

Quadriburge, daughter of king Cryda, 18/273.
Quadryburge, wife of king Edwyn, 19/304.
quere, 112/3113, choir, quire.

Ranulphus, a gibe at, for giving a Roman origin instead of a British, to the city of Chester, 144/386.
raunson, 108/2976, ransom.
raynynge, 22/411, reigning.
realte, 145/404, royalty.
recidiuacion, 146/453, backsliding.
reconforte, 44/1061, recomfort, refresh.
reconsylde, 82/2217, reconciled.
redact, 202/14, set up, enshrined.
rede, 177/1343, read.
redde, v., 83/2221, read.
redemptour, 108/2967, redeemer.
reders, 95/2591, readers.
redolent, 69/1815, 199/2018, sweet-smelling.
reduce, 146/438, subject, convert.
redy, 104/2859, ready.

Richard Clay and Sons, London and Bungay.

www.ingramcontent.com/pod-product-compliance
Lightning Source LLC
Chambersburg PA
CBHW020353030726
47496CB00007B/2119